In loving memory of my parents

謹以此書紀念我的父母

Contents

English Skills
for
Better
Writing

精進英文寫作力

Pedro Ng（吳白弢）

中華書局

□ 責任編輯：劉光宇　楊安琪
□ 裝幀設計：黃梓茵　龐雅美
□ 排　版：時潔
□ 印　務：劉漢舉

English Skills for Better Writing

□
著者
Pedro Ng（吳白弢）

□
出版
中華書局（香港）有限公司
香港北角英皇道 499 號北角工業大廈一樓 B
電話：(852) 2137 2338　傳真：(852) 2713 8202
電子郵件：info@chunghwabook.com.hk
網址：http://www.chunghwabook.com.hk

□
發行
香港聯合書刊物流有限公司
香港新界荃灣德士古道 220-248 號
荃灣工業中心 16 樓
電話：(852) 2150 2100　傳真：(852) 2407 3062
電子郵件：info@suplogistics.com.hk

□
版次
2022 年 5 月初版
2024 年 11 月第二次印刷
© 2022 2024 中華書局（香港）有限公司

□
規格
16 開（285 mm × 210 mm）

□
ISBN：978-988-8760-89-3

Acknowledgements

This book is a product of my life-long interest in the study and use of language. More specifically, it was motivated by my teaching of an English writing course for research in the social sciences for twenty years, which spanned nearly the second half of my academic career from 1971 to 2015 at The Chinese University of Hong Kong.

About 300 students, from 1995 to 2015, took my "Research Writing" course. I thank them all for giving me first-hand experience of seeing their problems in English writing. As the course was designed for a small class of not more than a dozen students, I was able to examine their writing closely to identify and understand their weaknesses in grammar, usage, and sentence construction. I corrected all the errors that I found and, where needed, offered better constructions in their prose. At my request, they revised their work with the help of my corrections and various changes. They learned more this way. In the process, I became increasingly involved in the art of expression through words.

I owe unmeasurable gratitude to my wife Meliza, a professional librarian, who has always been supportive and encouraging throughout the past three years of this book's preparation. She has sustained me in my task often with her good advice and inspiration. At her suggestion, I have included Chinese translations of "What you can learn in this chapter" at the beginning of all chapters and the instructions of all exercises (Chapters 4 to 22). This arrangement should be helpful to a larger readership whose first language is Chinese.

I am most grateful to Professor Ambrose Yeo-chi King, Emeritus Professor of Sociology of The Chinese University of Hong Kong and formerly Vice-Chancellor of the University, for his moral support and recommendation of my work to the present publisher. He has also kindly graced this book with an inspiring foreword, in which he eloquently points out that "deficiency in basic language skills and hence in writing is . . . tantamount to impotence in communication at the educated level". He also reminds us that "since we use writing as *the* means of expressing our ideas and feelings, our writing is associated closely with our identity".

My appreciation goes also to Dr. Zhao Dongxiao, formerly Managing Director of Chung Hwa Book Company (Hong Kong) and currently Vice President of Sino United Publishing (Holdings) Limited for his warm receptiveness to my proposal for this book. No less, I must thank Ms Gu Yu, Assistant Editor-in-Chief of Chung Hwa Book Company (Hong Kong), for her professionalism and all her unfailing effort in facilitating and guiding the publication of this work.

Pedro Pak-tao Ng
March 2021

We live in an "information age" characterized by exponential growth in audio-visual images giving priority to sensory experience. The pursuit of such experience seems to have much greater appeal, especially for the younger generation, than the study of language and its use in writing. The modern world is also marked by explosive expansion in different forms of digital communication in which the use of words often need not conform to traditional standards.

When young people are increasingly inseparable from vivid images and digital communication, it is not surprising that the decline in the general capacity to write among them has persisted. Nevertheless, it remains true that they need to have the skills of effective writing if they aspire to work in large firms, business corporations, government bodies or academic institutions. Not only do they use writing for communication in the work world, but writing is also their framework of conceptualization, analysis, elaboration, and, above all, thinking as an educated person.

Despite the importance of writing as a communication tool and as a framework of thinking, the foundational learning of English for many students is far from satisfactory. In this context, I am pleased to know that Professor Pedro Ng, my long-time colleague at the Chinese University of Hong Kong, has written this book specifically addressing the issue of acquiring adequate English skills for better writing. Its central message, it seems to me, is that learners and users of English should treat the skills of using the language seriously and apply such skills to write with a sharpened language awareness. Such awareness is not to be taken for granted but is to be acquired earnestly and systematically. I agree with his concern that learners of English need to realize that "in a global world of multifaceted communications across all fields and occupations, good English skills matter enormously." Deficiency in basic language skills and hence in writing is thus tantamount to impotence in communication at the educated level.

But to write effectively should be more than an instrumental goal. Since we use writing as *the* means of expressing our ideas and feelings, our writing is associated closely with our identity. When we read a person's writing, we see more than words and the meanings they represent; we see the quality of the person. If handwriting is one's costume, as an old Chinese saying puts it, then writing amounts to a disclosure of one's inner self. To the extent that this occurs, individuals who write well are not just competent communicators; they are also likely to become respected colleagues in their work with credibility and leadership potential, as Pedro also observes in his preface.

In this connection, Foucault's notion of "writing the self" reminds us of the significance of writing as a kind of ethical and mental exercise to reflect on the self for self-care and self-cultivation. Writing is seen as a process of creation of the self (as may be happening in today's personal blogs written in the first person), which is compatible with the Confucian emphasis on moral perfection of the individual. This, however, is often not what modern individuals are expecting to gain from writing. Viewed sociologically, therefore, the issue of writing is all the more important as it impinges upon the possibility of cultivating a truly autonomous and mature person, which is the ultimate ideal of liberal education.

Specifically, the contribution of Pedro's *English Skills for Better Writing* lies in its sensitivity to the peculiar linguistic need of students and other users of English. Before his retirement in 2015, he had taught the course "Research Writing" in the Chinese University of Hong Kong for 20 years since 1995. Over the years, he had accumulated considerable experience in handling students' problems in the learning of English in general and writing skills in particular.

This book addresses directly the linguistic competence of learners and users of English by first examining the obstacles to writing well and explaining what good written English ought to be. It then focuses on teaching the fundamental skills of understanding and applying the principles of how English works, supported with well-designed exercises. It also contains a rich compendium of the proper use of hundreds of troublesome words. Moreover, Pedro begins each chapter with a bilingual (English-Chinese) brief description of the chapter's content, a user-friendly feature to suit a wider readership.

Although books on the learning of English and writing guides are not lacking in the book market, Professor Pedro Ng adopts an approach that makes his work comprehensive in scope, enlightening to read, and practical for reference. True to what its title suggests, this book is intended to help students and other readers to solve their language problems as a prerequisite for improving their capacity to write. To this end I think Professor Pedro Ng has indeed offered a very good service to the community.

Ambrose Yeo-chi King
金耀基教授
Emeritus Professor of Sociology and former Vice-Chancellor
The Chinese University of Hong Kong

Why I wrote this book

Learning English is a common experience among students, but not many have learned it well enough to be able to use English competently and confidently. Errors of grammar and usage keep appearing in the writing of students at both secondary and tertiary levels. Deficiencies in English skills follow them as they enter the work world and could well hold them back in their career development. In a global world of multifaceted communications across all fields and occupations, good English skills matter enormously. The sooner learners of English realize this and the more actively they strengthen their English ability, the more likely they are to gain in confidence, self-esteem, and social recognition, and thus the greater their chances of doing better in life, whatever jobs they may hold.

I believe firmly that if one is willing and determined to put one's mind to learning the basic elements of how English words are organized into meaningful sentences and is ready to cultivate language-use habits that serve to sharpen language awareness, there is no reason why one cannot gradually master the language to express ideas properly and effectively. It is with this conviction that I have written this book, which, I hope, should help committed learners of English to attain their goal.

How this book came about

During my teaching career (in sociology) at The Chinese University of Hong Kong from 1971 to 2015, I often paid special attention to students' grammatical errors and various other deficiencies (e.g., incoherence, wordiness, inadequate vocabulary) in their English written work. In 1994, my Department recognized the need for offering a specially designed course to enhance students' English writing ability and asked me to fill this role. I gladly accepted and designed a new course, called initially "Writing for Sociology" and later "Research Writing". I started teaching it in 1995 until 2015 when I retired. The course covered the whole academic writing process, with considerable attention given to matters of grammar, proper usage, and effective sentences.

After teaching the writing course for about seven years, I wrote a text-cum-reference book titled *Effective Writing: A Guide for Social Science Students*, published by The Chinese University Press in 2003. The course, with *Effective Writing* as textbook, was warmly received by students every year. That rewarding experience inspired me to work on the present book soon after I retired. This new volume differs from *Effective Writing* in that it focuses on a much broader range of grammatical and usage topics. Familiarity with them surely helps to develop the ability to write well. This new work will offer help to students and non-students alike who want to improve their English writing competence.

What I have seen over the past four decades or so in the English writing of tertiary students shows there is clearly a burning need for improvement. Chinese-speaking learners of English have a variety of characteristic difficulties with English to cope with (e.g., the number attribute of nouns, verb tenses, use of articles and prepositions, choice and use of words, idiomatic combinations of words, sentence structure). Unless they make a conscious effort to overcome these difficulties, they will keep making the same kinds of errors that prevent their writing from being clear and effective. Teachers of English in schools also need to induce their students to pay much greater attention to the basic facts of grammar and usage simply because these matters can make a big difference between poor and good writing. This book is written with such a purpose in mind.

What does this book cover?

The content of this book is divided into three main parts:

Part 1 Getting oriented. Two important questions must be clarified to set you going in the right direction: First, what hinders you from writing good English? Second, what counts as good written English? They are discussed in the first two chapters. I hope and expect that you will read them carefully to (a) have a clear idea of what good written English is, and (b) be aware of what it is that you have not done enough and what kind of attitude you need to adopt to improve your ability to write well in English.

Part 2 Learning the skills. These skills are essential for writing good English. I have selected those skills that, in my opinion, play a significant role in writing sentences that are not only grammatically correct but also effective in expressing ideas clearly and idiomatically. Naturally, these skills cover a wide range of requirements that a careful writer should always bear in mind and strive to meet. I believe every learner of English should make a special effort to understand them well. Ideally, given sufficient attention and carefulness in writing practice, these skills should become habitual and even instinctive.

Exercises are given at the end of all the chapters (4 to 22) in this part of the book. I strongly encourage you to do them to reinforce your understanding of the material.

Part 3 Guide to using words properly. This is a convenient guide to about 300 troublesome words and phrases that are often misused because of insufficient or inadequate knowledge. By studying the given explanations and example sentences, you will soon learn to use these words and phrases properly. The words and phrases that I have included are based on a large amount of student writing I have read over several decades.

Who will benefit from this book?

All learners and users of English who wish to improve their command of English should benefit from this book, especially when it contains over 2,000 example sentences.   I have purposely written this book in English so that readers have more of an opportunity to accustom themselves to reading and understanding English. *Learning English through English can be immensely effective*. To maximize your English competence, it is necessary to see the language in action. As you become more competent, you will be thinking *in English* too.

You may be (a) a senior secondary, undergraduate, or postgraduate student, (b) a schoolteacher of English, or (c) a holder of a job in which written English is much used. You can use the book on your own and delve into any topic that interests you after reading the first three chapters.

Students. Students preparing for public examinations or tests such as the HKDSE and IELTS will find the book helpful. Undergraduates and postgraduates can also learn much from the book to write better papers and theses.

The language used in the book is, as far as possible, plain, and clear, although you may sometimes need to consult a good dictionary (with English explanations and example sentences to illustrate correct usage). *Looking up a dictionary is an important habit and a vital part of the effort needed to upgrade your English.* A good dictionary should be your constant companion. Pay close attention to how words and expressions are used in the context of sentences and try to become familiar with various sentence patterns, which can serve as models for your learning.

Teachers. Not only students but schoolteachers of English will also find this book useful. Teachers can use this book to strengthen their understanding of how good grammar and proper usage of words can facilitate effective expression of ideas. Teachers can also use material in this book as reference in selecting those aspects of English grammar and usage that they wish to teach their students.

At the same time, they can raise their students' awareness of the errors they commonly make and show them how such errors may be avoided. If little or no effort is made to recognize and correct language errors, they will tend to reappear and become ever harder to be got rid of. Writing infested with errors will remain poor in quality, becoming an obstacle to effective expression and communication.

Working adults. Adults working in jobs requiring much written communication in English can use this volume as a handbook to refresh and expand their knowledge of grammar and usage and to look up words whose use they are not sure of. This book can help them write better memos, announcements, business letters, minutes of meetings, project proposals, and reports of various kinds. A better writer can become a better colleague, team member, or manager because a better communicator earns more credibility and respect.

All set to go!

Now you are prepared to make the best use of this book to improve your English. Study it diligently and use it often to acquire a good grasp of how English works so that you will have a firm foundation upon which to develop your writing ability. Provided you work steadily and persistently through the book and do the exercises conscientiously (without looking at the answers first) and try to apply what you learn in anything you write, you will be surprised to see how much your written English will improve.

I hope you will find reading this book rewarding.

PART 1 Getting Oriented

Chapter 1 What Hinders You From Writing Good English?

What you will learn in this chapter

To write better English, you must first understand what has been keeping you from writing well. Hindering factors include (1) not serious about English, (2) not enough reading, (3) not enough knowledge of English grammar and usage, (4) inadequate ability to recognize errors, and (5) weak vocabulary. You should take concrete remedial action to become more competent and confident in using English to write better.

要改善你的英語寫作能力，首先你要明白有什麼障礙需要克服。障礙主要有五個：（1）對英語態度不夠認真，（2）閱讀不充分，（3）對英語語法和使用的認識不夠，（4）缺乏辨錯能力，（5）詞彙不足。你必須採取具體的補救行動提升你的英語能力，從而更有自信地用英語寫作。

1.1 Five hindering factors

1.2 A casual attitude towards the English language

1.3 Insufficient reading experience

1.4 Insufficient understanding of grammar and usage

1.5 Inadequate ability to recognize errors

1.6 Weak vocabulary

1.7 Vicious circle of avoidance of English

1.8 Conclusion: the strategy you need

1.1   Five hindering factors

Many learners and users of English want to do something to improve their English writing ability. As one of them, your first task is to examine what has been hindering you from writing well in English. In this chapter, let us have an overview of five possible factors. They may not exhaust all possibilities, but they are among the most common characteristics of those for whom writing well in English is difficult. The five factors are:

(1)   a casual attitude towards the English language,

(2)   insufficient reading experience,

(3)   insufficient understanding of grammar and usage,

(4)   inadequate ability to recognize errors, and

(5)   a weak vocabulary.

1.2   A casual attitude towards the English language

Take a moment to think about the place of the English language in your life. How have you looked at English as it relates to you? How much does it matter to you?

Let us be a little more specific. Do you attach great importance to English in your studies (if you are a student), your work, or your career advancement? Have you ever thought of English as your window to a wider world that extends beyond any boundary you can imagine? Do you feel the urge to know more about how English works as a language? Are you aware of your weakness in using English to write? Have you made an effort—a genuinely sustaining effort—to find out how to overcome that weakness? If you think you are generally satisfied with your English proficiency, do you want to improve and upgrade it?

If the answers to these questions are all or mostly "yes", then you have a rather serious attitude towards English. That is very good. You are on firm ground to strive for improvement. On the other hand, if your answers are mostly "unsure" or not clearly positive, then your attitude is largely casual. A casual attitude towards English as a language would not give you a strong enough driving force to strengthen your skills in using the language. It does not give you enough confidence; neither does it help you to set a goal to work towards. In short, it really hinders you from writing good English.

1.3   Insufficient reading experience

Reading offers an immensely valuable experience of becoming familiar with the use of words and phrases in sentences. If you have a habit of reading English material in newspapers, magazines and books, you are exposed to a great variety of sentence patterns that can demonstrate how standard written English looks like. Of course, you will also notice how ideas are connected through the sentences that make up paragraphs.

At the same time, you can also pick up many new or not-so-familiar words and colloquial expressions. In the process, you may even discover how familiar words are used in ways unfamiliar to you. For example, you may already know the meanings of **pay** and **handsome** but may have difficulty understanding the sentence **His rigorous training will probably pay off handsomely in the swimming**

gala. As a result, you can steadily expand and enrich your vocabulary, which means that you will get to know more words (a quantitative matter) and more about the words you know (a qualitative attainment).

So much can be learned and acquired from reading regularly that you will, in due course, cultivate an almost intuitive sense of what good standard written English is and looks like. Try reading an editorial from a local English newspaper and see how you take it. If you have no difficulty understanding its theme and main points laid out in some comprehensible structure, you probably have a *regular* reading habit over some years, which has expanded your vocabulary and given you the facility for recognizing and interpreting good written English.

I want to stress the word **regular** because, for reading to make a significant and positive impact on your language ability, it must be done regularly and consistently, such as if you set aside some time each day to read something, not while you are occupied by other thoughts and concerns but attentively and single-mindedly. It does require *self-discipline*.

By contrast, the lack of quality reading experience puts you in a very disadvantageous position, as far as language competence is concerned. You would not be familiar with good sentence forms; your vocabulary lacks healthy growth; and you would have inadequate knowledge of the idiomatic use of words and phrases.

1.4   Insufficient understanding of grammar and usage

Grammar is, simply put, the body of principles and rules about the structure of the language and the formation of sentences in that language. Usage, closely related to grammar, is how grammatical structures and words are used in ways that are both correct and idiomatic or natural.

1.4.1 Subject-verb agreement

To form a sentence properly, for example, the verb must agree with its subject. That is, a singular subject takes a singular verb and a plural subject takes a plural verb, as in the following three sentences:

	Remarks
Our new project starts in June.	Singular subject, **our new project**, and singular verb present tense, **starts**
We appreciate your understanding.	Plural subject, **we**, and plural verb, **appreciate**
What the doctor said makes a lot of sense.	**What the doctor said**, noun clause as singular subject, and singular verb present tense, **makes**

1.4.2 Word order and word form

Good (or correct) grammar requires us to pay attention to many points concerning word order or the use of different forms of a certain word, as the following two constructions show:

Incorrect	Correct
I don't know what is this?	*I don't know what this is.* (correct word order in an indirect question)
Keep this between you and I.	*Keep this between you and me.* (correct use of object form of pronoun)
They are working hardly on this project.	*They are working hard on this project.* (**Hard** is both adjective and adverb. Here, it is an adverb modifying *working*.)

1.4.3 Questions of usage

Of course, grammar and usage cover a lot of ground. Usage is about how words and phrases are used correctly and naturally (idiomatically) according to their grammatical function and precisely to show a particular meaning. Questions of usage are often also questions of grammar when grammatical forms or rules need to be considered. Thus, for example, the word **plan** may be used as a verb (e.g., **to plan a trip**) or as a noun (e.g., **a detailed vacation plan**). If you use **plan** as a verb, it refers to acting in preparation for something or making arrangements for something. That "something" is shown in the noun phrase **a trip**, serving as the object of the verb **plan**. But if you use **plan** as a noun, it is the description of the preparation or arrangement, which may be specified by another noun such as **vacation** and pre-modified by an adjective such as **detailed**.

1.4.4 Choosing the right word

Sometimes, the focus of usage can be primarily on choosing the right word or phrase to convey a particular meaning. Choosing the right word to express a meaning precisely or accurately is often an important task in writing. For instance, should a certain business proposal be described as **practical** or **practicable**? (**Practical** = worth doing; **practicable** = can be done.) When we write about what goes on between individuals, do we speak of their **relation** or **relationship**? (**Relation** = connection; **relationship** = quality of connection) Choosing the wrong word can distort your meaning and confuse your readers.

1.4.5 Usage is more than correct grammar.

At times, we may come across situations where the use of one word rather than another can make a big difference in the meaning of a sentence. Examine the following two sentences, both being grammatical in construction but different in meaning:

	Remarks
1. *Young people, who have many interests, find it difficult to identify what they really want to do.*	The clause, **who have many interests**, set off by two commas, is non-restrictive.
2. *Young people who have many interests find it difficult to identify what they really want to do.*	The clause, **who have many interests**, NOT set off by two commas, is restrictive.

In the first sentence, the **who-**clause (**who have many interests**, a relative clause) is "non-restrictive" (also called "non-defining") in that it does not restrict the reference of the subject **young people** to any particular individuals. That is, it applies to *all* young people. The content of the **who-**clause is not essential to the meaning of the sentence. To signify that such is the case, commas must be used to set off the non-restrictive **who**-clause.

In the second sentence, however, no commas are used to set off the **who**-clause. The sentence now means only those young people who have many interests would find it difficult to identify what they really want to do. As in the first sentence, the **who**-clause modifies the subject **young people**, but it now works as a "restrictive" or "defining" clause to limit the reference of **young people** to only those with many interests. Hence, correct usage is often more than just correct grammar. It can (and often does) include the proper use of punctuation so as to express an idea properly and clearly.

You will read more about matters of correct grammar and proper usage later in this book. They are treated in some detail because knowing them well is essential for using English with skill and confidence. A good foundation in grammar and usage is undoubtedly a prerequisite for writing good English.

1.5   Inadequate ability to recognize errors

If your understanding of grammar and usage is insufficient, you would not be able to recognize errors readily. You need to be familiar with the basic rules and principles governing sentence structure and with the use of words so that you can avoid many common errors and can recognize them as errors if you have made them carelessly. If you have a sharp awareness of what errors are and why they are errors, you will be able to correct them yourself, and thus you will be more able to minimize them in your writing.

As you can imagine, many kinds of errors may occur. The following is only a partial list to give you a general idea:

- Incorrect tense form of verbs
- Disagreement between subject and verb
- Disagreement between a pronoun and its antecedent
- Misuse of articles
- Improper use of singular and plural forms of nouns
- Improper use of restrictive and non-restrictive clauses
- Modifiers not modifying anything in a sentence
- Similar elements not put in similar grammatical forms
- Using the comma to link independent sentences
- Improper use of punctuation
- Unidiomatic use of word combinations

1.6   Weak vocabulary

A vocabulary is the whole set or collection of words that you know. To write good English, you need to have a vocabulary that contains not only the most commonly known words but also a good variety of words that have similar or opposite meanings. A good mastery of words with similar or opposite meanings comes handy when you need to describe objects, people, actions, and feelings with precision. If, for instance, you write about a discussion among a group on a certain topic, you may need to say something about the discussion. Your choice of adjectives may include **brief, congenial, constructive, enthusiastic, extensive, friendly, general, heated, in-depth, informal, lengthy, lively, productive,**

rambling, serious, sincere, warm, wide-ranging. The list can go on, but you need to know their meanings well enough to be able to understand differences in connotation between words that have similar meanings. Choosing the word that suitably expresses the meaning you want or the meaning that the situation in question requires is an important skill for writing effectively.

A rich vocabulary also contains words that are associated with new developments in such domains as technology, health care, international relations, arts, entertainment, mass communication, commerce, city planning, and even religion. If you know a broad range and variety of words referring to the various domains of modern life, you are well equipped to write about things such as social issues and a changing globalized world. Your description will be both specific and colourful.

In contrast, if your vocabulary is restricted and weak, you simply do not have enough words to express your ideas properly and accurately. What you write tends to sound dry and uninteresting, at times even confusing. You are also likely to lack both breadth and depth because your limited vocabulary prevents you from clarifying or elaborating your points.

1.7   Vicious circle of avoidance of English

These five factors together give rise to a low level of proficiency among many learners of English. This is usually accompanied by a general lack of confidence in using English for reading, writing, listening, and speaking. It can even develop into a phobia of English. I can recall what often happened when a university course was offered in two sections, one using Cantonese Chinese and the other using English as medium of instruction. Students usually shunned the English section and flocked to the Cantonese one, fearing that they might not do well in the first and thinking that they would feel more comfortable in the second.

The problem is that the avoidance or fear of English, in its turn, has a negative feedback on all the five factors. That is, such fear only exacerbates (= makes something worse) the casual attitude towards English, discourages reading English material and learning correct grammar and proper usage. It further weakens the ability to recognize errors and smothers the interest to strengthen one's English vocabulary.

The more you avoid English, the more unsatisfactory your English competence will be, resulting in a vicious circle. Some effort must be made to break through it.

1.8   Conclusion: the strategy you need

Clearly, if you want to write well in English, your strategy is to step up your effort on all the fronts described above. You need to

(1)   adopt a serious attitude towards the English language (however uncomfortable you may have been feeling about it) to become more sensitive to how the language works;

(2)   read various kinds of material in English more often and regularly (best daily) so that you can see the language *in action* and learn from how others write;

(3)   study the elements of grammar and usage and do your best to follow the principles you learn when you write in English;

(4) use the knowledge you gain from (2) and (3) to help you recognize errors when they occur in your writing;

(5) know how to correct your errors in your writing once you know or have been told (by a teacher, for example) that they are errors.

(6) increase your knowledge of English words to include their meanings, grammatical functions, and even their idiomatic combinations (collocations) with other words.

In the next chapter, we will see what good written English means.

Chapter 2   What is Good Written English?

What you will learn in this chapter

Good written English has these basic features: (1) It is grammatical, following principles and rules governing how words form sentences. (2) It is idiomatic, reflecting how native speakers use the language. (3) It contains careful and correct choice and use of words. (4) It is clear and readable, preferring the active voice and using plain words.

優秀的書面英語有以下基本特徵：（1）遣詞造句必須符合語法規則。（2）文句必須反映英語母語者的語言習慣。（3）選詞用字審慎正確。（4）行文簡練流暢，多用主動語態和易懂的文字。

2.1   Coming to grips with good written English

2.2   Good written English is grammatical.

2.3   Good written English is idiomatic.

2.4   Good written English is the result of choosing words carefully and using them correctly.

2.5   Good written English is clear.

2.6   Some basic points about clear writing

2.7   Conclusion

2.1 Coming to grips with good written English

Teachers of English no doubt want to teach their students adequate skills in using the English language, hoping that they will be capable of writing good English in their academic work, which is often a fairly good predictor of how they would write as adults. As all English teachers know, however, this goal is not easy to attain. This is especially so in Hong Kong where English is not a first language of the great majority of the population.

In the work world where English is often the language of international communication, corporate employers expect their staff to be competent in writing such documents as business letters, proposals, project contracts, reports, and other special-purpose papers. But such competency is not always what it should be.

Since you are reading this book, you are probably eager to learn how to write better English. What exactly is good written English? Different people tend to have different ideas about what good written English is. Indeed, this is a rather complex question.

Nevertheless, let us try to pin it down to a few important characteristics. First and foremost, good written English is grammatical. Second, it is idiomatic. That is, it reflects the way the language is used naturally by native speakers. Third, it uses words appropriately. Last but not least, good written English is clear so that it is easy to understand.

Let us consider briefly the meaning of each of these four essential characteristics.

2.2 Good written English is grammatical.

As mentioned in the first chapter (see 1.4), grammar is simply the body system of principles and rules that govern how words are put together to form meaningful and complete sentences. Rules determine such things as the order in which words occur and the form that given words take according to their function in the sentence. Rules make it possible for people to communicate efficiently if they are all familiar with such rules.

2.2.1 Grammar makes sentences sensible and readable.

To be able to write well, you need to have a good knowledge of grammar so that what you write does not violate the requirements of grammar, especially the basic ones that make sentences sensible and readable. In the preceding sentence, note the use of **does** but not **do** in **what you write does not violate the requirements of grammar.** Here, as in many other sentences, an important rule of grammar is that the verb must agree with the subject. **What you write** means anything that you write taken as a whole and is thus a singular subject. The verb that refers to it must then be a singular verb. **Does** is an auxiliary verb (or "helping verb") in the singular form. In the last part of that sentence, **the basic ones that make sentences sensible and readable**, the requirement of subject-verb agreement also applies. Here, **make** as a plural verb agrees with the plural subject **the basic ones.**

You have read about this subject-verb agreement rule in the preceding chapter (mentioned briefly in 1.4.1). Indeed, it is so important that you will have the chance to study it in some detail in Chapter 6.

2.2.2   Grammar helps us to write according to accepted standards.

In this book, you will come across rules about a variety of grammatical topics. They help us to write according to some generally accepted standards. They give us answers to many questions that arise when we write. For example: Can we use the present progressive (continuous) tense to refer to future events? When do we use **the** instead of **a** before a noun? Can an adverb (e.g., **certainly**) modify an entire sentence? What is the difference between **on time** and **in time**? Which is correct—**if I was** or **if I were**? I urge you to study the various grammatical topics carefully, because they will guide you in trying to write better English.

2.3   Good written English is idiomatic.

Writing a grammatical sentence, though necessary, does not guarantee that the sentence is well written. A well-written sentence is also idiomatic. That means it reflects how native speakers use the language. The following sentence is grammatically acceptable but is not idiomatic:

She spent much effort to collect money for the new project.

It would be idiomatic if rewritten to read:

She made a big effort to raise money for the new project.

In idiomatic or natural English, we do not say "spend an effort" or "pay much effort" but, quite often, "make an effort" or "make a big effort" or "put in a great deal of effort". Then, to reflect the effort involved in trying to ask for donated funds or some sort of financial contribution to a project, "raise money" is a better choice than "collect money". Certain words often combine or come together as "collocations" (further discussed in Chapter 18). A good knowledge of collocations will no doubt enable you to write in ways that sound more natural.

Let us see another example. The following sentence is taken from what a student wrote about her willingness to learn good English:

Learning good English could be painful, but pains walk with gains.

She starts off well in her sentence, but the second half of her sentence contains her own recast version of a commonly known proverb, "no pain, no gain". Since idioms and proverbs usually have a set expression, we cannot change them freely. Thus, her sentence may be revised to read:

Learning good English could be painful, but as we all know, "no pain, no gain".

Good writing is idiomatic. It should reflect natural usage (as what native speakers would do) of words and phrases, and the writer should pay great attention to choosing the right word that expresses more accurately what he or she tries to say.

2.4   Good written English is the result of choosing words carefully and using them correctly.

2.4.1   Choosing words carefully

Often, quite a number of words with similar meanings may all appear in natural usage but not all of them really express what you want to say. For example, all the following exclamations about a suggestion that you do not like are idiomatic, natural expressions, but you still need to find one (there may be more choices than those shown here) that suits your purpose.

What do you say about a suggestion you don't like?
What a bad suggestion!
What a bizarre suggestion!
What a crazy suggestion!
What a stupid suggestion!
What an absurd suggestion!
What a useless suggestion!
What a ridiculous suggestion!
What an outrageous suggestion!
What a preposterous suggestion!

As you write, you should be aware of the idea that concerns you and the context in which that idea occurs. For example, in referring to some sort of "discussion", you may want to indicate a particular kind of atmosphere or quality associated with it. You need to search for a suitable modifier before the word **discussion.** If your concern is time, the modifier could be **long, short,** or **brief.** If your concern is attitude of the people involved in the discussion, your choices include **candid, sincere, serious,** or **enthusiastic.** If your concern is the mood or atmosphere shown by the participants, you could think of **lively, intense, spirited,** or **heated.** Finally, if your concern is the depth of the discussion, you could consider **extensive, thorough, insightful,** or **thoughtful.**

As you think about these word choices, you should bear in mind the context of the discussion that you try to describe or write about. Is the discussion largely academic, political, professional, religious, business-related, serving certain interest groups, or perhaps some mixture of these? These are questions of context when you choose your words.

2.4.2 Using words correctly

What about using words correctly? This is indeed a huge question. For now, let us see a few examples.

Incorrect	Correct	Remarks
1. *We will **discuss about** this problem.*	*We will discuss this problem.*	**Discuss** is not followed by any preposition.
2. *This is a **most unique** performance.*	*This is a unique performance.*	**Unique** is an absolute term. No modifiers may be used.
3. *Their data set is not **update** enough.*	*Their data set is not up to date enough.*	**Update** is a verb. **Up to date** is a compound adjective, not hyphenated when placed after the noun it modifies.

Incorrect	Correct	Remarks
4. *Similar to* him, she enjoys reading novels.	*Like him, she enjoys reading novels.*	We use **like** (preposition) before a noun or pronoun to express similarity.
5. *I feel difficult* to learn a foreign language.	*I find it difficult to learn a foreign language.*	The task, not the person, is difficult. Thus, **I find it** (the task) **difficult.**

Learning to choose and use words appropriately is essential to good writing. Such learning is best cultivated by reading widely (to include diverse subject matter) which gives you exposure to words used in various contexts. You should also maintain the habit of consulting a good dictionary that can help you with the meanings and use of words, including collocations or the idiomatic combinations of words. Read Chapter 18 to see what good word skills involve. With good word skills, coupled with good knowledge of grammar and usage, you will be able to write better.

Part 3 of this book is on the proper use of many selected words and phrases. Such words and phrases often present problems to learners and users of English. I hope you will delve into that section frequently and make the best use of it to help yourself write better.

2.5   Good written English is clear.

The purpose of writing is essentially expressing yourself clearly. This means you want your readers to understand what you say without difficulty. Of course, if you write grammatically correct sentences, follow idiomatic ways of expression, choose the right words and use them properly, you stand a good chance of being understood. However, these are merely necessary but not sufficient requirements for clear writing, which is quite a complex matter and is indeed a goal that all writers, including experienced and professional ones, try to achieve.

Careful writers habitually read and read again, and again, what they have written to see how they can make their prose as clear as possible. They would ask themselves questions such as the following: Do my sentences contain unnecessary words and cumbersome phrases? Does my writing contain convoluted constructions that are complicated and difficult to understand? Are my paragraphs not coherent (not tightly organized to focus on a main idea)? Actions taken usually include cutting out superfluous words, simplifying phrases, using plain words, using ways to emphasize certain ideas, and reshaping sentence structures so that they become more straightforward and thus more readable.

2.6   Some basic points about clear writing

This book is intended to help you acquire important English skills that should equip you to write clearly. Study and apply them conscientiously, and you should be coming closer to that goal. For now, let us preview several basic points about clear writing. (Clear and effective writing will be discussed in Chapters 21 and 22.)

2.6.1   Characters (people, agents) and their actions should be clear.

Let characters, not abstract ideas, be the subjects in your sentences. Sentences should show clearly who does what. If your readers have to guess who your characters are, your writing is not clear. This means you should write in the *active voice* whenever possible. Examples:

The Government decided to increase land supply.

She has just accepted the appointment as director of research projects.

Our team developed a new procedure of ensuring product quality.

Sometimes, however, when it is difficult or awkward to specify the "doer", the passive would be better. Examples:

Ocean Park Hong Kong *was first opened* in 1977.

An error *was made* in our profit forecast for next year.

Ten million dollars *were raised* to help the victims of the earthquake.

2.6.2 Use plain words.

Plain or familiar words are easy to understand, as illustrated by the following examples:

Avoid	Use plain words
assistance	*help*
at this point in time	*now*
by means of	*by*
facilitate	*help, make easier*
for the purpose of	*to*
in order to	*to*
in a similar way	*similarly*
utilize	*use*
in connection with	*on, for, about*
with regard to	*of, on, for, about*

2.6.3 Vary the length of your sentences.

Common wisdom says it is desirable to write in short sentences. What counts as "short" is hard to say, although shorter sentences are easier to write and to understand. You should not, however, write *only* in short and simple sentences as your writing could sound choppy and even dull. Some sentences can be short (such as the opening sentence of this paragraph) while others may be longer (such as this sentence), depending on what you need to say and how you say it. If you wish to elaborate, you need longer sentences that are somewhat more complex in structure (such as this sentence and the one before it). Sometimes, shorter sentences are better combined to be more effective in expressing connection between ideas.

Good writing therefore includes a mixture of short and long sentences. With practice, you will find out what kind of mixture best serves your purpose. Of course, just as too many short and simple sentences will make your writing uninteresting, too many long and complex sentences will make your ideas more obscure and thus harder for your readers to follow and understand. A sensible variety of sentence lengths is likely to make your writing more appealing (= attractive) and readable.

2.6.4 Use punctuation marks carefully to enhance the flow of your ideas.

Learners of English tend to know not enough about the proper use of punctuation marks and usually pay little attention to them when they write. Unlike speaking, where the speaker can use different voice levels, facial expressions, hand gestures, and pauses to help listeners understand what they say, writing is silent and must depend on punctuation marks to help readers understand what you write because these marks show how ideas are related.

Careful writers pay as much attention to punctuation as to the choice of words. You should learn to use different punctuation marks for different purposes. Do not, for example, use a full stop or a comma casually. Find out, also, when to use a semicolon and when to use a colon. Improper use of punctuation is likely to mislead or confuse your readers. By contrast, competent use of punctuation will improve the clarity of your writing immensely. Read all about the proper use of various punctuation marks in Chapter 19.

2.6.5   Keep a habit of revising what you have written until it is clear enough.

Do you realize that good written English is often not achieved in one go but through repeated revising? Every good writer knows that revising or rewriting is the key to writing well. Rewriting calls for *rethinking*, *reshaping*, and *reorganizing*. Always make an effort to improve the clarity and effectiveness of what you have written. There may be errors of grammar and usage, unsuitable or imprecise choice of words, obscure characters, unfamiliar words or longwinded phrases, and sloppy punctuation. Some sentences may be too long; others may be badly constructed. As a result of careful revision, your writing will surely be much better than your first draft.

2.7   Conclusion

Writing good English is not an unattainable goal. To get there, keep the following points in mind:

(1)   Treat grammar and usage *seriously* as the foundation for writing well. Sometimes this may look more than you can handle. Remember, however, that grammar is just the reason why words can become meaningful and understandable sentences. If you maintain this frame of mind, grammar becomes more friendly and interesting.

(2)   Make an effort to find out what counts as "idiomatic" as opposed to "unidiomatic" when you want to express an idea. If you establish a habit of *reading widely* as much as you can, you will build up useful knowledge of what idiomatic English looks like.

(3)   As you read widely, your vocabulary will no doubt become richer for your use.

(4)   Pay attention to proper punctuation, use of active or passive voice, use of plain words, and variation in sentence length. All these will help you write clearly.

(5)   Always *review*, *revise*, and *rewrite* what you have written to get a better result.

Chapter 3　Learning English Skills

What you will learn in this chapter

Writing good English involves a variety of skills developed through the interaction between knowing more about English grammar and usage on the one hand and practising often on the other. There is a great deal to learn from theory, which is what grammar and usage rules tell you, and from practice, which is reading others' writing and writing your own pieces. If you keep working on both theory and practice, your English writing skills will improve significantly.

要想寫好英文，須具備多樣技巧。這些技巧，是通過掌握英語語法知識和多加實踐培養而成的。理論方面，有語法和詞語用法的學習；實踐方面，有從閱讀和寫作練習中的學習。如果你在這兩方面都持續下功夫，你的英語寫作技巧當會有顯著進步。

3.1　Writing good English is a matter of skill.

3.2　Skill is the combination of theory and practice.

3.3　Writing as skill

3.4　Skills can be enriched and strengthened.

3.5　Skills get better with practice.

3.6　Conclusion

3.1   Writing good English is a matter of skill.

Writing good English is a matter of skill. It is an ability built on the foundation of a good knowledge of English grammar and usage. This ability is developed through plenty of practice using such knowledge. Many learners of English, however, do not think seriously enough about English writing in terms of acquiring and developing a "skill". Yet, it remains true that "skill" is the ability to do something well, and the level of skill acquired determines the level of performance. Like all other skills, writing well has to be learned.

3.2   Skill is the combination of theory and practice.

The general idea of "skill" as the ability to do something well is the combination of theory and practice. Theory is a term we can apply loosely to the knowledge involved in any activity, and practice is simply the operational aspect of that knowledge. Thus, for example, a photographer must have some knowledge of such matters as perspective, space relationship between the camera and the object of interest, effect of light and shadow, aperture, exposure time, and aesthetics of a good picture. Armed with this knowledge, the photographer takes action to produce the pictures he or she desires. By putting knowledge into practice, the photographer has begun acquiring a skill (which consists of a variety of specific skills).

When we say that skill is the combination of theory and practice, a dynamic interaction goes on between theory and practice. The interaction is a process of learning, which occurs when you study something carefully and in detail. The photographer may study different effects obtained from varying the distance between the camera and the object of interest or varying the angle, horizontal and vertical, at which the picture is taken. Different conditions of light are also noted. As a result, the photographer gains more knowledge of what makes a good picture. Some of this experience is based on previous theoretical knowledge and some may become new knowledge. With more practice, more useful knowledge is gained. In turn, the new knowledge gained enriches the theory base.

Thus, a person who is interested in becoming a good photographer must have a good grasp of the theory of photography and combine it with frequent practice to gain new knowledge with which better results may be attained.

3.3   Writing as skill

Like taking good pictures, writing well has its theory or knowledge base. A considerable part of that base, known as grammar and usage, is covered in this book. It contains the basic knowledge necessary for producing good writing, which means writing that complies with the principles and rules of how words and phrases come together to form sentences.

Learning must occur when you engage in constant interaction between the theory base of writing and the practice of writing. The result of this interaction is the emergence of good writing skills. (While we can use the singular **skill** to refer to good writing in a general way, the plural **skills** can also be used when we have in mind the variety of specific skills involved in good writing, just as there are many specific skills in taking good pictures.)

Two important points must be made here, which concern not just good writing but many other activities as well (e.g., singing, playing an instrument, painting, public speaking, swimming). First, gaining the relevant theoretical knowledge is not a one-shot deal. There is much to know and learn; it ought to be learned patiently and carefully. Second, the practice part includes your exposure (seeing how good writers write) and your own involvement (doing exercises—such as those at the end of Chapters 4 to 22 of this book—and writing your own pieces). The practice is to inject *life* into your theoretical knowledge and to reinforce it. Without sufficient practice, what you have learned will remain partial and shaky. The more you practise, the stronger your acquired knowledge will stay with you like second instinct.

If you understand the significance of the two dimensions—theory and practice—of developing good writing skills, you will pay equal attention to mastering the principles and rules of grammar and usage on the one hand and grasping opportunities to practise writing on the other.

3.4   Skills can be enriched and strengthened.

Writing skills, like other skills, do not have to stay stagnant. You may not be a competent writer today because your knowledge base is not rich enough and you lack practice. But this can change. If you put your mind and heart to it, you can start to substantiate your knowledge of grammar and usage. Your previous knowledge may be shaky, but with help (as offered in this book) you can improve it.

There are always things you can do to enrich and strengthen your writing skills. For instance, do your best to understand how to use different verb tenses and how verbs can agree with their subjects. Try starting a sentence in different ways or combining two sentences into one. Learn new meanings and uses of words you already know. Also learn to put related items in the same grammatical form so that your writing becomes clearer and easier to read. Of course, there are more.

3.5   Skills get better with practice.

As we have said, skills are the combination of theory and practice. Learning occurs in just about every part of the process involving both theory and practice. As you read more (books, magazines, newspapers etc.), you will surely see how the principles and rules of grammar and usage (e.g., subject-verb agreement, use or non-use of articles, conditional sentences, parallel structures) are actually followed. If certain passages interest or impress you, copy them for your own study and reference. Never underestimate the power of learning from examples—examples of good sentences, good paragraphs, and good essays.

If you find that you are particularly weak in certain areas of grammar and usage, try study those areas again (and again if necessary) carefully and work on relevant exercises if these are available. (Remember: this book provides you with many exercises.) If you have difficulties with words, you can pay extra attention to their use, and some chapters of this book will be especially helpful (Chapter 7 on nouns, Chapter 8 on pronouns, Chapter 9 on articles, Chapter 10 on adjectives and adverbs, Chapter 11 on prepositions, Chapter 18 on word skills). With repeated attention, study, and practice, you should experience improvement coming your way.

When we say that writing skills will get better with practice, we include the possibility of becoming more aware of certain facts of words and their function. For example, if you pay enough attention to details through observation and examination, you may find that an adverb can modify a whole clause or sentence, that sometimes you can put the verb before the subject (inversion) for emphasis, and that even a long noun clause containing plural nouns can function as a singular subject and thus take a singular verb.

This way, it will not be surprising for your writing skills to get better.

3.6 Conclusion

Remember that English skills for good writing are not just knowledge on paper for you to learn. Of course, you need to learn that, but you must combine it with lots of practice. Use what you learn in real writing so that you will not forget. Also read how others write so that you can learn from them. To become a skilled writer, you must learn to treat with great respect the skills you are about to learn and be keen about honing them so that you will know and use them like the back of your hand.

Turn to the next chapter to begin your journey of learning to be a writer of good English.

PART 2　Learning the Skills

Chapter 4　Recognize the Main Word Classes

What you will learn in this chapter

Knowing the class to which an English word belongs is a basic skill for writing grammatical sentences. Such knowledge is gained from recognizing the various forms a word may take moving from one class to another, although some words that belong to two different classes may share the same form. More importantly, knowledge of word classes is built on understanding the use of the word in a sentence context.

Since there may be more than one way of expressing the same or about the same idea by wording a sentence differently, you will need to be able to use words appropriately according to their word class. At the same time, you should also be aware that, some words have different forms within the same word class. This is particularly true of words that have several adjective forms, each of which with a specific meaning different from the others.

要寫符合英語語法的句子，熟識單詞詞類是不可或缺的技巧。這也就是要明白一個詞從某一詞類轉為另一詞類時形式的變化（有些詞形式不變）。更重要的，這技巧是否熟練，有賴於你是否了解一個詞在句子裏的用法。

由於可以用不同的句式表達同一個意思，你必須根據詞類使用合適的詞。同時，有些詞可以詞類不變，但有多種形式，特別是一些形容詞有好幾種形式，意思卻迥異。這都是需要學習的。

4.1　**English word classes**

4.2　**Using words of different classes correctly**

4.3　**Alternative ways of expressing the same (or much the same) idea**

4.4　**Be familiar with variation in form across word classes.**

4.5　**Summing up**

4.1   English word classes

English words can be classified into a number of classes (traditionally called "parts of speech") according to the function they perform (such as nouns and verbs) in forming sentences. The most basic English skill you must have to write well is being able to recognize what word class a given English word belongs to when you see that word at work in a sentence so that, with enough practice, you will be able to use words of different classes properly in your sentences. If for any reason some words are not functioning the way they should, you should be able to spot that they are probably not being used properly.

The number of word classes is not fixed, for it depends on how detailed our analysis is. However, the more important word classes, for our present discussion, are (a) nouns, (b) verbs, (c) adjectives, and (d) adverbs. (Other word classes are: pronouns, prepositions, conjunctions, and determiners.) For your reference now, the following table shows the eight word classes and their functions.

Word class (Part of speech)	Function	Examples
Nouns	indicate people and things (anything)	*mother family idea cat bus trip peace love*
Verbs	indicate actions and states	*eat sing lose discuss imagine contain select*
Adjectives	modify nouns and pronouns	***large*** *table **delicious** cake **nice** day* *We were **anxious.***
Adverbs	modify verbs, adjectives, other adverbs, or whole sentences	*speak **softly** write **well very** careful* ***most** distinctly **Certainly,** this will work.*
Pronouns	substitute for nouns	*me you she ourselves everything something who*
Prepositions	relate a noun that follows the preposition to other parts of a sentence	***in*** *the park **on** time **after** class* ***because of** rain **according to** law*
Conjunctions	join elements, including clauses, together in a sentence	*and or but although while if when whereas so that*
Determiners (including articles)	show which or how many/much	*a/an the this some many most each every all*

As you should know, we use nouns to name anything (person, object, event, idea, feeling) that often serves as the subject and, if needed, the object of a sentence. We use verbs to say something about what the subject is or does, and adjectives and adverbs to qualify or modify. We shall see more later.

4.2   Using words of different classes correctly

How do we identify or recognize the class of a word? Sometimes, we do so by the word's form (spelling). Often, however, we tell the class of a word from the way it is used in the context of a sentence.

Recognizing the class of a word by its form:

beauty (noun)   *beautify* (verb)   *beautiful* (adjective)   *beautifully* (adverb)

Recognizing the class of a word from its use in a sentence:

Play (n) *is very* (adv) *important* (adj) *to a child's learning and development* (n).

Children **play** (v) *with toys* (n) *to enjoy themselves.*

Note that some words (such as **play**) belong to more than one word class.

Seeing how words are used in sentences is beneficial for developing your ability to use words correctly. One reason is that a word may have more than one grammatical form. Countable nouns have both a singular form (e.g., **egg, apple**) and a plural form (e.g., **eggs, apples**). Verbs have different forms according to the time sense it conveys. (e.g., base verb and present time: **open, write, sit**; past time: **opened, wrote, sat**). When different forms of words such as these come to your attention in your reading, you will gradually pick up patterns of correct use of words.

To express an idea properly, you often need to consider whether you should use a noun or a verb. For example: **The customer complained** (verb) **to the manager about the food**. You must be careful that the idea contained in the verb **complained** may have to be expressed as a noun in a different but related sentence: **The manager listened to the customer's complaint** (noun) **patiently**. It would be incorrect to say **The manager listened to the customer's complain** (verb) **patiently**.

4.2.1   Recognizing nouns and verbs

Nouns and verbs are the main building bricks of sentences. As society changes, many new words are added to these two word classes. It is worth your while to pay some attention to the correspondence between them. In many cases, there is noticeable resemblance in spelling between the noun form and the verb form. This is not too surprising when the noun form is a derivation from the verb. In some other cases, the noun form is the same as the verb form. When both forms are the same, they may or may not share the same meaning. These variations are illustrated below.

Nouns closely resembling verbs	
Verb	**Noun**
agree	agreement
begin	beginning
behave	behaviour
complete	completion, completeness*
continue	continuation, continuity*
differ	difference
discover	discovery
enjoy	enjoyment, joy
inform	information
know	knowledge
paint	paint, painter, painting*
waste	waste, wastage*
	*With different meanings

Nouns and verbs having the same form and sharing the same meaning	
Verb	**Noun**
answer	answer
approach	approach
benefit	benefit
claim	claim
cover	cover
damage	damage
debate	debate
end	end
love	love
mention	mention
reply	reply
stress	stress

Nouns and verbs having the same form but with different meanings

She borrowed a **book** (noun) from a library.
We will **book** (verb) a table for dinner this weekend.

Water **flows** (verb) from higher to lower levels.
Can you follow the **flow** (noun) of thought in this essay?

Ceiling **fans** (noun) used to be quite common in buildings.
Her controversial novel will certainly **fan** (verb) the flames of debate.

Turn (verb) right at the next junction and you will see the bus stop.
It is our son's **turn** (noun) this week to wash the dishes.

4.2.2 Recognizing adjectives and adverbs

Adjectives (adj) and adverbs (adv) are closely related in function. Basically, adjectives modify (= say something about) nouns (things, people, ideas, actions, events, etc.), while adverbs modify verbs (actions), adjectives, or other adverbs. Note the function of adjectives and adverbs in the following sentences:

Adjectives modifying nouns/pronouns
*He gave a **clear** (adj) **explanation** (n) of how the machine works.*
*The **orchestra** will perform an **interesting** (adj) **programme** (n).*
*This **orchestra** (n) is **famous** (adj) and **well funded** (adj).*
***She** (pronoun) seems **happy** (adj) today.* (**happy** modifies pronoun **she**)
***We** (pronoun) were **anxious** (adj) to start our trip.* (**anxious** modifies pronoun **we**)
Adverbs modifying verbs
*The orchestra **performed** (v) **impressively** (adv).*
*The preacher **speaks** (v) **emphatically** (adv).*
*We **arrived** (v) **early** (adv) to beat the lunchtime crowds.*
Adverbs modifying adjectives
*The teacher gave a **perfectly** (adv) **clear** (adj) explanation of the lesson.*
*"Mona Lisa" is a **famously** (adv) **beautiful** (adj) painting.*
*I bought some **almost** (adv) **ripe** (adj) avocadoes.*
Adverbs modifying other adverbs
*We need to examine this matter **very** (adv) **closely** (adv).*
*This news report is **simply** (adv) **totally** (adv) **confusing** (adj).*
*She speaks Spanish **extremely** (adv) **well** (adv).*

4.2.3 Different adverb forms

You should note that many adverbs are formed by adding **-ly** to an adjective. (In the above example sentences, **impressive → impressively, soft → softly, famous → famously, close → closely, total → totally**.) However, some adjectives end in **-ly**, such as **friendly, lively, costly, timely, heavenly**, and **masterly**.

At the same time, some adverbs referring to time, place, and frequency do not end in **-ly**: **now, today, tomorrow, soon, here, there, anywhere, somewhere, always, often, seldom, never**.

You should also note that some adverbs and adjectives have the same form:

Some adverbs and adjectives sharing the same form	
Adjective	Adverb
take a **close** look	don't stand too **close**
an **early** sunrise	she rose **early**
a **fast** sports car	it runs **fast**
a **hard** worker	we all work **hard**

4.3   Alternative ways of expressing the same (or much the same) idea

One useful way of testing your familiarity with the use of words belonging to different word classes is try rewriting a given sentence by changing the word class of its key words. For example, you can change **She has a problem that is difficult to solve** to **She has difficulty finding a solution to this problem.** In this change, **difficulty** (n) replaces **difficult** (adj) and **solution** (n) replaces **solve** (v). Of course, the sentence has to be reworded too. If you revise the sentence further to **She has a difficult problem,** it shows you understand how **difficult** as adjective can modify the noun **problem.** You will find that, very often, the "key words" of a sentence are likely to be nouns, verbs, adjectives, and adverbs.

4.3.1   Four important word classes: nouns, verbs, adjectives, adverbs

Nouns, verbs, adjectives, and adverbs are particularly important for learners of English to know well because they feature so much in all kinds of writing. You need them to write about what people do, how they do it, what conditions they may be in, how they respond to or take control of those conditions, what thoughts are being considered, and many other ideas. Consequently, you should try to know words of these four classes well. You should also study how they work with other words, such as prepositions, pronouns, and determiners (including articles), to be well equipped to write good sentences.

To illustrate this point, each of the following two sets of sentences represents different ways of writing about much the same, though not necessarily identical, idea:

Set 1
(Note that the third sentence in this set differs in meaning from the first two.)
(1) *She gave a **detailed** (adj) **description** (n) of how she became **interested** (adj) in psychology.*
(2) *She **described** (v) in **detail** (n) how she became **interested** (adj) in psychology.*
(3) *She **described** (v) the **details** (n) of her **interest** (n) in psychology.*

Set 2

(Note how sentences (4) and (5) in this set say something different from sentences (1) to (3). Further, sentence (5) contains some information not found in the other sentences.)

(1) *A good employer **treats** (v) his employees **kindly** (adv).*

(2) *A good employer is **kind** (adj) towards his employees.*

(3) *Good employers **treat** (v) their employees with **kindness** (n).*

(4) *Employees usually **expect** (v) their employers to **treat** (v) them **well** (adv).*

(5) *This employer's **kindness** (n) towards his employees is beyond their **expectation** (n).*

4.3.2   Using your knowledge of word classes in your writing

From the above, you can see that understanding the functions of nouns, verbs, adjectives, and adverbs is essential for forming a sentence to express accurately what you want to say. Sometimes, there is not much difference between one way and another, and your choice usually rests upon what comes before and after the sentence you are composing. At other times, one way of writing your sentence can be quite different in meaning from other possibilities. If it fits in well with your flow of thought as brought out by the set of sentences you are writing and if you feel it comes close enough to saying what you want to say, then you can consider adopting it.

4.4   Be familiar with variation in form across word classes.

If you are familiar with variation in form across the four main word classes we have been considering, you will find it easier to make sentences. You will be better equipped to put chosen words together as a sentence in different ways. Take the word **succeed** (v), for example. You could say **To succeed** (v) **makes me feel good** or **Success** (n) **makes me feel good** or **It gives me a good feeling to be successful** (adj) or **It feels good to be successful.** There could be more. You can then choose the one closest to what you mean to say. It is somewhat like an experienced chef putting together the ingredients he needs according to a recipe that he knows thoroughly well to prepare a delicious dish. He can modify the recipe to fit with the situation.

Now study the following two lists, each containing six selected words with their noun, verb, adjective, and adverb forms:

List 1

Noun	Verb	Adjective	Adverb
broadness breadth	broaden	broad	broadly
complaint complaining*	complain	complaining	complainingly
height	heighten	high	highly
newness	renew	new	newly
success succeeding*	succeed	successful	successfully
strength	strengthen	strong strengthened	strongly

*as a verbal noun

List 2

Noun	Verb	Adjective	Adverb
ability	enable	able enabled	ably
correction correctness	correct	correct corrected	correctly
confusion	confuse	confusing confused	confusingly confusedly
interest	interest	interesting interested	interestingly interestedly
satisfaction satisfactoriness	satisfy	satisfactory satisfying satisfied	satisfactorily satisfyingly satisfiedly
surprise	surprise	surprising surprised	surprisingly surprisedly

If you study the words in these two lists carefully, with the help of a good dictionary, you should discover that there is much to learn about the meaning of some words when they change their role from a noun or a verb to an adjective.

Referring to the words in List 1, we note that:

(1)   There is, in most cases, only one adjective form of the word.

(2)   The verb form of some words ends in **-en** (**broaden, heighten, strengthen**).

(3)   The noun form may sometimes look much like the verb form (**success** and **succeed**, **complaint** and **complain**), so you need to know the difference in spelling to distinguish between them.

(4) The noun form is sometimes the present participle (**-ing**) of a verb used as a verbal noun or a "gerund".

(5) There may be more than one noun form, but the meaning is likely to be somewhat different (**breadth** vs. **broadness**, **complaining** vs. **complaint**).

Referring to the words in List 2, we note that:

(1) All words have more than one adjective form, often each with a specific meaning used differently from the others. (e.g., A performance may be **satisfactory**; A meal can be quite **satisfying**; An employee may feel **satisfied** by how he or she is treated by the employer.)

(2) The same word may be both noun and verb (*interest, surprise*).

(3) As in the first list, two noun forms of the same word may have somewhat different meanings (*correction, correctness*; *satisfaction, satisfactoriness*).

4.5   Summing up

Make sure you bear in mind the following main points:

(1) When you learn a word, it is important that you know what class it belongs to. With the help of a dictionary, check what other classes that word (with possible spelling change) may become.

(2) If your dictionary offers example sentences, see how the word playing the role of different word classes is used in a sentence context.

(3) At the same time, try to write your own sentences using the various forms of this word. Make this a habit in your learning of the function of words, and it will help you develop a powerful skill for better writing.

(4) Of course, not every word has all the forms of noun, verb, adjective, and adverb. Some may have just a noun form and/or a verb form. As you come across more words, you will recognize what words come in multiple forms and what words exist in only one class.

(5) If a word has more than one form in the same word class (e.g., adjective), you should try to remember their difference in meaning (e.g., **satisfactory, satisfying, satisfied**). This knowledge and familiarity will sharpen your skill with words. (You will read more about word skills in Chapter 18.)

Exercises   Chapter 4

Exercise 4.1

Read the following passage in which 28 words are in boldface. Each of them belongs to one of the four main word classes: noun, verb, adjective, and adverb. Write them in the spaces under the appropriate label in the table that follows the passage. Of course, you will <u>not</u> be filling up all the provided spaces.

請閱讀下面這段文字，注意其中以粗體表示的 28 個詞各屬四個主要詞類之一（名詞、動詞 、形容詞和副詞）。請將這些詞按詞類寫在該段文字之下表中適當的空格裏。有部分空格是用不上的。

> As **is** **particularly** **typical** of **Chinese** **paintings**, **even** **seemingly** **empty** **space** **adds** a **certain** **philosophical** **meaning** or **aesthetic** **quality** to the painting. The **hermit**, the **pavilion**, the **stream**, the **trees**, and the **distant** **hills** at which the hermit **seems** to be **gazing** all **come** **together** **poetically** to **tell** a **story**.

Noun	Verb	Adjective	Adverb

Exercise 4.2

Is the underlined word a noun (n), verb (v), or an adjective (adj)? Write your answer in the parentheses at the beginning of each sentence.

下面句子中劃了線的詞是名詞 (n)、動詞 (v) 還是形容詞 (adj)？ 請把答案寫在括號裏。

1. (   )   We must <u>talk</u> to our group leader about this problem.

2. (   )   The doctor is going to give an online <u>talk</u> on the coronavirus.

3. (   )   Leonardo da Vinci's diagrams on machines will be on <u>display</u> at the Science Museum.

4. (   )   Many of Franz Liszt's piano pieces were composed to <u>display</u> the skills of the pianist.

5. (   )   Never be afraid to <u>correct</u> your mistakes.

6.   (   )   Correct table manners are most important in fine dining.

7.   (   )   That young girl surprises everybody with her amazing mathematical ability.

8.   (   )   I was happily surprised to find the old picture that had been missing a long time.

9.   (   )   There were many complaints about the quality of his work.

10.   (   )   She called the restaurant's manager to complain about the service she received at dinner.

11.   (   )   He almost mistook her for a well-known actress.

12.   (   )   You must be mistaken about seeing me in the park yesterday because I was at home all day.

13.   (   )   He was in high spirits from start to finish.

14.   (   )   From this point on the music starts to sound like a dance.

15   (   )   Are you finished with the books you borrowed from the library?

16.   (   )   They should have finished their business lunch by now.

17.   (   )   Chinese culture places great emphasis on filial piety.

18.   (   )   Some movies emphasize action much more than plot.

Exercise 4.3

Write the correct form (adjective or adverb) of the word in parentheses. If it is already correct, leave it as it is.

假如括號中的字（形容詞或副詞）不正確，請將它更正。

1. The apartment he saw is not (bad) at all. He wants the property (bad).

2. Have they thought of anything (different) (recent)?

3. The lady seemed (anxious) about something and uttered some words (nervous).

4. The soprano sang (beautiful) in such a (beautiful) concert hall.

5. Jimmy works very (hard) and does everything (good).

6. I will be (complete) happy with something (inexpensive).

7. We (ready) agreed with them about the procedure. We will have everything (ready).

8. I know (various) ways of doing this job (satisfactory).

9. We all feel (uneasy) in (difficult) situations.

10. You can get (tired) (fast) from working like (mad).

11. Look at that sentence (careful). Doesn't it look (incorrect)?

12. The company (usual) give all employees a (fair) evaluation.

Chapter 5　Use Verbs Correctly

What you will learn in this chapter

Verbs make up an important class of words that we need for thinking about and describing activities (actions), thought processes, and states of mind. You will learn about the five forms of verbs: base form, **-s** form, **-ing** form (present participle), past form, and past participle. Unlike regular verbs, though, irregular verbs express their past form and the past participle in a variety of ways. This may cause some difficulty to learners.

Further, you will have an overview of all the English verb tenses, of which four will be examined somewhat closely: (1) present simple, (2) present perfect, (3) past simple, and (4) past perfect. Finally, you will learn how two types of auxiliary verbs function: the "primary auxiliaries" (**be**, **have**, **do**) and the "modal auxiliaries" (such as **can**, **may**, **might**, **should**, **would**). They are put before ordinary verbs to make various senses.

動詞是一個重要的詞類，可以幫助我們思考及陳述各種行動、意念或狀況。在本章裏，你會學習動詞的五種形式：原式、-s 式、-ing 現在分詞、過去式和過去分詞。不規則動詞（irregular verbs）在過去式和過去分詞這兩種形式上有很多不同的變化，這有異於規則動詞（regular verbs）的情況，也令英語學習者感到些許困難。

此外，你需綜覽英語動詞的各種時態（tenses），並特別注意其中的四種：（1）一般現在時（present simple）（2）現在完成時（present perfect）（3）一般過去時（past simple）（4）過去完成時（past perfect）。最後，你將學習兩種助動詞（auxiliary verbs）的作用：基本助動詞（primary auxiliaries）（即 be、have、do）及情態助動詞（modal auxiliaries）（如 can、may、might、should、would）。這些助動詞都放在普通動詞之前使用，表達各種不同的意義。

5.1　The importance of verbs	**5.8　Verb tenses**
5.2　The base form	**5.9　More on four tenses: present simple, present perfect, past simple, past perfect**
5.3　The -*s* form	
5.4　The -*ing* form (present participle)	
5.5　The past form	**5.10　Auxiliary verbs**
5.6　The past participle (pp.)	**5.11　Modal auxiliaries**
5.7　Irregular verbs	**5.12　Summing up**

5.1   The importance of verbs

Have you ever noticed that when you write a sentence you cannot do without one or more verbs? A verb tells us something about the subject of a sentence. It is an "action word" if it says what the subject does, as in the following two sentences:

> I **have** dinner with my grandchildren every weekend.
>
> School classes generally **start** at eight o'clock in the morning.

A verb may also say something about thought and mental processes, as shown in the following:

> He **examines** the role of fast-food restaurants and **tries to understand** their future in Hong Kong.
>
> Chopin's music both **calms** our minds and **elevates** our spirits.

A verb may also be a "being word" if it says something about what the subject is or the subject's state, as in these sentences:

> My friend **is** a nice person.
>
> This new business plan **seems** too ambitious.

In learning to use verbs properly, you need to know that verbs take five forms: (1) the base form, (2) the **-s** form, (3) the **-ing** form (present participle), (4) the past form, and (5) the past participle.

Understanding these forms is important because they relate to how verbs are used according to such considerations as the person (first, second, third), variation for present and past tense, and whether the verbs are "regular" or "irregular". What follows here is only a brief statement of these matters.

5.2   The base form

The base form of a verb is simply a verb in its original spelling, with no added endings. It is as what you see in any verb's head entry in a dictionary. Its main uses are:

- Forming the infinitive after **to:**

> We want **to write** well.
>
> My friend likes **to watch** documentaries on television.

- Indicating the present tense for all persons except the third person singular (**he, she, it**):

> I/you/we/they **enjoy** listening to music.

- Expressing instructions and commands:

> Do not **cross** the road when the light is red.
>
> **Come** in and **take** a seat.

5.3   The -*s* form

Verbs used in the present tense for the third person singular (**he, she, it**) take an **-s** ending:

> She **works** for a large technology company.
>
> Johnny **sings** as a bass in the choir.

An idea, a problem, or a matter of attention, sometimes taking many words to describe, is usually treated like a third person singular and thus takes an -*s* form verb when stated in the present time:

> The rapid rise in property prices **causes** a great deal of public concern.
>
> The desirability of electric cars **becomes** a hotly debated topic.

Some special -*s* forms:

- Add **-es**, not just **-s**, when the base form verb ends in **-ch, -sh, -ss,** or **-x**:

> teach → teaches
>
> brush → brushes
>
> push → pushes
>
> discuss → discusses
>
> mix → mixes

- If the verb ends in **-y**, with one or more consonants before the **-y**, change the **-y** to **-ies**:

> cry → cries
>
> study → studies
>
> beautify → beautifies
>
> satisfy → satisfies
>
> verify → verifies

- Three verbs, **be, do,** and **have**, can be main verbs or auxiliary (helping) verbs. In either role, their equivalent **-s** forms follow this pattern:

> *be: he/she/it **is***
>
> *do: he/she/it **does***
>
> *have: he/she/it **has**.*

5.4 The *-ing* form (present participle)

The **-ing** form is also called the "present participle". (A participle is a word formed from a verb.) Its main uses are:

- Expressing an ongoing action when the **-ing** form verb follows the auxiliary verb **be**:

> *He **is gathering** information about the history of Hong Kong.*
>
> *Dark clouds **are forming**, which suggests possible bad weather.*
>
> *We **were having** lunch when the rain started.*

- As an adjective modifying a noun:

> | *an **exciting** journey* | *(base form: excite)* |
> | *the **coming** typhoon* | *(base form: come)* |
> | ***disturbing** news* | *(base form: disturb)* |
> | ***rotting** apples* | *(base form: rot)* |

- Without itself indicating tense (past or present), forming a phrase or clause (the underlined part in the following example sentences) that is related to the main idea of a sentence but cannot stand alone:

> *She played a piece of music **using** only her left hand.*
>
> *The boy sat in a corner of the room, **doing** nothing.*
>
> *Many people pick up more food than they can eat at buffets, **not knowing** that this is being irresponsible.*

- As a noun (traditionally called a "gerund"), or in a phrase that functions like a noun:

> *Cooking is not her strength.*
>
> *Swimming well takes a lot of practice.*
>
> *Using mobile phones is not allowed in this clubhouse.*

5.5   The past form

The past form of regular verbs ends in **-ed** to indicate the past tense (also called the "past simple tense" or "simple past tense"). This applies to all subjects (1st, 2nd, 3rd, singular and plural):

> *We watched a documentary on television last night.*
>
> *She decided to buy some flowers for her mother's birthday.*
>
> *I cooked breakfast this morning.*
>
> *Large groups of citizens gathered in the park.*

The past form of irregular verbs is variable (see later). This may be troublesome for learners of English, but can be mastered with care and patience.

5.6   The past participle (pp.)

The past participle takes various forms, especially for irregular verbs (see more later). For regular verbs, the **-ed** form also serves as the past participle. The past participle has the following main uses:

- Used with the auxiliary verb **have (has, had)** to indicate an action that is already done or completed:

> *I have tried to memorize this poem.*
>
> *Our boss has decided to change the date of the meeting.*
>
> *Someone had broken into the house before midnight.* (**Broken** is the pp. of the irregular verb **break**.)
>
> *Mr. Wong needs to travel a lot on business and has flown more than 20,000 miles since January this year.* (**Flown** is the pp. of the irregular verb **fly**.)

- Used with the auxiliary verb **be (am, is, are, was, were)** to form the passive voice:

> *The movie "Schindler's List" was directed by Steven Spielberg.*
>
> *Bananas are sold by weight.* (**Sold** is the pp. of the irregular verb **sell**.)
>
> *Einstein is widely considered a genius in science.*

- Forming a participial phrase to modify the subject of a sentence (hence the past participle can act like an adverbial):

> **Encouraged** by many supporters, he decided to face the challenge.
> (may also be written as: He, **encouraged** by many supporters, decided to face the challenge.)
>
> **Having been told** that the typhoon is coming, we will not be going out.
> (may also be written as: We, **having been told** that the typhoon is coming, will not be going out.)

- As an adjective modifying a noun immediately following it:

> **used** clothes   **lost** (pp. of **lose**) documents   the **excited** audience
>
> a **surprised** look   a **depressed** feeling   **stolen** (pp. of **steal**) merchandise

5.7   Irregular verbs

Change in the form of a verb is called "inflection". Most English verbs inflect as they go from the base form to the past form and the past participle form. Regular verbs take the **-ed** ending for both the past form and the past participle form. Some examples are:

Regular verbs		
Base form	Past form	Past participle
act	acted	acted
blend	blended	blended
care	cared	cared
divide	divided	divided
excel	excelled	excelled
follow	followed	followed
help	helped	helped
live	lived	lived
marry	married	married
perceive	perceived	perceived
rely	relied	relied
trace	traced	traced
Note that when the base form of a regular verb ends in **e** (as in **care**, **divide**, **live**, **perceive**, and **trace**), we simply add **d** in both the past form and the past participle.		

In comparison, irregular verbs take the past form and the past participle in many different ways. Sometimes, the past and the past participle take the same form. In some other cases, all three forms are the same. The following are some examples (see more in this book's Appendix):

Irregular verbs		
Base form	**Past form**	**Past participle**
begin	*began*	*begun*
buy	*bought*	*bought*
come	*came*	*come*
cut	*cut*	*cut*
deal	*dealt*	*dealt*
fall	*fell*	*fallen*
grow	*grew*	*grown*
hear	*heard*	*heard*
hurt	*hurt*	*hurt*
lead	*led*	*led*
learn	*learnt, learned*	*learnt, learned*
rise	*rose*	*risen*
spread	*spread*	*spread*
take	*took*	*taken*
write	*wrote*	*written*

5.8   Verb tenses

This is a topic that many learners of English are not quite comfortable with. "Tense" refers to time, which is divided for convenience into "past", "present", and "future". There are two points that you need to bear in mind when learning to use verb tenses properly:

- First, the three time divisions are largely relative, allowing for overlaps. Thus, for example, the "present" can be the present moment as one speaks or a certain vaguely understood time period covering the recent past and the "foreseeable" future.

- Second, the context is important for choosing how to write about things or events in the past or the future. "Context" means situation (as when telling a story, making an argument, analyzing a problem, formulating a plan, giving instructions, and so on). Thus, different tenses may be applicable within the same context. If these two points are not entirely clear to you, do not worry. Just read on, and they will more likely make greater sense to you.

5.8.1   Classification of verb tenses

Using the verb **study** as an example, English verb tenses can be classified as follows:

	Present	**Past**	**Future**
Simple	*I//we/you/they study. (He/she studies.)*	*I studied.* (same for all other persons)	*I will study.* (same for all other persons)
Progressive (Continuous)	*I am studying. (You/we/they are studying. He/she is studying.)*	*I/he/she was studying. (We/you/they were studying.)*	*I will be studying.* (same for all other persons)
Perfect	*I/we/you/they have studied. (He/she has studied.)*	*I had studied.* (same for all other persons)	*I will have studied.* (same for all other persons)
Perfect Progressive (Perfect continuous)	*I/we/you/they have been studying. (He/she has been studying.)*	*I had been studying.* (same for all other persons)	*I will have been studying.* (same for all other persons)

5.8.2 Using tenses

Once you have largely memorized the above pattern, you should pay more attention to how you use the various tenses in writing. The following points are important:

(1) The designation of "present", "past", and "future" is often not entirely clear or specific. There are varying overlaps between them.

- We can use the <u>present progressive</u> to say we are in the middle of some action.

  *I **am preparing** for next week's examination.*

- We can also use the <u>present progressive</u> to refer to something changing over a long period (perhaps since the recent past going into the near future).

  *Covid-19 infection cases **are** still **emerging** in many countries.*

- The <u>present progressive</u> can also refer to something we are involved in but may not be actually doing at this very moment.

  *We **are working** on a solution to this problem.*

- The <u>present perfect</u> tense contains both "past" and "present".

  *They **have lived** in Hong Kong for many years.* (from "many years" ago until right now)

  The sentence implies that these people may be leaving Hong Kong.

- The <u>present perfect progressive</u> contains "past", "present", and "future".

  *They **have been living** in Hong Kong for many years.* (from "many years" ago until now and continuing into the future)

  This sentence implies that these people will continue to live in Hong Kong.

---

(2) The "future" is particularly tricky. We can in fact use several different verb forms to refer to the future, as the following sentences show:

- **Be + going to** (indicating something we have decided to do)

  *We **are going to travel** in Switzerland next summer.*

- **Future simple** (simple statement of some possible action)

  *We **will take** a trip to Switzerland soon.*

- **Present simple** (announcing a timetable, not too different from the next two forms)

  *We **leave** for Switzerland tomorrow.*

- **Present progressive** (present continuous)

  *We **are flying** to Switzerland tomorrow.*

- **Future progressive** (future continuous)

> *We **will be leaving** for Switzerland tomorrow evening.*
>
> · **Present perfect + Future simple**
>
> *When we **have finished** with all the final rehearsals, we **will rest** briefly before performing on stage.*

5.9   More on four tenses: present simple, present perfect, past simple, past perfect

Let us now focus more on the use of four tenses: the present simple, the present perfect, the past simple, and the past perfect. They are much used when you review developments of events, describe characters and achievements, and analyze conditions and problems.

5.9.1   The present simple

Use the present simple for the following:

> · Habits or routines
>
> *I **go** to work at eight in the morning.*
>
> *We often **shop** at this supermarket.*
>
> · Thoughts and feelings that exist at the moment of writing
>
> *I **remember** this place very well.*
>
> *I **think** we need to work harder on language proficiency.*
>
> · Things and conditions that remain the same or true permanently or for a long time
>
> *We **see** lightning in the night sky moments before we **hear** the thunder.*
>
> *The earth **revolves** around the sun.*
>
> · Story of a journey as if things are happening as the reader reads
>
> *On the afternoon of our second cruise day at sea, we **discover** a huge "multi-purpose hall." Today it **is** an arena for bumper cars.*
>
> · Someone's ideas
>
> *Max Weber, a 19th century German sociologist, **argues** that there **is** a connection between the beliefs of Calvinism and the rise of capitalism.*
>
> · The future (see 5.8.2 above)

5.9.2   The present perfect

There are two main uses of the present perfect (***have/has* + past participle**):

> - To indicate that something happened at some time in the past. It could be a long time ago or only shortly before now. The activity may have happened just once or multiple times.
>
>   *I **have visited** Japan several times.*
>
>   *The Museum of History **has attracted** large numbers of visitors to its exhibits.*
>
> - To indicate that something or a situation began sometime in the past and continued to be still valid now. (Note the use of **for** and **since**.)
>
>   *We **have known** Mr. Chan for a long time.* (**For** is followed by a length of time.)
>
>   *They **have studied** English for many years.*
>
>   *The sovereignty of Hong Kong **has returned** to China **since** 1997.*
>   (**Since** is followed by a specific time point—a day, a month, a year—or a time clause, as in the next example.)
>
>   *She **has learned** to play the piano **since** she was a child.*

5.9.3 What is the significance of the present perfect?

The significance of the present perfect lies not so much in some past happening as in the effect of the happening on the present, at the time of speaking or writing. Take, for example, the sentence **They have studied English for many years**. Implied as an effect on the present is that they should now be quite competent in using English. Then, given the sentence **She has learned to play the piano since she was a child,** we may infer that as an adult, she now probably plays the piano quite well.

You should also note that, if the action that began sometime in the past is still in progress, you should use the **present perfect progressive** instead of the present perfect. Thus, instead of saying **They have studied English for many years**, you should say **They have been studying English for many years** if they are still studying English. Similarly, instead of **She has learned to play the piano since she was a child**, the sentence would become **She has been playing the piano since she was a child**, meaning she is still able to play the piano (and is probably quite good at it).

5.9.4 The past simple

At first glance, the past simple tense is simple to use because it refers to something that occurred in the past. As in telling a story or giving an account of past events, everything occurred in the past:

> *According to legend, Hua Mulan **was** a brave woman warrior in ancient China who **took** the place of her elderly father to fight in battle.*
>
> *On September 11, 2001, two hijacked planes **flew** into the twin towers of World Trade Center in New York and **killed** thousands of innocent people.*

Many learners of English, however, may have difficulty in using the past simple. Mainly, there are four points for your attention:

(1)   The regular past form of many regular verbs, as shown earlier in this chapter, ends in **-ed.** For some reason (perhaps insufficient attention or carelessness), this ending is often missing in learners' writing (and often omitted in speech too). The following spelling rules apply:

(a)   If the verb ends in **e**, just add **d.**

care → cared   *live → lived*

stage → staged   *underline → underlined*

(b)   If the verb ends with a consonant (letters other than **a, e, i, o, u**) + **y**, change **y** into **ied.**

carry → carried   *copy → copied*

magnify → magnified   *study → studied*

(c)   If a one-syllable verb ends with one vowel and one consonant, double the final consonant.

plan → planned   *stop → stopped*

dot → dotted   *trap → trapped*

(2)   Be careful with irregular verbs because their past form and past participle are irregular compared with regular verbs. If you are not sure, check with your dictionary. The following are some of the most common irregular verbs and their past forms:

become → became   *catch → caught*
drink → drank   *fly → flew*
know → knew   *lose → lost*
pay → paid   *ride → rode*
speak → spoke   *teach → taught*

(3)   The past simple of all verbs is the same for all persons, but the verb *be* is an exception. The past forms of *be* are *was* and *were*.

*I/he/she/it **was***   *I **was** rather impressed by his speech.*
                    *She **was** absent from work last week.*

*We/you/they **were***   *You **were** so excited watching the football game.*
                    *The choir members **were** totally immersed in their singing.*

(4)   Use the past form of the auxiliary verb **do (did)** in negative statements, questions, and emphatic forms. **Did** is used for all persons. Note carefully that the base form, not the past form, of the verb is used after **did.**

> Negative: They **did not want** to do anything to pollute the environment.
>
> Question: **Did** they **pollute** the environment? (not ~~Did they polluted~~)
>
> Emphasis: They **did follow** the instruction not to pollute the environment.
> (not ~~did followed~~)

5.9.5 The past perfect (*had* + past participle)

The past perfect can be particularly troublesome because it involves *two* reference points in time. Two events, A and B, both happened in the past, but one of them happened first. If event A happened before event B, the past perfect tense is used for event A and the past simple for event B.

> Event A happened earlier, followed by event B:
>
> I **had returned** the library books **before** I **left** for the trip.
>
> All workers at the office **had left** for home **when** the typhoon **struck**.
>
> **After** the choir **had sung** a hymn, the pastor **started** his sermon.

Note that the sequence of the two events is indicated by such words as **before**, **when**, and **after**. You can also use **already** or **just** after **had** to emphasize the completion of the event or action. However, if event A was still going on when event B occurred, you should use the past progressive tense for event A. Study the following sentences:

> We **had already finished** dinner when the telephone **rang**.
> (Alternatively: We **had already finished** dinner; then the telephone **rang**.)
>
> Beethoven **had already become** deaf before he **wrote** his fifth symphony.
>
> We **had just got** home when the plumber **arrived**.
>
> Now compare these two sentences:
>
> I **had just finished** watching television when you **called** me last night.
> (Usual pattern of one activity completed before another. **Watching television** here is a gerund phrase serving like a noun phrase as object of the verb **finished**.)
>
> I **was watching** television when you **called** me last night.
> (One activity was still in progress when another occurred. **Watching** is here the present participle that, when preceded by **was**, forms the past progressive tense.)
>
> Use the past progressive for the ongoing event (raining and looking for the cakeshop):
>
> It **was raining** heavily when we **arrived** at the MTR Central station.
>
> We **were looking for the cakeshop** when we **met** you at the mall.

Sometimes, two sentences are used to show that one event occurred first. Note that the later event may not be an "event" but some point in time or a certain condition:

> *It was 10 o'clock in the morning. They **had already checked out** of the hotel.*
>
> *Some people **arrived** late at the concert hall. The performance **had already started.***
>
> *My mobile phone **was** not in my bag. I **had left** it at home.*
>
> *The deadline for application **had just passed**. There was nothing she **could** do.*
>
> *An earlier event may also be introduced by **because**:*
>
> *We **did** not watch the dolphin show **because** we **had done** that many times before.*

5.9.6   Using the past perfect correctly

Remember the characteristic feature of the past perfect, namely, it does not just express past time but it indicates a relationship between two events at two different time points. When you use the past perfect, always check that you have both (a) a pre-occurring event or action and (b) another event or action or condition following it. Just writing about (a) without specifying (b) is not good practice unless (b) can be understood from the context (as shown in some sentences in the last box in 5.9.5).

If the event or action in (a) is something that happened over some time, you need to use the **past perfect progressive** along with (b), a condition or some happening as mentioned above. Thus, you may have:

> *She **felt** very tired because she **had been working** all day.*
>
> *I **had been waiting** for half an hour when the bus finally **came**.*

As you can see, there is some similarity with the use of the **past perfect**, but with the **past perfect progressive**, the length of the "pre-occurring" action is stressed.

5.10   Auxiliary verbs

Auxiliary verbs, as distinct from what are often called "main verbs", cannot be used alone to refer to an action or a state. They are "helping verbs" in the sense that they are put in front of a main verb to make a meaningful verb phrase that expresses the action or state. Three verbs, **be**, **have**, and **do** are called "primary verbs" because of their basic importance in expressing practically any idea. They can serve as main (ordinary) verbs as well as auxiliary verbs. When they function as auxiliary verbs, they are known as the "principal auxiliaries".

5.10.1 *Be*, *have*, and *do* as auxiliary verbs

Be (am, are, is, was, were)

Use **be** (**been** is the past participle of **be**) before a present participle to show a progressive or ongoing action or state:

*We **are learning** to write better.* (present progressive tense)

*She **was preparing** for her son's birthday party.* (past progressive tense)

*I **have been living** in Hong Kong since 1950.* (present perfect progressive tense)

*They **had been planning** for the trip for weeks.* (past perfect progressive tense)

*By Christmas, I **will have been working** on the project for over two years.* (future perfect progressive tense)

*When he visits his mother in Shanghai this summer, she **will have not been seeing** him for almost eight years.* (future perfect progressive tense for a negative statement)

Use **be** before a past participle to form the passive voice:

*This symphony **was composed** by Tchaikovsky.*

*This photo-editing software has **been updated**.*

*The examination had **been postponed** because of the typhoon.*

Have (have, has, had)

Use **have** before a past participle to form the present and past perfect tenses:

*I **have just finished** writing a book.* (present perfect tense)

*She **has completed** her contract with the company.* (present perfect tense)

*We **had considered** several options before you suggested yours.* (past perfect tense)

Do (do, does, did)

Use **do** as an auxiliary verb to ask a question and to make a negative statement with **not**:

***Do** you know the history of the Second World War?*
(Possible short answer: *Yes, **I do**.*)

***Did** it rain last week?*
(Possible short answer: *Yes, it did rain.* Or: *Yes, **it did**.*)

*Chinese people **do not drink** milk as much as Westerners do.*
(In speaking and in informal writing, **do not** is often shortened to **don't** and **does not** to **doesn't**.)

*She **does not** (doesn't) **think** that this is a good idea.*

5.10.2 *Be*, *have*, and *do* can also be used as ordinary (main) verbs

Be (am, are, is, was, were)

Use **be** to give information (including physical or mental condition) about a person or thing:

> Mr. Lee **is** the manager of this new restaurant.

> The snow-capped mountains in Switzerland **are** simply majestic and inspiring.

> He **is** polite. (implying he is usually polite)

> He **is** just being polite. (meaning he is trying or even pretending to be polite)

> Colour television **was** not available in Hong Kong until 1967.

Use **be** for age, size, weight:

> How old **are** the Egyptian pyramids? They **are** more than two thousand years old.

> How tall **are** you? I **am** 1.75 metres (*tall*).

> What **is** the weight of this parcel? or How much does this parcel weigh?

> It **is** less than 1 kilogramme or It weighs less than 1 kilogramme.

Use **be** in **there is/are/was/were** and **it is/was** constructions:

> **There is** bias in this statement.

> **There were** mistakes in his calculations.

> **There are** many problems of communication waiting to be fixed.

> **It was** cloudy and rainy last week.

> **It is** time to enjoy the show.

Have (have, has, had)

Have often means "possess".

> We **have** an old car that is not very reliable.

> We have **had** this old car for fifteen years.
> (**Have** here is an auxiliary verb; **had** is the past participle of **have** as an ordinary verb.)

Other uses of **have**:

> We usually **have** oatmeal and fruit for breakfast.

> The students **are having** an orientation camp this week.

> How many hours of driving lessons did you **have**?

> Did you **have** trouble getting tickets for the concert?

> I hope you **had** a wonderful time visiting your children in Vancouver.

> She **is having** all her best friends to her birthday party tomorrow.

Do (do, does, did, done)
Some common uses of **do** as an ordinary verb:
*What do you **do** for a living?* (The first **do** is an auxiliary verb; the second **do** is an ordinary verb.)
*I don't know how he **did** it, but he has **done** a great job.* (**Don't** is an auxiliary verb; **did** and **done** are ordinary verbs.)
*What is he **doing** these days?* (= What activities is he involved in?)
*How is he **doing** these days?* (= How is he getting on?)
*The boy does not **do** what his parents told him.* (**Does** here is an auxiliary verb.)
*It's all my fault and has nothing to **do** with you.* (= It doesn't concern you.)

5.11 Modal auxiliaries

The commonly used modal auxiliaries include **can**, **could**, **may**, **might**, **must**, **shall**, **should**, **will**, **would**, **be able to**, **have to**, **had better**, **ought to**, **be supposed to**, and **used to**.

Modal (from the noun **mode**, meaning a particular style of behaving) auxiliaries (or "modal verbs" or simply "modals") are, like the three common auxiliaries described above (**be, have, do**), "helping" verbs placed before an ordinary verb to make some particular sense.

However, modals are more than that. They are used generally to indicate the speaker's or writer's attitude or perspective about the nature of a situation or state of affairs (whether, for example, something is possibly the case or necessarily the case). Thus, there is clearly some important difference, reflecting the speaker's attitude, between the statements **It may be fine today** (expressing possibility) and **It must be fine today** (expressing necessity or certainty). **May** and **must** are two of many modal auxiliaries.

Modals are a rather broad topic in English grammar and usage. Understanding them well is instrumental in shaping your writing to express your intended ideas precisely. For the purposes of this book, however, only the more general uses of modals will be described.

5.11.1 Common characteristics of modal auxiliaries (modals)

There are several characteristics common to all modals:

(1)   Modals always occupy the first position in a verb phrase. *She **can sing** beautifully.* *We **would accept** any credit card.* ***May** I **see** your ID please?*
(2)   Modals are always used with the base form of an ordinary verb.(see the above three sentences).

> (3)   In short answers, only the auxiliary is used without repeating the original ordinary verb.
>
> **Can** *you play a trumpet?*   *Yes, I* **can***.*
>
> **Should** *we make a reservation?*   *Yes, we* **should***.*

5.11.2 Main uses of modals

The main uses of modals can be shown according to these categories: (1) permission, (2) polite requests and statements, (3) possibility, (4) ability, (5) obligation or necessity, (6) no necessity, (7) advisability, (8) expectation, and (9) repeated past action. The following only lists the more commonly used modals.

(1) Permission

may	*You **may** leave as soon as you have finished your work.*
can	*I **can** leave (=I am allowed to leave) early today.*
could	*The professor said exchange students **could** audit his course.* (**could** *is used here as a past form of* **can***.)*

(2) Polite requests and statements

may	***May** I have your attention please?*
can	***Can** you pass the salt please?* (informal)
could	***Could** you pass the salt please?* (more formal than **can**)
would	***Would** you mind helping me with the housework?*
	*We **would** be delighted to visit you in Canada next year.*

(3) Possibility

> **may** or **might** (less than 50% likelihood)
>
> **Present or future time:**
>
>   *They **may** come although it is getting late now.*
>
> Using *might* instead of *may* implies some doubt about the possibility:
>
>   *They **might** come although it is getting late now.*
>
>   *I always carry an umbrella because you never know when it **might** rain.*
>
> **Past time:**
>
>   *We knew that we **might** have to take a long time to go through customs.*
>
>   *I don't know where my brother went. He **might** have been at the library.*

You also use **might** to speak about a condition that is not fulfilled because some action did not happen (note the use of the past perfect tense for the action that did not happen). The following sentence thus refers to past possibility:

If we had waited longer (but we did not), *we **might** have got on a bus.*

could (less than 50% likelihood)

Present or future time:

*He is absent today. He **could be** sick.*

*She **could** do well in the interview tomorrow.*

Past time: *They **could have** decided to postpone the dinner gathering.*

should or **ought to** (90% likelihood) (expectation)

Future time:

*Wang has been practising hard. He **should** do well in the competition tomorrow.*

*Let's watch the movie this weekend. It **ought to be** interesting.*

must (95% likelihood)

Present time: *It's raining hard. She **must** be staying home.*

Past time: *Clearly, this **must have been** a misunderstanding.*

will (100% certainty)

Future time: *Don't worry, I **will** be there on time.*

(4) Ability

can	*She **can** cook for ten or fifteen people without difficulty.*
be able to	*To qualify for the job, you must **be able to** speak French and Putonghua.* (slightly more formal)
could	*I **could** not swim until about ten years ago.*
could	is also used to refer to an ability in the past but the action did not take place:
	*You **could** have called to make a new reservation; now we must sit more compactly.*

(5) Obligation or necessity

must	You **must** bring your passport when you travel to another country. (stronger than **have to**)
have to	Visitors to the temple **have to** leave their shoes outside.
should	We **should** arrive a little earlier to get seats.

had to provides the past tense of **must**:

Before the age of telecommunication, people **had to** rely on the post to contact overseas friends.

(6) No necessity

don't have to	Owing to bad weather, I **don't have to** go to work today.
	You **didn't have to** see a doctor as you said you had only a minor discomfort.
don't need to (= **don't have to**)	The two sentences above can be rewritten as:
	Owing to bad weather, I **don't need to** go to work today.
	You **didn't need to** see a doctor as you said you had only a minor discomfort.

(7) Advisability

ought to	As the examination is approaching, you **ought to** study more. (present or future time)
	She **ought to** have studied harder for her second test, but she didn't. (past time)
should	The preceding two sentences can be written with **should** in place of **ought to** without any change in meaning:
	As the examination is approaching, you **should** study more.
	She **should** have studied harder for her second test, but she didn't.

Like **must** and **have to, ought to** and **should** also carry the idea of obligation. However, while **must** and **have to** both express obligation with the expectation that it will be fulfilled, this is not necessarily true with **ought to** and **should.** Thus, if the advisable action is to be emphasized, **must** or **have to** is a better choice. For example:

As the examination is approaching, you **must** study more.

had better	**Had** in this modal is not a real past; its meaning is actually present or future. **Had better** is often used in giving advice, along with a stated or an implied threat of some unfavourable consequence.
	You **had better** be on time, or the tour group will leave without you.
	We **had better not** go to the Middle East at this time.

(8) Expectation

be supposed to	He **is supposed to** feel better after taking the medicine.
ought to	She **ought to** perform well after so much practice. (present or future)
	She **ought to have** passed the test, but she didn't. (past)
should	Our shuttle bus **should** arrive anytime now. (present or future)
	Our shuttle bus **should have** arrived ten minutes ago. (past)

(9) Repeated past action

Note that the time referred to in the following sentences is the past.

would When my mother was in the home for the elderly, I **would** visit her once or twice every week.

used to We **used to** go to church together on Sundays.

5.12 Summing up

Verbs play a central and instrumental role in all writing. The more you are familiar with the inflection (changes in form) and grammatical functions that verbs take and understand their proper usage, the better your writing will be. The following are the main points covered in this chapter.

(1) Verbs take five forms:

- the base form: **cook, try, go*, break*, forget*** (*irregular verbs)

- the **-s** form: **cooks, tries, goes, breaks, forgets** (for "third person" singular in present tense)

- the **-ing** form (present participle): **cooking, trying, going, breaking, forgetting**

- the past form: **cooked, tried, went, broke, forgot**

- the past participle: **cooked, tried, gone, broken, forgotten**

(2) Regular verbs have regular past and past participle forms, typically by having an **-ed** ending. Irregular verbs form their past tense and past participle in different ways (e.g., **come, came, come; do, did, done; hurt, hurt, hurt; lie, lay, lain**).

(3) Correct use of verb tenses is important because what you write almost always involves some reference to time—past, present, or future. You should know about all twelve possible English verb tenses although some of them are not as frequently used as others. The more frequently used tenses include (a) present simple, (b) present perfect, (c) past simple, and (d) past perfect. Some important points are:

- Many ways are possible to express future time, including using the present simple and the present progressive.

- The present perfect includes notions of past and present (e.g., **We *have lived* here for many years**). Closely related is the use of the present perfect progressive to include notions of past, present, and future (e.g., **We *have been living* here for many years**).

- The past perfect is usually used along with the past simple to reflect two reference points in time when one event happened before another (e.g., **He *had walked* for an hour before/when he *found* the old temple**).

(4)   The three "principal auxiliary verbs" (**be, have, do**) are "helping verbs" when they come before a main verb to make a meaningful phrase, including forming some tenses (e.g., ***am* writing, *had* finished, it *did* rain**). They can also double as main verbs (e.g., **She *is* polite; I *have* some trouble; He *is doing* well**).

(5)   There are a dozen or so "modal auxiliaries" (e.g., **can, could, may, might, must, should, would**) that you can use before a main verb to express how you feel about an action or a situation. You can use a suitable modal auxiliary to mean, for example, that some event is quite likely, that you are making a polite request, or that some action is necessary.

| Exercises | **Chapter 5** |

Exercise 5.1

For each of the following sentences, use the past simple tense form of a suitable verb selected from the given list.

試從附表中選一個適合的動詞，以其一般過去時形式填寫在空白處。

begin	buy	catch	cost	forget	hide
leave	review	spread	teach	wait	win

1. My friend _____ a new flat last month.

2. He _____ all his study notes thoroughly in preparation for the examination.

3. Their team _____ additional funding for the research project.

4. The meeting _____ at nine o'clock without any delay.

5. She _____ to bring her house keys when she left home this morning.

6. He _____ mathematics in a private school soon after he graduated.

7. We _____ for the shuttle bus for almost half an hour.

8. At breakfast the boy _____ a lot of butter on his toast.

9. Our neighbours the Wongs _____ for Tokyo last Saturday.

10. He _____ some money under a pile of magazines.

11. I remember your dog _____ the ball every time without miss.

12. In the 1960s a dish of dim sum _____ only about one dollar.

Exercise 5.2

Use the correct tense of the verb in parentheses.

把每句括號裏的動詞以正確時態寫在括號旁的空白處。

1. We (hear) _____ the Chief Executive's speech on television last evening.

2. It (rain) _____ not too much during the summer months.

3. When I got home in the afternoon, I (discover) _____ that the grocery I had bought (be) _____ already delivered in front of the door.

4. She (have) _____ no travel plans for the rest of the year.

5. I (work) _____ on my paper when you called me yesterday.

6. Up to now, no feedback (receive) _____ from our client.

7. Water (boil) _____ when it (reach) _____ 100° C.

8. They (fly) _____ from Hong Kong to Toronto, which took them 15 hours.

9. The Chens (live) _____ in Hong Kong for ten years when they (return) _____ to Sydney last Christmas.

10. For many months now, experts in several countries (try) _____ to develop an effective coronavirus vaccine.

11. I (believe) _____ strongly that practice can (improve) _____ your language proficiency.

12. My grandson (learn) _____ to play the violin since age three. He is still taking lessons.

13. We (visit) _____ Bangkok several times before but have never been to other places in Thailand.

14. The orchestra's musicians (be) _____ totally immersed in their playing last evening.

15. We did not watch the dolphin show because we (do) _____ that many times previously.

16. We have cruised in large ships quite a few times before, so we (plan) _____ to try a river cruise in Europe perhaps two years from now.

17. Conditions of Covid-19 are still uncertain; we hope things (be) _____ better next year.

18. What do you think he (go) _____ play as an encore?

19. When you (finish) _____ with all the exercises, you will be more familiar with the use of verb tenses.

20. After I (give) _____ the package to the courier this morning, I (feel) _____ much relieved.

Exercise 5.3

Be, **have**, and **do** are auxiliary verbs (AV), but can also be main verbs (MV). Underline them in the following sentences (each sentence containing one) and indicate their function as either AV or MV in the space to the right.

Be, have 和 do 是助動詞 (AV)，但也可以用作普通動詞（也稱主要動詞）(MV)。以下每句都含一個這樣的動詞，請在它的下面劃底線，並在右邊的空白處填 AV 或 MV，代表它在該句裏的作用。

AV or MV?

1. We are learning the skills necessary for writing better.   _____

53

2. Our team has been preparing for the event for weeks. _____

3. Mr. Szeto is our team leader. _____

4. She does not think that she should apply for the job. _____

5. We usually have noodles or pasta for lunch. _____

6. The meeting has just begun. _____

7. She had already left the office when you arrived. _____

8. This is easy to do if you follow the instructions. _____

9. How do you keep in contact with your former classmates? _____

10. He wants to do well in the next test. _____

11. They really had a pleasant time riding on the Glacier Express train. _____

12. There were many sunny days during their whole trip. _____

Exercise 5.4

The box below lists ten uses of modal auxiliaries. Identify the use of the modal auxiliary (in boldface) in each sentence and write in the parentheses the letter representing that use.

下面的方框裏列出了情態助動詞 (modal auxiliaries) 的十種功用。請辨認每句中的情態助動詞 (粗體字) 的功用，並在括號裏填寫代表該功用的英文字母。

a. Permission	b. Polite request	c. Possibility	d. Certainty
e. Ability	f. Obligation/necessity	g. No necessity	h. Advisability
i. Expectation	j. Repeated past action		

1. (　　) Our guests **should** be arriving anytime now.

2. (　　) Don't worry. You **might** do better next time.

3. (　　) All passengers arriving in Hong Kong **must** undergo quarantine for 14 days.

4. (　　) My daughter **does not need** to work at her office.

5. (　　) I **used to** buy groceries for my mother every weekend.

6. (　　) As I promised, I **will** be at the meeting.

7. (　　) **Could** I borrow your coffee maker please?

8. (　　) Our two children **could** swim before they were ten years old.

9. (　　) I **ought to** have gone to bed earlier last night, but I did not.

10. (   )   With the risk of viral infection still present, many people **don't have to** work at their offices.

11. (   )   Because of shortage of supply, each customer **may** not buy more than two bottles of hand sanitizer.

12. (   )   Our team **is supposed to** submit our project's interim report next week.

13. (   )   He said he **could not** spare the time to help me.

14. (   )   **Would** you mind if I left early?

15. (   )   Her boss said she **can** take the day off to help her sick mother.

16. (   )   Before there were computers and printers, people **had to** rely on typewriters to prepare documents.

17. (   )   In the 1950s I **would** visit the theatre in my neighbourhood on Sundays to watch the morning comedy show.

18. (   )   We **should** all exercise more to stay fit and healthy.

Chapter 6　Observe Subject-Verb Agreement

What you will learn in this chapter

One of the most common grammatical problems faced by learners and users of English is failure to achieve agreement between the subject and its verb in a sentence. You will learn the difference between singular and plural subjects and the difference between singular and plural verbs. You will also learn how the question of number (singular or plural) is associated with compound subjects, indefinite and relative pronouns, quantity expressions, collective nouns, and some commonly used phrases.

英語學習者和使用者經常遇到一個語法困難，就是句子中的主語與其動詞不一致 。在本章裏，你會學習單數主語和複數主語的區別，以及單數動詞和複數動詞的不同。此外，就主語與動詞達成一致這個問題，你更會學習怎樣就以下元素去判定單數和複數的不同：複合主語（compound subjects）、不定代詞（indefinite pronouns）與關係代詞（relative pronouns）、表示多少的詞語、集合名詞（collective nouns）和一些常用的短語。

6.1   What does subject-verb agreement mean?

The basic requirement that applies to any sentence you write is that there must be agreement between the subject and the verb that refers to it. Simply put, ***when you use a singular subject, its verb must be singular; when you use a plural subject, its verb must be plural***. Look at some examples below that show such agreement.

6.1.1   Singular verbs

The verbs (including auxiliaries, e.g., **be**, **have**, **do**) in the following sentences are all singular verbs because they apply to singular subjects:

---

*She **is** (aux. verb) just about to leave home.*

*Writing well **is** (main verb) always challenging.*

*Life in Hong Kong **was** (main verb) hard in the 1950s.*

*It **has** (aux. verb) been raining since this morning.*

*Only one of us **knows** (main verb) the answer to that question.*

*Communication **becomes** (main verb) so much easier with mobile phones.*

*What **does** (aux. verb) it mean to be a Christian in a high-tech society?*

6.1.2   Plural verbs

The verbs (including auxiliaries) in the following sentences are all plural verbs because they apply to plural subjects:

Note the plural subject in each of the following sentences:

*They **have** got wet in the heavy rain.*

*Children **learn** new things every day.*

*We **become** wiser as we grow older.*

*The books on the shelf **are** gathering dust.*

> *His son and daughter **have** both gone to study in Canada.*
>
> *My eyes **were** sore from some kind of inflammation.*

6.1.3 Singular/plural variation of *be, have,* and *do*

It is basic that you remember the singular/plural variations of the verbs **be, have,** and **do**, as given in the following table. (**This/that** represents any singular, and **these/those** any plural, subject in a sentence.) Variations of two irregular verbs, **give** and **take**, are also shown for comparison.

Verb	Singular Subject-Verb (past tense in parentheses)	Plural Subject-Verb (past tense in parentheses)
be	*I **am** (**was**)* *You **are** (**were**)* *He/she/it **is** (**was**)* *This/that **is** (**was**)*	*We **are** (**were**)* *You **are** (**were**)* *They **are** (**were**)* *These/those **are** (**were**)*
have	*I **have** (**had**)* *You **have** (**had**)* *He/she/it **has** (**had**)* *This/that **has** (**had**)*	*We **have** (**had**)* *You **have** (**had**)* *They **have** (**had**)* *These/those **have** (**had**)*
do	*I **do** (**did**)* *You **do** (**did**)* *He/she/it **does** (**did**)* *This/that **does** (**did**)*	*We **do** (**did**)* *You **do** (**did**)* *They **do** (**did**)* *These/those **do** (**did**)*
give	*I **give** (**gave**)* *You **give** (**gave**)* *He/she/it **gives** (**gave**)* *This/that **gives** (**gave**)*	*We **give** (**gave**)* *You **give** (**gave**)* *They **give** (**gave**)* *These/those **give** (**gave**)*
take	*I **take** (**took**)* *You **take** (**took**)* *He/she/it **takes** (**took**)* *This/that **takes** (**took**)*	*We **take** (**took**)* *You **take** (**took**)* *They **take** (**took**)* *These/those **take** (**took**)*

Note that, for the past tense of the verbs **have** and **do**, there is no distinction between the singular and the plural. Both singular and plural subjects take **had** and **did**. Indeed, in the past tense, the same past form of other verbs is used for both singular and plural subjects (e.g., **My mother** *gave* **me; My parents** *gave* **me**). *It is only in the present tense that you need to add an -s ending to a verb referring to a singular subject or a singular third-person, he/she/it, named or unnamed* (e.g., **This chair** *costs* **$500; He** *wants* **to try something new; It** *gives* **me joy to see you; This** *takes* **a moment**). For plural subjects in present time, you must not add an **-s** ending to the verb (e.g., **Her friends** *travel* **a lot every year; These cookies** *taste* **good**).

The important thing to remember about a "singular verb", then, is that it must end in **-s** when you use it in the present tense to talk about a "singular subject", which, in the case of person, is called a "third person". If you fail to follow this rule, you are causing disagreement between subject and verb.

Now we are ready for some specific situations of subject-verb agreement.

6.2   Main word of a noun phrase

When the subject consists of a noun phrase, however short or long, the main word (also called "head") of the noun phrase must agree with the verb that follows and refers to it.

The first boldfaced word in each sentence is the head of the noun phrase:

*The **rooms** of this apartment **are** quite spacious.*

*Physical **changes** in Hong Kong in the past two decades **have** been spectacular.*

*A **list** of references **appears** at the end of an academic article.*

*The **proposal** to build several man-made islands **has** aroused much debate.*

*The only **reason** that he gave for his resignation **was** that he wanted to spend more time with his family.*

6.3   Compound subjects

A compound subject is formed by joining two or more subjects with **and** or **both . . . and . . .** It is treated like a plural subject. Generally, you need to use a plural verb.

*Chopin and Liszt **were** contemporaries.*

*Hong Kong and Macau **are** both China's special administrative regions.*

*Both The Chinese University of Hong Kong and The University of Hong Kong **offer** medical training.*

6.3.1   Compound subjects formed with *or* or *nor*

If all parts of a compound subject joined by **or** or **nor** are singular, use a singular verb. If all parts are plural, use a plural verb:

*Either today or tomorrow **is** suitable for hiking since we do not have to work.*

*Neither this bookstore in Causeway Bay nor the one in Central **carries** the book you mentioned.*

*Chinese stir-fries or Western steaks **suit** me fine.*

If one part of a compound subject is singular and the other plural, the verb agrees with the nearer part. Sometimes, to make your sentence sound more natural, you can put the plural part closer to the verb that then becomes plural, as rewording of the third sentence below shows:

> *Neither Matthew nor his sisters **know** about their relatives in England.*
>
> *The manager or his assistants **are** authorized to handle customer complaints.*
>
> *Neither the employees nor the manager **is** responsible for business losses during the epidemic.*
>
> Better:
>
> *Neither the manager nor **his employees are** responsible for business losses during the epidemic.*

6.3.2 When *each* or *every* comes before a compound subject, the verb is singular.

> ***Each** school group and youth organization **is** entitled to a discount in the museum's admission fee.*
>
> ***Every** man, woman, and child **has** a right to receive medical care.*

6.3.3 When *each* follows a compound or plural subject, the verb is plural.

> *China and the United States **each have** different central values.*
>
> *The children **each get** a present from their parents.*
>
> *Brand A, Brand B, and Brand C **each have** their special appeal.*

Many learners make the mistake of using a singular verb (e.g., **each has, each gets**). In the above sentences, **each** functions adverbially (pointing to how some action or quality occurs) and *does not constitute the subject itself*. Thus, the verb should be plural to agree with the subject.

6.4 Indefinite pronouns

Many indefinite pronouns (so called because they stand for some person or thing without specifying which one: **anyone, anybody, anything, everyone, everybody, everything, no one, nobody, nothing, one, someone, somebody, something**) have a singular sense and thus take a singular verb:

> ***Anybody** who **cares** about climate change should know the global consequences of the melting of ice in the polar regions.*
>
> *Almost **everyone** in Hong Kong **loves** baked pork chop rice.*
>
> *This garment store is closing in a week; **everything has** to go!*
>
> *For little children, **nothing tastes** as good as ice cream.*
>
> ***Someone has** left a mobile phone in the toilet.*
>
> *Accidents occur often because **something** wrong **happens** with human control.*

6.5   Relative pronouns in relative clauses

The relative pronoun (e.g., **who**, **which**, **that**) that begins a relative clause points back to the noun, the head word of the noun phrase. This noun is called the "antecedent" of the relative pronoun. The relative pronoun must take a verb that agrees with its antecedent.

> ***Those*** *who **exercise** regularly **are** likely to be healthier.* (plural subject)
>
> *This is a **story** which **attracts** people of all ages.* (singular subject)
>
> *The only **thing** that **matters** now **is** to make the best use of our time.* (singular subject)
>
> *They **are** among the best **orchestras** that **have** ever visited Hong Kong.* (plural subject)

6.6   Quantity words and expressions

Quantity words and expressions like **all, any, some, most, a lot of, all of, some of, plenty of,** and **most of** have a singular sense when used with uncountable nouns and a plural sense when used with plural countable nouns.

Singular	***All*** *that description **is** designed to attract customers.* (**Description** is used in this sentence as an uncountable noun taking the singular form.)
Plural	***All*** *students **are** expected to take examinations.* (**Students** is a plural countable noun.)
Singular	***Any*** *improvement **is** gained by hard work and practice.*
Plural	***Any*** *tickets left at this time **are** likely to be all sold in a matter of minutes.*
Singular	***Some*** *help **comes** from those who know.*
Plural	***Some*** *people **find** cruising very attractive.*
Singular	*Take it easy. There **is plenty of** time.*
Plural	***Plenty of*** *cleansing agents **are** available in supermarkets.*
Singular	***Most*** *fruit in this supermarket **is** inexpensive.*
Plural	***Most*** *restaurants **accept** telephone reservations.*
Singular	***A lot of*** *money **is** spent on building a mass transit railway line.*
Plural	***A lot of*** *new banknotes **are** used for red packets at Chinese New Year.*
Singular	***All of*** *the seafood served at this restaurant **is** fresh.*
Plural	***All of*** *the eateries in Central **are** full at lunchtime.*
Singular	***Some of*** *the conducting we see on stage **involves** plenty of bodily movement.*
Plural	***Some of*** *the vegetables sold here **come** from Australia.*
Singular	***Most of*** *her work time **is** spent on telephone conferences.*
Plural	***Most of*** *the members of this church **live** on Hong Kong Island.*

6.7   Other quantity expressions

6.7.1 *One of, the only one of*

These phrases always come before a plural count noun. Note, however, that the verb used is plural in (a) but singular in (b) and (c). Study them closely to see why.

> (a) *She is **one of** hundreds of fresh graduates who **are** applying for this position.*
>
> (b) ***One of the reasons** she took the job **was** that it provided solid on-the-job training.*
>
> (c) *This is **the only one of** the movies currently showing that **is** really worth seeing.*

6.7.2 *More than one*

Be careful when using this phrase. While it suggests a plurality of things, the verb that is used depends on the main word associated with the phrase. The main word is **way** in (a), but **ways** in (b):

> (a   *There **is more than one way** to peel an orange.*
>
>   Alternatively: ***More than one way** to peel an orange **is** possible.*
>
> (b) *There **are more ways than one** to peel an orange.*
>
>   Alternatively: ***More ways than one** to peel an orange **are** possible.*

6.7.3 *A great deal of, a large amount of*

These two expressions are usually used with uncountable nouns and a singular verb.

> ***A great deal of** money **is** needed to keep a professional orchestra operating.*
>
> ***A large amount of** food **is** offered on several buffet tables.*

6.7.4 *The majority of*

The majority of is generally used with plural countable nouns and plural verbs.

> ***The majority of** consumers **do** their grocery shopping in supermarkets.*
>
> ***The majority of** Hong Kong people **have** travelled to other Asian countries.*

6.7.5 *None of*

When **none of** is followed by a plural noun or pronoun, you can use a singular verb (more formal) or a plural verb (more informal):

> ***None of*** *the children **has** heard of Einstein.* (more formal)
>
> ***None of*** *the children **have** heard of Einstein.* (more informal)

When **none of** is followed by an uncountable noun, the verb is singular:

> ***None of*** *his work satisfaction **comes** from pay.*
>
> ***None of*** *your argument **is** built on evidence.*

6.7.6   *A number of, a large number of, the number of*

A number of means "many" and **a large number of** means "very many". They both are used before plural countable nouns and so always take a plural verb:

> *I know that **a number of** travel agencies **offer** tours to South America.*
>
> *These young entrepreneurs know that **a large number of** obstacles **are** standing in their way.*

The number of refers to a certain number of things or people. So, it takes a singular verb:

> ***The number of*** *graduates applying for management jobs **is** quite large.*

6.7.7   *A variety of*

A variety of people/things means different types or kinds of people or things. It thus takes a plural verb:

> ***A variety of*** *treatment **methods exist** for the common cold.*
>
> ***A great variety of*** *animals **live** in Africa.* (You can modify **variety** with such adjectives as **wide, large, huge, considerable, amazing,** and **infinite**.)

When you speak of a particular variety (type) of something, *a variety of* takes a singular verb. You can speak of **this, that,** or **each** variety of something as a singular entity. Of course, you can also speak of **many varieties**, in which case you will use a plural verb. Sometimes, you can refer to **the variety of** something as a whole, using a singular verb.

> *I remember **a rare variety of** rose that **has** a refreshing fragrance.*
>
> ***This variety of*** *tea **is** widely available in Guangdong Province.*
>
> ***Each variety of*** *ice cream **has** its own special texture.*
>
> ***Many varieties of*** *apple **are** available at supermarkets.*
>
> ***The variety of*** *wines available for dining **is** unfamiliar to the inexperienced beginner.*

6.7.8 *A series of*

A series of, followed by a plural countable noun, takes a plural verb:

> *A series of events have occurred and aroused great attention by the media.*

But the word **series** can also refer to a TV programme consisting of a number of episodes. Used in this sense, **series** takes a singular verb (see also 6.8.1).

> *The series "Great Continental Railway Journeys" brings us to the history of many European countries.*

6.7.9 *As well as*, *together with*, *in addition to*

In the construction *X, as well as Y*, the subject is X; *as well as Y* is not part of the subject. The verb that follows therefore must agree with X. If X is singular, the verb is singular. The same reasoning applies to *together with* and *in addition to*:

> *Chan Fai, as well as his friends, decides to go hiking this weekend.*
>
> *The project leader, together with his team members, tries to find a solution to the problem.*
>
> *Tiramisu, in addition to ice cream, is his favourite dessert.*

6.8 Nouns plural in form (ending in -*s*) but often singular in meaning

6.8.1 The nouns (*news, means, series*) in the following sentences may look like plural, but they take singular verbs:

> *The news reported in newspapers is sometimes not accurate.*
>
> *Some people believe that the means is not important, the end is. (means = method; end = purpose)*
>
> *This documentary series on Rome's history sounds interesting.*

6.8.2 Some academic disciplines, with names ending in -s and a singular meaning, also take singular verbs, e.g., *economics, linguistics, mathematics, phonetics, physics, politics, statistics.* The same is true of the names of some diseases, e.g., *diabetes, measles, mumps, herpes.*

> *Economics studies the relationship between supply and demand.*
>
> *Mathematics has a long history.*
>
> *Diabetes is caused by a lack of insulin that controls the sugar level in the blood.*
>
> (Note that in the -**that** clause, **controls**, a singular verb, agrees with its singular subject **insulin** just as **is** agrees with the singular subject **diabetes** of the whole sentence.)

6.8.3   However, whereas the names of some academic studies are singular in meaning, they can also have a plural but somewhat different meaning in general use:

Singular	**Politics is** *his major field in graduate school.*
Plural	*Their* **politics** *(political views)* **are** *largely anti-establishment.*
Singular	**Statistics is** *a required course for social science students.*
Plural	**Statistics** *(numerical figures)* **show** *that the economy is improving.*
Singular	**Mechanics is** *a topic in physics.*
Plural	*The* **mechanics** *(work processes) of electronic payment* **are** *not easy to understand.*

6.8.4   Proper nouns ending in -*s* used with singular verbs

These include literary works, artistic productions, books in the Bible, and names of some countries and international organizations.

Gulliver's Travels   A Tale of Two Cities   Cats (musical)
Psalms (book in Old Testament)   Romans (book in New Testament)
Starbucks   United Nations   The Netherlands   United States

Psalms **is** *the longest book in the Bible.*
The United Nations, an intergovernmental organization aiming to maintain international peace and security, **was** *established in 1945.*
The United States **has** *an area that is about the same as that of China.*
"Cats", Andrew Lloyd Webber's musical, **has** *won numerous awards.*

6.9   Nouns ending in -*s* referring to an amount or measurement as a unit

Phrases such as the following are considered as singular when they refer to a quantity taken as a unit. Thus, they take singular verbs:

Time	**Three years separates** *the two sisters.*
	Ten minutes seems *a long time when you are waiting for a bus.*
Distance	**Ten kilometres is** *too far to walk.*
Money	**One hundred dollars is** *not too much to pay for a good meal.*
Space	**Three-quarters** *of the space of his apartment* **is** *used as storage.*

6.10 Expressions of two coordinated subjects commonly treated as singular

These expressions refer to food items (**bacon and eggs, fish and chips, surf and turf**), others to acts or activities (**hit and run, track and field, trial and error, wear and tear**). Some are designations of departments or tasks in an organization (**research and development, marketing and sales, scholarships and loans**). These expressions are all treated as single units and thus take singular verbs.

Bacon and eggs in this restaurant **is** served in generous portions.

Hit and run **is** a very serious offence in traffic accidents.

Research and development in high-tech companies **receives** great attention.

She now works in **scholarships and loans**, which **has** six staff members.

6.11 Plural nouns with no singular form

Many plural nouns (mostly ending in **-s**) have no singular form. They are used with plural verbs.

---

clothes	customs (at airports)	crew	earnings	glasses	groceries
headquarters	jeans	leftovers	logistics	manners	outskirts	police
refreshments	regards	surroundings	thanks	wages	

Customs **are** checking his bags now.

Her new glasses **are** quite costly.

The outskirts of the city **have** become easily accessible by public transport.

These refreshments for the reception **look** rather attractive.

Our thanks **go** to all the volunteer workers.

Proper table manners **are** important in our family.

The police **are** investigating this robbery case.

We all enjoy working in surroundings that **are** pleasant and friendly.

Some of these plural nouns may take both singular and plural verbs with a slight difference in meaning. Two examples are **logistics** and **headquarters**.

Singular	Logistics **is** a newly developed industry to move goods and equipment.
Plural	Complicated logistics **are** involved in planning a large arts exhibition.
Singular	Their company's headquarters **is** in New York.
Plural	Our headquarters **have** agreed to launch the new product line here.

6.12   Collective nouns

When a collective noun refers to a group acting or treated as one unit, it takes a singular verb. These nouns include **audience, class, committee, company, family, government, orchestra, school, staff,** and **team.**

> *The **audience** is waiting quietly for the concert to start.*
>
> *The **interview committee has** selected only ten out of more than a hundred applicants.*
>
> *A strong **government is** what we need now.*
>
> *This **class has** many gifted pupils.*

When a collective noun refers to group members as individuals acting in various ways within the group, it takes a plural verb:

> *The **audience have** various reactions to the orchestra's performance.*
>
> *The **committee have** not yet reached a decision.*
>
> *The **government are** planning measures to control the spread of Covid-19.*
>
> *The **class have** all passed the final examination.*
>
> Note: In British English collective nouns can be used with both singular and plural verbs, but in American English singular verbs are common with many collective nouns.

If you specify the components of the group, you always have a plural subject (e.g., **members** of the committee, **directors** of the organization, **students** of the school, **officials** of the government), thus requiring a plural verb:

> ***Workers of the factory have** just heard the newly announced bonus package.*
>
> ***Members of the committee have** yet to find a way to carry out the recently-reached decision.*

6.13   Phrases and clauses as singular subject

When you use a phrase (such as an infinitive phrase or a gerund phrase) or a clause (such as a **that** or **what** noun clause) as the subject of a sentence referring to a single idea or event, use a singular verb:

> ***To sing well takes** constant practice in the control of voice. (Subject is an infinitive phrase.)*
>
> ***Playing with burning candles is** highly dangerous. (Subject is a gerund phrase.)*
>
> ***That Yundi Li won the first prize in the International Chopin Piano Competition in 2000 at age 18 was** a great achievement. (Subject in this and the next sentence is a **that** noun clause.)*
>
> ***That health is the essence of true happiness is** well understood.*
>
> ***What actually happened to the disappeared flight remains** a mystery. (Subject is a **what** noun clause.)*

6.14   When the verb comes before the subject

In sentences starting with **There + be,** use a singular verb if the subject is singular and a plural verb if the subject is plural:

> *There **is** a large lookout **platform** on the peak.*
>
> *There **are** many different **opinions** on this controversial matter.*

Use **There + has been** (to indicate the present perfect tense) when the subject is singular and **There + have been** when the subject is plural:

> *There **has been** not enough **attention** given to improving English standards.*
>
> *There **have been** many **debates** on what freedom of speech really means.*

When you write direct questions starting with words such as **what, where, when, why,** and **how,** followed by **be** or **have/has,** e.g., **What + be** or **How + have,** make sure that the verb **be** or **have** agrees with the subject that comes after the verb:

> *What **is** the **purpose** of general education?*
>
> *What **are** your **reasons** for resigning from this company?*
>
> *Why **have** so many **migrants** moved from Mexico to the United States?*
>
> *How **has** global **warming** affected the world's climate?*
>
> *Where **have** courtesy and good manners gone?*

6.15   *Be* as a linking verb

When you use the verb **be** to link a subject to the "subject complement" (word or phrase that provides information about the subject), the linking verb agrees with its subject, not the subject complement. Study the following three pairs of sentences:

> *One **reason** for her outstanding performance **is** her teachers.* (**Reason** is the subject; **her teachers** is the subject complement.)
>
> *Her **teachers are** one reason for her outstanding performance.* (**Teachers** is the subject; **one reason for her outstanding performance** is the subject complement.)

> *The **cause** of congestion in this part of the road **is** parking violations.*
>
> *Parking **violations are** the cause of congestion in this part of the road.*

> ***What troubles students most is*** *grammar errors.* (The **what** clause, a noun clause, is a singular subject.)
>
> *Grammar **errors are** what troubles students most.*

6.16 *Per cent*

Following **per cent** or **per cent of,** use a singular verb if the phrase refers to a singular noun and a plural verb if it refers to a plural noun:

> *An **increase** of 1 per cent in bank interest rates **makes** a big difference in mortgage repayments.*
>
> *About 70 per cent of **visitors** to Hong Kong **are** from mainland China.*

6.17 Summing up

Subject-verb agreement is one of the most basic requirements in English grammar and usage. Of course, you need to be able to tell, first of all, which part of your sentence is the subject. Then, you must have a clear notion of the singularity or plurality of the subject. If you make no mistake about these two points, it should then be easy enough for you to decide whether to supply a singular or a plural verb to agree with your subject.

As you have noticed from reading this chapter, some subjects have certain special (or you might say "peculiar") qualities about them that call for using either a singular or a plural verb. Some words ending in **-s** are actually singular in meaning, while others (such as collective nouns) can have both singular and plural meanings depending on how they are used. If you have studied them carefully, you should find these points not difficult to understand or remember.

Exercises   Chapter 6

Exercise 6.1

Identify the subject in each sentence and write it in the space at the right.

試找出每句的主語並把它寫在右邊的空白處。

1. There are many reasons for visiting a public library.   _____

2. They insist on keeping their original plan.   _____

3. Do you know where your friends are?   _____

4. The pressures of work and children's schooling have become too stressful for many middle-class parents.   _____

5. Not stopping for a red traffic light is a serious offence.   _____

6. The single mother faces many problems.   _____

7. Swimming and ice-skating are my granddaughter's favourite leisure activities.   _____

8. Tai Chi, like yoga, enables you to relax.   _____

9. The old clock tower near the waterfront has been preserved.   _____

10. Most of his time is spent on restoring old furniture.   _____

Exercise 6.2

Use the correct form of the given verb(s) in parentheses.

把每句括號裏的動詞的正確形式寫在右邊的空白處。

1. What she always enjoys (be) reading and listening to music.   _____

2. What (do) Hong Kong and Macau have in common?   _____

3. Disputes over wages and benefits (be) often hard to resolve.   _____

4. He (work) best when he is not closely supervised.   _____

5. Members of this group (have) contributed much to attaining its goals.   _____

6. Very little space in their flat (have) been used for storage.   _____

7. What she (hope) to eat (be) not on the menu.   _____

8. After the accident, everybody in this and neighbouring apartments (be) questioned by the police.   _____

9. The agreement is not valid until all relevant papers (be) signed.   _____

10.　Our boss always (think) we (be) not working hard enough.　　　　_____

Exercise 6.3

Use the correct form of the given verb(s) in parentheses.

把每句括號裏的動詞的正確形式寫在右邊的空白處。

1.　Games on mobile phones (remain) the most popular pastime for young people.　_____

2.　What influences (have) online technology brought to our daily life?　　　　_____

3.　When she was a student, her roommate in the hostel (give) her a lot of problems.　_____

4.　There (have) been not enough attention (pay) to global climate change.　　　_____

5.　Fish and chips (be) a great favourite of my children.　　　　　　　_____

6.　All local residents will each (get) a one-time subsidy of ten thousand dollars from the government.　　　　　　　　　　　　　　　　　_____

7.　The only thing that (worry) managers is the lack of cooperation of their staff.　_____

8.　All of the seafood offered at this restaurant (be) fresh.　　　　　　_____

9.　There (be) more than one way to cook a steak.　　　　　　　　_____

10.　A thousand years (be) like a second in the history of the universe.　　　_____

11.　Any vacancies left (be) likely to be taken up in no time.　　　　　_____

12.　Statistics (be) used by researchers as evidence to demonstrate their claims.　_____

Exercise 6.4

If the verb in parentheses is correct, do nothing. If it is wrong, write the correct verb in the space at the right.

檢視每句括號裏的動詞，如果形式不正確，把正確的形式寫在右邊的空白處。

1.　She is one of the applicants who (has) a master's degree.　　　　　_____

2.　Her win in the singing contest, as well as her getting good grades in her school subjects, (make) her very happy.　　　　　　　　　　　　　_____

3.　*Gulliver's Travels* (were) written by Jonathan Swift.　　　　　　_____

4.　Two-thirds of his wealth (has) been donated to charity.　　　　　_____

5.　A special committee (have) been set up to look into this matter.　　　_____

6.　That society always (have) problems (are) well recognized.　　　　_____

7.　A great variety of birds (lives) in the woods.　　　　　　　　_____

8.   The number of learners of foreign languages (is) quite large.   _____

9.   Some members of her class (find) mathematics very difficult.   _____

10. Apple pie is the only one of the desserts that (are) really good here.   _____

11. To speak well (require) much more than language fluency.   _____

12. Everything that they (has) done (do) not quite make sense.   _____

13. His parents (is) an important reason for his polite behaviour.   _____

14. Only about 1 per cent of his toys (is) from his parents.   _____

15. Quite a number of the members of the committee (are) prepared to
     support this proposal.   _____

Chapter 7 Distinguish between Countable and Uncountable Nouns

What you will learn in this chapter

When you use nouns to name people, things, ideas, and actions, you have to be aware of their number aspect (singular or plural) often because they, if used as subject, must agree in number with their verb. This awareness is also needed when you put a determiner before the noun to identify which or how many or how much. You will learn about the nature and use of countable and uncountable nouns and nouns that have both countable and uncountable uses. Other useful topics include possessive forms, compound nouns, and complements following nouns.

名詞可以作為人、事物、意念和行動的名稱，在句子中用作主語時，必須和動詞在數（number）的方面一致，因此你須留意所用的名詞是否有單數和複數之分。如果在名詞前面有限定詞（determiner）來指明哪個或多少，也需要留意這個問題。在本章裏，你會學習可數名詞（countable nouns）和不可數名詞（uncountable nouns）的特性和用法，也會學習使用一些既可數又不可數的名詞。本章其他有關內容包括所有格形式（possessive forms）、複合名詞（compound nouns）和名詞後面的補語（complements）。

7.1   What do we use nouns for?

7.2   Using the wrong form of nouns

7.3   Countable and uncountable nouns: basics

7.4   More about countable nouns

7.5   More about uncountable nouns

7.6   Variable nouns

7.7   Possessives

7.8   Compound nouns (noun + noun combinations)

7.9   Possible structures after a noun

7.10 Verbal nouns (gerunds)

7.11 Summing up

7.1 What do we use nouns for?

When we write a sentence, we can hardly avoid using nouns. In general, we use nouns

- to name things (**paper, bus, steak**), places (**park, mall, theatre**), ideas (**plan, pleasure, unity**), people (**residents, politicians, employees**), actions (**travel, cooperation, singing**), and any other item or entity we refer to;

- as the subject of some statement (***Students* need to study hard**);

- as the object of some statement (**Let us examine the *plan* carefully**).

7.2 Using the wrong form of nouns

Nouns in English, if countable, may take a singular and a plural form. Since this is not the case with nouns in Chinese, Chinese-speaking learners of English may often use the wrong number form of nouns when they write or speak.

Look at the following items and decide whether they contain incorrect use of the singular/plural form of nouns:

Item 1: Business hour: 10 a.m. to 6 p.m. (a sign at the entrance of a shop)

Item 2: ABC Luxury Home or XYZ Property (a realty agency's name)

Item 3: ABC Property Agency

Item 4: PQR Watch and Jewellery (a jewellery shop's name)

Item 5: PQR Watch Company

Item 6: Please listen to my advices.

Item 7: There are many equipments in this laboratory.

Item 8: AA Noodle (a restaurant specializing in this food item)

Did you spot any errors in the above eight items? Congratulations to you if you saw errors in most of them.

Item 1: **Hour** is a countable noun. "Business hour" should be "Business hours" because the operation of business on a working day usually includes a number of hours. This is probably the most noticeable error all over Hong Kong. It appears on signs, advertisement pamphlets, and business cards.

Item 2: "ABC Luxury Home" or "XYZ Property" should be "ABC Luxury Homes" or "XYZ Properties". This type of error is common in Hong Kong. When you refer to something generally (without specifying which one) that is countable (existing as individuals or individual units), the noun (e.g., **home, property**) that names it should be in the plural form. Thus, the realty agency should say "luxury homes" or "properties" (both **home** and **property** are countable nouns) simply because it is in the business of selling or leasing "homes" or "properties" and not just one particular "home" or "property".

Item 3: "ABC Property Agency" uses the singular form **property** correctly because **property agency** is a compound noun (noun + noun) in which the first noun, which modifies the second, is usually singular (see 7.8.2 in this chapter).

Item 4: "PQR Watch and Jewellery" should be "PQR Watches and Jewellery". Why? First, **jewellery** is an uncountable noun (also called mass noun) with no plural form. So, it stays as "jewellery". But **watch** is a countable noun, and surely the jewellery shop sells watches, not just one watch.

Item 5: "PQR Watch Company" Here, unlike Item 4, the use of "watch" (singular) is correct because it is the first part of the compound noun "watch company". This is similar to the situation in Item 3.

Item 6: "Please listen to my advices" should be "Pleasc listen to my advice" because **advice**, an abstract noun, is uncountable.

Item 7: "There are many equipments in this laboratory" should be "There are many pieces of equipment in this laboratory". **Equipment** is uncountable as it refers to things or machinery in general needed for some purpose. It can become countable if you put "a piece of" in front of it.

Item 8: "AA Noodle" **Noodle**, a countable noun, is usually used in the plural **noodles.** Noodles typically come in long strips or strings. On a menu, all noodle items (note the singular **noodle** in the compound noun **noodle items**) come under the category label "Noodles" (plural). Individual items may include such descriptions as "stir-fried rice **noodles** Singapore style" (星洲炒米粉) and "shredded pork with stir-fried **noodles**" (肉絲炒麵). In short, the **-s** ending should be present in the restaurant's name "AA Noodles" and all the names of its noodle items on the menu (except for those in which **noodle** is the first part of a compound noun, e.g., **chicken noodle soup**). This is like the name of a restaurant chain that specializes in sandwiches and various snacks, "OK Super Sandwiches". The plural **sandwiches** is used correctly. On the menu a major category of items for customers' choice is, as we should expect, "sandwiches" and not "sandwich".

7.3   Countable and uncountable nouns: basics

7.3.1   Countable nouns

We use countable nouns to name things, people, ideas, places, events, and so on which exist separately and can therefore be counted. They have a singular and a plural form (usually ending in **-s**). The singular form may be preceded by **a, an,** or **any.** The plural form may be preceded by a number or words called "determiners", such as **all, any, few, many,** and **some** (these words tell us "which" or "how many/much"): (See also 9.1.1, Chapter 9.)

a desk	*a building*	*a policeman*	*an engineer*	*a concert*	*a pier*	*a district*
any suggestion	*any volunteer*	*two sisters*	*some birds*	*many trips*	*few attempts*	
a couple of (used colloquially to mean "a few" or "several") *days*		*all participants*				

Some example sentences:

> *A concert* will be held to raise funds for the orchestra.
>
> You may borrow *any book* you like from the library.
>
> Check carefully for *any mistakes* you may have made in your essay.
>
> I have got *some ideas* that I want to share with you.
>
> Now that we are both retired, we can take *several trips* each year.
>
> Spending a lot of time at home during the pandemic, we may find many *things* to do.

7.3.2 Uncountable nouns

By contrast, uncountable nouns refer to substances ("mass nouns" such as materials, liquids, gases), abstract qualities and concepts ("abstract nouns") which we do not see as separate objects but as shapeless things or notions in our mind. Because we cannot count them, we do not use numbers with uncountable nouns, which typically have no plurals. Some examples of uncountable nouns:

> air   water   rice   clothing   jewellery   equipment   courage   happiness
> honesty   integrity   knowledge   grace   love   peace   friendship   education

Some example sentences:

> You can find a lot of *clothing* in a department store.
>
> It takes much *courage* for a young child to sing on stage.
>
> His *knowledge* of Chinese language and culture is unsurpassed.
>
> *Integrity* makes a leader respectable and trustworthy.
>
> True *friendship* is marked by trust and loyalty.
>
> *Education* is much more than what one learns at school.

7.3.3 *A/an* before uncountable nouns

In general, do not use **a/an** in front of an uncountable noun. (Incorrect: ~~a clothing, an equipment, a beautiful jewellery.~~) But we can use **a/an** with some uncountable nouns that refer to feelings and mental activity when we qualify the noun in some way with an adjective:

> It is not easy to have *a clear understanding* of the law concerning privacy.
>
> Through studying as classmates in university, they have developed *a long-lasting friendship.*
>
> Although her parents had limited means, they wanted her to have *a good education.*
>
> He has *a fine knowledge* of art history.

7.3.4   Determiners before nouns

Be careful when you use determiners such as **many, few, much, little,** and **some** in front of countable and uncountable nouns. **Many, few, every** are used with countable nouns; **much, little,** and **less** with uncountable nouns. **Some, more, all,** and **any** can be used with both types. The following table shows examples of countable and uncountable nouns used with different determiners:

Countable nouns	Uncountable nouns
many pedestrians	*much rain*
many ideas	*much business*
few suggestions	*little support*
any solutions	*any money*
some proposals	*some clothing*
some restaurants	*some understanding*
all the people	*more food*
all options	*all music*
every member	*no time*
more participants	*less support*
a lot of ships	*a lot of water*
several beauticians	*much beauty*

If you understand the above table, you can also understand that it is incorrect to say "use less plastic bags", a sign displayed in some shops, when the correct advice should be "use fewer plastic bags".

7.4   More about countable nouns

7.4.1   General statements

Use plural countable nouns when you make statements about them in a general way.

Cruise companies now offer plenty of *itineraries*.

Many *jewellery shops* also sell *watches*.

Attendants can be rather helpful to *customers*.

Postgraduate students usually need to write a thesis.

This shop is open on *Saturdays, Sundays*, and public *holidays.*

Children under three years old are admitted free.

My granddaughter loves *cakes* and *desserts*. All *children* do!

Visitors to Hong Kong are impressed by its efficient public transport system.

7.4.2   *On foot*

Some countable nouns take only the singular form when used to mean a certain mode, form, or medium of some action.

> *She goes to school **on foot**.*
>
> *Some professionals charge fees **by the hour**.*
>
> *We can now go from Hong Kong to Macao **by bus** via the mega bridge.*
>
> *This watch is made almost entirely **by hand**.*
>
> *Some restaurants do not accept reservations **by telephone**.*

7.4.3 *Authorities* vs. *authority*

Some countable nouns used in the plural form have a meaning somewhat different from their singular form. They are used with plural verbs (e.g., **are, have, make**).

> *The health **authorities are** investigating the problem concerning possible contamination of influenza vaccines.*
> (**authority** = power; **authorities** = official organizations or government departments)
>
> *Human **resources are** what a society must develop to upgrade its economic strength.*
>
> ***Relations** between China and the United States **have** become strained.*
>
> *The **essentials** of grammar and usage **make** up most of the content of this book.*

Other examples of nouns usually used in the plural form and phrases using them:

Plural nouns	Example phrases
basics	*the **basics** of writing business letters*
conditions	*changing social **conditions***
contents	*a book's table of **contents***
feelings	*having mixed **feelings***
means	*living within one's **means***
particulars	*personal **particulars** required by the application form*

7.4.4 Collective nouns

A collective noun (also called "group noun") refers to a group of people, such as **family, school**, and **company**. Singular verbs are more commonly used with collective nouns. (Sometimes, plural verbs may be used. See also 6.12 in Chapter 6.)

A collective noun can be treated as a whole unit, thus taking a singular verb and a singular pronoun:

> My **school is** in a quiet area of town. **It** was established over a century ago.

It can also be thought of as individuals acting within the unit, thus using a plural verb and a plural pronoun:

> My **company have** decided to expand the marketing department. **They** are looking at long term development.

Other examples of collective nouns:

bank	board (of directors or governors)	choir	church	group	class
committee	firm	government	orchestra	public	staff	team

Note that in American English, using singular verbs with collective nouns is more common than in British English:

> The **orchestra has** planned to perform in various communities in its new season.
>
> The **government wants** very much to improve its relations with the public.
>
> The **public is** well informed each day about the number of new Covid-19 cases.

7.5   More about uncountable nouns

7.5.1   Uncountable made countable

Many uncountable nouns, including "mass nouns", can be made countable if you supply a unit noun before it. Commonly, **piece** is used to mean a small quantity (of some material or substance): **a piece of bread/cake/meat/paper**. For abstract nouns and mass nouns, you can also use **piece** to refer to some amount of that which is referred to: **a piece of advice/information/news.**

Other examples of different unit words to make uncountable nouns countable:

a drop of water	a cup of tea	a grain of rice	a bar of chocolate
a sheet of paper	a block of wood	a loaf of bread	a speck of dust
a pile of rubbish	a round of applause	a sum of money	an item of clothing
a slice of meat/bread	a bag of flour	a lump of sugar	a puff of air/smoke

7.5.2   Some uncountable nouns are plural in form.

No singular forms with the same meaning are possible, and you cannot use them with numbers.

> You can see chapter titles in the table of **contents**.
>
> The **customs** officers have found large quantities of cocaine in that man's bags.
>
> Music has the effect of bringing out our **feelings**.
>
> We have bought the **groceries** we need for next week.
>
> Children learn good **manners** from their parents.
>
> Clean **leftovers** can be used to make new dishes.
>
> The **logistics** of staging an open-air orchestral concert are complex indeed.
>
> Many **thanks** to you for your generous support.

7.5.3 Countable nouns used uncountably

Some countable nouns can have uncountable use when preceded by determiners such as **any, some, enough, little,** and **much**:

> In the following sentences, the use of the noun in boldface is indicated at the end of each sentence (U = uncountable; C = countable).
>
> **attempt**
>
> > Although he has been living in Japan for some years, he has not made **any attempt** to learn Japanese. (U)
> >
> > She made several unsuccessful **attempts** at passing the driving test. (C)
>
> **change**
>
> > There is not **much change** in his financial condition. (U)
> >
> > Technology has brought about many **changes** in social life. (C)
>
> **difficulty**
>
> > I have **some difficulty** in remembering names. (U)
> >
> > Their research project has run into **difficulties**. (C)
>
> **difference**
>
> > There is **little difference** between "safe" and "secure". (U)
> >
> > They need to make an effort to settle their **differences**. (C)
>
> **thought**
>
> > Not enough **thought** had gone into the business proposal. (U)
> >
> > The **thought** of failing again really disturbs him. (C)

More examples of such nouns:

chance	choice	contact	demand	point	question	idea
indication	criticism	doubt	examination	hope	talent	

7.6   Variable nouns

Many abstract nouns can have countable use when they have a more particular meaning and uncountable use when they have a more general meaning. The context shown in a sentence determines the appropriate use. These nouns are similar to those mentioned in the preceding section (7.5.3) except that their uncountable use does not necessarily require placing a determiner (such as **little** and **much**) before the noun in question.

Study the following sentences (again, U = uncountable; C = countable):

concern

*There is widespread **concern** that global warming is causing unusual climatic conditions.* (U)

*What are your main **concerns** as a young parent?* (C)

experience

*You have accumulated enough **experience** for this job.* (U)

*My friend had some eye-opening **experiences** when travelling in Europe last month.* (C)

life

***Life** is not simple for most people.* (U)

*She has had a hard **life**.* (C)

strength

*His remarkable **strength** in going through such difficulty comes from his faith.* (U)

*You need to know both the **strengths** and the weaknesses of an argument.* (C)

time

*The passing of **time** is always a mystery.* (U)

*Every **time** I go to Beijing I visit the Forbidden City Palace Museum.* (C)

Other examples of variable nouns :

behaviour	comfort	comparison	competition	conflict	connection
danger	democracy	emphasis	excitement	fact	loss	love	meaning
obligation	performance	power	reality	research	society	sport
structure	struggle	success	theory	trial	youth	victory

7.7 Possessives

7.7.1 Basic forms of possessives

The apostrophe mark (') placed before or after the letter **s** at the end of a noun indicates that something belongs to someone:

Type of noun	Examples
Singular noun	*my friend's favourite cafe, the principal's office*
Plural noun	*my parents' home, visitors' parking spaces*
Irregular plural	*children's books, men's department*
Names ending in -**s**	*Charles' school, the Wongs' children,* *Paris' attractions*
Note: Pay attention to the names of some churches, schools and restaurants which involve the use of 's, such as St. John's Cathedral, St. Stephen's Girls' School ('**s** after **Stephen** but just ' after **Girls**), St. Paul's College, and McDonald's (always include '**s** when referring to this fast food chain).	

7.7.2 The *'s* possessive form

Use the **'s** form when the noun refers to a person, a group of people, an organization, or time to indicate possessions, relationships, actions, characteristics:

When the noun refers to	Examples of 's
a person	*my granddaughter's homework* *her mother's eyes*
a group of people	*the new students' adjustment to the school* *customers' complaint*
an organization	*the company's board of directors* *the club's rules*
time	*next year's property prices* *an hour's flight*

7.7.3 The *the . . . of* + noun possessive form

Use *the . . . of* + **noun** structure when the noun is inanimate (not alive):

the front of the building	(not preferred: *the building's front*)
the beginning of the story	(not preferred: *the story's beginning*)
the history of the war	(not preferred: *the war's history*)
the enjoyment of music	(not preferred: *music's enjoyment*)

the development of technology	(not preferred: *technology's development*)
the majority of the votes	(not preferred: *the votes' majority*)

Both *the . . . of* + **noun** structure and the *'s* form are possible in some expressions, such as the following:

the centre of the circle	OR	*the circle's centre*
the importance of reading	OR	*reading's importance*
the departure of this flight	OR	*this flight's departure*
the work of the artist	OR	*the artist's work*
the faithfulness of God	OR	*God's faithfulness*
the speed of the train	OR	*the train's speed*
the value of money	OR	*money's value*
the mystery of the moon	OR	*the moon's mystery*

7.8   Compound nouns (noun + noun combinations)

7.8.1   First noun modifies second noun

A noun may be followed by another noun to form a compound noun. The first noun modifies the second.

the Peak tram	*the airport bus*	*the lunch buffet*	*the ferry pier*
the construction site	*the trade war*	*a holiday camp*	*a stone monument*
a furniture shop	*an art museum*	*a theme park*	*a concert hall* *a news reporter*
a role model	*the mass media*	*lifestyle habits*	*air travel* *group leader*

7.8.2   First noun singular in form

As you can see in 7.8.1, the first noun is usually singular. This is also true of combinations in which the first noun has a plural meaning but is usually in the singular form when used to modify another noun. (For example, **bus stop** = a stop for buses; **stamp dealer** = a dealer who sells and buys stamps; **bookshop** = a shop that sells books.) Note that some such combinations are commonly spelled as one word (e.g., **bodyguard, bookshop, playground, footprint, teapot**).

bus stop	*stamp dealer*	*bookshop/bookstore*	*ticket booth/office*	*photo shop*
snack bar	*toy shop*	*taxi stand*	*toothbrush*	*vegetable market* *eyeglasses*

7.8.3 First noun plural in form

This type of combination includes nouns that are often used in the plural form (e.g., **savings**) and nouns whose singular form has a different meaning (e.g., **glasses, customs**).

> *a **savings** account*   *a **customs** officer*   *a **sports** event*   *a **sales** manager*
>
> *the **sales** department*   *the **repairs** department*   *the **Lotteries** Fund*   *a **goods** vehicle*
>
> *the **Arts** Festival*   *the **admissions** office*   *the **desserts** menu*   *a **clothes** hanger*
>
> *the **amenities** building*   *the **drinks** machine*   *the **outpatients** department*

7.8.4 Combinations of more than two nouns

These are often found in mass media reports on economic, technological, and political matters. The following are some examples:

> *a customer relations manager*   *a sports apparel company*
>
> *the food and beverage sector*   *the trade war situation*
>
> *law enforcement officers*   *government support measures*
>
> *personnel management problems*   *population policy research institute*
>
> *energy production costs*   *digital age innovations*

7.8.5 Distances, time periods, and various measurements

A number comes before the first noun and is usually joined to it by a hyphen (-). You must note that, after hyphenation, the first noun is singular in form. Adding an **-s** at the end of the first noun would be an error. For example, while you can say **This restaurant opens twenty-four hours a day,** you cannot say **This is a twenty-four-hours restaurant**. You should say **This is a twenty-four-hour restaurant.**

> *a two-hour movie* (not ~~a two-hours movie~~)   *a ten-year-old girl* (not ~~a ten-years-old girl~~)
>
> *a seven-passenger car*   *a five-kilometre walk*   *a fifty-page book*
>
> *a twenty-four-hour outpatients clinic*   *a three-day drive*
>
> *a three-month course*   *a hundred-dollar banknote*   *a one-litre bottle*
>
> *a fifty-storey building*   *a four-person table*   *a two-week cruise*
>
> All such compound nouns can be expressed in the plural, such as:
>
> *several seven-passenger cars*   *a few three-month courses*

7.9   Possible structures after a noun

Many structures can come after a noun in a sentence, depending on what you want to say. When you need to say something about a noun to complete your meaning, what you say after the noun is called its "complement". The following are some common possibilities:

Prepositional phrases containing a noun phrase

*I like your suggestion **concerning the redesign of language education**.*

*The thought **of global warming** worries us.*

Prepositional phrases containing a gerund (verbal noun) phrase

*I have no intention **of buying any more decorative objects**.*

*We have a good chance **of completing the project in time**.*

Infinitive phrases (may include prepositional phrases)

*All these years he has the desire **to buy a new apartment**.*

*Do you feel the need **to do something about improving your language skills**?*
(**about improving your language skills** is a prepositional phrase, here forming part of an infinitive phrase)

Noun clauses introduced by *that, what, whether*

*She has the idea **that she might be a lawyer someday**.*

*Here is the story of **what really happened**.*

*They have an urgent question **whether there is any alternative plan**.*

7.10   Verbal nouns (gerunds)

Before we leave this brief survey of using nouns, a few words about verbal nouns (called "gerunds" or "**-ing** forms") are in place. The **-ing** form of a verb is used to show the present or past progressive (continuous) tense. (e.g., **We are raising money for the poor. She was working in the kitchen when her phone rang.**) Besides this use, the **-ing** form of a verb can also act as a noun, hence the term "verbal noun". It can form a phrase that can function as the (a) subject, (b) direct object of the main verb, (c) complement of a subject, or (d) object of a preposition.

(a) Subject

> ***Playing mah-jong** is a favourite pastime of many Hong Kong people.*

> *Under our present financial situation, **repaying our debts** will be difficult.*

(b) Direct object of the main verb

> *He enjoys **reading books on art**.*

> *She loves **staying at resort hotels** in Thailand.*

(c) Complement of a subject

> *His part-time work is **counselling young people**.*

> *They were so excited that they felt like **celebrating immediately**.*

(d) Object of a preposition

> *He insisted on **paying the food bill** for everybody.*

> *Now they are already planning on **going to Iceland** next summer.*

As you can see, the verbal nouns or gerunds in the above sentences all function as nouns. You will also note that the verbal noun can be the first word in a phrase called a **gerund phrase.** The noun function is served by all the gerund phrases in the above example sentences.

7.11 Summing up

Nouns are commonly used words that are part of almost anything you write. Exercise care when you use nouns. Most importantly, pay great attention to the difference between countable and uncountable nouns. Some main points concerning these two types of nouns and some related topics are as follows:

(1)   Countable nouns have singular and plural forms (**-s** endings).

(2)   Uncountable nouns include mass nouns and abstract nouns. They must not be preceded by **a** or **an**.

(3)   Some determiners (**some, few, many, much,** etc.) apply to only countable nouns (**many users**) or only uncountable nouns (**much congestion**); some others can apply to both kinds (**any ideas, any time**).

(4)   Use the plural form of countable nouns in general statements. Remember that this is a guideline often not given sufficient attention among Chinese speakers. (Note the use of the plural **speakers** in this sentence, which qualifies as a general statement or a statement that applies to people generally.)

(5)   Collective or group nouns can take singular or plural verbs depending on intended sense. (Do we focus on the group as a single unit or on members of the group as individual actors?)

(6)   Many uncountable nouns can become countable by having a unit noun before them (e.g., **a piece of advice, a cup of tea**).

(7)   Some uncountable nouns are plural and have no singular forms (e.g., a **customs** officer).

(8)   Many nouns have both countable (e.g., **Life is precious**) and uncountable use (e.g., **What a happy life**).

(9)   Note the use of the apostrophe mark (') (e.g., **McDonald's**) and the structure of **the . . . of + noun** (e.g., **the joy of love**) for the possessive form of various nouns.

(10)   Compound nouns are formed by the combination of two or more nouns (e.g., **mud bath**).

(11)   After a noun you can have a prepositional phrase, an infinitive phrase, or a noun clause.

(12)   Nouns formed from verbs (**-ing** forms), called **gerunds**, can form **gerund phrases** that function just like nouns.

Exercises | Chapter 7

Exercise 7.1

Select a suitable determiner from the ones given and write it in the blank of each sentence.

從下面所列的限定詞中選擇合適的一個，填寫在每句的空白處。

| some   many   much   more   few   several   little   every   fewer   less |

1. _____ primary school pupil knows how to do multiplication.

2. Restaurants have lost _____ business during the past half year.

3. China consumes _____ rice than it produces, so it needs to import some rice.

4. Let us protect our environment by using _____ plastic bags.

5. Hot weather can cause _____ spoilage to fruit and vegetables.

6. Not many, but _____ pedestrians are too impatient to wait for the green crossing light.

7. Electric cars are becoming popular because they cause _____ air pollution than petrol-cars do.

8. _____ people really understand how an aeroplane can fly.

9. _____ banks now offer their customers a great diversity of investment plans.

10. People in Switzerland speak _____ different languages.

11. Many bars now have _____ customers than was the case before the pandemic.

12. Many grass-roots families have _____ hardware support for their children's online learning.

Exercise 7.2

The singular and plural forms of a noun are given in parentheses appearing in each sentence. Choose the form that fits the sentence. Write your chosen word in the blank before the parentheses.

下面每句中的括號裏有一個名詞的單數與複數形式。選擇符合該句的正確形式，把你所選的填寫在括號前的空白處。

1. She accompanied her mother to buy _____ (grocery, groceries) at the supermarket.

2. He has lost _____ (contact, contacts) with his former English teacher.

3. The price of goods is influenced by _____ (demand, demands) in the market.

4. Her faith in God gives her tremendous _____ (strength, strengths) for overcoming great obstacles.

5. This shop has rather unusual business _____ (hour, hours).

6. Some restaurants do not accept _____ (reservation, reservations).

7. Vegetables are usually sold by _____ (weight, weights).

8. It is not difficult to learn the _____ (essential, essentials) of swimming.

9. The misuse of _____ (power, powers) can lead to political instability.

10. The training of musicians places a great deal of _____ (emphasis, emphases) on practice.

Exercise 7.3

From the given phrases in the box, select one or more suitable phrases to make each of the 12 uncountable nouns countable. Write the letter(s) in the appropriate blank.

從方框內的短語中，選擇適當的短語 (可以多於一個)，把代表所選短語的字母填入下面每個不可數名詞之前的空白裏，使該名詞能作可數名詞用。

a) *a bar of*	d) *a grain of*	g) *a set of*	j) *a speck of*
b) *a bottle of*	e) *an item of*	h) *a sheet of*	k) *a strip of*
c) *a glass of*	f) *a piece of*	i) *a slice of*	m) *a sum of*

1. _____ advice

2. _____ money

3. _____ water

4. _____ cake

5. _____ wine

6. _____ chocolate

7. _____ paper

8. _____ dust

9. _____ sand

10. _____ news

11. _____ land

12. _____ data

Exercise 7.4

Examine the underlined word(s) in each sentence. If you see something wrong, write the whole underlined part after correction in the space provided at the right. If you think the underlined part is correct, write the word CORRECT.

細心留意下面每句劃了底線的部分。假如它有錯，試改正然後把整個劃了底線的部分寫在右邊的空白處。假如你認為它沒有錯，請在空白處寫 CORRECT 一詞。

1. Most people have a saving account in a bank. _____

2. Children usually love dessert. _____

3. This shop is known for selling expensive jewellery and watch. _____

4. I wonder if there is a taxis stand nearby. _____

5. We look forward to having lunch with you. _____

6. My short-sightedness is worsening: I think my <u>eyeglass needs</u> replacing   _____

7. The <u>women department</u> is on the second floor.   _____

8. Have you eaten at <u>McDonald</u> recently?   _____

9. She just returned from a <u>five days vacation</u>.   _____

10. We had some unforgettable <u>experiences</u> when travelling in Japan.   _____

11. This beautiful embroidered dress is made entirely <u>by hands</u>.   _____

12. Our <u>twelve-years-old</u> granddaughter is now a Secondary One student.   _____

Chapter 8   Observe Pronoun-Antecedent Agreement and Keep Pronoun References Clear

What you will learn in this chapter

In writing, you often need pronouns to refer to persons or things. The person or thing referred to by a pronoun is the pronoun's "antecedent" (= a word to which the word that follows refers). You will learn that the pronoun must agree with its antecedent in person, number (singular or plural), and gender. This is one important condition for clear pronoun reference. There are other conditions you should take note of to ensure all pronoun references are clear and unambiguous.

在英文寫作中，我們常用代詞（pronouns）來表示人、物或事。所指代的人、物或事稱為代詞的先行詞（antecedent）。代詞必須和它的先行詞保持一致（agree）。這包括三方面：人稱、單數或複數和性別。只有代詞與先行詞達成一致，而且也符合一些其他條件，代詞的指涉（reference）才可以清晰明確。

8.1   Pronouns referring to people

8.2   What does pronoun-antecedent agreement mean?

8.3   Pronoun reference

8.4   Summing up

8.1 Pronouns referring to people

This should not be new to you, but it would be good if you use the following table to refresh your memory of the various forms of pronouns referring to people. It serves as a background for our discussion in this chapter of pronoun-antecedent agreement and clear pronoun reference.

Person	Number	As subject	As object	Possessive as determiner (before a noun)	Possessive as pronoun (without a following noun)	Reflexive
1st	Singular	I	me	my (*This is **my** book.*)	mine (*This book is **mine**.*)	myself
	Plural	we	us	our	ours	ourselves
2nd	Singular	you	you	your	yours	yourself
	Plural	you	you	your	yours	yourselves
3rd	Singular (gender distinction applies) *	M he F she N it	him her it	his her its	his hers its	himself herself itself
	Plural	they	them	their	theirs	themselves

*M = masculine; F = feminine; N = neuter

Thus, using the first person singular as example, we can write sentences such as the following:

Subject	*I bought a fruit cake yesterday.*
Object	*The salesperson put it in a box for **me**.*
Possessive as determiner	*This is **my** fruit cake.*
Possessive as pronoun	*This fruit cake is **mine**.*
Reflexive pronoun	*I chose the fruit cake **myself**.*

8.2 What does pronoun-antecedent agreement mean?

Although the term sounds daunting (= making you feel nervous), the idea is actually quite simple. Since the meaning of a pronoun derives from its antecedent, the word it refers to, the two must be in agreement.

A pronoun must agree with its antecedent in person, number, and gender.

If you are already familiar with the basic forms of personal pronouns as given in 8.1 and are careful in writing your sentences, complying with pronoun-antecedent agreement should not be difficult.

> *My granddaughter practises every day for her weekly violin lesson.*
>
> *Our pastor told all choir members that he will hold a Zoom meeting with them this evening.*
>
> *Hong Kong is known for its beautiful natural harbour.*

8.2.1   Antecedents joined by *and* (Compound antecedents)

If you have two or more antecedents joined by **and**, refer to them with a plural pronoun.

> *Our friend John **and** his wife went to the States to witness the wedding of **their** daughter.*
>
> *The restaurant manager **and** his staff believe that **they** are doing the right thing to win the trust of **their** customers.*
>
> ***My wife and I** admit that **we** have not been to the movies for nearly a year.*
>
> Exceptions:
>
> - If the compound antecedent is a single person, thing, or idea, use a singular pronoun.
>
>   *My **ex-colleague and former classmate** told us how **he** went to college by chance.*
>
> - If *each* or *every* is placed before a compound antecedent, use a singular pronoun.
>
>   ***Each** grants and loans applicant is required to submit a statement of **his** or **her** study plan.*

8.2.2   Antecedents joined by *or/nor*

When you use **or** or **nor** (or **either . . . or . . . , neither . . . nor . . .**) to join the parts of an antecedent, the pronoun that follows agrees with the part that is closer.

> (1) *Either long work hours **or** stress will take **its** toll on the office worker.*
>
> (2) *Either stress **or** long work hours will take **their** toll on the office worker.*
>
> (3) *Neither the conductor **nor** the musicians were using scores when **they** played the encore piece.*
>
> Note: If one part of the antecedent is plural and the other singular, it is better to put the plural part second. The plural pronoun that follows will make the sentence sound more natural, as in sentences (2) and (3). Here is another example:
>
> *We hope that either Ho and Lee or Tam will present an innovative plan in **his** proposal.*
>
> Better: *We hope that either Tam or Ho and Lee will present an innovative plan in **their** proposal.* (Ho and Lee is a two-person team.)

8.2.3   Collective nouns as antecedents (see also 6.12, Chapter 6, on collective nouns)

Collective nouns such as **audience, committee, family, group,** and **team** can have singular meaning when treated as a whole unit or plural meaning when considered as individuals capable of acting differently.

> Collective noun antecedent with singular meaning intended:
>
> *The audience there showed **its** distinctive manner of approval by clapping in a strong rhythm.*
>
> Collective noun antecedent with plural meaning intended:
>
> *The audience **were** thrilled by the orchestra's performance: **they** cheered wildly for many long minutes.*

8.2.4 Indefinite pronouns (e.g., *everyone, somebody, anyone, everything*) as antecedents

Indefinite pronouns ending in **-one, -body,** and **-thing** are singular and must be referred to by singular pronouns. Follow this rule in writing although in informal speech it is considered acceptable to use plural pronouns when the singular indefinite pronoun antecedent is plural in meaning. (**Everyone dining in this club cannot use *their* mobile phones.**)

> *Everyone should hand in **his** or **her** assignment tomorrow.* (This is correct in standard English but may create awkwardness if **his or her** appears more than occasionally.)
>
> *Everyone should hand in **their** assignments tomorrow.* (Only in conversation.)
>
> You can revise the sentence in the following ways:
>
> • Change the antecedent to a plural word, and use a plural pronoun.
>
>   *All students should hand in **their** assignments tomorrow.*
>
> • Rewrite the sentence to avoid the pronoun.
>
>   *Everyone should hand in this assignment tomorrow.*

8.3 Pronoun reference

If you observe basic pronoun-antecedent agreement, you have already done well in achieving clear pronoun reference. However, there are several points requiring your attention to ensure clear and unmistakable pronoun reference:

- Be careful when there are several possible antecedents.

- Watch for pronouns that are too far away from their antecedents.

- Make sure that a pronoun refers to a specific, not implied, antecedent.

8.3.1 Be careful when there are several possible antecedents.

When this happens, it is not clear which antecedent the pronoun refers to. As a writer, you may not be aware of it because you know which one you have in mind. It is just not clear to readers from the way you present the sentence. To correct the ambiguity, you need to revise the sentence.

> *Hong Kong is sometimes compared with Shanghai, but **it** is quite different.*
>
> The ambiguity: What does **it** refer to—Hong Kong or Shanghai?
> To correct the ambiguity, you may revise as follows:
>
> > *Hong Kong is sometimes compared with Shanghai, but Shanghai [or Hong Kong] is quite different.*
>
> Or: *Hong Kong is sometimes compared with Shanghai, but **they** are quite different from each other.*

You may also create ambiguity when you use **said** or **told** to quote indirectly what someone has said.

> *When Siu Ling was finished with her DSE exams, her mother said **she** needed a good rest because **she** had not been sleeping enough.*
>
> The ambiguity (or confusion): Who needed a good rest, Siu Ling or her mother?
> To remove the confusion, use direct quotation or rewrite the sentence:
>
> > *When Siu Ling was finished with her DSE exams, her mother said, "**You** need a good rest because **you** have not been sleeping enough."*
>
> Or: *When Siu Ling was finished with her DSE exams, her mother said that **Siu Ling** needed a good rest because **she** had not been sleeping enough.*

8.3.2   Watch for pronouns that are too far away from their antecedents.

A pronoun's reference may be unclear when it is widely separated from its antecedent because readers may be distracted by the information between the two. This problem is likely to occur in long sentences and in adjacent sentences.

> The connection between the pronoun **it** near the end of the passage and its antecedent is unclear.
>
> > *Plastic bag levy was introduced in 2009. For a long time, we have been using far too many plastic bags. Since 2009, however, the number of these bags ending up in landfills has decreased, so **it** is clearly working.*
>
> To clarify the connection, drop the pronoun and mention the noun to which it refers.
>
> > *Plastic bag levy was introduced in 2009. For a long time, we have been using far too many plastic bags. Since 2009, however, the number of these bags ending up in landfills has decreased, so **the levy** is clearly working.*

A similar situation applies to the use of relative pronouns such as **who, which,** and **that.** Make sure that they are placed **immediately after the antecedent to which they refer.**

> Not clear:
>
> *I found **a valuable old photo of my wife and me** as I went through some old things **that** was taken when we were newly married.*
>
> Clear:
>
> *As I went through some old things, I found **a valuable old photo of my wife and me that** was taken when we were newly married.*

8.3.3   Make sure that a pronoun refers to a specific, not implied, antecedent.

Be particularly careful when you use **it, which, this,** or **that** (**this** and **that** can function as "demonstrative pronouns") to refer to a whole idea mentioned in the preceding clause, sentence, or passage. Be careful also when **it** or **they** refers to an **implied antecedent that is not actually stated.** Your readers may find it uneasy to relate that pronoun to its proper antecedent.

> The following example uses **this** to sum up the idea contained in the first two sentences:
>
> *The number of tourists visiting Hong Kong has dropped drastically since the emergence of Covid-19. Many shops have lost a lot of business. **This** shows that the pandemic can hurt the economy.*
>
> In the next example, the relative pronoun **which** refers not to a single word before it but to the entire preceding clause:
>
> *We have an excellent system of public transport in Hong Kong, **which** is rarely the case in North American cities.*
>
> Sometimes, the reference of **it** or **they** is not clear, as in the next three examples. You can correct this problem by stating the antecedent explicitly in place of the pronoun.
>
> Unclear: (1) *The management agreed on adjusting employees' pay, but **it** took time.*
> (Did the agreement of the management or the adjustment of employees' pay take time?)
>
> Better: *The management agreed on adjusting employees' pay, but the adjustment took time.*
>
> Unclear: (2) *She is so interested in buying dresses that **it** simply becomes greater each day.*
> (**It** may refer to one of two implied antecedents: interest or collection of dresses. The modifier **interested** and the gerund phrase **buying dresses** suggest possible antecedents. Instead of making readers guess what you actually mean, it is better if you supply a specific antecedent.)
>
> Clear: *Her interest in buying dresses simply becomes greater each day.*
>
> Or: *She is so interested in buying dresses that her collection of dresses becomes greater each day.*
>
> Unclear: (3) *The typhoon damaged many vegetable fields in the New Territories, but **they** have not yet been able to estimate the loss.*
> (Who are **they**? The government? The farmers?)
>
> Clear: *The typhoon damaged many vegetable fields in the New Territories, but **the farmers** have not yet been able to estimate the loss.*

If you use the relative pronouns **who, which,** and **that,** make sure that they refer to appropriate antecedents. Note that they are all placed immediately after the antecedent.

Who refers to people.
*Sun Yat-sen, **who** was instrumental in the overthrow of the Qing dynasty, studied medicine in Hong Kong.*
Which refers to animals, things, and ideas. Sometimes, **which** can refer to the idea or condition described by the entire clause before it (as also shown in the first part of the preceding box).
*The Bank of China Tower, **which** is a unique landmark in Hong Kong, was completed in 1990.*
*The weather will be fine tomorrow, **which** is good news to everybody.*
That refers to animals, things, ideas, and sometimes to people considered collectively.
*Covid-19 is a disease **that** affects the lungs and even other organs of the body.*
*Customers **that** buy groceries at this supermarket mostly live in the neighbourhood.*

8.4   Summing up

Pronouns are words that stand for a noun. Consequently, its meaning is determined by its antecedent, the word it refers to. You must, firstly, make sure that a pronoun agrees with its antecedent in person, number, and gender. Secondly, make sure that the pronoun refers unmistakably to a specific antecedent. The main points are as follows:

(1)   Singular antecedents take singular pronouns; plural antecedents take plural pronouns.

(2)   Antecedents taking the form **A and B** take plural pronouns.

(3)   Antecedents taking the form **A or B** take pronouns that agree with B.

(4)   Indefinite pronouns ending in **-one, -body,** or **-thing** take singular pronouns.

(5)   Collective nouns with singular meaning take singular pronouns; collective nouns with plural meaning take plural pronouns.

(6)   Be careful when there are several possible antecedents.

(7)   Make sure that a pronoun is close enough to its antecedent.

(8)   Make sure that a pronoun's reference is specific, not implied.

Exercises Chapter 8

Exercise 8.1

Choose the correct words in italics and write them in the blanks to the right.

選擇斜體字中的正確詞語並填寫在右邊的空白處。

1. Rainwater and sunshine *has/have* done *its/their* damage to the paintwork.   _____

2. A man is known by the company *he/they keep/keeps*.   _____

3. China is known for *their/its* expansiveness and large population.   _____

4. Will everyone please have *his or her/their* ID cards ready?   _____

5. My friend and I *am/are* exchanging stories of *my/our* recent travels.   _____

6. When will the new cruise ship sail on *his/its* maiden voyage?   _____

7. Neither the moderator nor the speakers did *his/their* best to create a useful discussion of the question.   _____

8. The opposing sides in the dispute are ready to settle *its/their* differences.   _____

9. Either the tour guide or the tourists in his group had to make up *his/their mind/minds* about the itinerary changes.   _____

10. The chorus rose to perform *its/their* important part in the final movement of Beethoven's Ninth Symphony.   _____

Exercise 8.2

The pronoun (in italics) in most of the following sentences does not agree with its antecedent. Write the correct pronoun in the space to the right. If the given pronoun is correct, write CORRECT.

下面的句子中，很多所含的代詞（斜體）都與其先行詞不一致。請將改正後的代詞寫在右邊的空白處。假如原本的代詞沒有用錯，可在空白處寫 CORRECT。

1. He chooses to major in economics because he finds *them* interesting.   _____

2. Time is a river of passing events, and powerful is *their* current.   _____

3. One should not easily believe what *one* hears from others.   _____

4. All customers of the bank are entitled to *his* or *her* privacy.   _____

5. He asked me to sign the contract, *that* I did.   _____

6. My friend and mentor offered *their* valuable advice.   _____

7. The children are old enough to look after *himself*.   _____

8.   Each of those lofty mountains has *its* own beauty.   _____

9.   When global health problems arise, the World Health Organization should
       help to solve *it*.   _____

10.   Anyone who applies for a job should submit a resumé along with *their* application.   _____

Chapter 9 Know When to Use Articles (a/an, the)

What you will learn in this chapter

Articles (belonging to the word class of determiners) are among the most troublesome topics of English grammar and usage for English learners. There are only two articles: the indefinite article **a/an** and the definite article **the**. They are used, when certain conditions are met, before a noun. You will learn that the use or non-use of articles has to do with three considerations: (1) the kind of noun involved, (2) general vs particular meaning, and (3) definite vs indefinite reference.

冠詞（限定詞中的一種）對英語學習者來説，是英語語法和使用中最棘手的問題之一。冠詞只有兩個：不定冠詞（indefinite article: **a/an**）和定冠詞（definite article: **the**）。在適當情況下，它們可以用於名詞或名詞性短語之前。在本章裏，你將學習從三個因素去決定使用冠詞與否。這三個因素是：(1)冠詞後跟隨的名詞類型，(2)泛指抑或特指，(3)確切説明抑或不確切説明。

9.1 **Basics about articles**

9.2 **Three main considerations**

9.3 **The kind of noun used**

9.4 **General meaning and indefinite reference**

9.5 **Particular meaning**

9.6 **Review chart showing the relationship between meaning and reference when using articles and some other determiners**

9.7 **Summing up**

9.1   Basics about articles

The proper use of articles (**a/an**, **the**, and **zero article** when no article is necessary) in English is not easy. Improper use of articles (in particular, the indiscriminate use of **the**) is one of the most noticeable weaknesses in the writing of students for whom English is not a first language. Study this chapter carefully: it should help you a lot.

9.1.1   Articles are determiners

Articles (**a, an, the**) belong to a group of words called "determiners", which are placed before a noun or noun phrase to determine or limit its reference. Generally, they show which one or how many/much we are talking about.

The words in boldface are all determiners. All of them are used before nouns or noun phrases:

the school   *the* piano that Chopin used   *a* tasty meal   *an* umbrella   *our* family
this restaurant   *the* restaurant near *the* MTR entrance   *those* waves   *all* citizens
each country park   *some* workers   *any* water   *any* friends   *either* hand   *both* parents
less money   *several* tall buildings   *most* people   *many* companies   *every* day

---

9.1.2   Use or non-use of articles

The use or non-use of articles allows us to think of nouns (and noun phrases) in different ways to indicate the kind of reference or meaning intended:

Using *a*	I have bought ***a book***. (some book, but we do not know which one)
Using *the*	Is this ***the book*** you have bought? (we now know which one)
Using no article	***Books*** are important sources of knowledge. (a general statement)

9.1.3   Pronunciation of *a, an, the*

Many learners of English do not pay enough attention to how the three "little words" (**a, an, the**) are pronounced. Most of them pronounce the articles "heavily" regardless of context. That is incorrect. In normal usage, these three words are pronounced *softly* before a noun. When you want to stress the reference shown by these words, not only do you use a stronger utterance, the pronunciation changes too.

The is usually pronounced /ðə/* (as in the world), but changes to /ði/ before a vowel sound (such as **the earth, the environment**) or when used as a stressed form, (as in ***the*** only one, ***the*** big day, *the* great master). (*Note: The **th** sound /ð/ is like the initial sound of **they,** and not the /d/ sound of **day.** Proper pronunciation is shown in IPA, International Phonetic Alphabet. Consult your dictionary if you are not familiar with how the symbols are pronounced.)

A is normally pronounced /ə/ (as in *a* **house,** *a* **tree**), but /eɪ/ when stressed (as in *a* **special treatment,** *a* **great achievement,** *a* **strange story**).

An is usually pronounced /ən/ (as in *an* **idea,** *an* **envelope**), but /æn/ when stressed (as in *an* **empty apartment,** *an* **everyday habit**).

9.1.4 *A* or *an*?

A is used with words that begin with a consonant sound (remember: sound, not letter):

> *a concept   a game   a month   a plan   a university*
>
> *a usual routine* (As in **university**, u in **usual** is pronounced /ju/, a consonant sound.)

An is used with words that begin with a vowel sound:

> *an event   an idea   an hour* (silent h)   *an honest* (silent h) *person*
>
> *an organization   an unusual arrangement   an answer   an end*

If you understand the above rules for using **a** and **an**, you should understand the following:

> *a usual arrangement,* but *an unusual arrangement*
>
> *a lowest common multiple,* but *an LCM* (L, pronounced /el/, is a vowel sound.)
>
> *a Master of Arts degree,* but *an MA degree* (M, pronounced /em/, is a vowel sound.)
>
> *a sailor, but an SOS signal* (S, pronounced /es/, is a vowel sound.)

9.2 Three main considerations

To understand the general principles of using or not using articles, we consider three main aspects:

- The kind of noun used

- General or particular meaning

- Definite or indefinite reference

9.3 The kind of noun used

9.3.1 *A* or *an*

The indefinite article **a/an** can only be used with singular countable nouns:

> *a father   a group   a problem   a city   a bus*
>
> *an idea   an organization   an envelope   an ant*

9.3.2 *The*

The definite article **the** can be used with both countable and uncountable nouns:

Countable nouns:

the father   *the group*   *the problem*   *the city*   *the cities*   *the bus*   *the buses*

the idea   *the ideas*   *the organization*   *the organizations*   *the ant*   *the ants*

Uncountable nouns (only in singular form) :

the advice   *the cooperation*   *the patience*   *the knowledge*   *the integrity*

the progress   *the support*   *the trust*   *the worth*   *the honour*   *the beauty*

When we want to express general meaning, we do not use any article (zero article) before plural countable nouns (**Groups are formed to deal with *problems* arising from controversial *issues*.**) and uncountable nouns (**How can one develop *patience* and *confidence?***) We will see more of this later (9.4.2) when we consider the other two aspects.

9.3.3   Never use *a/an* with uncountable nouns.

You CANNOT say:

~~a confidence~~   ~~a cooperation~~   ~~a news~~   ~~an advice~~

~~a knowledge~~   ~~a health~~   ~~a sleep~~   ~~a money~~   ~~a traffic~~

However, you can use **a/an** with some uncountable nouns when they are qualified:

a father's confidence   *a doctor's advice*   *a talk about money*

a great help   *a rare cooperation*   *an interesting news item*

a little knowledge   *a deep sleep*   *a health problem*

9.3.4   Making an uncountable noun part of a countable phrase

When we have a noun phrase containing an uncountable noun preceded by a countable noun that becomes the main word of the phrase, we can put **a/an** before the main word. The whole phrase is made countable.

Thus, **piece**, **bit**, **vote**, **instance**, and **item** are all countable nouns and main words in the following noun phrases. If needed, we can insert an adjective between **a/an** and the main word.

a piece of advice	*a valuable piece of advice*
a bit of advice	*an honest bit of advice*
a vote of confidence	*a strong vote of confidence*
an instance of cooperation	*a rare instance of cooperation*
a piece of equipment	*a fine piece of equipment*
an item of news	*an important item of news*
a talk about money	*an informative talk about money*

9.3.5 Expressions without articles

Normally a singular count noun is preceded by either the indefinite article (e.g., **a day**), the definite article (e.g., **the day**), or some other determiner (e.g., **any day, this town, another way, each person, every road**), but there are some exceptions. Certain nouns in expressions involving time, place, situation, and movement are normally used without articles:

---

at night   *finish school*   *enter university*   *in class*   *at work*

in office (= holding a job)   *on time* (= at the correct time)

in time (= before the designated time)   *out of town*   *by bus*

by train   *on foot*   *go home*   *after lunch*   *by phone*

by fax   *by post*   *by email*   *in house*   *in school*

on/behind schedule   *on vacation*   *from strength to strength*

9.3.6 Proper nouns

Articles do not normally appear before proper names, especially personal names, except when we wish to refer to people who share certain qualities with particular individuals:

---

*the **Lees** and **Chans*** (Lee and Chan are among the most common Chinese surnames)

*the **Bill Gates** of China* (someone who is wealthiest in China, like Bill Gates globally)

*a **Scrooge*** (someone who is as miserly as Scrooge in Charles Dickens' story of "A Christmas Carol")

Other examples of using the definite article **the** before proper nouns:

- (Some) countries

  the People's Republic of China (but just **China**)   *the Philippines*   *the United States*
  the United Kingdom (but just **Britain**)   *the Netherlands*   *the Vatican*

- Mountain ranges

  the Himalayas   *the Kunlun Mountains*   *the Rockies*   *the Alps*

- Large regions

  the Far East   *the Middle East*   *the West*   *the Sahara*   *the Arctic*

- Rivers

  the Yangtse   *the Mekong*   *the Amazon*   *the Thames*   *the Danube*   *the Nile*

- Oceans and seas

  the Pacific   *the Atlantic*   *the South China Sea*   *the Mediterranean*

- Unique buildings and museums

  the Forbidden City (China)　　*the National Palace Museum* (China)
  the White House (USA)
  the Taj Mahal (India)　　*the Acropolis* (Greece)　　*the Louvre* (France)

- Organizations

  the United Nations　　*the World Health Organization*　　*the International Olympic Committee*

- Newspapers

  the South China Morning Post (Hong Kong)　　*the New York Times* (New York)
  the Times (London)

9.4　General meaning and indefinite reference

When we write about entities in general or whole classes, we are expressing general meaning. In so doing, we are concerned with generalities, not individual particular cases:

> *Schools are instrumental in the fundamental learning of children.*

In the above sentence, it does not matter which school(s) or which child(ren). These questions are irrelevant to the validity of the sentence.

Therefore, when we want to express general meaning, there is no need to identify which ones we are talking about. This means *the reference is necessarily indefinite*. The distinction between indefinite and definite reference is important only when we want to express not general, but particular meaning.

9.4.1　All forms of the article (definite, indefinite, and zero article) may be used.

> (a) ***the: The library*** *is a place for keeping books and other information resources.*
>
> (b) ***a: A library*** *is a place for keeping books and other information resources.*
>
> (c) ***zero article: Libraries are*** *places for keeping books and other information resources.*

Essentially the same general meaning is expressed in the above three sentences. Note, however, that reference is to all libraries generally as a kind of institution both in (a) **the library** and in (c) **libraries,** whereas reference is to *any* library in (b) **a library.**

9.4.2　Most natural way of expressing general or generic meaning

To express general or generic meaning naturally, use *zero article* with uncountable nouns or plural countable nouns:

> *Cooperation* between *management* and *workers* is necessary to minimize *industrial disputes*.
> (**Cooperation** and **management** are uncountable nouns; **workers** and **disputes** are plural countable nouns.)
>
> *Both **parents** and **teachers** have **influence** on the development of **children**.*
> (**Parents**, **teachers**, and **children** are plural countable nouns; **influence** is an uncountable noun.)

9.4.3 Using *the* with a singular count noun to indicate a generic class (less common)

> *The cell* is the smallest unit of living matter that can exist independently.
>
> The above is a statement that defines or classifies something, and it means about the same as:
>
> *Cells* are the smallest unit of living matter that can exist independently.
>
> *A cell* is the smallest unit of living matter that can exist independently.

In the same way, the following three sentences are similar in meaning:

> *The church* is an organization.
>
> *Churches* are organizations.
>
> *A church* is an organization.

9.4.4 Using *a/an* with a singular countable noun to make a generic phrase (also less common)

Two examples (**a cell, a church**) were given in 9.4.3. Here is another example in which the generic phrase **an opinion poll** is used to define or classify something:

> *An opinion poll* conducted properly is supposed to be reliable.
>
> It means about the same as:
>
> *Opinion polls* conducted properly are supposed to be reliable.
>
> *The opinion poll* conducted properly is supposed to be reliable.

But since **a** means "any", its use in some contexts cannot adequately express generic meaning, as when the statement does not define or classify something. Then, we cannot use **a/an** in front of the noun.

We can say:	*The computer* has brought pervasive changes to society.
	Computers have brought pervasive changes to society.
But not:	~~A computer has brought pervasive changes to society.~~

9.4.5   Using *the* to express general meaning

Before adjectives (behaving as nouns) that refer to <u>classes of people</u>:

the rich   the poor   the young   the old   the religious   the healthy
the sick   the privileged   the deprived   the talented   the better educated
the highly trained   the disabled   the locally born   the overseas Chinese

*It is often said that the gap between **the rich** and **the poor** is widening.*

***The better educated** in the population are more likely to be working as professionals.*

Before group nouns that refer to <u>collectivities or aggregates taken as wholes</u>:

the public   the audience   the administration   the middle class
the state   the government   (to be distinguished from **the Government** or just
                                Government, both indicating particular meaning)

*Many people aspire to become members of **the middle class**.*

*When the economy declines, people tend to blame it on **the government**.*

Before nouns that refer to our <u>physical environment</u> or to stereotypes or institutions that are part
of our <u>shared social world</u> or our <u>common experience</u> (***a/an** is also possible):

the weather   the future   the past*   the environment*   the media*
the news   the cinema   the city*   the bank*   the civil service**
the political system   the workaholic*   the countryside   the world   the atmosphere*
*the bureaucracy** (sometimes used with no article when using **bureaucracy** as a concept)

*Part of our social greeting is some brief talk about **the weather**.*

***The environment** means different things to different people.*

*Sociologists believe that **bureaucracy** exists in all large organizations.*

*One may wonder whether good leaders or good managers have an edge (= have an advantage) in
career advancement in **the bureaucracy** of the civil service.*

*We all value **an environment** that is healthy and sustainable.*

*What **the future** holds for humanity is an extremely complicated question.*

*We have reasons to doubt the authenticity of the reality presented by **the media**.*

9.4.6   The word *society*

Use *zero article* with *society* when it means "the society that we as human beings all live in". That is,
society takes no article when it is used as a general and abstract idea that can include any society we can
think of. I point this out because non-native speakers attach **the** to **society** too often and too easily.

> *What is the relationship between **society** and **the individual**?* (Notice that **the individual** refers to the entire class of human individuals.)
>
> *As concepts, culture and **society** are two sides of the same coin.*
>
> *Roles of men and women are changing in today's **society**.*
>
> *The computer has revolutionized **society**.*

9.5 Particular meaning

We express particular meaning when we refer to particular, or specific, individual entities (objects, persons, ideas, etc.) rather than things in general or classes of things.

9.5.1 Distinction between definite reference and indefinite reference

In referring to particular entities, we need to distinguish between definite reference and indefinite reference. For general meaning, which concerns classes rather than specific individuals, such distinction is irrelevant (as stated in 9.4) as the reference is necessarily indefinite.

Definite reference applies when the reader can identify the things or persons referred to [as in sentence (a) below]. That is, the reader can tell which thing or person is referred to. By contrast, indefinite reference occurs if the reader cannot identify them [as in sentence (b)].

> (a) *This is **the student** who has surpassed all others in the test.*
>   (The who-clause indicates the identity of the student.)
>
> (b) ***Some students** have failed the test.*
>   Although we know that certain individual students have failed the test, we cannot, or do not intend to tell who they are.)

9.5.2 Particular meaning with definite reference

9.5.2.1 Use **the** to indicate which one(s) we mean:

> (a) Back-pointing use of **the** (to refer to things or persons mentioned before):
>
>   *First you select **a destination** and **a travel agency**; then you go to **the agency** to ask for information about **the destination**.*
>
>   *Sometimes you start with **a good idea**, but later find that **the idea** is really too complex to write about in a short paper.*
>
> (b) Forward-pointing use of **the** (to refer to things or persons to be discussed):
>
>   *This is **the document** that has caused so much controversy.*
>
>   *We were disappointed by **the response** the legislator gave to our query.*
>
>   *Nobody is interested in **the story** about how he came to power.*
>
>   ***The opinions** of others can affect how we see ourselves.*

9.5.2.2 Many phrases contain the structure **the B of A**, where **B** is an aspect or feature of **A**. **B** can be either a countable noun (singular or plural) (e.g., **the effects of the pandemic**) or an uncountable noun (e.g., **the challenge of competition**).

the joy of music	*the characteristics of globalization*
the use of computers	*the effects of the trade war**
the essence of Chinese culture	*the fascination of magic*
the love of paintings	*the satisfaction of helping others*

* If **A** has particular meaning, we use **the** before it (e.g., ***the effects of the trade war** that occurred last year*).

9.5.2.3 Use **the** to refer to the only one(s) in existence (assuming our reader understands what is referred to from general knowledge or from knowledge of the situation concerned):

the digital age   the tourism industry   the British Prime Minister   the China market the Internet   the West   the United Nations   the WHO (World Health Organization) the Renaissance   the Cultural Revolution   the Second World War   the pandemic

The world *has become much smaller because of the convenience of communication***.*

*With a huge continuing surge in the number of Covid-19 infections,** **the Government** has to consider much stricter methods of containing the spread of **the virus.*** *

*China has become the third country to have successfully obtained soil samples from the surface of **the moon.*** *

** Note the structure **the B of A**

9.5.3   Particular meaning with indefinite reference

Use **a/an** or an indefinite determiner (e.g., **some, several, many, most, no**) to refer to certain individual entities (objects, persons, ideas, etc.) without really identifying which one(s):

*I recently came across **an insightful book** on the clash of civilizations.*

*Medical experts are working steadfastly for **an effective vaccine** against Covid-19.*

*Everyone is hoping for **a better year** in 2021 after so much worry in 2020.*

***An old classmate of mine** sent me a nice digital Christmas card from Hawaii.*

***A good father** disciplines his children with love so that they will learn proper behaviour.*

*We need to include **some discussion** of the practical implications of the study.*

***Many videos on health** have appeared online during the past year.*

***Several possible solutions of the problem** have been suggested by our team.*

***No sensible person** would believe that the media can really print anything they want.*

9.6 Review chart showing the relationship between meaning and reference when using articles and some other determiners

Meaning \ Reference	Definite (with identifying which ones)	Indefinite (without identifying which ones)
General (whole classes)	Not applicable	**a/an** ***A group*** *has members.* **the** ***The family*** *is an institution.* ***The young*** *and* ***the aged*** *are quite different.* **Ø** ***Groups*** *are different from* ***crowds.*** ***People*** *respond to* ***social rules.*** *They turned to* ***science*** *for an answer.* *Science studies* ***physical phenomena.*** ***Trust*** *and* ***leadership*** *are personal qualities.* *We are all* ***members*** *of* ***society.***
Particular (specific entities)	**the** ***the idea*** *of progress* ***The digital age*** *is here.* ***the study*** *of law* ***the cause*** *of conflict* ***the scientific method*** ***the*** *past 150 years* ***the honour*** *of being a good leader* ***the society*** *of post-1997 Hong Kong*	**a/an** *We have* ***an idea.*** *They visited* ***a university*** *there.* *He gave* ***an explanation*** *of their behaviour.* **many*** *It took* ***many years*** *to succeed.* **some*** ***Some people*** *like it.* **no*** ***No solution*** *was found.* **most*** ***Most children*** *love to play.* **several*** ***Several*** *letters arrived.* **all*** ***All*** *my friends know.* Ø Zero article (no article used) * These are called **indefinite determiners.**

9.7 Summing up

Using or not using articles in front of nouns or noun phrases is a skill that helps you write idiomatic English. You need to bear in mind three things: (1) the kind of noun used, (2) general vs. particular meaning, and (3) definite vs. indefinite reference. The following are some main points:

The kind of noun used

(1)   **A/an** can only be used with singular countable nouns but never uncountable nouns.

(2)   **The** can be used with both countable and uncountable nouns.

(3)   Many nouns in expressions about time, place, situation, and movement are used without articles.

(4)   **The** is used with many names of places and countries.

General (with indefinite reference) vs. particular meaning (with definite vs. indefinite reference)

(5)   We express general meaning when we are concerned with classes, not individual entities.

(6)   We express particular meaning when we have specific individual entities in mind.

(7)   In general meaning, our reference is necessarily indefinite. That is, we do not identify which one(s).

(8)   When expressing particular meaning, our reference can be either definite or indefinite.

You can often refer to the diagram in 9.6 that illustrates the relationship between general vs. particular meaning and definite vs. indefinite reference. The example phrases and sentences there should help you remember how articles are or are not used.

Exercises Chapter 9

Exercise 9.1

Write T for "true" or F for "false" in the parentheses at the beginning of each statement.

假如下列陳述句所說正確，在括號內寫 T，不正確則寫 F。

1. (   )   Articles are determiners placed before a noun or noun phrase.

2. (   )   **An** is used with words that begin with a vowel letter.

3. (   )   The definite article **the** can be used with both countable and uncountable nouns.

4. (   )   We cannot use the indefinite article (**a**, **an**) immediately before uncountable nouns (e.g., **an advice**).

5. (   )   Articles can always be used before proper nouns.

6. (   )   No articles may be used when expressing general meanings.

7. (   )   Normally, either **a** or **the** can come before a singular countable noun.

8. (   )   When we express general meaning, our reference is necessarily indefinite.

9. (   )   When our reference is indefinite and the meaning is general, we can only use the indefinite article.

10. (   )   The most natural way of expressing general meaning is to use zero article with uncountable nouns or plural countable nouns.

11. (   )   In expressing particular meaning, our reference can be definite or indefinite.

12. (   )   In the structure **the B of A**, **B** is some feature or quality of **A** and can be either a countable noun (singular or plural) or an uncountable noun.

Exercise 9.2

Write a suitable article (**a**, **an**, or **the**) in each space provided. If no article is needed, write Ø.

在每句的空白處填寫適當的冠詞 (a, an 或 the)。假如毋需冠詞，填寫 Ø。

1. What's _____ weather like tomorrow?

2. Zhongshan is one of _____ main cities in _____ Pearl River Delta region.

3. _____ workaholics are _____ people who find it difficult to stop _____ working.

4. _____ thesaurus is _____ dictionary of _____ synonyms.

5. You may begin with _____ simple idea and gradually develop _____ idea into _____ interesting proposal.

6. _____ joy of _____ music is hard to describe clearly, but Leonard Bernstein, _____ famous composer and conductor, wrote _____ book on it.

7. _____ fascination of magic lies in its ability to keep us in _____ awe and _____ puzzlement.

8. He is _____ very gifted scientist who can give us _____ simple explanations of _____ very complex phenomena.

9. _____ aged and _____ young are quite different in their reaction to _____ Covid-19 virus.

10. This is _____ candidate who has surpassed all others in _____ job interview.

11. As _____ saying goes, _____ bird in _____ hand is worth two in _____ bush.

12. How do we study _____ relationship between _____ society and _____ individual?

Exercise 9.3

The following passage is about the art of Chinese calligraphy. In each numbered space write a suitable article (**a, an**, or **the**). If no article is needed, write Ø.

以下這段文字略述了中國書法的藝術。在每個標有號碼的空白處，填寫合適的冠詞 (**a, an** 或 **the**)。假如毋需冠詞，填寫 Ø。

Chinese calligraphy is considered __(1)__ art. Writing of __(2)__ Chinese characters is performed with __(3)__ brush of __(4)__ particular kind depending on __(5)__ size of characters, using specially prepared black ink and __(6)__ fine paper. Various skills, such as how __(7)__ brush is held and how different strokes and dots are formed by __(8)__ brush, are involved in producing characters that are __(9)__ representation of "style". __(10)__ calligrapher uses his or her skills to blend many elements into __(11)__ art form, such as __(12)__ smoothness, __(13)__ force, __(14)__ balance, and __(15)__ elegance. When writing, __(16)__ calligrapher must have __(17)__ calm mind and __(18)__ perfect positioning. In such __(19)__ state, he hopes to have every line or stroke of __(20)__ character he is writing to be properly located. Good calligraphy is __(21)__ result of __(22)__ long learning process, often using __(23)__ work of __(24)__ outstanding calligrapher as example to follow. With sufficient practice, one begins to develop __(25)__ personal style, showing not just skills but also __(26)__ spirit of __(27)__ fine artistic calligraphy.

Chapter 10 Use Adjectives and Adverbs to Modify

What you will learn in this chapter

Adjectives and adverbs are major word classes. Adjectives, by introducing certain details, describe or limit the meaning of nouns, whereas adverbs can modify verbs, adjectives, other adverbs, or even whole sentences. Obviously, given their function of describing or shaping meanings associated with what we write, how they operate needs to be well understood. What you will learn include recognizing adjectives and adverbs, positioning them in sentences, choosing the right adjective and adverb for various purposes, and making comparisons with these modifying words.

形容詞和副詞都是主要的詞類。形容詞通過展示一些細節來描述或修飾名詞,而副詞可用以修飾動詞、形容詞和其他副詞,甚至整個句子。既然形容詞和副詞可以給予我們所寫的文字更豐富的意思,我們尤其應該清楚理解它們的功能和用法。你在本章裏可以學到的包括:辨認形容詞和副詞、認識它們在句子裏的位置、就各種不同目的而選擇適當的形容詞和副詞,還有怎樣用這兩種詞作不同程度的比較。

10.1   **What do adjectives and adverbs do?**

10.2   **Topics to be covered**

10.3   **Two positions of adjectives**

10.4   **Recognizing adjectives**

10.5   **Choosing the right adjective**

10.6   **Using adjectives and adverbs**

10.7   **Types of adverbs**

10.8   **Position of adverbs**

10.9   **Gradation (comparison) of adjectives**

10.10 **Comparing adverbs**

10.11 **Using adverbs with graded and ungraded adjectives**

10.12 **Adverbs from adjectives**

10.13 **Adverbs modifying adjectives in ways other than showing gradation**

10.14 **Summing up**

10.1   What do adjectives and adverbs do?

10.1.1 You already know them (to some extent).

You are probably already familiar with adjectives and adverbs. As you may recall, adjectives are used to modify (describe or limit the meaning of) nouns and pronouns, and adverbs are mostly used to modify verbs, adjectives, or other adverbs. In the first sentence of this paragraph, **familiar** is an adjective modifying the pronoun **you**, subject of the sentence; **already** is an adverb modifying the adjective **familiar**, and **probably** is an adverb modifying both **already** and **familiar**.

10.1.2 An important part of the English language

Closely (adverb, adv) related (adjective, adj) word classes, adjectives and adverbs are indispensable (adj) for communication and writing about what happens anywhere (adv) and what we can make of events in our world. Without adjectives and adverbs, there is perhaps (adv) little (adv) we can say about how (adv) we feel under the wide-ranging (adj) influence of the global (adj) coronavirus pandemic. You can easily (adv) see that we cannot do much (adv again) without them in the language. In this short passage you just read, we used four adjectives and seven adverbs.

10.1.3 Many adverbs formed from adding -*ly* to adjectives

Many adjectives can be turned into adverbs by adding -**ly** at the end. Thus, for example, **angry → angrily, easy → easily, quick → quickly, cold → coldly, nice → nicely, careful → carefully**. (Note: For adjectives ending in **y**, change the **y** to **i** before adding -**ly**.) To strengthen your recognition of the modifying functions of adjectives and adverbs, you can study the following pairs of sentences:

*He thought it was an **easy** examination.*
*He answered the questions **easily** in the examination.*
*She took a **brief** glance of the headlines on the front page.*
*She glanced **briefly** the headlines on the front page.*
*You seem **careful** in money matters.*
*You seem capable of managing money matters **carefully**.*

10.1.4 Some words ending in -*ly* are adjectives.

But a few words ending in -**ly** are actually adjectives: **costly, deadly, elderly, friendly, likely, lovely, lonely, silly, timely, ugly, unlikely.** Read the following sentences and try to identify which -**ly** words are adjectives and which -**ly** words are adverbs:

*We decided **easily** that such a **poorly** planned project was **unlikely** to succeed.*
*On that **terribly** cold morning, it would be **silly** to go out wearing only a T-shirt.*
*You should realize **quickly** that the people of this community are very **friendly**.*

10.2   Topics to be covered

What you will learn in the rest of this chapter includes the following important topics:

- the position of adjectives

- recognizing adjectives

- choosing the right adjective

- the same word as both adjective and adverb

- the kinds of adverbs

- the position of adverbs

- comparative and superlative forms of adjectives and adverbs

10.3   Two positions of adjectives

10.3.1 Most adjectives can be placed in one of two positions ("attributive" and "predicative") in a sentence:

Before a noun (the "attributive position")	After a linking verb (the "predicative position"), which joins the adjective to a subject. Examples of linking verbs: *be, seem, look, become, feel, get, smell, taste, turn.*
*It was a **fascinating trip**.*	*The trip **was fascinating**.*
*We had a **fruitful discussion**.*	*Our discussion **was fruitful**.*
*She has got a **new dress**.*	*Her dress **is new**.*
*This is **delicious dessert**.*	*This dessert **tastes delicious**.*
*This is seemingly a **luxurious hotel**.*	*This hotel **looks luxurious**.*
*We are having **colder** weather now.*	*It's **becoming colder** now.*
*She has **grey** hair.*	*Her hair is **turning grey**.*
*People think of him as an **intelligent** man.*	*He **seems intelligent**.*

10.3.2 Some adjectives can only be used in the attributive position (before a noun):

*I like to swim in an **outdoor** pool.*
*This is the **only** Turkish restaurant in town.*
*Our **main** problem is we do not have enough time.*
*The **former** pianist now works mainly as a conductor.*
*No standing is allowed on the **upper** deck of buses.*

10.3.3 Some adjectives can only go in the predicative position (after a linking verb). You can sometimes use other words, with an adjective before a noun, to achieve a similar meaning.

> *The man **felt unwell** after running.* (Do not say: ~~the unwell man~~, but you can say: *the **sick** man*)
>
> *The baby **is** already **asleep**.* (Do not say: ~~the asleep baby~~, but you can say: *the **sleeping** baby*)
>
> *These two girls **look alike**.* (Do not say: ~~two alike girls~~)
>
> *We **are pleased** to meet you.*
>
> *It is getting late and I cannot **stay awake** for much longer.*

10.4   Recognizing adjectives

10.4.1 No fixed pattern

The adjectives that you have seen in the examples so far are among the more common ones. There is no fixed pattern to such adjectives as **big**, **cold**, **good**, **new**, **nice**, **poor**, and **quick**.   If you read a lot, you will become familiar with them and many others as descriptive words. In addition, you should note that words that can act as adjectives include:

Words acting as adjectives	Examples
Present participles (**-ing** words)	*fascinating* (*a **fascinating** story*)
	smiling (*the **smiling** child*)
	running (*a **fast-running** athlete*) (***fast*** here is an adverb modifying ***running***)
	operating (*trying to reduce the **operating** costs*)
	working (*a clock in good **working** condition*)
Past participles (**-ed** or **-en** words)	*damaged* (*a door **damaged** beyond repair*)
	excited (*an **excited** winner*)
	surprised (*We were **surprised** at his failure.*)
	broken (*Mind the **broken** glass on the floor!*)
	taken (*This seat is already **taken**.*)
Nouns (used before another noun or a noun phrase)	*work* schedule
	church groups
	fusion cuisines popular among professionals (**Cuisines popular among professionals** is a noun phrase, and so is the whole phrase including **fusion**.)
	museum visits
	travel itinerary containing museum visits (**Itinerary containing museum visits** is a noun phrase, and so is the whole phrase including **travel**.)

10.4.2 Suffixes as cues

Some suffixes (word endings) added to a noun or verb typically tell you that the word so formed is an adjective. Study the following examples. See if you can add some more on your own going through the given suffixes.

suffix	+	this word	=	this adjective	suffix	+	this word	=	this adjective
-able		count (v)*		countable	-ive		act (v)		active
-al		nation (n)*		national	-less		home (n)		homeless
-ant		vigil (n)		vigilant	-like		dream (n)		dreamlike
-ary		discipline (n)		disciplinary	-ly		month (n)		monthly
-ed		culture (n)		cultured	-ory		contradict (v)		contradictory
-ent		persist (v)		persistent	-ous		fame (n)		famous
-esque		picture (n)		picturesque	-some		trouble (n)		troublesome
-ful		success (n)		successful	-ual		fact (n)		factual
-ible		flex (v)		flexible	-uous		continue (v)		continuous
-ic		metal (n)		metallic	-worthy		trust (n)		trustworthy
-ish		child (n)		childish	-y		water (n)		watery

*v = verb, n = noun

10.5   Choosing the right adjective

10.5.1 Knowing what characteristics you want in your description

Since an adjective is a descriptive word to modify a noun (person, thing, idea, event, situation), think carefully about what quality or attribute you want to say about the noun in question. Think of several options and see which one offers you the most adequate description or modification.

If, for example, you are referring to a trip you took recently, many adjectives may come to mind, such as **exciting, enjoyable, fun-filled,** and **wonderful**. If, let us say, your trip included several days' outdoor physical activities such as hang-gliding and white-water rafting, then indeed your trip must have been both **fun-filled** and **exciting**. You may want to elaborate on the ways in which your activities have been **fun-filled** and **exciting**. You may then conclude, justifiably, that your trip was **enjoyable** and **wonderful**.

Suppose your friend also came back from a trip which, however, involved him in activities quite different from yours. His itinerary included visits to museums, art galleries, parks, historic trails, and evening concerts because he loves art, nature, and orchestral music. In telling you about his trip, he probably would think of such adjectives as **enriching, refreshing, relaxing, and even educational.** He would describe his trip as **enriching** and **educational** because of the historic trails, art and music elements. The trip was also **refreshing** and **relaxing** because of the many visits to parks. On this basis, he can claim that his trip was **enjoyable** and **wonderful,** and maybe **exciting,** too, because he experienced so much that is valuable to him.

There you are. You need to be mindful of the qualities and characteristics that you want to bring to others' attention when looking for the right descriptive words. If you are careful and patient enough, you will find what you want. It is all right if the same adjectives (e.g., **enjoyable, wonderful**) are chosen by different writers to refer to not the same experiences, as long as enough details are given.

10.5.2 Learning more about synonyms in your descriptive vocabulary

As descriptive words, adjectives can come in a variety of words that have nearly the same (or similar) meanings. These are called synonyms, which you can find in a general learner's dictionary or, for more details, a thesaurus (dictionary of synonyms). Of course, a thesaurus gives you synonyms of not just adjectives but other word classes such as nouns and verbs as well.

A very helpful feature of a thesaurus is that synonyms of a given word are arranged in different groups of meaning. If you see the group whose meaning matches what you have in mind, you can then check the synonyms in that group to see which one or ones suit you best. With more use of a thesaurus, you will soon realize that adjectives that appear to be similar in meaning are in fact not quite the same in reference or connotation (implied or suggested meaning) although they may be based on the same broad idea. Further, differences exist not only between different groups of meaning but also within the same group.

Let us illustrate the usefulness of finding the right adjective to express your idea with the seemingly simple word **rich.** The following table shows the various possible meaning groups of this adjective and some synonyms within each meaning group for the user's consideration and choice.

Meaning group of *rich*	Possible synonyms (other adjectives with similar meaning)
1. wealthy (*a rich banker*)	*well-off, well-to-do, affluent, prosperous*
2. precious (*rich fabrics*)	*fine, expensive, valuable, priceless*
3. flavourful (*a rich dessert*)	*full-bodied, delicious, sweet, tasty*
4. intense (*a rich voice*)	*deep, warm, resonant, mellow, bright*
5. well-endowed (*a rich garden*)	*abundant, lush, exuberant, splendid*
6. productive (*a rich harvest*)	*fruitful, fertile, bountiful*
7. varied (*a rich culture*)	*dynamic, lively, vigorous, vivid, vibrant*
8. containing something (*rich in minerals*)	*plentiful, well-provided, copious, ample*

If you study the above table carefully and use a good dictionary to check the meaning of the words given in each meaning group, you will see that the synonyms in each group are not identical in meaning. There could be differences in emphasis or connotation. Thus, for instance, in the "flavourful" meaning group, **delicious** means having a pleasant or enjoyable taste, whereas **full-bodied** implies the pleasant or enjoyable taste is quite strong and even somewhat heavy. In choosing the right adjective that suits your purpose, you need to understand subtle differences in meaning. The context of writing often allows us to know which meaning is contained in a certain adjective, as when we say that **China has a *rich* culture, with its *long* history and *vibrant customs.*** Using the right adjectives to convey meaning accurately is no doubt a valuable skill.

10.5.3 Caution in describing experiences and feelings: *exciting* and *excited*

When you see an action-packed movie, you can say it is **exciting, interesting,** or **thrilling.** That is what the movie does to you. It is your experience. On the other hand, you feel **excited, interested,** or **thrilled.** That is how you react to the movie. Do not confuse the two different meanings.

When describing feelings and experiences, you have many pairs of adjectives (**-ing and -ed**) to choose from. You need to be careful to choose the correct member of the pair. Remember: the **-ing** adjective is for describing the external agent that does something to you, whereas the **-ed** adjective is for describing how you feel as a result. Many learners of English use the wrong adjective if they do not distinguish clearly between these two types of adjectives. The following table lists many such adjectives.

-ing (Something or someone is like this)	*-ed* (You are or feel like this)
amusing	amused
annoying	annoyed
comforting	comforted
confusing	confused
depressing	depressed
disappointing	disappointed
discouraging	discouraged
disturbing	disturbed
encouraging	encouraged
entertaining	entertained
exciting	excited
exhausting	exhausted
fascinating	fascinated
frightening	frightened
heartening	heartened
horrifying	horrified
inspiring	inspired
insulting	insulted
interesting	interested
motivating	motivated
moving	moved
overwhelming	overwhelmed
puzzling	puzzled
relaxing	relaxed
satisfying	satisfied
shocking	shocked
soothing	soothed
stimulating	stimulated
surprising	surprised
terrifying	terrified
threatening	threatened
thrilling	thrilled
tiring	tired
troubling	troubled
uplifting	uplifted
worrying	worried

10.6   Using adjectives and adverbs

10.6.1 Remember that you use adjectives to modify nouns and adverbs to modify verbs mainly but also adjectives or other adverbs. The following sentences will help you remember this:

Adjectives	Adverbs
He is a **quick** runner.	He runs **quickly**. (**Quickly** modifies verb *runs*.)
The library is a **quiet** place.	You may speak **quietly** in a library. (**Quietly** modifies verb *speak*.)
She bought some **cheap** clothes at this shop.	She bought some clothes **cheaply** at this shop. (**Cheaply** modifies verb *bought*.)
It was a **hot** day.	It was a **very** hot day. (**Very** modifies adjective *hot*.)
Better give your car's tyres a **careful** check.	Better check your car's tyres **really** carefully. (**Really** modifies adverb *carefully*.)

10.6.2 Note, however, that sometimes the same word can be both adjective and adverb, depending on how it is used, as in the following:

Adjectives	Adverbs
You will take an **early** train tomorrow.	You need to get up **early** tomorrow.
We did some **hard** work on the problem.	We worked **hard** on the problem.
The water of this pool is not **deep**.	They stayed up and chatted **deep** into the night.
Parents have **high** hopes for their children.	His teacher encourages him to aim **high** in examinations.
Beijing is a **long** way from Hong Kong.	Have you known her **long**?
He is their **only** son.	This song takes **only** two minutes to sing.

Other words that can work as both adjectives and adverbs include **fast**, **late**, **low**, **near**, **right**, **wrong**. Make sure, however, that you know their proper use.

10.6.3 Adverbs with two forms

Some adverbs take two forms, one with **-ly** ending and one without. They usually have different meanings. Here are a few examples:

Without *-ly* ending	With *-ly* ending
fine (to be satisfactory) *I am doing **fine**.*	**finely** (into very small pieces) *She added some **finely** chopped onions to the ground beef.*
hard (with force) *Press the two glued parts **hard** so they can bond well.*	**hardly** (almost none) *There is **hardly** any rice left.*

Without *-ly* ending	With *-ly* ending
high (a long way up)	**highly** (with praise)
*Passenger planes can fly **high** above the clouds.*	*Your teacher speaks **highly** of you.*
late (after the expected time)	**lately** (recently)
*The concert started **late** last evening.*	*We have been very busy **lately**.*
near (a short distance or time away)	**nearly** (almost)
*The final exams are drawing **near**.*	*It took him **nearly** two hours to get to work yesterday.*
short (little is left)	**shortly** (soon)
*Time is running **short**; we must hurry.*	*Our guest will arrive **shortly**.*

10.7 Types of adverbs

10.7.1 Six main types

Adverbs that modify a verb, an adjective, another adverb, or part of a sentence may be grouped under six main types: (1) manner, (2) place, (3) time, (4) degree, (5) focus (emphasis), and (6) connection. See some examples of one-word adverbs and adverbial phrases in the table below:

(1) Adverbs of manner (to show how something happens):
*She did not damage the toaster **deliberately.***
*The conductor bowed **respectfully** to the audience.*
carefully   deliberately   eagerly   generously   happily *honestly   nervously   quietly   respectfully   skillfully*
(2) Adverbs of place:
*I could not find my phone in this room; I must look **elsewhere**.*
*Once we are **off** this highway, we will be in busy city traffic.*
above   anywhere   behind   elsewhere   here *home   inside   off   outside   somewhere   there*
(3) Adverbs of time (including fixed time, duration, and frequency):
*People **nowadays** care more about rights rather than obligations.*
*The gas company man comes **occasionally** to check the meter reading.*
afterwards   always   earlier   immediately   now   nowadays *often   rarely   sometimes   soon   today   usually   normally* *occasionally   every day   once a week   some years ago*

(4) Adverbs of degree:

*Have you recovered from your cold **completely?***

***Surely** the Covid-19 pandemic is not going to disappear anytime soon.*

absolutely   certainly   completely   definitely   fairly   really
much   slightly/a bit   surely   too   undoubtedly   very

(5) Focusing adverbs (to focus attention on a specific part of a sentence):

*This plan is **simply** impractical. (**simply** focuses on impractical)*

*I like Charles Dickens' novels, **particularly** his "A Tale of Two Cities".*

also   entirely   exactly   fully   indeed   just   only
mainly   mostly   particularly   simply   solely

(6) Connecting adverbs (to show the logical relation to a previous sentence):

*He had his passport stolen before returning to Hong Kong. **As a result**, he had to go through a lot of trouble to obtain a replacement passport from the Chinese Embassy there.*

*I usually do not like crowded places. **Besides**, with the Covid pandemic still around, it is safer to avoid crowds.*

after all   as a result   besides   consequently   for example
furthermore   however   in addition   in a nutshell   in conclusion
on the other hand   in other words   so   still

10.7.2 Sentence adverbs

Some adverbs can modify not individual words (verbs, adjectives, adverbs) but whole sentences. A sentence adverb usually says something about the situation stated in the sentence or shows our comment on what we are saying. The following illustrate some commonly used sentence adverbs:

***Obviously**, eating in a fine-dining restaurant will not be cheap.*

***Surprisingly**, she did very well in her examination.*

*They **kindly** offered to put us up for all three days of our visit.*

***Fortunately**, we had fine weather when we were there.*

*We **probably** will be late for the show.*

*That is **certainly** a great idea.*

***Perhaps** we can discuss with other team members to see whether this is possible.*

*Environmental protection needs a lot of education, **of course.***

10.8 Position of adverbs

10.8.1 Three positions in a sentence to place an adverb: *front, mid*, and *end*.

Front position (at the beginning, before the subject)
Sentence adverbs are often in the front position although mid or end positions are possible:
Economically, *Hong Kong has been developing well.*
Presumably, *entertainment programmes are most popular among television audiences.* (Or: *Entertainment programmes are **presumably** most popular among television audiences.*)
Of course, *she was late as usual.* (Or: *She was late as usual, **of course**.*)
Connecting adverbs generally go in front position:
He did not prepare well before the exams. ***Consequently***, *he did poorly.*
You need not be so troubled. ***After all***, *it is not really your problem.* (Or: *It is not really your problem, **after all**.*)

Mid position (close to the main verb)
Adverbs of time, before the main verb:
*They **sometimes** watch a movie on weekends.*
*I will **soon** deal with that problem.*
Adverbs of degree, before the main verb or an adjective:
*She **really** loves ice cream.*
*The concert was **absolutely** wonderful.*
Adverbs of time (frequency), immediately after **be** as a main verb (but before it for emphasis on **be**):
*I am **usually** back home by 7 p.m.* (*I usually **am** back home by 7 p.m.*)
*He is **always** late for school.* (*He always **is** late for school.*)
Adverbs of time (frequency), immediately after the first auxiliary, if any (but before it for emphasis on the auxiliary):
*Ann has **always** liked biology.* (*Ann always **has** liked biology.*)
*We would **normally** go to church on Sundays.* (*We normally **would** go to church on Sundays.*)
Focusing adverbs, immediately after the first auxiliary, if any (but before it for emphasis on the auxiliary):
*The children have **certainly** been enjoying their play.* (*The children certainly **have** been enjoying their play.*)
*She can **only** read books in Chinese.* (*She only **can** read books in Chinese.*)

End position (end of sentence)

Adverbs of time (fixed time, such as **today**; and frequency, such as **daily**) usually come in end position:

> They will celebrate their mother's birthday **tomorrow**. (Or: **Tomorrow**, they will celebrate their mother's birthday.)

> We meet for lunch **once a month**. (Or: **Once a month** we meet for lunch.)

> We did not have smart phones **then**.

Adverbs of place also usually come in end position:

> Is there a supermarket **nearby**?

> I will meet you this afternoon **at the gift shop**.

Adverbs of manner often take end position:

> You will make fewer mistakes if you work **carefully**.

Some adverbs of degree come in end position:

> I like impressionist paintings **very much**.

> We examined the situation **carefully.**

(The adverb can be placed before a long object: We examined **carefully** the situation involving dispute between the manager and his subordinates.)

10.8.2 Position of two commonly used focusing adverbs: *only* and *even*

Only, in front position, can refer to (focus on) the subject:

> **Only** my mother can make such a tasty banana cake.

> **Only** the ticking of the clock broke the silence.

Only can refer to other parts of a sentence. You put **only** in mid position before the main verb, or after an auxiliary or after **be** as a main verb. Sometimes, you can also put **only** immediately before the part it refers to.

> I **only** like swimming in the outdoor pool when the weather is warm.
> (Or: I like swimming in the outdoor pool **only** when the weather is warm.)

> They have **only** lived in Hong Kong for a few months.
> (Or: They have lived in Hong Kong **only** (for) a few months.)

> You can **only** borrow this reference book for two days.
> (Or: You can borrow this reference book, but **only** for two days.)

> She is **only** responsible for checking the accuracy of the data.

Be careful when your sentence containing **only** becomes ambiguous:

> We **only** go to dim-sum lunch on Sundays. (and do nothing else?)

If you mean that you would not have any other kind of lunch, you may say:

> We go to **only** dim-sum lunch on Sundays.

If you mean that this kind of lunch happens only on Sundays, you may say:

*We go to dim-sum lunch **only** on Sundays.*

Even, in front position, can refer to (focus on) the subject:

***Even** a six-year-old child can enjoy Mozart's music.*

***Even** boarding a bus can be difficult for an elderly person.*

Like **only**, **even** can refer to other parts of a sentence. You put **even** in mid position before the main verb, or after an auxiliary or after **be** as a main verb. For emphasis, you can also put **even** immediately before the part it refers to.

*She can **even** speak Korean.* (**Can** is a modal auxiliary.)
(Not: ~~She can speak even Korean.~~)

*He can't **even** remember his way home.* (**Can't** is a modal auxiliary.)
(Not: ~~He can't remember even his way home.~~)

*Most shops are **even** open on Sundays.*
(Or: *Most shops are open **even** on Sundays.*
But not: ~~Most shops are open on Sundays even.~~)

*He is **even** too tired to pick up the phone.* (**Is** is a main verb here.)
(Not: ~~He is too tired to pick up his phone even.~~)

*They love football so much that they would play it **even** in the rain.* (**Would** is a modal auxiliary.)
(Or: *They love football so much that they would **even** play it in the rain.*
But not: ~~They love football so much that they would play it in the rain even.~~)

10.9 Gradation (comparison) of adjectives

10.9.1 The idea of gradation

When you think of adjectives as qualities (of people, things, actions, events), you may also think about whether there is more or less of the quality you have in mind. This is what gradation means.

If an adjective is about a quality that can vary in degree (more or less), it is a graded (or gradable) adjective. Some examples are (you can think of more):

Graded adjectives:						
brave	cold	difficult	expensive	efficient	eloquent	exciting
familiar	happy	important	interesting	long	modern	new
patient	reliable	sentimental	strong	successful	tall	young

If an adjective refers to a quality that is either present or not present and no distinction of "more or less" is usually made, it is an ungraded (or non-gradable) adjective. The following are some examples:

Ungraded adjectives:

absolute	*alive*	*awful*	*complete*	*dead*	*deserted*	*empty*
excellent	*exhausted*	*ideal*	*immediate*	*impossible*	*permanent*	
perfect	*separate*	*spiritual*	*sufficient*	*traditional*	*unique*	

10.9.2 Basic comparative and superlative forms

There are various ways of saying how persons or things differ in certain qualities, as in the following sentences:

> *Chen is **not as tall as** Wang.*
>
> *Chen is **shorter than** Wang.*
>
> *Wang is **taller than** Chen.*
>
> *This coffee shop is **more popular** with white-collar workers.*
>
> *Have you tried the dim sum served at Hong Kong's **oldest** tea-house?*
>
> *It is difficult to tell which restaurant in this district offers the **most efficient** service.*

In the box above, the first three sentences say the same thing about Chen's and Wang's height. Their tallness is compared. In the last three sentences, comparison of an eatery in question and others not directly mentioned is implicit. In these sentences, **shorter**, **taller**, and **more popular** are called the "comparative form"; **oldest** and **most efficient** are called the "superlative form".

One way to see how the comparative form differs from the superlative form is by noting "short" versus "long" adjectives as a rough guideline:

	Comparative	**Superlative**

Short adjectives, such as:
  tall
  deep
  hot
	Pattern A
	  taller
	  deeper
	  hotter
		Pattern A
		  tallest
		  deepest
		  hottest

Long adjectives, such as:
  beautiful
  exciting
  impossible
	Pattern B
	  more beautiful
	  more exciting
	  more impossible
		Pattern B
		  most beautiful
		  most exciting
		  most impossible

10.9.3 One-syllable and two-syllable adjectives

Another rough guideline to help you remember comparative and superlative forms of adjectives is noting the number of syllables that the adjective has.

Many one-syllable and some two-syllable adjectives follow Pattern A (**-er** and **-est**):

One-syllable adjectives: (*bigger, biggest*)

   big   cold   deep   high   hot   large   long   nice   small   short

Two-syllable adjectives: (*easier, easiest*)

   crazy   easy   fancy   happy   heavy   lovely   noisy   pretty

However, some two-syllable adjectives can take either Pattern A (**-er** and **-est**) or Pattern B (**more** and **most**) when forming the comparative and superlative.

Some two-syllable adjectives that take either Pattern A or Pattern B:

   busy   clever   common   gentle   handsome   narrow

   pleasant   polite   quiet   remote   simple   stupid

Thus, for example, the comparative and superlative forms of **busy** are, respectively, **busier** and **busiest**, and also **more busy** and **most busy**. Both forms are possible, but in general Pattern A (**- er** and **-est**) is less formal. Thus, **Nathan Road is one of the busiest roads in Hong Kong** sounds less formal than **Nathan Road is one of the most busy roads in Hong Kong.**

At the same time, some of these adjectives more commonly take Pattern A while others take Pattern B. For example, with **simple, simpler** and **simplest** are usually used. With **pleasant**, however, **more pleasant** and **most pleasant** are more common. (**Taking a walk in the park is** *more pleasant* **in early morning when the air is** *fresher* **and the park is not crowded.**)

For adjectives ending in **-ed**, regardless of the number of syllables, only Pattern B (**more** and **most**) is used:

(*more amazed, most amazed*)

   amazed   delighted   disciplined   enlarged   excited

   favoured   honoured   impressed   isolated   motivated

   mystified   pleased   reserved   strengthened   surprised

Only Pattern B (**more** and **most**) also applies to some two-syllable adjectives:

(*more complex, most complex*)

   complex   correct   curious   current   eager   exact   famous

   foolish   honest   Ideal   likely   nervous   recent   rigid   usual

10.9.4 Multi-syllable adjectives

With adjectives of three or more syllables, Pattern B (**more** and **most**) is typically used. A partial list follows:

Adjectives ending in **-ful** and **-less** (**more beautiful, most beautiful**)
beautiful   careful   careless   colourful   effortless   fearful   fearless   graceful *grateful   powerful   resentful   respectful   senseless   tactful   thoughtful*

Adjectives ending in **-ing** (**more amazing, most amazing**)
amazing   appealing   boring   caring   confusing   embarrassing   encouraging *exciting   fascinating   frightening   insulting   interesting   promising   willing*

Adjectives ending in **-able** (**more acceptable, most acceptable**)
acceptable   adaptable   agreeable   believable   comfortable   comparable *inevitable   laughable   preferable   probable   reasonable   remarkable* *tolerable   vulnerable*

Other multi-syllable adjectives (**more appropriate, most appropriate**)
appropriate   characteristic   complicated   convenient   dangerous *different   difficult   feasible   fortunate   horrible   impressive* *isolated   marvellous   ordinary   practical   realistic   responsible* *significant   sufficient   tremendous   unusual*

10.9.5 *Less, least, much, a lot, far*

Since gradation can vary in decreasing as well as increasing degrees, the comparative and superlative degrees can be expressed by **less** and **least**, the opposites of **more** and **most**. The following are a few examples of using **less** and **least**:

*Sequels to an action story are often **less exciting than** the original.* *Taking a bus is always **less expensive than** taking a taxi.* *It is not easy to decide which of three outdoor activities—white-water rafting, hang-gliding, and rock climbing—is the **least** dangerous.* *Going to a fast-food restaurant is the **least expensive** way to eat out.*

Much, **a lot**, and **far** can be used with the comparative degree to add emphasis.

*The food at this small restaurant is **much better than** that at our usual place.* *The air in the southern parts of Hong Kong Island is **a lot cleaner than** in Central.* *Dogs are **far more intelligent than** you think.*

10.9.6 Other ways of making comparisons

as . . . as (both in positive and in negative statements)
*The club sandwich is **as expensive as** the jumbo hot dog.*
*His present project is just about **as costly as** his previous one.*
*Apartments in Canada are not **as small as** those in Hong Kong.*
so . . . as (only in negative statements)
*Apartments in Canada are **not so small as** those in Hong Kong.*
*Computers are **not nearly/quite so bulky as** they were twenty or thirty years ago.*
so . . . that
*She closed the door **so lightly that** I did not notice her coming in at all.*
*The morning air in the park is **so fresh that** it is really worth getting up early.*
as + many/much/little/few + noun + as
*Our church does not have **as many members as** theirs.*
*I have never seen this popular café having **as few customers as** it has now.*
as + adjective + a + noun + as
*The investment was not **as bad a performance as** we had earlier expected.*
*Or: The investment was not **such a bad performance as** we had earlier expected.*
the more/less . . . , the more/less . . .
***The more famous** the pianist (is), **the more** he or she is **in demand**.*
***The older** we get, **the weaker** our joints and muscles become.*
***The more complicated** the subject (is), **the less attentive** the audience becomes.*
too
*She is spending **too much time** on trivial matters.*
enough
*Your son is **old enough** to take care of himself.*

10.10   Comparing adverbs

10.10.1 Adverbs that are also adjectives

Adverbs that are also adjectives (see also 10.6.2) take **-er** and **-est** to form the comparative and superlative. Some examples are: **close, early, fast, hard, high, late, long.**

> *We live **closer** to our daughter than to our son.*
>
> *The repair work may take **longer** than we expected.*
>
> *We will rise **earlier** tomorrow because we have many places to visit.*
>
> *Hannah works the **hardest** in her class, as her grades clearly show.*
>
> *Emotions run **highest** in places **worst** hit by the earthquake.*

10.10.2 Adverbs ending in *-ly*

Adverbs ending in **-ly** take **more** and **most** to form the comparative and superlative.

> *We can solve this problem **more quickly** if we work together closely.*
>
> *The pastor gave his sermon **more convincingly** by citing some actual life episodes.*
>
> *He resigned from the committee **most unexpectedly** when his expertise was needed.*
>
> *This must be **the most historically accurate** documentary on Rome I have ever seen.*
>
> *With advancing age, we need to take our health **much more seriously**.*

10.10.3 Irregular adverbs

Adverb	Comparative	Superlative
well	*better*	*best*
badly	*worse*	*worst*
much	*more*	*most*
a lot	*more*	*most*
little	*less*	*least*

> *Her son did **well** in school last year; this year he may do even **better**.*
>
> *However, her daughter Amy did **less well.***
>
> *He was laid off last month and, **worst** of all, he was badly injured in an accident.*

10.10.4 Other ways of making comparisons (objects of comparison sometimes implied)

> ***as . . . as*** (both in positive and in negative statements)
>
> *Music has no boundaries: Asians love classical music **as enthusiastically as** Westerners.*
>
> *My French friend who lives in Beijing speaks Putonghua almost **as well as** the locals there.*
>
> *I did not enjoy the film **quite as much as** you did.*

> ***so . . . as*** (only in negative statements)
>
> *The chariot race scene in the new Ben Hur movie is **not nearly so thrillingly produced as** that in the older Ben Hur movie over 60 years ago.*

so . . . that
*She performed her gymnastics **so beautifully** that nearly all the judges gave her the highest score.*
too
*He seems to be playing his role in the movie **too seriously.***
enough
*If you do not work **hard enough**, you will not succeed.*

10.11 Using adverbs with graded and ungraded adjectives

Remember that adverbs can modify verbs, adjectives, and other adverbs. **More** and **most**, used to form the comparative and superlative of adjectives, are, in such a capacity, adverbs. Indeed, adverbs combined with adjectives may be used to describe feelings, actions, objects, places, and situations. To do this properly, it is important to note whether the adjective is graded or ungraded (see 10.9.1 for a quick review) because it is on this distinction that the pairing with a suitable adverb depends.

10.11.1 Grading adverbs used with graded adjectives

Grading adverbs	Graded adjectives
a bit, considerably, equally, extremely, fairly, highly, hugely, immensely, intensely, most, quite, rather, reasonably, relatively, slightly, somewhat, sufficiently, terribly, very	*busy, clever, cold/hot, difficult, efficient, exciting, expensive, famous, friendly, happy, important, intelligent, large, long, outstanding, rich, reliable, remarkable, serious, strong, successful, valuable, weak*

Not all combinations are possible or advisable. For example, we can say **extremely rich** and **immensely/very famous** but would not say **highly rich** and **slightly famous**. The following illustrate some possible combinations:

*Her new domestic helper is **highly efficient** with both household chores and childcare.*
*I need to attend a **most important** meeting today.*
*Hong Kong is a **rather successful** city.*
*He is **reasonably happy** despite the long hours of his work.*

10.11.2 Non-grading adverbs used with ungraded adjectives

Non-grading adverbs	Ungraded adjectives
absolutely, almost, completely, entirely, fully, just, largely, mainly, nearly, perfectly, purely, simply, thoroughly, totally, truly, utterly	*absurd, amazing, complete, correct, excellent, exhausted, free, full/empty, ideal, impossible, marvellous, modern, right, sentimental, strict, sufficient, superb, traditional, unique, unknown, wrong*

Again, not all combinations are possible or desirable. For example, we can say **absolutely ideal**, **simply marvellous**, or **totally unknown**, but would not say **fully ideal**, **almost marvellous**, or **extremely unknown**. Some possible combinations are illustrated as follows:

> *The show was **absolutely marvellous** .*
>
> *We were **completely exhausted** after hiking for five hours.*
>
> *This ten-year-old girl's skills in mental arithmetic are **simply excellent**.*
>
> *The design of the glass pyramid entrance to the Louvre Museum in Paris is **truly unique**.*

10.11.3 Some acceptable mixed patterns

Sometimes, adverbs such as **absolutely**, **completely**, **just,** and **totally**, all non-grading, are used to modify gradable adjectives. Then, grading adverbs such as **extremely**, **rather**, **quite,** and **very** are used to modify ungraded adjectives. This is acceptable for expressing *special emphasis*.

> Non-grading adverbs modifying graded adjectives
>
> > *It is **absolutely important** that you have backed up your mobile phone's data.*
> >
> > *Eating out is **simply expensive.***
> >
> > *That he can solve the puzzle so quickly is **just remarkable**.*
> >
> > *What we read in the news report may not be **totally reliable.***
>
> Grading adverbs modifying ungraded adjectives
>
> > *Disrespectful and disorderly behaviour of legislators is **extremely wrong**.*
> >
> > *The soprano's performance was **quite amazing**.*
> >
> > *He believes living so close to public transport is **rather ideal**.*
> >
> > *In Japan, we find the coexistence of the **very modern** along with the **very traditional**.*

10.11.4 Five commonly used grading adverbs: *fairly, pretty, quite, rather, really*

These five grading adverbs are commonly used before both graded and ungraded adjectives. They differ in strength, starting with **fairly** (= to some extent), which is about the same as **pretty** (more used in informal speech). Then, the strength increases roughly as follows:

fairly   <   **quite**   <   **rather**   <   **really**
(**pretty**)

Quite means to some degree, but stronger than **fairly**. Sometimes, it could mean "very" if spoken emphatically. **Rather** is stronger than **quite**, often implying "more than expected". **Really** is strongest, meaning "very" or even "extremely".

Used with graded adjectives	Used with ungraded adjectives
She bought a **fairly expensive** dress.	The music of this piece has some **fairly emotional** moments.
The exam was **pretty difficult**.	
	He joined a **pretty exclusive** club.
Government's economic statistics are **quite reliable**.	Her parents are **quite strict**.
This game's rules are **rather simple.**	
	The repairman did a **rather terrible** job.
Good language skills are **really essential** for this job.	
	What he did was **really wrong.**

10.11.5 Some adjectives have both graded and ungraded senses.

You will recall that a "graded" adjective refers to a quality that can vary in degree (greater or smaller; more or less) whereas an "ungraded" adjective refers to a quality that is either present or absent. Thus, for example, **expensive** is graded and **separate** is ungraded.

You must not, however, think that all adjectives are either graded or ungraded. Many adjectives are both graded and ungraded, depending on the meaning they are intended to express in the context of a given sentence. Take **emotional**, for example. If used to describe an approach that is the opposite of **rational**, **emotional** is ungraded. If **emotional** describes some music passage that, more than another, tends to stir feelings, then it can have a graded sense.

In the following box, you will see some adjectives that have both graded and ungraded senses. For each of six adjectives selected from this list, two example sentences are given. The first uses the adjective in an ungraded sense, the second in a graded sense. Please study them carefully.

Some adjectives with both graded and ungraded senses	comfortable common conservative contemporary creative different educational effective emotional fast formal fresh fundamental good grand ideal immediate impossible independent intelligent intellectual liberal long mobile musical necessary new nice old open original outstanding political popular positive practical professional proper quiet read safe serious simple short solid strict strong technical unknown wrong
comfortable	People usually chase after a **comfortable** life. The hotel we stayed at was **rather comfortable**.
educational	Universities are **educational** institutions. We believe that television documentaries can be **highly educational**.
emotional	Music often has an **emotional** content. He plays Chopin's music with a **very emotional** approach.
immediate	The government promised **immediate** action to clean up those areas where rats are rampant. They are trying to solve the **most immediate** problem of housing.

musical	In Hong Kong, three universities and an academy of performing arts offer **musical** education to those who intend to pursue a career in music.
	She is **very musical**: she loves singing and playing the piano.
positive	We are bound to have both **positive** and negative life experiences.
	Her parents have been a **very positive** influence.

10.12   Adverbs from adjectives

You have already met many adverbs and adjectives in this chapter. The following points are worth noting:

- Many adverbs are formed by adding **-ly** to the adjective:
  careful → carefully
  effective → effectively
  fair → fairly
  nice → nicely
  traditional → traditionally
  undoubted → undoubtedly

- If the adjective ends in **-le**, change **-le** to **-ly:**
  gentle → gently
  possible → possibly
  remarkable → remarkably
  sensible → sensibly
  simple → simply
  terrible → terribly

- If the adjective ends in **-y**, change **-y** to **-ily:**
  easy → easily
  heavy → heavily
  lazy → lazily
  noisy → noisily
  ready → readily
  steady → steadily

- If the adjective ends in **-ic**, add **-ally:**
  basic → basically
  drastic → drastically
  logic → logically
  music → musically
  specific → specifically
  tragic → tragically

10.13   Adverbs modifying adjectives in ways other than showing gradation

Earlier, you have seen how we can use grading adverbs (e.g., **fairly, highly, rather, very**) to modify graded adjectives and sometimes ungraded adjectives as well. There are times, however, when we are not so much concerned with gradation or strength of the presence of some quality as we are with the manner in which that quality exists. Take the adjective **surprised**, for example. If we are concerned with gradation, we could say that someone is **rather surprised** or **very surprised**. But if we consider the manner in which the quality of being surprised is expressed, we could say **happily surprised, pleasantly surprised, completely surprised**, or, in a different direction, **hardly surprised, not particularly surprised**, or **not at all surprised**.

In descriptive writing, we sometimes need to search for appropriate modifiers to present something (person, object, place, event, action, etc.) in a particular way. We usually first select the adjective serving to describe the key attribute or quality and then choose from a variety of adverbs the one that does the job suitably. The following are examples of some such phrases (adverb + adjective):

actively involved	*firmly committed*	*not at all interested*
painfully lengthy	*downright boring*	*totally shocked*
formally separate	*irreparably damaged*	*uncontrollably obsessed*
directly influenced	*forever grateful*	*unspeakably sad*
bitterly disappointing	*incredibly entertaining*	*wildly enthusiastic*

10.14   Summing up

Adjectives and adverbs are modifiers: adjectives modify nouns and pronouns; adverbs modify verbs, adjectives, other adverbs, and even whole sentences. Remember the following main points:

(1)   Adjectives may be used attributively before a noun or predicatively after a linking verb. Some adjectives may be used in only one of these two positions. Make sure you understand this. (Review 10.3)

(2)   It is important to use adverbs in appropriate positions in a sentence. They can be placed in front, mid, and end positions. The right sense is not properly conveyed if you use them not in the correct position. (Review 10.8, especially 10.8.2 concerning **only** and **even**.)

(3)   When you use adjectives and adverbs, it helps if you are familiar with their comparative and superlative forms, enabling you to make comparisons. For both adjectives and adverbs, the comparative form uses an **-er** ending or **more** before the word. The superlative either ends in **-est** or takes **most** before the word.

Some adjectives take both the (**-er** and **-est**) pattern and the (**more** and **most**) pattern while for most multiple-syllable adjectives only the (**more** and **most**) pattern applies. To learners of English, this could be troublesome. (Review 10.9.3 and 10.9.4)   But when you have pretty much mastered it, you will become more confident in choosing modifiers to grace your writing.

(4)   The comparative and superlative forms of adjectives and adverbs are used when you are comparing two or more entities (persons, objects, actions, etc.) or focusing on the current characteristic of someone or something with implied comparison (e.g., **The economy is growing stronger**; **Mt. Everest is the tallest mountain in the world**; **His business has been expanding most rapidly**).

(5)   Sometimes, the characteristic quality of someone or something is stated not by using the comparative or superlative forms of adjectives and adverbs. Instead, you can describe the extent to which or the manner in which the quality exists in the person or thing. You do this by placing a suitable adverb before the adjective that refers to the quality. This is an area that requires some careful study and practice. You need to develop a vocabulary of adjectives and adverbs, and learn, from reading, various combinations of adverbs and adjectives that are both logical and idiomatic. The material in 10.11 and 10.13 should be helpful.

(6)   When you use an adverb to modify an adjective (e.g., **extremely happy, simply impossible**), you need to distinguish between "grading adverbs" and "non-grading adverbs" on the one hand and, on the other, between "graded adjectives" and "ungraded adjectives". (10.11.1 to 10.11.4) There are both common patterns of combination and acceptable variations.

Throughout the presentation of these patterns in this chapter, the idea of gradation of adjectives should be well understood. Of course, this is complicated as many adjectives have both a graded and an ungraded sense, often with different meanings (10.11.5). This is something you must keep in mind.

Exercises　Chapter 10

Exercise 10.1

In the parentheses at the left, write T for "true" or F for "false".

假如陳述的內容正確，在左邊的括號裏寫 T，否則寫 F。

1. (　　　) All adverbs are formed by adding **-ly** to an adjective.

2. (　　　) These words are adverbs: *costly, friendly, timely, likely*.

3. (　　　) Some adjectives can only be used in the attributive position (before a noun).

4. (　　　) *Energetic* is used in the predicative position in this sentence: *Our discussion was energetic and useful.*

5. (　　　) Adjectives include present participles and past participles.

6. (　　　) **-ing** adjectives (such as *exciting*) are for describing how a person feels as a result of some activity that he or she has taken part in.

7. (　　　) Sometimes, the same word can be both adjective and adverb.

8. (　　　) *Hardly* means the same as *hard*.

9. (　　　) Connecting adverbs (such as *in addition*) show the logical relation to a previous sentence.

10. (　　　) Some adverbs can be used to modify a whole sentence.

Exercise 10.2

If the underlined word is an adjective, write ADJ in the space at the right. If it is an adverb, write ADV.

假如劃了底線的字是形容詞，在右方的空白處寫 ADJ。假如是副詞，寫 ADV。

1. These days the sun rises very early.　　　　　_____

2. Traffic in the fast lane can be hectic.　　　　　_____

3. Small businesses are being hit hard by the economic downturn.　　　　　_____

4. This recipe calls for finely chopped ginger mixed with minced pork.　　　　　_____

5. We are taking an early plane tomorrow morning.　　　　　_____

6. Don't stand too near the hot stove.　　　　　_____

7. Shenzhen is fast becoming a high tech centre of China.　　　　　_____

8. Notice the fine brushwork in this landscape painting.　　　　　_____

9.   They all think he is the <u>right</u> person for the job.   _____

10. She came to the meeting <u>right</u> on time.   _____

11. The problem is likely to be solved in the <u>near</u> future.   _____

12. Honest and reliable domestic helpers are <u>hard</u> to come by.   _____

Exercise 10.3

Fill in the blanks with appropriate adjectives in the list or adverbs based on them. Use the comparative or superlative form where necessary.

選擇合適的形容詞或由以下形容詞衍生的副詞填在空白處。需要時，選用比較級或最高級。

bad   careful   chilly   close   demanding   efficient   fast
frequent   good   hard   honest   interesting   pleasant   warm

1.   In winter, my cousin usually avoids Vancouver and comes to Hong Kong where it is _____.

2.   You must drive _____ than your brother, who is, _____ speaking, not a safe driver.

3.   The exercise routine you recommended is not nearly as _____ as I thought it would be.

4.   The _____ she got to getting admitted to university was being interviewed.

5.   Costs are running high and much time is wasted—the company must try to operate _____.

6.   This is the _____ wet market in the city; I will not buy from it again.

7.   You must practise _____ than before if you really want to win.

8.   If you don't hit _____, the nut will not crack.

9.   After entering the highway the car started to go _____ and _____.

10. The movie starts with a thrilling action sequence, but soon gets _____.

11. The stroll near the beach was quite relaxing but would have been _____ if it had been _____.

12. She didn't play her instrument sufficiently _____ in the audition to qualify.

Exercise 10.4

Normally, grading adverbs may modify graded adjectives while non-grading adverbs may modify ungraded adjectives. Following this guideline, which of the following statements are problematic? Write OK in the space at the right if the statement follows the guideline; write P if the statement is problematic.

表分級的副詞 (grading adverbs) 通常可修飾有分級性的形容詞 (graded adjectives)，而不能表分級的

的副詞 (non-grading adverbs) 則可修飾無分級性的形容詞 (ungraded adjectives)。依此準則,下面哪些陳述會有問題? 假如是符合該準則的,在右方的空白處寫 OK,否則寫 P。

1. Tax evasion is a considerably serious offence. _____

2. Many collectors consider this antique violin extremely valuable. _____

3. He is reasonably happy despite his meagre income. _____

4. She bought a completely expensive bag simply because she liked its design. _____

5. We were totally exhausted after walking the whole day. _____

6. Her authentic acting in the film is simply excellent. _____

7. This part of the history of Hong Kong about 150 years ago is rather unknown. _____

8. His truly unique carving of pictures on leaves has to be seen to believe. _____

9. Their huge project is now somewhat complete. _____

10. We are keeping all these old pictures for largely sentimental reasons. _____

11. She has difficulty complying with all the requirements of her very strict violin teacher. _____

12. The magic show we saw was mainly outstanding. _____

Chapter 11　Use Prepositions to Say Many Different Things

What you will learn in this chapter

Prepositions (words like **in, on, to** and phrases like **because of, together with, in front of**) are used to show how two parts of a sentence are related in time, space, cause and effect, or some other way. Different prepositions may serve a similar purpose, and a given preposition can have many uses. You will learn a variety of structures involving prepositions, including common prepositional phrases, **to** followed by **-ing** forms, prepositions at the end of sentences, prepositions in relative clauses, and prepositions that commonly follow nouns, adjectives, and verbs to express many different ideas.

介詞（單詞如 in, on, to 及短語如 because of, together with, in front of）可用以表示一個句子裏一部分與另一部分在時間、空間、因果或其他方面的關係。不同的介詞可用以表達大致相同的意義，而一個特定的介詞又可用以表達一些很不同的意義。在這章裏，你會學到很多含有介詞的結構，包括：常用的介詞短語、to 之後跟 -ing 形式、放在句末的介詞、在關係從句裏的介詞。你也會認識到很多常跟在名詞、形容詞和動詞後面的介詞，可以表達許多不同的意思。

11.1 Basics about prepositions

11.1.1 Prepositions give life to what you say.

Even when you have understood the use of verbs, nouns, pronouns, and articles (and other determiners), you cannot do much without a good knowledge of prepositions. In a practical sense, prepositions give life to what you want to say.

A preposition is a word or phrase that links two parts of a sentence to show how they are related in space, time, or some other manner. Examine the following two sentences:

> (1) *Some thieves climbed **over** the fence.*
>
> (2) *She continued to try again **in spite of** another failure.*

In both sentences, you can see how the preposition (in boldface) links the two parts. In sentence (1), **over** links the thieves' climbing and the fence to show a relationship in space. In sentence (2), **in spite of** links the subject's continued trying and her failure, showing a relationship of concession (= allowance).

11.1.2 Before a noun or noun phrase

A preposition is usually placed before a noun or noun phrase (e.g., **on the table**, **over the fence**). It may also come before some clause (usually one beginning with a **wh**-word or **how)**. In the following two sentences, the preposition is followed by a noun clause, one beginning with **what** and another with **how**:

> *Are you listening **to what the pastor is saying***?
>
> *This is an article **about how leisure relates to social life.***

The noun phrase or noun clause that follows the preposition is called a "prepositional complement". The preposition and its complement together make up a "prepositional phrase". Thus, in the above two sentences, **to what the pastor is saying** and **about how leisure relates to social life** are prepositional phrases. So are **over the fence** and **in spite of another failure** in the two sentences in 11.1.1.

11.1.3 The prepositional complement may be another prepositional phrase.

> *The dog appeared **from across the road***.
>
> *We did not meet the artist **until after the concert.***

11.1.4 Many prepositions are simple one-word prepositions.

above	about	after	at	before	between	beside	by
concerning	despite	down	during	for	from	in	into
like	of	on	over	past	since	through	to
towards	under	until	up	with	within	without	

11.1.5 Some two-word prepositions:

according to	along with	apart from	away from	because of
contrary to	due to	except for	out of	prior to	together with

11.1.6 Some three-word and four-word prepositions:

as well as	as a result of	at the risk of	by means of	in addition to
in accordance with	in comparison with	in contrast to	in front of	
in relation to	in spite of	on account of	on top of	with reference to

11.2   Prepositions of time and place

Many commonly used prepositions refer to time and place. The use includes literal (e.g., a time point) and customary (e.g., using **in** for time periods but **on** for named days) elements. The choice of one or another preposition in referring to a time or place can have different meanings (e.g., **in** a place vs. **at** a place). Let us see some common examples.

11.2.1 Time

Some common prepositional phrases of time using **in**, **on**, and **at**:

in
in 2019   in June   in summer   in the third quarter   in the 19th century in the morning   in the afternoon   in the evening
on
on Friday   on 10 September   on that day   on Christmas Day on her birthday   on Monday morning   on Friday evening   on Sunday night
at
at nine o'clock   at lunchtime   at Christmas (= a few days around Christmas) at the weekend   at breakfast   at noon   at midnight   at bedtime

Time prepositions in sentences:

at, *from*, *on*
Classes start *at* 8:30 a.m.
Afternoon tea is available *from* 2 p.m. *to* 4 p.m.
We plan to visit the science museum *on* Thursday, the 21st of February.
However, if which Thursday (or any day of the week) is specified by words such as **this** or **next**, the preposition is not used:
We plan to visit the science museum *this* Thursday.

over*, *during*, *throughout*, *within (You can use **over** or **during** to refer to something that occurs within a certain time period, either for part of that period or for all of it.)

> **Over** the weekend, we had a dinner gathering with our children and grandchildren.

> The weather will be colder **during** (or **over**) the next few days.

> It rained **throughout** last week.

> We have to leave **within** the next half-hour, otherwise we will be late.

on time*, *in time

> I need to be at the reception **on** time. (=I must not be late for the reception.)

> We will be **in** time for the concert. (=We will arrive before the start of the concert.)

for some time*, *over time*, *in some time

> They are going to take a short trip **for** just a day or two.

> I haven't seen you **for** a long time.

> Social values change **over** time. (=Social values change as time passes.)

> She completed the questionnaire **in** only ten minutes.

> The photos will be ready **in** an hour. (=an hour from now)

since*, *for*, *until

> They have been living in Hong Kong **since** 2009.

> They have been living here **for** ten years now.

> You can keep this book **until** next Monday.

> The escalators will be under repair **up to** (or **until**) the end of February.

> Few people have known about this small restaurant **until** now.

> **Until** 2015 they had always been living in Shanghai. (They left Shanghai in 2015.)

NOTE:

- **Since** and **for** are used with the present perfect progressive tense to refer to something continuing up to now.

- **Until** means up to a specified time point, which determines the tense of the verb of the action.

- Do not use **in**, **on** or **at** before these words: **this**, **next**, **last**, and **every**:

> The new show starts **this** Thursday.
> (Not: ~~The new show starts on **this** Thursday.~~)

> Rev. Chan will be the speaker **next** Sunday.
> (Not: ~~Rev. Chan will be the speaker on **next** Sunday.~~)

> I had a big reunion with my former classmates **last** Christmas.
> (Not: ~~I had a big reunion with my former classmates at **last** Christmas.~~)

> Back then, we visited our children in Canada **every** summer.
> (Not: ~~Back then, we visited our children in Canada in **every** summer.~~)

11.2.2 Place

Some common prepositional phrases of place using **in**, **on**, and **at**:

in			
in the living room	in/inside the hotel lobby	in/inside the park	in the market
in the pool	in the airport	in the New Territories	in the city in China
on			
on the floor	on the ground	on the door	on the second floor
on the beach	on the grass	on Nathan Road	on the computer screen
at			
at the school	at the bus stop	at the next traffic lights	at the taxi stand
at Ocean Park station	at the clubhouse	at 97 Caine Road	at the party

11.2.3 Position and movement

Included in the general idea of place is the notion of position and movement. Position can be thought of as a specific location and movement is going from one location to another. Thus, when we say that **The alarm clock is *on* a table *beside* the bed**, we are stating the exact place or position of the alarm clock. Similarly, we point to specifically where the post office is in a sentence such as **The post office is *across* the street from the fruit store**. Then, there are times when we describe movement, such as when we say that **Many cars are going *through* the new tunnel** or that **We can hear an aeroplane flying high *above* the clouds**.

The following are some examples of sentences using various prepositions of place, including those referring to position and movement:

in*, *on*, *at
Many new towns have been established **in** the New Territories during the last four or five decades.
Traffic **on** Queen's Road Central is unbearably crowded most of the day.
Our flight is scheduled to arrive **at** Haneda Airport, Tokyo on time.
across, over
I saw my friend **across** the auditorium at the concert last evening.
The use of smart phones has spread all **over** the world.
along, through
We walked **along** the aisle until we came to some vacant seats in front.
Our taxi inched along **through** heavy traffic late afternoon yesterday.

above*, *over (***above*** is not directly over; ***over*** is suggesting closeness)
*They live in a spacious house in the hills **above** the sea.*
*There are several footbridges **over** the busy road.*
below*, *under (***below*** is not directly under)
*Many places in the Netherlands are **below** sea level.*
*Owing to lack of space, they put some of their clothes in boxes **under** their bed.*
onto*, *into*, *out of
*Take care as you step **out of** the train **onto** the platform.*
*The truck crashed **into** a parked taxi.*
*He was so tired that he took a long while to get **out of** bed.*
between*, *among
*Shanghai is **between** Hong Kong and Beijing.*
*Support for the rule of law is common **among** the people of Hong Kong.*
along*, *around*, *past
*We like to take a stroll after dinner **along** the waterfront road.*
*Some twenty runners are training **around** the track.*
*My friend lives in the apartment block just **past** the hotel.*
from*, *away from
*Tokyo is about four hours by air **from** Hong Kong.*
***From my home**, I can see the Botanical and Zoological Gardens.*
*People ran **away from** the beach when they saw a big tidal wave coming.*
next to*, *in front of*, *behind
*Who is sitting **next to** the host at the head table?*
*The tall man sitting **in front of** me blocks my view of the stage.*
*Someone **behind** me is doing something with his mobile phone.*
inside*, *outside*, *opposite
*The audience **inside** the hall is waiting anxiously for the concert to begin.*
*Latecomers must wait **outside** the hall until a suitable break.*
*The concertmaster (principal violinist) sits almost directly **opposite** the principal cellist.*

NOTE:

- What is the difference between **in** a place and **at** a place? You use **at** to emphasize the place as a location, like an address; you use **in** to emphasize the space of the place, like the space within the boundaries of a school or all the public space within a city. Thus, you say **I expect to arrive at Chek Lap Kok Airport about noon**, but you say **I expect to arrive in Hong Kong about noon**.

- When you use **home** in a sentence like **I will go home soon**, **home** is an adverb and you cannot use any preposition, such as **at** or **to**, before **home.**

11.3   Prepositions with meanings other than place and time

Accompaniment	
with	*We are having dinner **with** some friends.*
along with	*The children went **along with** their teacher.*

Belonging to/part of	
of	*He is the most experienced member **of** the team.*
in	*We enjoyed being **in** the party last night.*

Possession/carrying/involvement	
with (possession)	*Angela is resting at home **with** a bad cold.*
with (carrying)	*Jerry is at the bus stop **with** a cup of coffee.*
with (involvement)	*You have been **with** the company for years.*

Cause	
because of	***Because of** heavy rain, the meeting has been cancelled.*
on account of	*She obtained poor results **on account of** insufficient preparation.*
owing to	***Owing to** lack of relevant experience, he was not accepted for the position.*
for	*He was fined **for** illegal parking.*
from	*Illness may result **from** drinking unclean water.*

Concerning	
of	*This is the story **of** his success from rags to riches.*
	*Here is an updated map **of** the entire territory of Hong Kong.*
about	*This book is **about** English grammar and usage.*
	*It is not healthy to worry **about** many things all the time.*

Concession (admission that something is true)	
despite	***Despite** trying hard to control himself, he was shaking once on stage.*
in spite of (= despite)	*She continued trying **in spite of** her previous failures.*
for all (= in spite of)	***For all** his shortcomings, he is still a likeable person.*
	For all can also mean considering how much or little something is. For example, the phrase **for all I know** means what I know is really not much:
	***For all** I know, he may not be working at all.*

Exception and addition	
except	She knew the answer to all the questions **except** the last one.
besides	They have a lot in common **besides** popular music.
	Besides working as an architect, he also travels to take pictures of old cathedrals in Europe. (Note the use of an -**ing** form here, a gerund, as part of a noun phrase, **working as an architect**, as the object of **besides**.)
as well as	German is spoken in Austria **as well as** Germany.
together with	My friend, **together with** his family, is visiting Japan soon. (Note that the verb **is** agrees with the singular subject **friend**.)
	apart from (or **aside from**) **Apart from** fatigue, jet lags tend to confuse your sense of time.

Manner and means	
like	The flu epidemic spread **like** wildfire.
as	You can use lemon juice **as** a cleaning agent.
with	**With** the help of some friends, she started running a small gift shop.
without	After his eye operation, he can now see **without** glasses.
by	They went to Ocean Park **by** the mass transit railway.

Support/cooperation and opposition	
for	Most citizens are **for** protecting the environment.
with	We have to comply **with** the rules.
	As roommates, they get along **with** each other well.
against	Some people are **against** the idea of constructing artificial islands to increase land supply for housing.

11.4   Many uses of prepositions

In learning to use prepositions correctly, you need to realize that any one preposition can be used in different senses. Thus, for example, you have seen in the preceding section that **of** can refer to membership or "concerning". You have also seen that **with** has a wide range of uses.

Indeed, **with** is so versatile that it is worth our while to examine further its uses in sentences. After that, we will also examine **over**, another multi-functional preposition.

11.4.1 *With*

Meaning of *with*	Example sentence
• Accompaniment	*He went out **with** his dog.*
• Manner or behaviour	*She responded **with** a smile.*
	*We usually sleep **with** all windows open.*
• Condition	***With** or without your help, he will proceed as planned.*
• Using something	*We can now prepare many dishes **with** a food processor.*
• Together with	*I will have my coffee **with** cream and sugar.*
• Having	*This is a fine piano **with** exquisite sound.*
• What an action is related to	*After all the preparation, he is ready to go ahead **with** his project.*
• Result	*She felt sorry **with** embarrassment.*
• Situation	*We must speed up our work, **with** the deadline so near.*
• Against	*He had an argument **with** his assistant.*
• Supported by	*The opera is sung in Italian, **with** English and Chinese surtitles.*
• Including	*The meal **with** dessert and coffee is reasonably priced.*

11.4.2 *Over*

Meaning of *over*	Example sentence
• Above	*We can reach the library by a footbridge **over** the road.*
• Across	*From the observation deck on the 100th floor, you have a magnificent view **over** the harbour.*
• On the opposite side	*There is a pharmacy just **over** the street.*
• Covering	*Walking by a dusty area, he put his hand **over** his nose and mouth.*
• Concerning	*They rejoiced **over** their daughter's recovery after a long illness.*
• Better than	*WhatsApp has many advantages **over** email.*
• During	*We plan to visit friends in Canada **over** the New Year holiday.*
• Control/authority	*A good leader has influence **over** his or her followers.*
• More than	*Drivers who go **over** the road's speed limit are simply risking their lives.*
• In many parts of	*Irresponsible users of the public barbecue pitches have left rubbish all **over** the place.*
• Past a difficult time	*It took him several weeks to get **over** his infection.*
• Falling from a place	*It is quite awesome to see the edge of the mighty glacier toppling **over** into the sea.*

11.5   Some common prepositional phrases

The following are some common phrases starting with a preposition (preposition + noun). They should be an important part of your vocabulary. Make sure you know how to use them correctly in your writing (and your speaking).

at	*in*	*on*
at all times	in advance	on average
at the moment	in brief	on balance
at the beginning	in control	on behalf of
at lunch	in due course	on condition that
at the bus stop	in danger	on second thought
at the MTR exit	in general	on the whole
at first	in other words	on purpose
at last	in cash	on the other hand
at the end	in future	on arrival
at home	in time	on duty
at once	in haste	on the face of it
at least	in addition	on the left/right
at the same time	in addition to	on the ground
at the centre	in deep water (= in trouble)	on the phone
at school	in my opinion	on television
at work	in writing	on holiday/vacation

by	*for*	*out of*	*from*
by accident	for a change	out of breath	from day to day
by all means	for ages	out of control	from place to place
by chance	for lunch	out of danger	from my point of view
by cheque/credit card	for fear of	out of date	from bad to worse
by heart	for fun/pleasure	out of fashion	from beginning to end
by means of	for good	out of luck	from cover to cover
by mistake	for ever	out of money	from start to finish
by no means	for life	out of order	from strength to strength
by air/land/sea	for free	out of practice	from top to bottom
by email/fax/phone	for nothing	out of print	from morning till night
by far	for sale	out of reach	from time to time
by hand	for short	out of sight	from what I know
by hook or by crook (= by	for a walk	out of stock	from now on
any method)	for a while	out of sympathy	from rags to riches
by the rules	for now	out of time	from A to Z
by the way	for better or (for) worse	out of touch	from one to another
by any standard	for whatever it is worth	out of tune	

11.6   Prepositions followed by *-ing* forms

The **-ing** form of a verb (e.g., **reading**, **walking**) can be used like a noun (e.g., **reading is good for you**, **too much walking can hurt**). A phrase containing an **-ing** form can then function as a noun phrase (sometimes called a "gerund phrase"), which may follow a preposition, as in this sentence: **I was thinking *about finding* a place to eat**. (**finding a place to eat** is a gerund phrase)

The following are more examples:

*You can learn to play a music instrument well **by practising** often.*

*She just bought a gadget **for crushing** garlic.*

*Passenger aeroplanes can now fly for fifteen hours or more **without stopping**.*

*Remember to close all windows **before leaving** home.*

*He has become a happier person **since taking up** his new job.*

11.6.1 Using the *-ing* form after the preposition *to*

When you use **look forward to**, be careful about what you say after that. Remember that **to** here is a preposition. You can say, for instance, **I look forward *to seeing* you again soon**, but not ~~I look forward to see you again soon~~.

Similarly, **to** is a preposition in the constructions **be used to** and **get used to**. Thus, you can say **I am used *to* drinking my coffee black** (meaning this has been my habit) or **I can get used to drinking my coffee black** (meaning although not my habit, it can be fine with me).

Here are a few more examples showing the use of the **-ing** form of a verb after the preposition **to:**

*We are looking forward **to visiting** our friends in Sydney.*

*She looks forward **to regaining** her health after a long rest.*

*People in Hong Kong are used **to living** in small flats.*

*He is trying to get used **to washing** the dishes every day.*

11.6.2 Modal auxiliary *used to*

Note that if you say **I used to**, you must continue with a base verb form. Accordingly, you can say **I used to drink my coffee black** (meaning this habit no longer exists). In this construction, **used to** is a modal auxiliary verb that exists only in the simple past tense.

11.7   Prepositions at the end of a sentence

Normally, as pointed out at the beginning of this chapter, a preposition is followed by a complement, as in **I am thinking *about* going to the library**. Note that the preposition can come at the end of the sentence in the following constructions (especially in questions):

*There is something (that) I am thinking **about**.*

*What am I thinking **about**?*

*What are you looking **at**?*

*Who did she talk **to**?*

In formal style, the questions are written as:

About what am I thinking?

At what are you looking?

To whom did she talk?

However, the informal style, with the preposition at the end, is more common.

11.8   Placing a preposition before *which*

We are familiar with this article may be rewritten as **This is the article *with which* we are familiar** to emphasize this particular article. Placing the preposition before **which** like this is more formal. Alternatively, **This is the article we are familiar *with***, placing the preposition at the end of the sentence, is acceptable in informal style. Study the following similar constructions:

*This is a question **to which** we do not have an easy answer.*

*It is an issue **about which** we are all concerned.*

*We have a situation **in which** all parties have something to gain.*

*This is a task **on which** they have spent much time.*

*They are merely repeating an idea **of which** most citizens have heard.*

*Have we considered the resources **with which** we carry out our plan?*

11.9   Prepositions following nouns, adjectives, and verbs

By now, you probably have the impression that prepositions are indeed versatile (=having many different uses) words that show the relationship between two parts of a sentence. You should note that prepositions often come after three commonly used word classes: nouns, adjectives, and verbs. There are numerous phrases that show such connections. Often, there can be more than one choice of preposition depending on the meaning intended. The connection is largely a matter of custom.

Let us now examine some selected phrases that include an object of the preposition for your reference. See if you can supply your own object of the preposition so that you may remember better the noun/ adjective/verb + preposition structure.

11.9.1 Noun + preposition

students' **access to** the library's books	some **knowledge of** music
doctors' **association with** other doctors	a **lack of** support
her **attitude to/towards** her new friends	a new **method of** editing photographs
the **cause of** the failure	an urgent **need for** more housing
his **concern for** the disadvantaged	my **opinion of** the new play
their **concern with** social justice	their frequent **participation in** church
my **difficulty with** French	a habitual **preference for** coffee
his **difficulty in** finding a good job	the **reason for** (not of) the delay
an **emphasis on** quality	a detailed **report on/about** this problem
some **familiarity with** Japanese	an unconfirmed **report of** a missing girl
little **hope of** winning	great **respect for** the environment
the **implication of** the new policy **for** our daily life	a gradual **rise in** the price
the **importance of** being honest	a new **rise of** ten dollars in the toll
a strong **interest in** sports	your **view about/on** the price increase
your **introduction to** investment	his optimistic **view of** (not towards) life

11.9.2 Adjective + preposition

Note that some adjectives may be followed by one of several prepositions. If there is no difference in meaning using one or another preposition, it is listed as one entry (e.g., **angry at/about**). If there is difference, separate entries are given (e.g., **anxious about**, **anxious for**). To practise the use of the adjective + preposition structure, try replacing the prepositional objects with your own.

accustomed to the noise	*familiar to* us
anxious about (=worried) *the interview*	*familiar with* a new environment
anxious for (=wanting) *work*	*famous for* his interpretation of Chopin
afraid of heights	*free from* all previous restrictions
amazed at/by his impressive results	*full of* old and useless things
angry at/about something	*full of* challenge
angry at/with someone	*grateful to* someone for something
aware of the news	*happy about/with* the improvement
based on the facts	*important to* her for sentimental reasons
capable of looking after herself	*important for* someone to do something
comparable to (=similar) *someone/something*	*interested in* hiking
compatible with existing system	*involved in* many cultural activities
composed of several parts	*necessary for* maintaining health
concerned about (=worried about)	*nervous of* (=frightened of) *darkness*
concerned for (=worried about someone's welfare or safety)	*nervous about* (=anxious about) *exams*
	proud of his achievement
concerned with (=is about, involved with, interested in)	all is *ready for* display
confident about/of something	ideas *relevant to* this study
confident in/of your ability	*responsible for* law and order
consistent with the general practice	*safe from* intruders
contrary to what he expected	the *same as* last year
different from the old method	*satisfied with* the gains
eager for her parents' approval	*similar to* his original design
excited about the trip	*surprised at/by* the child's learning progress
excited at/by the prospect of promotion	*tired of* so much repetitive work
	worried about passengers' safety

11.9.3 Verb + preposition

Many verbs are used with a preposition to determine the intended meaning (e.g., When you **argue for** something, you support it; When you **argue against** it, you oppose it). Sometimes, the same verb may take either one of two different prepositions without change in meaning (e.g., **concern yourself about/ with something**). The following is a select list of commonly used verbs and the prepositions they are usually associated with. (Note the last two words in this sentence, showing the verb **associate + with**.)

To strengthen your familiarity with the verb + preposition structure, you can supply your own prepositional object and an object of the verb, where suitable, after reading through each of the following entries.

agree with *someone on/about something*	***listen to*** *music*
associate with *a group or event*	***look at*** *the stars*
argue about *something with someone*	***look for*** (=search for; expect) *a place to eat*
argue for/against *an action*	***look into*** *something* (=consider something carefully)
ask *someone* ***for*** *an explanation*	***look up*** (=search for information about) *a word*
believe in *keeping promises*	***provide*** *someone* ***with*** *something*
care about/for *the elderly*	***provide*** *something* ***for*** *someone*
compare *A* ***with*** *B* (=identify their similarities and differences)	***remind*** *someone* ***of*** *something*
	replace *A* ***with*** *B* (Passive: *A is* ***replaced by*** *B.*)
compare *A* ***to*** *B* (=A is like B)	***reply to*** *a request*
complain *to someone* ***about/of*** *something*	***result from*** *a cause*
concentrate on *your homework*	***result in*** *a consequence*
contribute *his time* ***to*** *the project*	***search for*** *job opportunities*
concern *yourself* ***with/about*** *something*	***strive for*** *perfection*
consist of *many parts*	***substitute*** *B* ***for*** *A* (=replace A with B)
happiness ***consists in*** (=is based on) *doing your best*	***succeed in*** *becoming a leader*
cope with *a difficult situation*	***succeed as*** *a film director*
deal with *this problem*	***suffer from*** *pain*
decide on *a date for the meeting*	***think of*** *someone/something* ***as . . .***
depend on *good tactics for success*	***transform into*** *a different person*
deprive *someone* ***of*** *something*	***withdraw from*** *reality*

11.9.4 Phrasal verbs

Some of the items in 11.9.3 also belong to a rather large class of verb + preposition and verb + adverb constructions known as "phrasal verbs". (The preposition and adverb in these constructions are called "particles".) Sometimes, the meaning of a phrasal verb may not be directly evident from the words themselves, because the combination may have one or more idiomatic meanings.

Thus, **look for**, **look into**, and **look up** are among the most common phrasal verbs. Their meaning is not immediately obvious from the literal meaning of **look**. Even the expression **agree with**, legitimately a prepositional verb like so many listed in 11.9.3, can mean making you feel good or healthy when you say **Spicy foods don't agree with me** (=they make you feel sick). Used this way, **agree with** does not carry the literal meaning of approving of something. So, **agree with** is also a phrasal verb.

In the table below, I have selected two dozen phrasal verbs formed from four simple and commonly used verbs: **come**, **get**, **put**, **take**. One meaning for each is shown, although there are often more meanings. To help you use such phrasal verbs correctly, the grammar pattern of each one is given, using these symbols: v = verb, adv = adverb, prep = preposition, n = noun, pron = pronoun, sth = something. Of course, it is only a very brief overview here; you can find out more about phrasal verbs if you use a good general dictionary or consult a dictionary of phrasal verbs.

Phrasal verb	Meaning	Grammatical pattern
Come		
come about	to happen	v + adv
come by	to visit briefly and casually	v + adv
come up	to happen unexpectedly	v + adv
come up with something*##	to have an idea	v + adv + prep + n
come round	to happen at the usual time	v + adv
come through	to recover from a serious illness	v + adv
Get		
get at sth*	to find out sth	v + prep + n
get sth across*##	to make some idea clear to someone	v + n + adv
get away with sth*##	to do sth wrong without getting punished	v + adv + prep + n
get back to someone*##	to contact or reply to someone	v + adv + prep +pron
get by	to manage to live with limited resources	v + adv
get down to sth*##	to begin to do sth seriously	v + adv + prep + n
Put		
put sth across*#	to explain your ideas to someone successfully	v + n + adv
put sth behind you*##	to forget sth unpleasant and not let it affect your future	v + n + prep + pron
put someone off*##	to make someone lose interest in sth	v + pron + adv
put sth forward*#	to suggest an idea for dicussion	v + n + adv
put sth together*#	to produce sth by collecting ideas	v + n + adv
put someone up*##	to have someone stay at your home	v + pron + adv
put up with someone/sth*##	to accept an unpleasant person or situation without complaining	v + adv + prep + n/pron
Take		
take after someone*##	to look like or behave like someone older in your family	v + prep + n
take sth in*#	to notice or undertand sth you hear or read	v + n + adv
take on sth*##	to have a particular quality	v + adv + n
take over	to take responsibility for sth after someone else has done it	v + adv
take up sth*##	to begin doing sth new for pleasure	v + adv + n
take someone through sth*##	to explain sth to someone as to how to do it	v + pron + prep + n

* These phrasal verbs have objects.

With these phrasal verbs, for the specified meaning, the object can come either between the verb and the adverb/preposition particle or after the particle.

For the specified meaning, the object comes in the position as indicated.

11.10   Prepositional phrases and sentence objects

Two general situations require special attention when using prepositions. First, you may be writing a sentence in which more than one noun, adjective, or verb may refer to the same object that forms part of the prepositional phrase. Second, your sentence may contain a direct object and an indirect object that is contained in a prepositional phrase.

11.10.1   More than one noun or adjective or verb referring to the same object

When you have more than one noun or verb or adjective referring to something, these words may be associated with different prepositions, in which case you will need to use the appropriate preposition for each noun or verb or adjective. In each of the following sentences, the same object word is part of two prepositional phrases.

Nouns

*The social environment we live in profoundly influences our **feelings about** and **perceptions of** the world. (=The social environment we live in profoundly influences our **feelings about** the world and our **perceptions of** it.)*

Verbs

*Given a rich variety of leisure facilities and services, we can **look for** and **participate in** those activities that suit our interest. (= Given a rich variety of leisure facilities and services, we can **look for** those activities that suit our interest and **participate in** them.)*

Adjectives

*Japanese culture is both **similar to** and **different from** Chinese culture. (= Japanese culture is both **similar to** Chinese culture and **different from** it.)*

11.10.2   The preposition in relation to object(s) in a sentence

Objects usually follow the subject and verb in a sentence:

I gave *him* a present. (him is "indirect object"; **a present** is "direct object".)

This sentence can be rewritten as:

I gave a present *to him.* (The indirect object is changed into a prepositional phrase **to him** and is placed after the direct object **a present**.)

Examine the following sentences that illustrate the same kind of dual arrangement:

---

*We can easily send **our friends** pictures any time.*

*We can easily send pictures **to our friends** any time.*

*Cruise companies offer **holiday makers** numerous itineraries.*

*Cruise companies offer numerous itineraries **to holiday makers**.*

*The violinist played **for the audience** a beautiful encore.*

*The violinist played a beautiful encore **for the audience**.*

You can keep a long indirect object as a prepositional phrase placed after the direct object:

> *The teacher gave a detailed explanation* **to students who have just joined the class.**
>   (direct object)   (indirect object)

But if you have a long direct object, you should put it after a **to** (or sometimes **for**) phrase containing the indirect object:

> *Newton gave* **to the world** *an understanding of mechanical forces.*
>   (indirect object)   (direct object)
>
> *The violinist played* **for the audience** *an exciting and technically brilliant encore.*
>   (indirect object)   (direct object)

The **to** phrase must come first if the direct object is a **that** noun clause after such verbs as **explain, propose, demonstrate, recommend,** and **suggest**:

> *Scholars explain* **to** *general readers* **that organizations operate like a system.**
>   (indirect object)   (direct object: noun clause)
>
> *Doctors suggest* **to** *their patients* **that eating egg yolk is not really harmful.**
>   (indirect object)   (direct object: noun clause)

11.10.3 Sentences in which there is no distinction between direct and indirect objects

In such sentences, the main verb is usually followed by its object, and a prepositional phrase comes in to say something that has to do with this object. The pattern, verb + object + prepositional phrase, is rather often used. Study the following examples:

> *Angry passengers blamed the airline* **for the delay of their flight.**
>
> *In the crowded restaurant, we had to share a table* **with another couple.**
>
> *A sign warned drivers* **about strong wind on the bridge.**
>
> *The waitress cut the birthday cake* **into eight portions.**
>
> *He concerns himself primarily* **with earning enough money to support his family.**
>
> *We congratulated Siu Fong* **on her outstanding performance.**

11.11   Some confusable prepositions

As you have seen earlier in this chapter, a given preposition can have many possible uses while some different prepositions may have similar uses. Here, let us examine a few prepositions and compare some of their similar uses. If you are not careful, you may be confused and end up choosing the wrong preposition for your purpose. With care, you can learn to use these prepositions correctly to reflect the specific use you have in mind. We shall review the following pairs:

- **in** and **at**

- **by** and **until**

- **during** and **for**

- **for** and **since**

- **to** and **for**

- **between** and **among**

11.11.1 *In* and *at*

In is more definite about being within some space; **at** is more commonly used to refer to a location generally. Sometimes, the space or location may be more that of time rather than place, as in the last pair of sentences in the box below.

In	At
They live **in** Singapore.	Our plane will stop **at** Singapore on the way to Sydney.
His office is **in** this building.	His office is **at** the top of this building.
There are many shops **in** the two terminals of the airport.	We have to be **at** the airport before 8 a.m.
The concert was cancelled **in** the end because the artist had been injured in a ski trip only days before the concert.	The music is loud and rousing **at** the end of the symphony.

11.11.2 *By* and *until*

You use **by** to say that something will happen at or before a certain time; you use **until** to say that a condition will remain up to a certain time.

By	Until
These books must be returned to the library **by** next Thursday at the latest.	We have rented the games room **until** 4 p.m. today.
Our friends will be back in Hong Kong **by** the end of this month.	Our friends will not return to Hong Kong **until** the end of this month.

11.11.3 *During* and *for*

Both these prepositions can be used when referring to time. **During** means in or within some time period; **for**, among its many different uses, can show a length of time. That is, while **during** tells us when something happens or happened, **for** tells us how long something happens or happened. Note that you can use **during** and **for** with the simple present and the simple past tenses. You can also use these two prepositions in the same sentence, as shown in the box below.

During	For
She became a Canadian citizen **during** winter of 1991.	I first visited Japan **for** a month **during** summer of 1963.
Their baby girl cries a lot **during** the night.	Last night, I was wide awake a long while, so I simply read **for** an hour or two.

11.11.4 *For* and *since*

You just saw that **for** tells us how long something happens or happened. **For** also allows you to say how long something has been going on up to now, using the present perfect or the present perfect progressive tenses. These tenses are also applicable to the use of **since**, which tells when something started. Remember that **since** requires mentioning a specific time point (not a period).

For	Since
We have known each other **for** ten years.	We have known each other **since** 2009.
They have been watching television **for** two hours.	They have been watching television **since** two hours ago.

11.11.5 *To* and *for*

Bear in mind that these two prepositions have many different uses, including when some aspect of time is involved. Here, however, we focus on their uses in relation to people (e.g., **What is this *to* you? That is good *for* you!**) Only some of their possible uses are mentioned in the box below. Study them carefully.

To	For
Showing how somebody thinks or feels about something or what somebody knows: *Exercising regularly is important **to** me.*	Concerning somebody or something: *Luckily **for** us, today's weather will be excellent for hiking.*
***To** some people, failure is but a prerequisite of success.* ***To** my knowledge, no one knew what he was planning to do.*	Showing how difficult, valuable, exceptional, rare, and so on something is that somebody has done: *It was so remarkable **for** her to have crossed the Atlantic in a boat all by herself.*
Showing somebody's reaction to something: *Rock music isn't really **to** his taste.* ***To** her surprise, she got acceptance by three prestigious universities in the States.*	Considering what you can expect from someone: *That's too amazing a keyboard performance **for** a five-year-old child!*

11.11.6 *Between* and *among*

A widespread belief is that **between** should be applied to two things and **among** to three or more. This advice is useful up to a point. When we have a small number of parties involved in some interaction, it is possible to use **between** to refer to such interaction as occurs between musicians of an orchestra, their conductor, and members of the audience listening to their music making. The sentence concerning South Korea in the box below also illustrates the logical use of **between** to refer to its location relative to its three neighbouring countries of China, North Korea, and Japan.

An important note: When you use **between**, the basic structure is always **between . . . and . . .** Do not say something like **This room can accommodate** *between* **30** *to* **50 persons** (should be **This room can accommodate** *between* **30** *and* **50 persons**).

Between	Among
*Today's temperature will be **between** 20 **and** 24 degrees.*	*Today's temperature will vary greatly **among** different areas of the city.*
*No agreement has been reached in the summit meeting **between** North Korea **and** the United States.*	*Britain's leaving the European Union is a hot topic **among** members of the Union.*
*South Korea is located **between** China, North Korea, **and** Japan.*	*There is considerable interest in Korean cuisine **among** the people of Hong Kong.*

11.12   Summing up

Although many prepositions are seemingly little words (some of them, such as **of**, **to**, **in**, **on**, **at**, **by**, **for**, **with**, are among the most frequently used words in English), they are powerful in pointing to the relationship between different parts of a sentence. At the same time, you must not forget that there are quite a few two-word and three-word prepositions (**according to**, **together with**, **as well as**, **in contrast to**). They add a great deal of language choices to what you can do to express ideas about the relationship between people, actions, and things.

The correct use of prepositions is not easy to learn and master, especially for non-native speakers. To become more familiar with them, you have to learn them as vocabulary units and pay careful attention to the sentence patterns in which they appear.

This chapter has been an overview of the use of prepositions. The following are some main features of prepositions that should be well understood:

(1)   Prepositions must be followed by a noun, pronoun, or noun phrase (**e.g., I was talking** *with* **these people**), but it is possible to reverse the order (**e.g., these are** *the people* **I was talking** *with*).

(2)   A given preposition can have more than one meaning or use (**e.g.,** *over* **the street**, *over* **the Easter holiday**, *over* **my face**).

(3)   The same meaning or use can be shown by two or more prepositions (**e.g., the reason** *for* **the delay**, **the cause** *of* **the delay**, **something leading** *to* **the delay**). Sometimes these prepositions are interchangeable in the same sentence:

*He is excited **by** new smart phones.*

*He is excited **about** new smart phones.*

Sometimes they are not interchangeable:

*He is obsessed **by** new smart phones.* (but not ***in***)

*He is interested **in** new smart phones.* (but not ***with***)

(4) Many prepositions can be followed by **-ing** forms (*before starting* **our journey**, *without lingering* **any longer**, **look forward** *to seeing* **you**).

(5) Many nouns, adjectives, and verbs take a preposition or one of several possible prepositions. Sometimes, only one preposition is suitable (**understanding of**, not **understanding on**). Sometimes, changing the preposition also changes the meaning (**concerned with** vs. **concerned about**; **agree on** vs. **agree with**).

(6) Prepositions appear in a great number of **phrasal verbs (verb + preposition/adverb)** whose meanings may be different from the separate meanings of the component words. Unlike the usual prepositions, phrasal verbs do not have to be followed by nouns or pronouns.

| Exercises | **Chapter 11** |

Exercise 11.1

Fill in the blanks with the appropriate preposition chosen from the two given in the parentheses.

選擇括號裏一個合適的介詞，填寫在空白處。

1.   We have been living in Hong Kong _____ thirty years. (**for, since**)

2.   I do not want to be late: I must get to the clinic _____ time. (**on, at**)

3.   There is a long line of people _____ the taxi stand. (**in, at**)

4.   Some people hide valuables _____ their bed. (**below, under**)

5.   The use of smart phones has spread all _____ the world. (**around, over**)

6.   Our friends used to live _____ the New Territories. (**at, in**)

7.   She was so tired that she took a long while to get _____ her bed. (**away from, out of**)

8.   It is hard to get _____ such heavy rush hour traffic. (**along, through**)

9.   For decades, the Star Ferry has been a convenient means of transport _____ the harbour. (**over, across**)

10.   _____ insufficient experience, he did not get the job. (**because, owing to**)

11.   German is spoken in Austria _____ Germany. (**as well as, from**)

12.   He was standing _____ (**in, at**) the queue _____ (**at, near**) the bus stop.

13.   I had never been _____ (**at, to**) the United States before 1964.

14.   When the plane arrived _____ (**in, at**) the airport in San Francisco _____ (**at, on**) that spring morning in 1964, I was excited indeed.

15.   Let us look at the problem _____ (**in, from**) their point of view.

Exercise 11.2

Fill in the blanks with **at, for, in, on, to, with** or no preposition (write **NP**).

在空白處填寫適當的介詞 (**at, for, in, on, to, with**)。假如不需用介詞，就填寫 **NP**。

1.   Our neighbours are _____ holiday; they won't be back until next Monday.

2.   They were married _____ 1968.

3.   I will always remember _____ that day in winter 1989 when it snowed heavily in Vancouver.

4.   Let us get together _____ a leisurely lunch soon.

5.   Our Austrian friend is coming _____ Hong Kong _____ Christmas.

6.   We are going _____ Ocean Park _____ the kids this weekend.

7.   He thinks he can learn swimming _____ just a week.

8.   This hall is reserved _____ the orchestra's weekly rehearsal.

9.   The fellowship group meets _____ every other Saturday evening.

10.   There is an East Rail station _____ the university.

11.   Which is the quickest way _____ the Government Headquarters?

12.   I wonder why there are no children _____ this tour to Greece.

Exercise 11.3

Fill in the blanks with the appropriate multi-word preposition from the given list.

從下列複合介詞中選擇合適的填寫在空白處。

except for	away from	by means of	prior to	because of	in spite of
along with	in front of	in contrast to	in relation to	next to	for all

1.   _____ the pandemic, many concerts at the Cultural Centre have been cancelled.

2.   Their daughter, _____ two other classmates, was awarded first prize in the prose reading contest.

3.   All passengers on the cruise ship must take part in a safety drill _____ the ship's departure.

4.   It is good if you have the chance to get _____ the crowds and noise of the city.

5.   The Museum of History is _____ the Museum of Science.

6.   She did not stop caring for her children _____ her illness.

7.   _____ we know, our company may have to downsize to reduce costs.

8.   I could not see part of the stage because there was a tall person sitting _____ me.

9.   She liked the material and design of the hat _____ the colour.

10.   Boys' academic ability is about the same _____ girls'.

11.   Containers are lifted and moved _____ powerful cranes.

12.   In the 1960s, trains going to the New Territories ran every hour or so _____ every few minutes today.

Exercise 11.4

Rewrite the following sentences without changing the meaning, replacing each underlined phrase with a **phrasal verb.** You may need to modify some words.

Example: He will not be attending the meeting because something <u>unexpected happened</u>.

He will not be attending the meeting because something <u>came up</u>.

試重寫下面的句子。保持意思不變,但須用一個適當的短語動詞 (phrasal verb) 取代了底線的短語。某些詞可能需要改動。參看上面舉例。

> Phrasal verbs for this exercise:
>
> come about   put up with someone/something   agree with   take up something
>
> take after someone   put something across   get at something
>
> get away with something   come through   come up with something

1. She said she <u>has an idea</u> to share with us.

    _____ .

2. My granddaughter recently <u>began learning to play</u> the recorder.

    _____ .

3. He is doing all he can to <u>discover</u> the truth of the matter.

    _____ .

4. Harmony between two conflicting parties can <u>happen</u> if both sides agree to compromise.

    _____ .

5. I don't know how you could <u>tolerate</u> the noise from the renovation work next door.

    _____ .

6. He was lucky to <u>survive</u> the dangerous operation.

    _____ .

7. She <u>resembles</u> her father in the pursuit of excellence.

    _____ .

8. Mango ice cream is a great dessert, but it <u>can make me feel sick</u>.

    _____ .

9. Don't ever think you can <u>go unpunished when you lie</u> in your tax return.

    _____ .

10. Politicians need to be good at <u>telling their ideas</u> to the public.

    _____ .

Chapter 12   Know Your Phrases and Clauses

What you will learn in this chapter

Phrases and clauses are important structures of writing. Phrases, without a subject and a finite verb, cannot make complete sense or stand on their own. By comparison, clauses contain a subject and at least one finite verb to make complete sense. A sentence may contain just one clause, called a main clause, and, if needed, a subordinate clause. You will learn to recognize six kinds of phrases and their function in sentences: noun phrase, gerund phrase, infinitive phrase, adjective phrase, participial phrase, and prepositional phrase. You will also learn the basics of sentence types (simple, compound, complex).

短語（phrases）和從句（clauses）是寫作的重要結構。短語沒有主語，也沒有限定動詞（finite verb），所以沒有完整的意義，也不能獨自成句。相比之下，從句有主語，也有至少一個限定動詞，因而有完整的意義。一個句子可以只含一個主句（main clause），也可以（如有需要）含一個從屬分句（subordinate clause）。你會在本章裏認識六種短語：名詞短語（noun phrase）、動名詞短語（gerund phrase）、不定式短語（infinitive phrase）、形容詞短語（adjective phrase）、分詞短語（participial phrase）和介詞短語（prepositional phrase）。你也會學習三種句型的概要：簡單句（simple sentence）、複合句（compound sentence）和複雜句（complex sentence）。

12.1 Two short passages

12.2 Why you should be familiar with phrases and clauses

12.3 What are phrases?

12.4 Some types of phrases you should know about

12.5 Restrictive and non-restrictive phrases

12.6 What are clauses?

12.7 Simple, compound, and complex sentences

12.8 Clauses in action

12.9 Summing up

12.1 Two short passages

Read the following two passages:

- *It was the 12ᵗʰ of May. We flew to Shanghai. We soon arrived. It was almost 6 p.m. We did not have any check-in baggage. We went through customs quickly. We had earlier appointed a driver. He came to meet us. He drove us to our hotel. Traffic on the highway was smooth. Traffic in the city was slow. It was rush hour.*

- *On 12ᵗʰ May, we flew to Shanghai,* **arriving** *there almost 6 p.m.* **Not having** *any check-in baggage, we went through customs quickly. A* **pre-appointed driver** *came to take us to our hotel. Traffic was smooth on the highway but slow in the city* **because** *it was rush hour.*

The first paragraph consists of twelve short simple sentences. Although the description is clear, the sentences sound choppy and the flow of ideas seem awkward. By contrast, the second paragraph is much more readable. Phrases and clauses are used in a way that connects ideas naturally, making their flow smooth and easy in four sentences.

12.2 Why you should be familiar with phrases and clauses

When you are familiar with the structure and functions of various phrases and clauses, you are more likely to write in the style of the second paragraph in 12.1 rather than in the style of the first. Chances are that you are already using phrases and clauses in your writing. They are not particularly difficult to understand. Consequently, sharpening your skills of using phrases and clauses properly will help you write accurately and effectively.

12.3 What are phrases?

A phrase is a group of words containing an idea, but it does not have complete sense because it has neither a subject nor a finite verb. A finite verb is a verb with a specific tense (present, past, future, etc.), number (singular or plural) and person (first, second, third) as required by a subject, such as **she plays; they will come; we are studying**. When both subject and a finite verb are present, a sentence with complete meaning is formed.

(Short) sentences	Phrases
She plays often.	*playing digital games*
They will come here.	*to come to a decision*
He had a good time.	*to have a good time*
They surely will visit us.	*sometime next year*
My cousin invited me to dinner.	*happy as ever*

The sentences above all contain a subject and a finite verb. Each sentence has complete meaning and can stand on its own. The phrases, as you can see, all do not have a subject and a finite verb. The first three phrases contain a non-finite form of a verb, which cannot make complete sense. The last two phrases contain no verbal form at all. All five phrases thus do not have complete sense and cannot stand on their own although they contain some fragmentary ideas. To have complete sense, they need to be connected to another group of words containing both a subject and a finite verb, as in the following two examples:

*They surely will visit us **sometime next year**.*

*My cousin, **happy as ever**, invited me to dinner.*

12.4   Some types of phrases you should know about

Sentences necessarily contain phrases of various kinds. If you have a good knowledge of the types of phrases that commonly occur in sentences, you are more likely to write sentences rich in content and varied in structure.

You should know something about six types of phrases: (1) noun phrase, (2) gerund phrase, (3) infinitive phrase, (4) adjective phrase, (5) participial phrase, and (6) prepositional phrase. With information given in the following box, study the example sentences in which a particular type of phrase occurs and note the function of the phrase in the sentence. When acting as a noun, the phrase is "nominal". If the phrase modifies some word in the sentence, the phrase can be "adjectival" (like an adjective) or "adverbial" (like an adverb).

Type of phrase	Example sentence	Function
Noun phrase		
a table for two	*I have reserved **a table for two**.*	nominal, object
close friends	*Her **close friends** helped her.*	nominal, subject
Gerund phrase		
eating a healthy breakfast	***Eating a healthy breakfast** is a good idea.*	nominal, subject
getting so much attention	*She resents her little sister's **getting so much attention** from their parents.*	nominal, object
Infinitive phrase		
to eat too many sweets	***To eat too many sweets** is bad for your teeth.*	nominal, subject
to memorize this poem	*His teacher wants him **to memorize this poem**.*	nominal, object
to see you	*Her excitement **to see you** is obvious.*	adjectival (modifies **excitement**)

Type of phrase	Example sentence	Function
Adjective phrase		
very famous	*We were looking for a* **very famous** *cafe.*	premodifies a noun (**café**)
quite busy	*I have been* **quite busy**.	complement of subject (**I**)
much prettier	*The new paint makes the house* **much prettier.**	modifies object (**house**)
Participial phrase		
arriving late	*Those* **arriving late** *will not be admitted.*	adjectival (modifies **those**)
having made up her mind	***Having made up her mind***, *she will not listen to anything you say.*	adverbial (modifies **she**)
packing for our trip	*We will be busy* **packing for our trip**.	adverbial (modifies **busy**)
Prepositional phrase		
about rest	*His ideas* **about rest** *are very different from ours.*	adjectival (modifies **ideas**)
for many weeks	*They have been studying the problem* **for many weeks**.	adverbial (modifies **studying**)
to your case	*The rules are applicable* **to your case**.	adverbial (modifies **applicable**)

12.5   Restrictive and non-restrictive phrases

Examine the following two sentences:

(a) **Oranges,** *selling at six dollars each***, are a good buy today.**

(b) **Oranges** *selling at six dollars each* **are a good buy today.**

Sentence (a) tells us that all oranges are a good buy today; by the way, they are selling at six dollars each. The phrase **selling at six dollars each** is a participial phrase (formed from the present participle **selling**) modifying **oranges**. In this sentence, it does not restrict the main idea that all oranges are a good buy today.

The main idea remains the same even if you take out the phrase, which is thus called "non-restrictive". Note that *a non-restrictive phrase is set off by two commas if it appears in mid-sentence.*

By contrast, sentence (b) says that not all oranges but *only* those selling at six dollars each are a good buy today. Thus, the phrase **selling at six dollars each** is restrictive because it restricts or limits the meaning of the sentence. The main idea of the sentence changes if you remove the phrase from the sentence. It is the same phrase as that used in sentence (a), but its role has changed. No commas are used to set off a restrictive phrase in a sentence. This last point is most important because it is how you tell your readers that the phrase has a restrictive or limiting sense.

The difference between non-restrictive and restrictive phrases applies also to clauses. You need to remember that if what you say about the subject of the sentence does not affect the main idea of the sentence, you are using a non-restrictive element (phrase or clause). You will read more about this in Chapter 13 on restrictive and non-restrictive relative clauses.

12.6   What are clauses?

A clause, different from a phrase, is a group of words that has *both* a subject and a finite verb acting with that subject. It may be a whole sentence (**She was happy**) or part of a sentence (**She smiled** *because she was happy*).

A sentence may consist of only one clause (**She felt good about everything**) or more than one clause (**She felt good about everything because she was happy**). If a clause makes complete sense on its own, we call it a main or independent clause (**She felt good about everything**). If a clause depends on the main clause to make complete sense, we call it a subordinate or dependent clause (**because she was happy**).

12.7   Simple, compound, and complex sentences

A simple sentence consists of only one main clause. The length of the sentence depends on whether you add phrases and various modifiers. Thus, a simple sentence is not necessarily short.

All these are simple sentences (containing only one main clause):
I stood.
I stood near the information counter.
I stood near the information counter waiting for my friend.
I stood near the brightly lit information counter waiting patiently for my friend.
I stood near the brightly lit information counter shortly before noon waiting patiently for my friend.

A compound sentence has two or more main clauses connected by a "coordinating conjunction" (e.g., **and**, **but**, **or**, **so**) and a comma. The clauses may also be joined by a "conjunctive adverb" (e.g., **however**, **therefore**, **indeed**, **moreover**) and a semicolon.

*She met her friend at the square, **and** they went shopping at the mall nearby.*

*We had tickets for the concert, **but** the concert was later cancelled.*

*She wants to become a doctor, **so** she is applying for admission to a medical school.*

*We can take a tour to Phuket, **or** we can join a cruise to Japan, **but** we do not have enough time for both.*

(Note: A semicolon is required to separate two clauses in the next four sentences.)

*Freedom is valuable; **however**, it must not infringe on others' rights.*

*He thinks the rent is affordable; **moreover,** the location is convenient with shops and public transport.*

*All cultures have their own customs; **therefore,** a visitor needs to follow local practices.*

*The Covid pandemic has changed our lives; **indeed,** we have adapted to a new normalcy.*

A complex sentence has a main clause and one or more subordinate clauses. A subordinate clause says something more about the main clause. It may be an adverb clause, an adjective clause, or a noun clause, and is typically introduced by such words as **although**, **because**, **if**, **since**, **so that**, **that**, **how**, **while**, **whereas**, **whether**, **which**, and **who**. In the following box, all subordinate clauses are in boldface.

Complex sentence	Function of the subordinate clause
Although he meant good, his plan was faulty.	adverb clause, indicating concession
He lost in the competition ***because he had not practised enough***.	adverb clause, indicating cause
We changed the date of the gathering to a Saturday ***so that more people could come.***	adverb clause, indicating purpose
They decided to cancel the hiking ***since the weather was unstable.***	adverb clause, indicating cause
The public library, ***which is open seven days a week***, is much used by the community.	adjective clause, modifying subject (**public library**)
All candidates ***who apply for the position of management trainee*** must be a university graduate.	adjective clause, modifying subject (**all candidates**)
The committee discussed ***whether they needed another fund-raising programme.***	noun clause, object of verb (**discussed**)
How he uses his money is his own affair.	noun clause, subject of sentence

A compound-complex sentence contains at least two main clauses and one or more subordinate clauses. In the following two examples of compound-complex sentences, clauses are introduced by **but**, **because**, **when**, **however**, **before**, and **since**. You will read more about constructing compound sentences for achieving coordination and complex sentences for subordination in Chapter 15.

*This bookstore has been here for several decades, **but** it will have to close soon **because it can no longer make enough profit to sustain its business**.* (two main clauses and one subordinate clause)

*He wanted to go to university **when** he finished secondary school; **however**, he had to work to earn enough money **before** he could do that **since** his father had just passed away.* (two main clauses and three subordinate clauses)

12.8   Clauses in action

Think of clauses as units of thought. They are highly useful when you write. Some clauses can be simple sentences; other clauses can work together in compound or complex sentences to serve different purposes. Of course, you may begin with single clauses and add other clauses to them as needed.

To demonstrate how you can put clauses in action, let us use three examples, each starting with a simple sentence:

Example 1

Eating vegetables is good for health.

You can add an idea to contrast it, as in this compound sentence:

*Eating vegetables is good for health, **but** many people do not follow this advice.*

Alternatively, you can turn the original sentence into a noun clause:

*We have long been told **that eating vegetables is good for health**.*

Example 2

John will not be joining us today.

You can insert an adjective clause after the subject, and set off the inserted clause by two commas:

*John, **who is not feeling well**, will not be joining us today.*

You can also add a clause to expand the original statement:

*John will not be joining us today, **so** he has sent David to represent him at the meeting.*

As suggested in the first example, you can also use the original statement as a noun clause introduced by **that**:

*We did not know **that** John will not be joining us today.*

Example 3

All work and no play makes life monotonous.

Try adding a short main clause in front, making the original statement a noun clause:

*Even children would agree **that** all work and no play makes life monotonous.*

Or, let the original statement be a main clause, and place an adverb clause of concession in front:

***Although we must work to earn a living**, all work and no play makes life monotonous.*

12.9 Summing up

Knowing the nature and function of phrases and clauses is useful for constructing sentences to serve your communication purposes. Be sure you understand the following main points:

(1)   Phrases do not contain a subject and a finite verb. So, phrases by themselves cannot stand alone; they need to combine with other words to form a complete sentence that has a subject and at least one finite verb (which is required by the subject).

(2)   A phrase can contain other phrases (e.g., **for many weeks**, a prepositional phrase containing **many weeks** as a noun phrase).

(3)   Phrases are always incomplete in meaning, but they can be brought to good use to serve nominal, adjectival, and adverbial functions in clauses and sentences.

(4)   Clauses always have both a subject and a finite verb. Sometimes one clause works well enough as a simple sentence, but at other times you need to put multiple clauses together to combine ideas.

(5)   Beyond the simple sentence, a compound sentence contains two or more coordinated independent clauses. A complex sentence has one main clause and one or more subordinate or dependent clauses.

(6)   You can try to shape your sentences in different ways by choosing and placing clauses in different positions to discover which way will serve your purpose best.

Exercises   Chapter 12

Exercise 12.1

Write T in the parentheses if the statement is true, write F if it is false.

下列陳述假如是對的，在括號裏寫 T，不對的，寫 F。

1.　(　　　)　A phrase does not have a subject.

2.　(　　　)　A phrase may contain a finite verb.

3.　(　　　)　A phrase may contain no verbal form at all.

4.　(　　　)　A clause has both a subject and a finite verb.

5.　(　　　)　A clause can only be part of a sentence.

6.　(　　　)　A simple sentence must be also short (a few words).

7.　(　　　)　We use coordinating conjunctions (e.g., **and, but, or**) to construct a compound sentence.

8.　(　　　)　A compound sentence has only two main clauses.

9.　(　　　)　One or more subordinate clauses may be present in a complex sentence.

10.　(　　　)　A prepositional phrase can function adverbially.

11.　(　　　)　This sentence contains a non-restrictive phrase: **Avocados grown in California are tastier than those grown in Mexico.**

12.　(　　　)　Because phrases are always incomplete in meaning, they have little use in sentence writing.

13.　(　　　)　A phrase can contain other phrases (as when a prepositional phrase contains a noun phrase).

14.　(　　　)　The underlined part in this sentence is an adjective clause: **This clinic, which opens on Sundays, has a dermatology section.**

15.　(　　　)　Adverb clauses always contain adverbs.

Exercise 12.2

For each sentence in this exercise, do the following: (A) Identify the type of phrase underlined, using letters (a to f) representing the six types of phrases mentioned in this chapter. See the box below.
(B) Identify the function of the phrase in the sentence, using numbers 1 to 7 as explained below. Write your answers in the spaces under A and B at the right.

請為此練習的每個句子作兩項回答：(A) 識別劃了底線的短語屬於哪一種短語（參看以下方框，用字母 a 至 f 作答）。(B) 識別該短語在句子中的功用（參看以下方框，用數字 1 至 7 作答）。

A. Type of phrase
a = noun phrase   b = gerund phrase   c = infinitive phrase   d = adjective phrase
e = participial phrase   f = prepositional phrase

B. Function of the phrase
1 = adjectival (like an adjective), modifying subject
2 = adjectival, modifying object
3 = adverbial (like an adverb), modifying an adjective
4 = adverbial, modifying a verb
5 = adverbial, modifying an entire sentence
6 = nominal (like a noun), as subject
7 = nominal, as object

		A	B
1.	Her idea of a relaxing holiday is not at all like ours.		
2.	To be able to play the piano so well is truly amazing for a blind musician.		
3.	She was clearly confident that she would win.		
4.	The meeting on next Tuesday is cancelled.		
5.	Originally written for children, J.K. Rowling's Harry Potter stories have been turned into blockbuster movies for people of all ages.		
6.	Mrs Lee was lucky enough to get a grand prize.		
7.	The situation is more complicated than it looks.		
8.	His interest to study law is still quite strong.		
9.	These privileges are all applicable to you.		
10.	The books on this shelf are mostly new acquisitions.		
11.	We have the new painting hung in the living room.		
12.	Her parents want her to focus more on her studies.		
13.	He complained that the beer was not cold enough.		
14.	We will be busy getting ready for a family reunion in Hong Kong.		
15.	Because of insufficient time in the oven, the meat roast was not quite ready to eat.		
16.	Learning a new language is so much fun for him.		
17.	I am looking forward to seeing you all soon.		

18. The discussion must not drift <u>away from the original theme</u>.   _____   _____

19. <u>The fashion shop on the corner</u> is always crowded on weekends.   _____   _____

20. <u>Not having seen my friend for nearly thirty years</u>, I wonder if I can   _____   _____
     still recognize her when we meet next week.

Chapter 13

Distinguish between Restrictive and Non-restrictive Relative Clauses

Relative clauses are adjective clauses beginning with a relative pronoun to modify a noun in the main clause of a sentence. They function to (1) give more information about people and things, or (2) limit our reference to particular people and things. If they perform the first function, they are called "non-restrictive relative clauses"; if they perform the second function, they are called "restrictive relative clauses". You will learn about the difference between these two functions and how you can show, by using or not using commas, which function applies to the sentence you are writing.

關係從句（relative clause）是以一個以關係代詞（relative pronoun）開頭的形容詞從句（adjective clause），用以修飾主句中的名詞。關係從句有兩種不同功用：（1）給人或物添加更多信息，（2）限定指稱的是哪一個人或物。具有第一種功用的關係從句稱為非限定關係從句（non-restrictive relative clause）；具有第二種功用的關係從句稱為限定從句（restrictive relative clause）。你會在本章裏了解這兩種功用的區別並學會通過使用逗號與否來分別表達這兩種功用。

13.1 **What are relative clauses?**

13.2 **Focusing on the relative pronoun in a relative clause**

13.3 **Use commas for non-restrictive clauses but not for restrictive clauses.**

13.4 **Prepositions may appear in relative clauses.**

13.5 **Summing up**

13.1   What are relative clauses?

Relative clauses are adjective clauses, which begin with a relative pronoun (e.g., **who, which, whom, whose, that, when, where**), that refer to or modify a noun in the main clause (as in this sentence where **that** refers to the word **clauses**). We use relative clauses for two purposes:

- To give additional information about people and things (We call such relative clauses **non-restrictive**, non-defining, or non-identifying.)*

  *Mr. Leung, **who lives next door to me**, is very friendly.*
  (The clause **who lives next door to me** adds information about Mr. Leung.)

- To identify or limit our reference to particular people and things (We call such relative clauses **restrictive**, defining, or identifying.)*

  *The man **who lives next door to me** is very friendly.*
  (The clause **who lives next door to me** identifies which man is referred to.)

*Review the ideas of "non-restrictive" and "restrictive" introduced in 12.5 of Chapter 12.

13.1.1 The core meaning of "non-restrictive"

A "non-restrictive" (also called "non-defining" or "non-identifying") relative clause works only to give more information about someone or something mentioned in the main clause. It does not change the meaning of the main clause. When you write such a clause in mid-sentence position, you *must* set it off by two commas, one before and one after the clause.

13.1.2 The core meaning of "restrictive"

A "restrictive" (also called "defining" or "identifying") relative clause serves to identify or specify someone or something in the main clause. Without it, the reference of the person or thing in the main clause is unclear. A restrictive relative clause does not require commas before and after it.

13.2   Focusing on the relative pronoun in a relative clause

13.2.1 The relative pronoun in a relative clause can be subject or object:

Sentences containing a non-restrictive relative clause (Note: Set off the clause in mid-sentence by two commas. Place a comma before the clause if it comes in end position.)	Function of the relative pronoun in the relative clause
1) *The city of Shanghai, **which has been rapidly developing**, has a vast subway system.*	**which** functioning as subject
2) *His uncle, **who has lived in Canada many years**, will visit Hong Kong next month.*	**who** functioning as subject
3) *The City Hall, **which we often visit**, has a nice concert hall.*	**which** functioning as object
4) *This is Tsing Ma Bridge, **which was opened in 1997 to road and rail traffic.***	**which** functioning as object

Sentences containing a restrictive relative clause	Function of the relative pronoun in the relative clause
5) People **who exercise regularly** are healthier.	**who** functioning as subject
6) Do you know the Spanish restaurant **that is right by the sea**?	**that** functioning as subject
7) The hexagonal rock columns **that we saw in Sai Kung** were quite a sight.	**that** functioning as object
8) We received a post card from the woman **whom we met on a train in Germany**.	**whom** functioning as object

13.2.2 Using *who, which,* and *that*

Who, **which**, and **that** are three relative pronouns most often used in relative clauses referring to nouns in the main clause.   The following summarizes their use:

Relative pronoun	refers to	used in non-restrictive clause	used in restrictive clause
who (**whom** for object; **whose** for possessive)*	persons	✓	✓
which	things	✓	✓
that**	persons or things	X	✓

*****whom** for object; **whose** for possessive:

> These villagers, **whom the anthropologist has been studying**, are friendly people. (non-restrictive clause set off by two commas)

> I.M. Pei is a Chinese-American architect **whose designs include the Bank of China in Hong Kong.** (restrictive clause, no commas)

******In referring to things, **that** is more usual than **which**. **That** is also preferred when introducing a restrictive clause (no commas):

> The music shop **that was in this mall** has moved.

> The film **that many people have been talking about** will be screened soon.

13.2.3 Using *when, where,* and *why*

When, **where**, and **why** are called "relative adverbs" to introduce relative clauses as restrictive clauses that refer to nouns (in the main clause) of time, place, and reason, respectively. They are all equivalent to using **which** following a suitable preposition:

> I'll never forget the day **when my mother passed away**.
> (= I'll never forget the day **on which** my mother passed away.)
>
> Can you suggest a suitable place **where we can meet**?
> (= Can you suggest a suitable place **at which** we can meet?)
>
> This is the reason **why they left for Australia.**
> (= This is the reason **for which** they left for Australia.)

13.3   Use commas for non-restrictive clauses but not for restrictive clauses.

The use and non-use of commas surrounding or before a relative clause has been pointed out earlier (13.1.1, 13.1.2, 13.2.1, 13.2.2). These commas are so important that we must understand their use clearly.

Keep in mind that a relative clause is restrictive when it limits or specifies the reference of the noun (sometimes pronoun) in the main clause. The content of the following two boxes should help you. But first, we need to introduce a term, "antecedent", to facilitate the discussion. An antecedent is simply the noun (or pronoun) which comes before the relative pronoun of the relative clause. The relative pronoun refers to the antecedent.

Non-restrictive clauses (set off by commas)
When the antecedent refers to all of a class: **Our neighbours**, *who have lived in the building many years, are all very polite.*

When the antecedent is restricted in itself (i.e., itself limited in reference, or it is already identified):
 	
    The antecedent is a named person:
 	
      We all remember **Albert Einstein**, *who gave us the idea of relativity.*
 	
    The antecedent is one of a kind:
 	
      My uncle, *who lived in Boston, was very kind to me when I was there.*
 	
    The antecedent is identified by the preceding context:
 	
      In the afternoon, she ordered a pizza. **The pizza**, *which had been made for some hours, lost all its crunchiness.*

Restrictive clauses (no commas used)

When the antecedent is restricted by the relative clause to **some of a class**:
 	
     Those of our neighbours *who are short-time tenants are not too interested to know other people living in the same building.*
 	
     Anyone *visiting Beijing who has seen the Forbidden City is deeply impressed by its grandeur.*

When the antecedent is restricted by the relative clause:
 	
     Many academics congratulated **the scientist** *who had won the Shaw Prize for Physics.*
 	
     My uncle *who lived in Los Angeles last visited Hong Kong in 1991.* (I had more than one uncle. The relative clause specifies which one I meant.)
 	
     Pizzas *which were made hours ago would no longer be crunchy.*

13.4   Prepositions may appear in relative clauses.

Compare the following statements with the relative clauses made from them:

Statement	Relative clause
We go to the cinema.	*the cinema that we go to*
She has been talking about the coffee shop.	*the coffee shop that she has been talking about*
I am interested in the book.	*the book that I am interested in*
We are walking on the land.	*the land that we are walking on*

In the relative clauses above, the relative pronoun **that** is the object of a preposition. Note that using **that** and placing the preposition at the end only applies to restrictive clauses. In such cases, we often leave out the relative pronoun, especially when spoken:

*The cinema (that) we go **to** is around the next corner.*

*Do you know the coffee shop (that) she has been talking **about**?*

*This is the book (that) I am interested **in**.*

*The land (that) we are walking **on** was reclaimed from the sea ten years ago.*

13.4.1 The preposition may come at the beginning or at the end of the relative clause.

The four example sentences in 13.4 are written in an informal spoken style, with the preposition placed at the end of the relative clause (and leaving out the relative pronoun **that**). In formal written English, the preposition comes before the relative pronoun. Compare the two styles:

> *This is the book (that) I'm interested **in**.* (Informal)
>
> *This is the book **in which** I am interested.* (Formal)

The following are more examples of relative clauses containing a preposition written in the formal way:

> - *This is a question **to which** there is no easy answer.*
> - *Here is a topic **about which** we know very little.*
> - *The resolution of this problem will produce a situation **in which** all parties will have something to gain.*
> - *We are given a task **on which** we will need to spend a great deal of time.*
> - *This is the book **of which** you have heard a great deal.*
> - *That is the original novel **from which** an abridged version has been produced.*

13.4.2 Rewriting a sentence to change a restrictive clause into a non-restrictive one

By now, you should be able to see that the relative clauses in all the six sentences above are restrictive clauses (hence no commas are used). To strengthen your understanding of restrictive and non-restrictive relative clauses, all the six sentences are now rewritten to contain a non-restrictive clause (hence commas are used). Study them carefully to see why the clause in the rewritten sentence is non-restrictive.

- *All the questions, **to which there are no easy answers**, will be discussed.*

- *Various topics, **about which we know very little**, have already been selected for the seminar.*

- *Such a situation, **in which all parties have something to gain**, will be most welcome.*

- *Many tasks, **on which we will need to spend a great deal of time**, are involved in team building.*

- *The stories of Harry Potter, **of which** you must have heard, are all bestsellers.*

- *Shakespeare's plays, **from which** many abridged versions have been produced, are required readings for students of English literature.*

13.5   Summing up

Both non-restrictive and restrictive relative clauses are subordinate clauses. The clause is non-restrictive if it merely adds information about the noun in the main clause it refers to and so does not serve to identify that noun's reference in the sentence. The clause is restrictive if it does identify that noun's reference in the sentence and hence limits the meaning of the sentence. Distinguishing between them is an important and useful skill to master.

Of course, you need to be sure yourself which of the two situations applies to what you want to say. Make sure, too, that you use commas to set off a non-restrictive clause but no commas for a restrictive one. This punctuation requirement is essential for signalling your intended meaning to your readers. Do it correctly so that your readers will not be misled.

Prepositions may appear in restrictive relative clauses. In formal writing, the preposition comes before the relative pronoun **which.** In informal speech, however, two changes occur: (1) **which** is replaced by **that** (the word can be omitted), and (2) the preposition comes at sentence end.

Exercises **Chapter 13**

Exercise 13.1

Circle the letter representing the correct answer for each of the following:

把下面每題正確答案的字母代號圈起來：

1. Relative clauses are
   a) noun clauses
   b) adverb clauses
   c) adjective clauses
   d) independent clauses

2. Relative clauses may begin with
   a) who
   b) which
   c) that
   d) when
   e) any of the above

3. A non-restrictive relative clause gives this about someone or something mentioned in the main clause:
   a) less information
   b) limited information
   c) more information
   d) no information

4. Which of the following words is used to refer to things?
   a) who
   b) when
   c) that
   d) whose

5. Only one of the following sentences is correctly constructed: (Don't ignore punctuation.)
   a) The salesperson, who sold me the camera is not on duty today.
   b) The salesperson who sold me the camera, is not on duty today.
   c) The salesperson sold me the camera is not on duty today.
   d) The salesperson who sold me the camera is not on duty today.

6. A clause that identifies or specifies someone or something in the main clause us called
   a) dependent clause
   b) subordinate clause
   c) special relative clause
   d) restrictive relative clause

7.   The word **which** functions as an object in one of the following sentences:
a) Green minibuses, which run specific routes, are convenient for many people.
b) The pyramids, which tourists in Egypt often visit, have been in existence for thousands of years.
c) The MTR, which carries large numbers of commuters every day, started in 1980.
d) Custard tarts, which are my favourite dessert, are on special sale today.

8.   In one of the following sentences, the antecedent of the relative pronoun is restricted in itself (that is, it is already identified):
a) My mother, who had been a member of her church choir, was my first piano teacher.
b) New immigrants, who have little social support, have a hard time adjusting to life in an unfamiliar country.
c) The necklace which was stolen is worth thousands of dollars.
d) I remember the waitress who served us.

9.   Choose the word or phrase that completes the sentence: *I would like to see the picture ...*
a) she drew it.
b) that she drew.
c) that she drew it.
d) drew.

10. The relative pronoun **that** functions as subject in the following sentences except one:
a) I still remember the Star Ferry pier that used to be right here.
b) The smart phone is a gadget that has replaced the camera, the notebook, the calendar, and the computer.
c) The holiday resort in Bali that we visited is as large as a university campus.
d) This is the film that won 11 Oscar awards in 1960.

Exercise 13.2

Do the following: (A) Underline the relative clause in each sentence. (B) In the parentheses, write NR for a non-restrictive and R for a restrictive clause. (C) Add commas where necessary.

給下列句子做三項練習：(A) 在關係從句 (relative clause) 之下劃底線。(B) 如該從句屬非限定 (non-restrictive)，在括號裏寫 NR，如屬限定 (restrictive)，則寫 R。 (C) 如有需要，在句子適當處加逗號。

1.   (   )   The ability to write well which is not commonly found among learners of English can be consciously cultivated.

2.   (   )   We can all learn from the mistakes that we have made.

3.   (   )   She carelessly left in the taxi the gift that she had just bought.

4.   (   )   Symptoms of Covid-19 which can take a long time to emerge are not the same for all the infected.

5.   (   )   Hong Kong which began as a small fishing village has developed into a large cosmopolitan city.

6. (   )   I will see you at the City Hall where we met last time.

7. (   )   The Grand Canyon which is over 300 kilometres long has to be seen to be believed.

8. (   )   The concert that we are all looking forward to takes place next Sunday.

9. (   )   According to an article that appeared in National Geographic scientists are studying the possibility of travel to Mars.

10. (   )   This is the house where we lived while we were in Cambridge in 1977.

11. (   )   He does not like to drive at times when the roads are dark.

12. (   )   Albert whom you met yesterday works in an international company.

Exercise 13.3

Write a new sentence by changing the second sentence in each pair to a relative clause and combining it with the first sentence. Write your new sentence first in a formal pattern and then in an informal pattern.

將下面每一組句子的第二句改寫為關係從句，然後與第一句合併。請分別用正式（formal）和非正式（informal）形式寫出新句子。

1. Finding affordable housing in Hong Kong is a problem.

    Many young people are concerned about the problem.

        Formal pattern: _____

        Informal pattern: _____

2. We have a new task.

    We will need to spend a great deal of time on the task.

        Formal pattern: _____

        Informal pattern: _____

3. This is an attractive position.

    Everybody wants to apply for this position.

        Formal pattern: _____

        Informal pattern: _____

4. This is the medical research.

    He referred to this research.

        Formal pattern: _____

186

Informal pattern: _____

5.   Here are the buildings.

You have heard so much of these buildings.

Formal pattern: _____

Informal pattern: _____

6.   They are the main supplier.

Many wine sellers get their wines from this supplier.

Formal pattern: _____

Informal pattern: _____

| Chapter 14 | # Use Participial Phrases to Say Something About the Subject |

Participial phrases contain the **-ing** present participle or the **ed/en** past participle. They cannot stand alone but can work like an adjective or an adverb when connected to a main clause. You will learn to use **participial phrases** to say something about the subject and what that subject does in a main clause so as to enrich the content of your sentence. Participial phrases are particularly useful when you need to express a condition, a cause, a reason, a purpose, and the like, that sheds some light on an action.

分詞短語（participial phrase）含現在分詞（-ing present participle）或過去分詞（ed/en past participle），雖然不能獨自成句，但連接到一個主句時，就能發揮像形容詞或副詞的功用。在本章裏，你可以學習用分詞短語為主句裏的主語（subject）或該主語的某些行動添加一些信息，使整句的內容更為豐富。所以，如果需要說明行動的背後有什麼情況、原因、理由、目的等，分詞短語就會顯得尤其合用。

14.1 Using a participial phrase in a sentence

14.2 Review of some basics about the participle

14.3 Time reference of participial phrases

14.4 Function of participial phrases in sentences

14.5 Conversion from relative clauses to participial phrases

14.6 Conversion from adverbial clauses to participial phrases

14.7 Main types of participial phrases that commonly begin a sentence

14.8 Typical error of not properly modifying subject of main clause

14.9 Summing up

14.1   Using a participial phrase in a sentence

Imagine that you are going to say something like this in two sentences:

The new student does not know anyone in his class. He feels quite lonesome.

The two sentences are perfectly fine and grammatical, but you can also say the following:

Not knowing anyone in his class, *the new student feels quite lonesome.*

Read the rewritten sentence again (pausing at the comma in mid-sentence), and you should feel that it is more concise and more effective than the original two sentences. It is more effective in the sense that now, it sounds clearer why the new student feels lonesome in his class.

What you read above is changing the first of the two sentences into a **participial phrase** (so called because it contains a participle, **knowing**), which modifies (says something about) the subject (**the new student**) in the main clause.

14.2   Review of some basics about the participle

When a verb is limited (or specified) by tense (time), number (singular or plural), and person (first, second, third), it is a **finite verb** (e.g., **you know, she sings, they have left**). When there are no such limitations or specifications, the verb is in its non-finite form. (See also 12.4 in Chapter 12.) There are three non-finite verb forms: the infinitive (e.g., **to know**), the present participle (e.g., **knowing**), and the past participle (e.g., **known**).

14.2.1 Two non-finite participle forms

All verbs have two non-finite participle forms:

(1)   the **-ing** present participle [used for forming all progressive (continuous) tenses, pointing to action in progress]:

They will be *staying* in Hong Kong for some time.

(2)   the **-ed/-en** past participle (used for forming all perfect tenses, referring to action occurring before sometime in the past or before now):.

We have already *explained* the week-long programme with them.

The **-ed/-en** participle is also used to express the passive forms of all tenses:

This famous landmark *has been visited* often.

14.2.2 Participles can be used like adjectives.

You have seen earlier (10.4.1 in Chapter 10) that both present participles (**-ing**) and past participles (**-ed/-en**) can work as adjectives, as also demonstrated in the following sentences. Each of the sentences may be rewritten with an adjective clause that contains the participle.

---

*Beware of **falling** rocks.*
*(Beware of rocks **that are falling**.)*

*He must work harder in the **coming** school year.*
*(He must work harder in the school year **that is coming**.)*

*Many **broken** windows need to be repaired.*
*(Many windows **that have been broken** need to be repaired.)*

*Victoria Peak is probably the **most visited** landmark in Hong Kong.*
*(Victoria Peak is probably the landmark **that is most visited in Hong Kong**.)*

14.3 Time reference of participial phrases

A participial phrase by itself has no clear time reference. This reference depends on the main verb (of the main clause). That is, we can speak of the participial phrase having an "intended time" when it is connected to a main clause.

14.3.1 The present participle (-ing) can indicate the same time as that of the main verb.

Present time	*The guest **speaking in the talk show now** is a tree specialist.*
Past time	*Her baby sister, **wanting to attract attention**, talked continuously.*
Future time	*Anyone **planning to dine in this restaurant** will need to book early.*

14.3.2 The past participle (-ed/-en), despite its name, can show different times.

Same time as that of the main verb:	Panel A
Present simple	*She **enjoys** going to malls (which are) **crowded with people**.*
Past simple	*She **enjoyed** going to malls (which were) **crowded with people**.*
Before the time of the main verb	**Panel B**
Intended time in the participial phrase is past perfect when the main verb is past simple.	***Not having seen her parents in Hong Kong for nearly three years*** *(= Because she had not seen her parents in Hong Kong for nearly three years), she **flew** from the US to visit them for several weeks.*
Intended time in the participial phrase is present perfect when the main verb is future simple.	***Having made up my mind*** *(= after I have made up my mind), I **will stick with** my original plan.* ***Never having accepted failure*** *(= because I have never accepted failure), I **will keep on** trying.*

14.4   Function of participial phrases in sentences

Participial phrases can be adjectival (functioning like an adjective), as in the following sentences:

> Guests **arriving late** (= guests who arrive late) will *not be admitted until a suitable break.*
>
> We made casual wear selections (*that are*) **determined by personal taste**.

Participial phrases can also be adverbial (functioning like an adverb) when they refer to a condition, reason, or time relation, as in the following sentences:

> **Walking about the park**, *I felt invigorated by the fresh air.*
>
> **Having finished her homework**, *she watched television.*
>
> **Angered by the waiter's poor service**, *we complained to the manager.*
>
> **Not knowing anyone in his class**, *the new student feels quite lonesome.* (This sentence appeared at the beginning of this chapter, 14.1.)

14.5   Conversion from relative clauses to participial phrases

Because of the adjectival function of participial phrases, they can be formed by reducing relative clauses. This means you just delete the relative pronoun from the relative clause and change the verb in the relative clause to an appropriate (non-finite) participle. The two sentences in Panel A in 14.3.2 illustrate these basic steps. Study also the following sentences.

Sentence using relative clause	Sentence using participial phrase
Most domestic helpers **who work in Hong Kong** are from the Philippines.	Most domestic helpers **working in Hong Kong** are from the Philippines.
Everyone **who is taking a bus or the MTR** must wear a face mask.	Everyone **taking a bus or the MTR** must wear a face mask.
Applications **that are not submitted before the end of the month** will not be considered.	Applications **not submitted before the end of the month** will not be considered.
A question **that is currently being considered** is the safety of the various vaccines.	A question **currently being considered** is the safety of the various vaccines.
The waiters, **who all looked cheerful**, served us well throughout the whole dinner.	The waiters, **all looking cheerful**, served us well throughout the whole dinner.
	Or: **All looking cheerful,** the waiters served us well throughout the whole dinner.
Note: The relative clauses in the first four sentences are all restrictive, thus no commas are used. The fifth sentence contains a non-restrictive relative clause, which is set off by two commas. The participial phrase derived from this relative clause is therefore also non-restrictive and may precede or follow the subject (**the waiters**) it modifies.	

14.6   Conversion from adverbial clauses to participial phrases

Since participial phrases may be adverbial in function, they can also be formed from adverbial clauses, including those involving reason and time if the subject of the main clause is the same as that of the adverbial clause. The three sentences in Panel B in 14.3.2 illustrate this well. Let us now see how the four sentences containing participial phrases in the second box of 14.4 can be converted from sentences containing adverbial clauses.

The basic steps are: (1) Check that the subject of the adverbial clause (a clause always contains a subject) is the same as the subject of the main clause. (2) Delete the subject of the adverbial clause (sometimes, it is necessary to move it to the subject position of the main clause). (3) Change the verb in the adverbial clause to an appropriate (non-finite) participle. (4) Remove or keep the subordinator as the situation requires (make sure the sentence makes logical sense when you read it).

Sentence using adverbial clause	Sentence using participial phrase
While I was walking about the park, *I felt invigorated by the fresh air.*	*Walking about the park*, *I felt invigorated by the fresh air.*
As (since/because) she had finished her homework, *she watched television.*	*Having finished her homework*, *she watched television.*
As (since/because) we were angered by the waiter's poor service, *we complained to the manager.*	*Angered by the waiter's poor service*, *we complained to the manager.*
As (since/because) the new student does not know anyone in his class, *he feels quite lonesome.*	*Not knowing anyone in his class*, *the new student feels quite lonesome.*
	(Note how the adverbial clause subject **the new student** is moved to the subject position of the main clause.)
Note: A participial phrase by itself has no indication of time until it is used alongside a main clause. Its "intended time" either precedes or is the same as the time of the main clause. This aspect is mentioned also in 14.7.1 and 14.7.2.	

Did you notice that in all the four sentences above, the subordinator (called "subordinating conjunction") in the adverbial clause has been removed in the process of conversion. This includes **since** when it means "because". But **since** also means "from some past time". When **since** has this meaning in the adverbial clause, it is kept as the word introducing the participial phrase, as in the following example:

Sentence using adverbial clause	\Sentence using participial phrase
*Xiaolan has not been back to Shanghai **since she came to Hong Kong three years ago.***	***Since coming to Hong Kong three years ago**, Xiaolan has not been back to Shanghai.*

14.7   Main types of participial phrases that commonly begin a sentence

Let us now focus on the sentences using a participial phrase as those in the two boxes of 14.6. They all contain a participial phrase in the front position. Notice that *the subject of the main verb (of the main clause) is also the "subject" of the participial phrase* (in which the subject is "implied"). This is an important point, because if the two (subject of the main verb and that of the participial phrase) do not match, error results. We will return to this later in 14.8.

In describing the types of participial phrases, we consider two dimensions:

(a)   Distinction between a "general" form and a "perfect" (in the sense of "completed") form.

- In the general form, the time intended or implied in the participial phrase is determined by the main verb.

- In the perfect form, time intended in the participial phrase precedes that shown by the main verb.

(b)   Whether the action expressed by the participial phrase is in the active voice or the passive voice.

Taking these two dimensions together, we have four main types of participial phrases, as shown in the box below in 14.7.1.

14.7.1 Four main types of participial phrases

	Active Voice	**Passive Voice**
General form (intended time is same as that of main verb)	**Type 1** *Asking for members' support*, the chairman gave a moving speech.	**Type 3** *Asked to help the earthquake victims*, they responded enthusiastically.
Perfect form (intended time precedes that of main verb)	**Type 2** *Having asked for his friends' advice*, he now knows what to do.	**Type 4** *Having been asked by their teacher to lead the discussion*, the students had to read the material thoroughly.

14.7.2 More examples to show that participial phrases are used to combine sentences

Type 1 (General form, active voice, intended time same as main clause)   *I knew the complexity of the problem. I went to consult my project director.* → **Knowing the complexity of the problem,** *I went to consult my project director.*
Type 2 (Perfect form, active voice, intended time precedes that in main clause)   *I have watched the movie many times. I can tell you almost the whole story.* → **Having watched the movie many times,** *I can tell you almost the whole story.*
Type 3 (General form, passive voice, intended time same as main clause)   *I was never discouraged by repeated failures. I kept on trying.* → **Not discouraged by repeated failures**, *I kept on trying.*
Type 4 (Perfect form, passive voice, intended time precedes that in main clause)   *She had been invited to attend a formal dinner. She selected an elegant dress for the occasion.* → **Having been invited to attend a formal dinner**, *she selected an elegant dress for the occasion.*

14.7.3 Naming the subject

From the example sentences in the preceding box in 14.7.2, you can see that the subject of the entire sentence is at the beginning of the main clause. It is important to note that if the same person is mentioned in the participial phrase, only a suitable pronoun is used there. *If the person is named, the name appears not in the participial phrase but in the main clause*, as in the following:

> (**✗**) ~~Leaving Tom's house in early morning, he went straight to the park for a walk.~~
>
> (**✓**) *Leaving his house in early morning, Tom went straight to the park for a walk.*

14.8   Typical error of not properly modifying subject of main clause

When using participial phrases alongside a main clause, you must remember that the participial phrase has an "implied" subject although it does not actually appear in the phrase. This "implied" subject is the same as the subject of the main clause (see 14.7).

Therefore, when you use a participial phrase in the front position followed by a main clause, make sure that what is said in the preceding paragraph is true. Otherwise, you have an error known as "dangling modifier", which means that the modifier (the participial phrase) is not properly and meaningfully related to the subject of the main clause, as demonstrated in the following sentence:

(**✗**) ~~*Looking down from the observation point on Victoria Peak, Kowloon and Hong Kong Island spread out before our eyes.*~~

The subject of the main clause is **Kowloon and Hong Kong Island.** It is not sensible to say that **Kowloon and Hong Kong Island** can **look down from the observation point on Victoria Peak**. To correct this error, you can recast the sentence as follows:

*Looking down from the observation point on Victoria Peak, **we could see** Kowloon and Hong Kong Island spread out before our eyes.*

By inserting **we could see** in the initial position of the main clause, the participial phrase is meaningfully related to a legitimate subject **we** of the main clause. **We** is of course the implied subject of the participial phrase. Now study another example of an error of dangling modifier. Note again the need for placing a suitable subject at the beginning of the main clause so that the participial phrase can sensibly refer to that subject.

(**✗**) ~~*After having been in isolation for so long, the world seemed to have changed greatly.*~~

(**✓**) *After having been in isolation for so long, he found that the world seemed to have changed greatly.*

14.9   Summing up

The main points of this chapter are:

(1)   A participial phrase contains the present participle (**-ing**) or the past participle (**-ed/-en**).

(2)   We use a participial phrase alongside a main clause to say something adverbially about what the subject does in the main clause. This usually refers to things such as a condition, a reason, a time relation, a method, or a purpose.

(3)   Since participial phrases function adjectivally and adverbially, a sentence containing a relative clause can be converted to a sentence containing a participial phrase. Similarly, an adverbial clause in a sentence can be converted to a participial phrase modifying a main clause subject.

(4)   Four types of participial phrases are possible by considering (a) whether the time implied in the participial phrase is "general" (time same as main clause) or "perfect" (time precedes that of main clause), and (b) active versus passive voice.

(5)   The implied subject of the participial phrase should be the same as the subject of the main clause. If this is not so, an error of "dangling modifier" results. To correct the error, you must supply a sensible and legitimate subject in the main clause so that the participial phrase can meaningfully modify the subject. As you do so, you may need to reword the main clause.

Exercises	**Chapter 14**

Exercise 14.1

In each of the following sentences, examine whether it contains a participial phrase. If it does, write that phrase in the space to the right. If it does not, write NIL.

檢視下列每個句子是否含分詞短語 (participial phrase)。如有，把該短語寫在右面空白處；如沒有，則寫 NIL。

1. The man wearing a green jacket is my manager. _____

2. Generally speaking, the children in this class are well-behaved. _____

3. This restaurant serves delicious Italian cuisine. _____

4. Opened since 2018, this café is popular among office workers. _____

5. Always trying to do well, he feels quite stressed. _____

6. Many people spend their leisure playing with their phones. _____

7. Nothing feels better than enjoying a cup of good coffee. _____

8. She hates going to malls crowded with people. _____

9. We drove around looking for a place to park. _____

10. Calling his opponent a liar, Mr. M boasted about his integrity. _____

Exercise 14.2

Use a suitable participial phrase to combine the pairs of sentences or rewrite the sentence. Underline the participial phrase.

試用適當的分詞短語將下面每組句子合併或把原句重寫，並在你所用的分詞短語之下劃底線。

1. John had completed the project. He took a vacation.

   _____

2. When they arrived at the party, they found that everyone was singing.

   _____

3. She did not know where the Museum of History was. She asked for directions at the Tourist Information Office.

   _____

4. Einstein is widely known as an influential physicist. He has given us the idea of relativity.

   _____

5.　I have been invited to give a speech at the meeting. I better get prepared.

_____

6.　An old lady was hit by a car while she was crossing the road.

_____

7.　The audience was applauding excitedly when the concert ended. The audience would not leave.

_____

8.　She has read the book many times. She can tell you the whole story.

_____

9.　The new employee does not know anyone in her department. She feels quite disoriented at times.

_____

10.　The company chairman was surrounded by reporters. He made an important announcement.

_____

Exercise 14.3

Some of the following sentences contain a "dangling modifier". Identify them by underlining the dangling modifier. Then, in the space provided, rewrite the sentence to correct the error. Some rewording will be necessary. If you think the sentence contains no such error, write CORRECT.

下面有些句子含有一個懸垂修飾語 (dangling modifier)。找出該懸垂修飾語並在其下劃底線。然後將句中的錯誤改正，在空白處寫出正確的句子 (用詞可能需要有些改動)。假如你認為原句沒有錯誤，在空白處寫 CORRECT。

1.　Now growing a beard, he looks very different.

_____

2.　Having failed numerous times, success was finally hers.

_____

3.　Playing with Lego pieces, the children had a great time.

_____

4.　Passing by the village, some rice fields were visible.

_____

5.　Looking out of the window, a fantastic view of the harbour was before our eyes.

_____

197

6. Holding two full-time jobs, he has no time at all for recreation.

    _____

7. Completely absorbed in watching her drama videos, hours went by without notice.

    _____

8. Never having learned to swim properly, swimming in the deep pool was too scary for him.

    _____

9. Comparing television and news magazines, each type of medium has its strengths and limitations.

    _____

10. Hoping to sustain the economy, large sums of employment subsidy are being given to both big and small companies.

    _____

Chapter 15

Use Coordination or Subordination to Show the Relative Importance of Two Ideas

When you have two related and equally important ideas, each expressed in a clause, you can link them as a compound sentence with two ideas in coordination. The linking words or expressions include coordinating conjunctions, conjunctive adverbs, and correlative conjunctions. If one idea is more important than another, you write a complex sentence with the more important idea as the main clause and the other idea as the subordinate clause attached to the main clause by, for instance, subordinating conjunctions, relative pronouns, and participial phrases.

當你表達兩種具有某種關係而同等重要的想法時，可以用兩個分句分別表示，然後將它們連接，構成一個複合句，使兩種想法並列。用來連接的詞或用語有：並列連詞（coordinating conjunctions）、連接性副詞（conjunctive adverbs）和互聯連詞（correlative conjunctions）。如果兩個意念中有一個比較重要，就讓它作為主句（main clause），次要的則作為從句（subordinate clause），兩者相連構成一個複雜句（complex sentence）。用作連接的詞或用語包括：從屬連詞（subordinating conjunctions）、關係代詞（relative pronouns）和分詞短語（participial phrases）。

15.1 Make your writing more readable by showing relations between ideas.

15.2 Coordination

15.3 Subordination

15.4 Subordination and coordination compared

15.5 Summing up

15.1 Make your writing more readable by showing relations between ideas.

When you write, you want to convey to readers how you treat the relations between ideas. Some ideas are equally important (shown by "coordination"). Others may be less important (shown by "subordination"). In either case, your readers need to know such differences, so they can follow your writing with greater ease and interest.

15.2 Coordination

To achieve coordination, you join equally important ideas with "coordinators". Three kinds of coordinators may be used: (1) coordinating conjunctions, (2) conjunctive adverbs, and (3) correlative conjunctions.

15.2.1 Coordination using coordinating conjunctions

Coordinating conjunction	Two ideas joined
and	The principal gave a speech, **and** he also presented prizes.
but	I wanted to buy that classic novel, **but** it was out of print.
or	We can visit Ocean Park, **or** we can go to Disneyland.
nor	We don't like oily food, **nor** do we like hot and spicy dishes.
so	Things are expensive here, **so** you must plan your spending.
for	Use fewer plastic bags, **for** we need to save the environment.

15.2.2 Coordination using conjunctive adverbs

Conjunctive adverbs are adverb-like words or phrases that indicate logical relationships (e.g., reason, concession, condition, confirmation, emphasis, contrast, result) between clauses. Note that *when two independent clauses are joined by a conjunctive adverb, a semicolon must follow the first clause and a comma must follow the conjunctive adverb*. There are more than twenty commonly used conjunctive adverbs. Ten of them are used in the following sentences. Try to use them and some of the ones listed at the bottom of the box to enrich your sentence-making ability.

Conjunctive adverbs (relationship)	Two ideas joined (Note the semicolon separating the two clauses and the comma following the conjunctive adverb.)
however (concession)	Freedom is valuable**; however,** it must not infringe on others' rights.
therefore (reason and result)	All societies have their own customs**; therefore,** a visitor should follow local practices.
in addition (addition)	Bernstein was a famous conductor**; in addition,** he was an outstanding music educator.
in contrast (contrast)	She is outgoing and likes to talk**; in contrast,** her brother is much less active and does not talk much.
consequently (result)	My cousin has lived in the United States since childhood**; consequently,** she speaks English like an American.

Conjunctive adverbs (relationship)	Two ideas joined (Note the semicolon separating the two clauses and the comma following the conjunctive adverb.)
in fact (confirmation/ emphasis)	*People in China increasingly use their mobile phones to pay for various expenses**; in fact,** many shops and taxis do not accept cash.*
indeed (confirmation)	*Social constraints are part of our life**; indeed,** they affect us even if we are unaware of them.*
otherwise (condition)	*You must dress appropriately in a fine-dining restaurant**; otherwise,** you might feel out of place.*
on the other hand (concession)	*The press always say readers have the right to know**; on the other hand,** it is also important to respect the privacy of individuals whose stories become public knowledge.*
nonetheless (concession)	*Modern paintings can be quite abstract**; nonetheless,** they have special appeal to some people.*
Other conjunctive adverbs: **alternatively, besides, hence, similarly, in the same way, further, moreover, that is to say, in other words, in addition, instead, likewise, thus, as a result, for example, meanwhile**	

Note the following:

• It is possible to place the conjunctive adverb in mid-position in the second clause. Three of the sentences from the preceding box are rewritten as examples:

> *Freedom is valuable**;** it must not, **however,** infringe on others' rights.*
>
> *She is outgoing and likes to talk**;** her brother, **in contrast,** is much less active and does not talk much.*
>
> *The press always say readers have the right to know**;** it is also important, **on the other hand,** to respect the privacy of individuals whose stories become public knowledge.*

• Each of the sentences in the larger box above can also be written as two sentences. The conjunctive adverb can begin the second sentence or may be placed after the subject of that sentence. Thus, the same idea can be expressed in any of the following ways:

> *Freedom is valuable**; however,** it must not infringe on others' rights.*
>
> *Freedom is valuable**;** it must not, **however,** infringe on others' rights.*
>
> *Freedom is valuable. **However,** it must not infringe on others' rights.*
>
> *Freedom is valuable. It, **however,** must not infringe on others' rights.*
>
> *Freedom is valuable. It must not, **however,** infringe on others' rights.*

If the two ideas are not too long, you can join them as one "compound sentence", which shows that the two ideas are equally important. With two longer ideas, you can express them in two separate sentences.

15.2.3 Coordination using correlative conjunctions

Correlative conjunctions are pairs of connecting words, such as **both . . . and . . . , either . . . or . . . , not only . . . but also . . .** You use them to link sentence elements that are grammatically equal and expressed in a parallel form (see Chapter 17) to show a relationship or a contrast.

Correlative conjunctions	Two ideas joined
both . . . and . . .	**Both** effective delivery **and** a good sense of humour are important in public speaking.
either . . . or . . .	**Either** we vote for candidate A **or** we vote for candidate B.
*not only . . . , but also	Education is about **not only** acquiring knowledge, **but also** developing one's character.
*if . . . , then . . .	**If** she practises on the piano two or three hours every day, **then** she will surely perform well.
*just as . . . , so . . .	**Just as** television is our window to the world, **so** the smart phone is our instantaneous link with other people.
*Note that, for these correlative conjunctions, a comma follows the first clause.	

15.3 Subordination

Subordination is the use of words or word groups to show that one element in a sentence is less important than another. To do this, you can use any of the following: (1) subordinating conjunctions, (2) relative pronouns, (3) noun clauses, (4) appositives, (5) prepositional phrases, and (6) participial phrases. When clauses are used for the subordinate part (as when introduced by subordinating conjunctions or relative pronouns), the resulting sentence is a "complex sentence".

15.3.1 Subordination using subordinating conjunctions

Subordinate clauses, functioning as "adverbial clauses", begin with a subordinating conjunction (e.g., **although, because, while**) to express a cause, a condition, a comparison, or a concession. Some common subordinating conjunctions are:

- Cause: **because, since, so that**

- Comparison or contrast: **as if, whereas, while**

- Condition: **even if, if, provided that, given that, whenever, whether**

- Concession: **although, even though, though**

- Purpose: **so that, in order that**

Subordinating conjunctions	Two clauses joined
even though	**Even though** we have been to Japan before, we have never gone there by cruise ship.
while	**While** her academic performance places her at the top of her class, she is not well received by her classmates.
provided that	**Provided that** the location is accessible by the mass transit system, he will consider buying a home there.

Subordinating conjunctions	Two clauses joined
as if	*He looked totally exhausted, **as if** he had been beaten up.*
so that	*She has been practising intensively **so that** she will stand a better chance of passing the test.*
because	*I cannot communicate with anyone today **because** I left my phone at home.*
whether	***Whether** we win or lose, we will have done our best.*

Note:

- It is customary to place the subordinate adverbial clause first, followed by the main clause. But it is also possible to reverse the order, starting with the main clause (as in sentences in the above box using **as if, so that, and because**).

- If you start with the subordinate clause, you usually need to use a comma after it. But if you start with the main clause, a comma is not necessary before the subordinate clause.

15.3.2 Subordination using relative clauses

Relative pronouns such as **who, that**, and **which** introduce subordinate adjective or relative clauses (see also 13.1 in Chapter 13) that say something about the main subject. By comparison, the information contained in the adjective clauses is considered not as important as the content of the main clause (also called "independent clause").

Relative pronouns	Two clauses joined
who	*New immigrants, **who** lack social networks here, will have a hard time.**
which	*Ocean Park, **which** has a low-level area and a high-level area, was established over 40 years ago.**
whom	*This is the manager to **whom** we complained about the food.***
that	*The violin is a string instrument **that** produces sounds resembling the human voice.***
*As you may recall (from Chapter 12), the subordinate clauses introduced by **who** and **which** in these sentences are "non-restrictive", meaning that they do not affect or restrict the meaning of the main clause. Commas must be used to set off the subordinate clause.	
The subordinate clauses introduced by **whom and **that** in these sentences are "restrictive" in that they limit the meaning of the main clause. They tell us which person or thing is referred to. No commas are used to set off the subordinate clause.	

15.3.3 Subordination using noun clauses

Noun clauses function like nouns. It may be the sentence subject, object of the main verb, complement of the subject, or object of a preposition. The content of noun clauses thus plays a secondary role in giving substance to what the main clause tries to say.

Function of the noun clause	Noun Clause (in boldface)
Sentence subject	The news **that his fever has gone down** is comforting. It doesn't concern me **whether or not the task is done.**
Object of the main verb	The chairman explained **what the meeting's main purpose was.**
Complement of subject	The question is **how the conflict can be resolved**.
Object of a preposition	Parents are sometimes anxious about **what their children actually learn at school**. I am astonished at **how small Hong Kong's flats are**.

15.3.4 Subordination using appositives

An appositive is a word or phrase that describes or identifies a noun in a sentence. Its function is to add some information about a certain word in the main clause. It is usually not essential (non-restrictive) to the meaning of the sentence and is thus set off with commas or dashes. Appositive phrases often appear in mid-sentence.

> Psychology, **the study of the mind**, helps our understanding of human behaviour.
>
> My friend, **eager to be successful in his career**, works extremely hard.
>
> Our new manager—**efficient and friendly**—soon gained the respect of members of his team.

The appositive phrase may sometimes come at the front. A comma must follow the phrase.

> **A world-class violinist**, Anne-Sophie Mutter has performed in Hong Kong several times in recent years.
>
> **Angry at the poor service of the waitress**, they left without leaving any tip.

The appositive phrase may also follow the main clause:

> When in Paris you should visit the Louvre, **one of the world's best museums**.
>
> She is an outstanding young musician, **one who should be successful in whichever orchestra she chooses to join.**

Most appositive phrases are non-restrictive (non-essential to the meaning of the sentence), hence the commas setting them off. But sometimes an appositive phrase is restrictive (essential to the meaning of the sentence); it then must not be set off by commas.

> They want to hold their concert in a hall **large enough to seat 1000 people.**
>
> The gentleman **sitting next to the chairman** is the newly appointed secretary.
>
> The accidents and emergency unit is trying to have more nurses **willing to work overtime**.

15.3.5 Subordination using prepositional phrases

As mentioned in Chapter 12 on phrases and clauses, a prepositional phrase is headed by a preposition followed by a noun or noun phrase (e.g., **because of careful planning, according to official statistics**). Many prepositional phrases perform an adverbial function in that they refer to such matters as causes, conditions, comparisons, and concessions. They express a subordinate idea alongside a main clause. Such a prepositional phrase may take an initial, middle, or final position in the sentence, as in the following example. Note the use of comma(s) in the initial and middle positions but not in the final position:

Initial position	***Because of the popularity of mobile phones***, *interpersonal communication has never been more convenient.*
Middle position	*Interpersonal communication,* ***because of the popularity of mobile phones****, has never been more convenient.*
Final position	*Interpersonal communication has never been more convenient* ***because of the popularity of mobile phones****.*

The following are more examples of subordination using prepositional phrases:

Accompaniment: **along with, together with**
Together with a main course, *you can have a salad, a dessert, and tea or coffee.*
Addition: **apart from, in addition to**
Apart from a few minor errors, *her presentation was quite acceptable.*
Cause/Reason: **because of, as a result of, on account of**
His business, ***as a result of hard work and sensitivity to consumer needs****, thrived successfully.*
Comparison: **like, in comparison with, as contrasted with, contrary to**
Contrary to popular belief, *people are having less leisure time as society becomes more affluent.*
Concession: **in spite of, despite, regardless of**
In spite of fierce competition, *this small bookstore is still doing well.*
Condition: **given, in case of, in the event of**
Given the complexity of the problem, *we need to study it carefully.*
Degree: **according to**
We normally allocate time to tasks ***according to their relative priority****.*
Purpose: **for the purpose of** (or just **for**)
I went to the box office early ***for the purpose of getting tickets for the best seats****.*

15.3.6 Subordination using participial phrases

As you may recall from Chapter 14, participial phrases use the non-finite present participle (**-ing**) or past participle (**-ed/en**) to introduce a phrase that is about a certain state or condition, whose intended time is either the same as or before that in the main clause. The content of the participial phrase is subordinate to that of the main clause.

To understand this better, let us think of a scenario consisting of two parts: (A) You have been trying hard to get something done without much success so far, and (B) you already know this is a difficult task because you have failed before, but you remind yourself that you must persist and never give up.

With these two ideas in mind, here are some sentences you can write, each consisting of part (A) and part (B):

The intended time in (A) (participial phrase) is the same as the time in (B) (main clause):	
(A)	(B)
(Type 1)* **Knowing** the difficulty of success,	I kept on trying.
(Type 3)* **Not discouraged** by repeated failures,	I continued trying.
The intended time in (A) precedes the time in (B):	
(A)	(B)
(Type 2)* **Having tried** many times,	I still failed badly.
(Type 4)* **Having been convinced** that I must reach my goal,	I persisted.
*For the meaning of the four types, see 14.7.1 in Chapter 14.	

As you can see, each participial phrase is about a certain previous experience or a mental condition that sets the stage for the action in the main clause. The four types of sentences shown in the box all use a participial phrase to express a subordinate element. They differ in subtle ways involving a "general" form (Types 1, 3) versus a "perfect" form (Types 2, 4). They also differ in using the active voice (Types 1, 2) versus the passive (Types 3, 4). You can review these points in more detail in 14.3 (time reference) and 14.7 (the four main types) of Chapter 14.

15.4 Subordination and coordination compared

The four sentences in the box in 15.3.6 are all constructed to show subordination, placing emphasis on the main clause. Each of them can be reworded to show coordination, putting both parts on equal status.

Try reading them to feel their difference. It may help if you read the main clause somewhat louder and more emphatically in the subordination pattern but keep your tone the same in both independent clauses in the coordination pattern. Make sure you also see the use of coordinating conjunctions (**but, so**) and conjunctive adverbs (**however, therefore**) in the sentences showing coordination.

Subordination	Coordination
Knowing the difficulty of success, I kept on trying.	I knew the difficulty of success, **but** I kept on trying.
Not discouraged by repeated failures, I continued trying.	I was not discouraged by repeated failures, **so** I continued trying.
Having tried many times, I still failed badly.	I had tried many times; **however,** I still failed badly.
Having been convinced that I must reach my goal, I persisted.	I had been convinced that I must reach my goal; **therefore,** I persisted.

15.5   Summing up

When writing sentences involving two ideas, you should always bear in mind the question of whether coordination or subordination would better serve your purpose. This is all about showing the relationship between ideas or elements so your sentences would become more readable.

Use coordination to relate two equally important elements by linking two main clauses with:

(1)   a coordinating conjunction (e.g., **and, but, or, so**) preceded by a comma;

(2)   a conjunctive adverb (e.g., **however, therefore, on the contrary**) preceded by a semicolon and followed by a comma;

(3)   a pair of correlative conjunctions (e.g., **both . . . and . . . ,   not only . . . but also . . . , either . . . or . . .**).

Use subordination to emphasize one element rather than another. You can show the less important element with:

(1)   a subordinate clause introduced by a subordinating conjunction (e.g., **although, because, while**);

(2)   a subordinate clause introduced by a relative pronoun (e.g., **who, that, which**);

(3)   a noun clause introduced by such words as **that, whether, what, why,** and **how**;

(4)   an appositive phrase that describes or identifies a noun in the main clause;

(5)   a prepositional phrase beginning with a preposition (e.g., **because of, in spite of, like, given**);

(6)   a participial phrase that contains a present participle (**-ing**) or a past participle (**-ed/-en**).

This may seem like a long list of skills to learn and understand. However, if you have studied this chapter carefully step by step, you should find the material useful for helping you write better sentences that are sufficiently clear to your readers. Such clarity is desirable in good written English.

Exercises Chapter 15

Exercise 15.1

a) **however**	b) **indeed**	c) **but**	d) **if . . . then . . .**	e) **although**
f) **or**	g) **who**	h) **both . . . and . . .**		i) **while**	j) **and**
k) **in fact**	m) **given that**	n) **therefore**		o) **that**

Find the words in the above list that may be used as . . .

上面所列的詞有哪些可以作為以下詞類使用？

1.   coordinating conjunctions: _____

2.   conjunctive adverbs: _____

3.   correlative conjunctions: _____

4.   subordinating conjunctions: _____

5.   relative pronouns: _____

Exercise 15.2

Combine each of the following pairs of sentences into one sentence using coordination. Use the construction specified in the parentheses. You may need to change some wording.

用括號內指定的詞類把下面每組句子連接為一個並列句。原句文字或需改動。

1.   Swimming allows movement of the whole body. It is enjoyable and relaxing. (coordinating conjunction)

      _____

2.   The project is highly challenging. We managed to complete it in time. (coordinating conjunction)

      _____

3.   This is our rough plan. It will be modified and improved. (conjunctive adverb)

      _____

4.   Writing well is not easy. You need to have good language skills and well-organized ideas. (conjunctive adverb)

      _____

5.   We learn to recognize errors. We are more likely to avoid those errors when we write. (correlative conjunctions)

_____

6.   We cannot work effectively without a good plan. A good plan cannot succeed without a good leader. (coordinating conjunction)

_____

7.   Television serves as our window to the world. The smart phone acts as our connector with people. (correlative conjunctions)

_____

8.   She put in many hours of practice every day. She won first prize in the public speaking contest. (conjunctive adverb)

_____

9.   Writing grammatical sentences is important for writing well. The same is true of using words properly. (correlative conjunctions)

_____

10. Credit cards make consumption easy. Consumers are lured into debt. (coordinating conjunction)

_____

Exercise 15.3

Combine each of the following pairs of sentences into one sentence using subordination. Use the construction specified in the parentheses. You may need to change some wording.

用括號內指定的詞類把下面每組句子連接為一個主從複雜句。原句文字或需改動。

1.   You may not succeed right away. You should keep on trying. (subordinating conjunction)

_____

2.   They were impressed by the young lady's qualifications. They offered her the position. (participial phrase)

_____

3.   Tourists are unfamiliar with places here. They often need to ask locals for directions. (subordinating conjunction)

_____

4.   The task is difficult. We did it successfully. (prepositional phrase)

_____

5.   The new hospital is located at a quiet setting. It has over 500 beds. (relative clause)

_____

6.   He will consider setting up a shop there. The condition is that the site is easily accessible.
        (subordinating conjunction)

_____

7.   The project operated at a great loss. The reason is poor planning. (prepositional phrase)

_____

8.   The new teacher was eloquent and friendly. She soon gained the trust and respect of her students.
        (appositive)

_____

9.   We have seen sunrise on the peak many times. We still enjoy the view these days. (subordinating
        conjunction)

_____

10.   The daily number of locally infected Covid-19 cases remains at low single digits. This news is
        comforting. (noun clause)

_____

Chapter 16

Use Conditional Sentences to Talk about Real and Unreal Possibilities

You may sometimes write about real possibilities such as when you heat up water, it will eventually boil. Sometimes, you may point to possible results of an "unreal" condition such as what you would do if you suddenly had a million dollars. At other times, you may even talk about the results of something that did not happen in the past. For example, if you obtained low marks because you did not prepare well for a test, you can say you would have done much better if you had prepared well (but you did not). To talk about these things, you need conditional sentences. In this chapter you will learn about the basic types of conditional sentences and some main variations in each type.

寫作時，你或會提及一些在現實中很可能發生的事，例如水加熱終會沸騰。有時你或需表達在某種虛擬的情況下事情會如何，比如你的財富暴增，你會如何應對？也有些時候，你可能就一些沒有發生的事而探討其後果，例如，倘若你因為沒有在考試之前好好溫習而成績欠佳，你可以說假如有充分的溫習（但事實上沒有），成績應該會好得多。談論這些事情，就必須使用條件句（conditional sentences）。在這章裏，你將學到條件句的幾個基本類別及每一類別中的一些不同寫法。

16.1 Conditional sentences contain an *if*-clause and a main clause.

16.2 Type 1 conditionals. *Typical sentence: If it rains, our picnic will be postponed.*

16.3 Type 2 conditionals. *Typical sentence: If I knew the answer, I would tell you.* (But I don't know the answer.)

16.4 Type 3 conditionals. *Typical sentence: If we had left home earlier, we would not have been late.*

16.5 Using *will/would* and *should* in *if*-clauses

16.6 Inversion of subject and auxiliary (*were, had, should*)

16.7 *If it was/were not for* and *if it had not been for*

16.8 Some other ways of expressing unreal events, wishes, and instrumental conditions

16.9 Summing up

16.1 Conditional sentences contain an *if*-clause and a main clause.

Conditional sentences (also referred to as "conditionals") consist of (a) a subordinate clause usually introduced by **if** to show the condition under consideration and (b) a main clause for the "result" given the condition stated in the **if**-clause. This is one of the structures used in subordination (15.3.1 in Chapter 15).

As a description of a condition, the **if**-clause is also an adverbial clause that modifies and gives meaning to the main clause.

16.1.1 Contractions commonly used (especially in speech)

Contractions in speech are common in conditionals. When writing involves reported or indirect speech, contractions are thus often used. The following list is worth reviewing:

Panel A
will
I'll = I will   *I won't = I will not*
we'll = we will   *we won't = we will not*
(The same for all other persons, singular and plural, in this panel and in panels B, C)
Panel B
would, had
you'd = you would or you had
If you'd called me, I'd have come earlier = If you had called me, I would have come earlier.
Panel C
would not, could not, had not, did not
I wouldn't = I would not
they couldn't = they could not
she hadn't = she had not
he didn't = he did not
Panel D
were not for, had not been for
if it weren't for = if it were not for
if it hadn't been for = if it had not been for
hadn't it been for = had it not been for

16.2   Type 1 conditionals. *Typical sentence: If it rains, our picnic will be postponed.*

This type of conditional sentence expresses possible events or actions and what they will lead to. They also include descriptions of natural phenomena and universal truths. The time is the present or the future.

Verb in *if*-clause: Present time (Situation is true in the present or future)	Verb in main clause: Future simple tense
If we **miss** the bus, we'll certainly be late for the meeting.	
If the Number 8 typhoon signal **is** up, we all must leave the workplace.	
If your books **are** overdue, you'll have to pay the library a fine.	
If the polar ice **melts** too quickly, sea levels will rise dangerously.	

16.2.1 Variations of Type 1

Use the present progressive (continuous) or the present perfect in the **if**-clause:
If you **are looking** for a care-free holiday, you will find many choices of cruises.
If you **have** already **seen** this movie, we will pick another.
Use **may, might, can, must** or **should** in the main clause:
If it rains, our party **may** be postponed.
If you want to stay healthy, you **must** eat more vegetables.
If you have a respiratory illness, you **should** wear a mask.
Use the present tense in both the **if**-clause and the main clause to mean that one thing always follows another:
If demand for a product **increases**, the price of that product **goes** up.
If you **press** the emergency button, the alarm **rings**.

16.3   Type 2 conditionals. *Typical sentence: If I knew the answer, I would tell you.* (But I don't know the answer.)

Like Type1, the time of Type 2 is the present or the future. The past tense in the **if**-clause is not a true past tense but merely expresses non-factual or hypothetical meaning. You can use this type of sentence to refer to hypothetical conditions that are not true (non-factual) or not expected to be true.

Verb in *if*-clause: **Past simple tense (but not a true past)** (Situation is untrue in the present or future.)	Verb in main clause: *would* + **infinitive**
If we **lived** in Japan, we **would** have to know Japanese.	
If I **were** you, I **would** consult a doctor for advice.	
If she **ate** ice cream, she **would** gain weight.	
If we **did not have** a car while living in Canada, we **would** find it difficult to get about.	

16.3.1 Variations of Type 2

Use **might** or **could** in the main clause:
If he **worked** harder, he **might** pass the test.
If I **had** a printer, I **could** make some copies for you.
Use **would be** or **might be + -ing** in the main clause:
If I **were** you, I **would be eating** much less red meat.
If she **was** on holiday, she **might be cruising** in the Mediterranean too.
Use the past progressive (continuous) in the **-if** clause:
If we **were going** by ship, we **would feel** much more relaxed.
If my printer **was working** properly, you **could use** it to print your letters.

16.4 Type 3 conditionals. *Typical sentence: If we had left home earlier, we would not have been late.*

The time is past. The event or action in the **if**-clause did *not* happen, so what the main clause says is not true. The typical sentence above means that *we actually did not leave home earlier and so we were late.* Thus, Type 3 conditionals are used when we look back to the past and guess about what might have been. In other words, it is like, in hindsight, imagining a picture of things happening differently from how things really happened. Sometimes, this means pointing out people's mistakes; it may also mean regretting about the past.

Verb in **if**-clause Past perfect tense	Verb in main clause **would have** + past participle
If I **had known** that the sale was on, I **would have** gone to look for bargains.	
If you **had worked** more carefully, you **would have** passed the test.	
If he **had not answered** the phone call, he **would not have** burned his pizza in the oven.	

16.4.1 Variations of Type 3

Use **might** or **could** instead of **would** in the main clause:
*If I **had known** that the sale was on, I **might have** gone to look for bargains.*
*If he **had given** greater attention to the details of expression, he **could** have won.*
Use the continuous form of **would have been -ing** in the main clause:
*If I **had** not **fallen** ill last week, we **would have been touring** with our children in Europe now.*
Use the past perfect progressive (continuous) in the **if**-clause:
*If I **had** not **been wearing** a seat belt, I **would have been** badly **injured** in the accident.*
Had in the **if**-clause (in all sentences above) can be placed first before the subject, and omit **if**:
***Had I known** that the sale was on, I **would have** gone to look for bargains.*
***Had I not been wearing** a seat belt, I **would have been** badly **injured** in the accident.*

16.4.2 Mixing Type 2 and Type 3

You can mix Type 2 and Type 3, depending on what you want to express or stress in the **if-** clause and in the main clause.

Type 3 for the **if**-clause (for something that did not happen) and Type 2 (or some variation of it) for the main clause:
*If he **had worked** harder, he **would pass** the test.*
*If you **had not forgotten** your password, you **would have** no problem completing the transaction.*
*If we **had reserved** a table, we **wouldn't be waiting** here in a queue.*
Type 2 for the **if**-clause and Type 3 (or some variation of it) for the main clause:
*If your son **was** more careful, he **would have obtained** much better results.*
*If I **didn't have to take** the conference call, I **would have** joined your outing.*
*If you **needed** anything, you **could have** asked me.*

16.5   Using *will/would* and *should* in if-clauses

So far, you have not seen the auxiliaries **will/would** and **should** in **if**-clauses of conditional sentences. The following are some of their special uses.

---

if . . . will referring to a result:

Normally, a present simple tense in the **if**-clause expresses a condition under which some action is likely in the future, as in:

If I have time, I will write you.

Similarly, the **if**-clause is a condition in:

*We'll split the bill **if** it exceeds $1,000.*

But in the following sentence the **if**-clause is a result:

*We'll split the bill **if that will** make everybody feel better.*

---

if . . . will/would referring to willingness: (Using **would** is more polite.)

If you'll *tell me what you like to see, I'll make the arrangement.*

If you would *like to help, we would all be happy.*

If you'll *do as I tell you, you'll be safe.*

---

if . . . will/would used in polite requests: (Using **would** is more polite.)

(In a clinic)   ***If you'll*** *take a seat, the doctor will see you soon.*

(In a restaurant)   ***If you would*** *come this way, I'll show you to your table.*

(In a shoe shop)   ***If you would like*** *to try some other styles, I'll bring them round.*

(In a library)   ***If you would take the lift to the third floor****, you'll find the reference librarian's desk facing you a short walk after you exit from the lift.*

16.6 Inversion of subject and auxiliary (*were, had, should*)

The auxiliaries **were**, **had**, and **should**, which may appear in the **if**-clause, normally come after the subject. In more formal English, they may be placed before the subject. This is called "inversion". In this pattern, **if** is omitted, as illustrated in the second of each pair of sentences in the following box.

---

were (in a Type 2 conditional; this is the "subjunctive" use of **were** for unreal situations)

*If I **were** in his position, I **would do** something about time management.*

Were *I in his position, I **would do** something about time management.*

---

had (in a Type 3 conditional)

*If she **had** taken my advice, she **would have done** a better job.*

Had *she taken my advice, she **would have done** a better job.*

---

should (in a Type 1 conditional to mean that the action or condition is possible but not likely)

*If you **should** have any problems, just let me know.*

Should *you have any problems, just let me know.*

16.6.1 More examples of inversion of subject and auxiliary in conditionals

The following examples show only the part containing the inversion. You can always reconstruct the **if**-clause by restoring **if** and placing the auxiliary after the subject. The dots represent the main clause, which you may try to supply. The first sentence is done for you.

---

were (more common than **was** for unreal situations)

Were I to start all over again, . . .
(If I *were* to start all over again, I *would choose* a different career.)

Were I in her shoes, . . .

Were Johnny to apply for the job, . . .

had

Had he realized the significance of the project, . . .

Had I not lost my mobile phone, . . .

should

Should you decide to change your mind, . . .

Should I run into David whom I haven't seen a long time, . . .

16.7 *If it was/were not for* and *if it had not been for*

This is a common (and useful) way of saying that one particular event or situation is very influential or has important consequences. After **for**, you need to supply a noun or noun phrase.

To talk about the present or future: *If it was/were not for (If it wasn't/weren't for)*

If it wasn't/weren't for the ubiquitous mobile phone, taking pictures *would remain* a

laborious activity. (You can consider this as a variation of a Type 2 conditional.)

You can put **were** (but customarily not **was**) at the beginning and omit **if**:

Were it not for the ubiquitous mobile phone, taking pictures *would remain* a

laborious activity.

To talk about the past: *If it had not been for (If it hadn't been for)*

If it hadn't been for my cataract surgery, I *would have been* able to join your trip.
(You can consider this as a variation of a Type 3 conditional.)

You can put **had** in front and omit **if:**

Had it not been for my cataract surgery, I *would have been* able to join your trip.

More examples:

If it wasn't (or *weren't*) *for* your encouragement, I *would feel* totally helpless.

If it hadn't been for your support, I *could not have* done anything.

16.8 Some other ways of expressing unreal events, wishes, and instrumental conditions

As you can see by now, conditionals can come in different forms, sometimes even without using an obvious **if**-clause. Other ways of talking about unreal events, wishes, and instrumental conditions that make something happen include the use of **even if**, **unless**, **whether**, **otherwise**, **provided (that)**, and **if only.**

Clauses with **even if**, **unless**, **whether**, and **provided** (**that**) usually use the present tense.

even if

> She will not be absent from the examination **even if** she is not feeling well.

unless

> **Unless** you can catch the 8:30 shuttle bus you will be late for work. (= *If you cannot catch the 8:30 shuttle bus, you will be late for work.*)

whether

> You have to say something **whether** you know the answer or not. (= *You have to say something **even if** you do not know the answer.*)

otherwise

> You better put on a coat; **otherwise**, you will catch a cold. (= *If you do not put on a coat, you will catch a cold.*)

provided (that)

> We can return the merchandize for refund **provided that** we have the receipt.

if only

(a) Used with an unreal past, **if only** expresses hope or wish with a present meaning:

   (Note the use of the basic Type 2 conditional pattern.)

   If only I *had* more time (= I *wish* I had more time, but *If only* is more emphatic), I *would be able* to listen to a lot more music.

   When the topic of interest is clear from the context, the **if only** clause can stand by itself, without a main clause:

   If only I *had* more time!

(b) Used with a past perfect, **if only** expresses regret (about the past): (Note the adoption of the basic Type 3 conditional pattern.)

   If only we *hadn't forgotten* to shut the windows when we were out, the room *would have stayed* dry during the heavy rain.

   If only you *had been* more careful, you *would have avoided* the overdue fine.

(c) Used with **would** + infinitive (base form of a verb), **if only** expresses a wish for something to happen or to stop happening:

   If only more cruises *would* start from Hong Kong, we *could have* more voyages to choose from.

   If only the Covid-19 pandemic *would* come under efficient control, the gloom of a battered economy *could be* driven away.

16.9 Summing up

(1) **General logic**. Conditional sentences typically contain an **if**-clause, a subordinate adverbial clause, to refer to situations (A) that may or may not be true. Given these situations, an outcome statement (B) is made. The general logic is that the validity of (B) depends on the situation described in (A).

(2) **Basic structures.** There are three common basic structures:

1st conditional for factual or probable situations (**If he hurries, he'll make it**.)

2nd conditional for speculative situations (**If he hurried, he would make it**.)

3rd conditional for hypothetical and untrue situations (**If he had hurried, he would have made it**.)

(3) **Use of comma.** The **if**-clause often comes at sentence beginning. If so, a comma follows it (as in the three examples above). If the **if**-clause follows the main clause, no comma is used to separate them (**He'll make it if he hurries**).

(4) **Use of *would*.** Typically, but not necessarily, the word **would** is used only in the outcome statement (main clause).

(5) **Time reference.** The time reference in conditional sentences is not directly related to the verb tense used. Thus, for instance, in **if I won the competition**, the past tense verb **won** is not a real past pointing to past time but a statement about a speculative or imaginary event. Further, the use of a past perfect in, say, **if she had worked harder**, actually refers to something that did not happen at all.

(6) **Variations.** The three common structures of conditional sentences are not the only possible ones. As you have learned in this chapter, there are variations within each of the three common types. Mixtures of 2nd and 3rd conditionals are also possible. Indeed, **if** can be used with any normal combination of verb tenses (e.g., **If no one answered the phone last night and this morning, then he is probably out of town.**)

(7) **Other possibilities.** Other than **if**-clauses, a number of words and phrases may be used to construct conditional sentences to refer to unreal events, wishes, regrets, and certain instrumental conditions making things happen or not happen. These include **even if**, **unless**, **whether**, **otherwise**, **provided (that)**, and **if only.**

Exercises | **Chapter 16**

Exercise 16.1

Identify each of the following conditional sentences as Type 1 (possible situations), Type 2 (hypothetical situations), or Type 3 (events that did not happen):

辨認下面的條件句屬於哪類：第一類（可能的情況）、第二類（假設的情況）、第三類（不曾發生的事情）。

1. If I don't leave home before 8 a.m., I'll be late for work.   Type _____

2. Mr. Chu might have wanted to go to the show if he had known about it.   Type _____

3. If I were you, I would do some research on the company before the job interview.   Type _____

4. If she was playing her saxophone at midnight, her neighbours would complain.   Type _____

5. If I miss this train, I'll take the next one.   Type _____

6. If you had a million dollars, what would you do with the money?   Type _____

7. If I had not left my phone at home yesterday, I could have called you.   Type _____

8. Had I known that it was your birthday, I would have brought you a present.   Type _____

9. The audience would understand you better if you spoke more slowly.   Type _____

10. The accident would have never happened if the driver had seen the stop sign at the junction.   Type _____

Exercise 16.2

Complete the sentences by choosing the correct clause (a, b, or c):

選擇正確的從句 (a，b 或 c)，使每句得以完整。

1. If I had more money,
    a) I'll buy a new home.
    b) I had bought another home.
    c) I would redecorate my home.

2. If we had known that you planned to visit Hong Kong,
    a) we might be happy.
    b) we would look forward to it.
    c) we would have taken a few days off to show you around.

3. If you really cared about your son,
    a) you can take him to Ocean Park.
    b) you would spend more time with him.
    c) you will give him a good book.

4. If the weather worsens,
    a) we'll go home earlier.
    b) we would hide somewhere.
    c) we had to cancel the trip.

5.   If only you had come to the party,
     a) then you would not be sorry.
     b) then we would have had a great time.
     c) then it will be great fun.

6.   If you hurry up,
     a) you will be late.
     b) you may be late.
     c) you won't be late.

7.   If you have finished eating,
     a) I finished too.
     b) I would soon finish.
     c) I will clear the table.

8.   Were it not for Typhoon signal number 8,
     a) the ferries would be operating as usual.
     b) all bus services had been suspended.
     c) all subway lines are still running.

9.   I might have gone there
     a) if I knew that the book exhibition was on.
     b) if I know that the book exhibition was on.
     c) if I had known that the book exhibition was on.

10. She wouldn't accept that job
     a) even if she had been offered the job.
     b) even if she was offered the job.
     c) even if she will be offered the job.

Exercise 16.3

Fill in the blanks with the correct form of the verb given in parentheses, using **also, could, should,** or **would** where necessary.

在下列句子空白處填上括號中的動詞的正確形式。視乎需要，還可選擇使用 **also**、**could**、**should** 或 **would**。

1.   If I had known what to do, I _____ (do) it.

2.   It would have cost the company too much money if it _____ (agree to) the compensation package.

3.   Our project _____ (fall) behind schedule if it were not for her help.

4.   Had it not been for the sudden bad weather, our cruise ship _____ (berth) at the last port of call.

5.   If you _____ (run into) Ben (but not likely), give him my regards.

6.   I _____ (think about) it again if I were in your position.

7.   If you _____ (wait) here, I'll see if the manager is free.

8.   If you liked to go to that concert, you _____ (ask) me.

9.   She probably _____ (study) if she had known that there was a test yesterday.

10. I am not a good cook, but if I _____ (be) I would not have to eat out so often.

| Chapter 17 | **Put Related Items in Parallel Structure** |

What you will learn in this chapter

Parallel structure is the use of the same grammatical form (words, phrases, or clauses) to express related elements in a sentence. You will learn to recognize various patterns of parallel structure, including those using coordinating conjunctions (**and, but, or,** etc.) or correlative conjunctions (**both . . . and . . . , not only . . . but also . . . ,** etc.). You need to be sensitive to these conjunctions and some other words (**some, the, should, that,** etc.) as they may signal a need for parallel structure. Lists should also contain parallel forms. In short, through skillful use of parallel structure, your writing becomes clearer and more readable.

平行結構（parallel structure）是用同樣的語法形式（詞、短語或分句）來表達句子裏一些相關的元素。你會在本章裏學習辨認各種不同的平行結構，包括由並列連詞（如 and, but, or）或互聯連詞（如 both . . . and . . . , not only . . . but also . . . ）帶出的平行結構。你需要特別留意這些連詞和一些其他的詞（如 some, the, should, that），它們都可能表示這個句子需要用平行結構。此外，凡是列表項目都需依循平行結構寫出。簡言之，善用平行結構，你的寫作會更清楚易讀。

17.1   What is parallel structure?

Parallel structure (also called "parallel construction") is the use of the same grammatical form to express similar ideas or elements. Parallel words, phrases, and even clauses can indicate a close relation between sentence elements. When used appropriately, parallel structure helps to create coherence in a paragraph. That is, sentences in a paragraph "hang together" well around some theme.

17.1.1 Same grammatical forms

Examine the following sentence:

> *I have quite a few hobbies, such as taking pictures, go to swim, music, and travel.*

First, the sentence is ungrammatical. The hobbies named ought to be nouns or equivalents of nouns. **Go to swim** is not in the form of a noun-equivalent. For our purpose here, the problem with this sentence is how the hobbies are expressed. They should be expressed not in the way you just saw in the sentence, using different grammatical forms (**taking pictures** is a gerund phrase, **go to swim** is a verb phrase using a finite verb, and **music** and **travel** are nouns). Instead, they should all take the same grammatical form (gerund phrases for this sentence) as follows:

> *I have quite a few hobbies, such as taking pictures, swimming, listening to music, and travelling.*

17.1.2 Items in a series

The hobbies mentioned in the above sentence make up a "series", which is the simplest and the most common form of parallel structure. Now examine another sentence constructed with infinitives or infinitive phrases in a parallel structure to refer to a series:

> *My cousin loves to read, to sing, and to attend concerts.*
>
> Notice that the word **to** is placed before each item or before the first item only:
>
> > *My cousin loves to read, sing, and attend concerts.*
> >
> > (✗) *My cousin loves to read, sing, and to attend concerts.*

Alternatively, the same sentence can be written using gerund (**-ing**) phrases:

> *My cousin loves reading, singing, and attending concerts.*

17.2   Parallel structure in proverbs

It may be a helpful, though brief, exercise to see the presence of parallel structure in proverbs. Proverbs are usually concise and insightful statements of wisdom and good advice. Their messages tend to be quite effectively delivered through elements expressed in the same grammatical form. The following are some examples:

(1) *A bird in the hand is worth two in the bush.*

(2) *Two is company; three is a crowd.*

(3) *Man proposes; God disposes.*

(4) *The spirit is willing, but the flesh is weak.*

(5) *To err is human; to forgive divine.*

(6) *Where there is a will, there is a way.*

To recognize parallel structure, mainly you need to look for similarity in grammatical form. Take, for example, the third, the fourth, and the fifth proverbs from the above list:

Man proposes; God disposes. (subject + verb)

The spirit is willing, but the flesh is weak. (subject + be + adjective)

To err is human; to forgive is divine. (infinitive phrase + be + adjective)

You can see that the same grammatical structure is present in each of the two parts of each sentence. This is especially effective to show the contrast between two different ideas in each statement (man vs. God; spirit vs. flesh; to err vs. to forgive).

17.3 Why parallel structure?

The following are the main benefits of using parallel structure in writing:

- The relation between equally important elements is clearly shown (e.g., **spirit** versus **flesh**).

- The sentence holds together well (when its details point to the main message).

- The sameness in grammatical form tightens the prose through balance and rhythm and aids reading with understanding because a sentence containing parallel structure reads smoothly and easily.

17.4 Parallel words, phrases, and clauses

The elements appearing in a parallel construction can be single words, phrases, or clauses. You should become more familiar with parallel structure after examining the following examples carefully:

Single words in parallel structure

*Culture consists of the learned pattern of **thinking**, **feeling**, and **acting** that characterize a society.* (gerunds)

*His argument in defence of his innocence is **simple** but **convincing**.* (adjectives placed after the nouns they modify)

*A group of good friends enjoy a **direct**, **intimate**, and **cohesive** relationship with one another.* (adjectives placed before the nouns they modify)

*He didn't go to work on **Monday** nor on **Tuesday**.* (nouns)

Phrases in parallel structure

***Choosing a topic** and **drafting an outline** are the first steps in the writing process.* (gerund phrases)

*For main course, I think I will have the **roasted duck breast** rather than the **grilled lobster**.* (noun phrases)

***To lower costs** and **to maintain operating efficiency**, fast-food restaurants adopt standardization as far as possible.* (infinitive phrases)

*Students spend their time **reading books**, **doing assignments**, and **hanging out with their friends**.* (participial phrases)

Clauses in parallel structure

*A community is made up of people **who share a feeling of common identity** and **who are held together by some form of interaction**.* (adjective clauses)

***Whether the story was true** or **whether some rumour was being circulated**, you should not have believed it so easily.* (adverbial clauses)

*I have no idea **how the dispute started** and **how things have become so messy**.* (noun clauses)

17.5 Uses of parallel structure

From the above, you should have noticed that conjunctions—more specifically, coordinating conjunctions (**and**, **or**, **but** are among the most common ones)—are used to connect elements in parallel structure. This is one main use of parallel structure. There are two other main uses, as shown below.

Parallel structure is used for:
(a) Elements connected by coordinating conjunctions (**and**, **but**, **or**, **nor**, **yet**) See most of the sentences in box in 17.4.
(b) Elements connected by paired correlative conjunctions (**both . . . and**; **either . . . or**; **neither . . . nor**; **not . . . but**; **not . . . but rather**; **not only . . . but also**; **whether . . . or**) *The subtitles of the film are **both** in English **and** in Chinese.* *Great statesmen **both** profess noble governing aims **and** make wise political decisions.* *We can vote for **either** candidate A **or** candidate B.* (Alternatively: ***Either** we vote for candidate A **or** we vote for candidate B.*) *Competition is **not** just about winning **but** about doing one's best.* *What is important in one's education is **not** grades **but rather** learning new things.* *Doctors work **not only** to diagnose ailments **but** (**also**) to prescribe treatment.* (The word **also** may be omitted. See more in 17.5.1) ***Whether** you want to choose from the set dinner menu **or** you want to select a la carte is all up to you.*
(c) Elements being compared or contrasted (using, for example, **rather than**, **as opposed to**, **more . . . than**) *Nowadays children enjoy watching animation films **rather than** reading books.* (The two parallel elements are gerund phrases.) *Most tourists want to take photographs **rather than** buy picture post cards.* (Note that when simple verbs appear on both sides, **rather than** is usually followed by the bare infinitive without **to**.) *Members of my family habitually like Chinese food **as opposed to** Western cuisine.* *The focus of this movie is **more** on action **than** on plot.* *Righteousness in God's eyes is **more** about faith **than** about good deeds.* (Note carefully that the prepositions **on** and **about** must be repeated in the last two sentences.)

17.5.1 Special attention when you use *not only . . . , but also . . .*

> You use **not only . . . , but also . . .** when you have, for example, these two clauses in mind (note how the words **also** and **but** may be omitted):
>
> *We watch movies to be entertained.*
>
> *We watch movies to appreciate good acting.*
>
> ⇨ **(A)** *We watch movies **not only** to be entertained **but** (**also**) to appreciate good acting.*

Alternatively, you can start the sentence with **not only**, followed by the auxiliary **do**, before the subject **we**:

> **(B)** *Not only do* *we watch movies to be entertained,* (**but**) *we also do so to appreciate good acting.*

Note that both forms, (A) and (B), are possible when the original two clauses have the same subject (**we**). However, when the two clauses have different subjects, only form (B), starting with **not only**, is possible. Study the following:

> *The movie was highly entertaining.* (subject: **the movie**)

> *We saw a lot of good acting.* (subject: **we**)

> ⇨ *Not only was* *the movie highly entertaining,* (**but**) *we also saw a lot of good acting.*

(✘) ~~The movie was not only highly entertaining, but we also saw a lot of good acting.~~

17.6   Some useful tips on using parallel structure

(1)   Check how you present a series of infinitives or infinitive phrases. The word **to** can be put before each item of the series or just before the first item, as mentioned earlier (17.1.2). However, if you have long items, it is better to place **to** before each infinitive phrase:

> *A beginner swimmer needs **to feel** comfortable with water, **to practise** modified breathing, and **to learn** the correct movement of hands and feet.*

(2)   Coordinating conjunctions are often used in creating parallel structure. Each time you do so, check carefully that the elements linked by these conjunctions (such as **and**, **or**, **but**, **yet**) are in the same grammatical form.

>   adv   adj   adv   adj   adv   adj
> *She is unmistakably modest **yet** easily approachable **and** genuinely sincere without*
>   n   n
> *aloofness **or** coldness.*

Inspect this sentence closely and you should notice that this sentence takes the pattern:

> **She is** A **yet** B **and** C.

To achieve parallelism, A, B, and C each consists of an adjective premodified by an adverb. C is then extended to: **without** D **or** E (where both D and E are nouns)

(3)   Distinguish between (a) a compound sentence containing two subject-verb parts and (b) two verbs referring to one subject:

(a) ***She made*** *a large bowl of salad, and **she prepared** a cake as dessert.*

(b) *She **made** a large bowl of salad and **prepared** a cake as dessert.*

You need to place a comma before **and** in a) but not in b). Both sentences contain parallel structure. The second sentence is more natural.

(4) Parallel structure is not always word for word. The essential requirement is that the elements connected are in the same grammatical form.

*He attributes the rise of these Chinese technology firms to **being** at the right time and **being** focused on execution and after-sales service.*

In this sentence, two gerund phrases (**being** + adjective phrase) make up the parallel structure. The adjective phrase in the first part is a prepositional phrase with adjectival function here. The adjective phrase in the second part contains adjective + preposition + noun phrase. When introduced by **being**, the combination becomes a gerund phrase.

(5) Parallel structure can be established not only within but also across sentences. You can use parallel structure with variation and flexibility to make your writing clear and readable. The following example illustrates this.

*The coronavirus pandemic has brought **not only** anguish and suffering to those infected **but also** a feeling of uncertainty and helplessness to many others. Even for those who are fortunate enough to remain healthy and uninfected, life has already been significantly different. Indeed, this global pandemic has been an unprecedented reckoning. It has been a time **to consider what life means**, a time **to re-evaluate priorities and commitments**. It has also been a time for Christians **to examine how they may still relate meaningfully to God and other people.***

Note how **not only** and **but also** introduce parallel elements (long noun phrases) in the first sentence. Note also that parallel structure is used across the last two sentences, each containing one or more infinitive phrase (in boldface).

(6) Pay attention to parallel structure signals. These are words (e.g., articles; determiners like **some**, **other**, and **any**; auxiliaries like **can** and **should**; prepositions like **for**; and conjunctions like **that** used to introduce clauses) that are often (though not always) repeated to make the parallel structure stand out. This is important especially when you have long parallel items as illustrated by the sentences in the box

below. To strengthen your familiarity with parallel structure, try to identify and recognize the structure of the parallel items in these sentences.

Some news reports are to be skimmed, others to be digested in detail.

There are basically three kinds of workers: the uncommitted who can't wait to be off work, the orderly ones who just want to do their job, and the dedicated who are simply workaholics. (Note the presence of relative clauses that help to form parallel items here.)

A good leader should always be willing to listen to others and should never fail to let his followers see the larger picture.

This film is for people who like music and for those who enjoy stories set in the 18th and 19th centuries.

She told her parents that she likes to draw and that she wants to be an artist.

Parents' praise for their children can keep them well behaved, but indiscriminate and excessive praise can make them complacent and proud.

17.7   Maintaining parallel structure in vertical lists

You create a vertical list (vertical so that it may be more easily read) to enumerate components of something, or to summarize important points, descriptions, instructions, or stages in a process. The elements of your list should be parallel in structure to enhance reading and understanding.

A faulty list (elements not parallel)	An improved list (elements parallel)
The government will consider these tasks seriously:	The government will consider these tasks seriously:
1. Build more public housing	1. Building of more public housing
2. Reviewing education system	2. Review of education system
3. Scientific research should be supported	3. Increased support of scientific research
4. A growing promotion of the arts	4. Greater promotion of the arts

17.8   Examples of parallel structure in the words of famous characters in history

Now that you have seen and learned the basic patterns of parallel structure, it will be good for you to take a close look at the following selected words of some well-known characters in the Bible, in literature, and in history. See how parallel structure containing similar grammatical forms is used to capture main ideas clearly for the reader with considerable impact. The effect is direct and forceful.

---

(1) *"I am the bread of life. Whoever comes to me will never go hungry, and whoever believes in me will never be thirsty."* (Jesus Christ, in Holy Bible, John 6: 35)

(2) *"Love does not delight in evil but rejoices with the truth. It always protects, always trusts, always hopes, always perseveres."* (Apostle Paul, in Holy Bible, 1 Corinthians 13: 6-7)

(3) *"It is a far, far better thing that I do than I have ever done; it is a far, far better rest that I go to than I have ever known."* (Last statement in Charles Dickens, *A Tale of Two Cities*,1859)

(4) *"Ask not what your country can do for you; ask what you can do for your country."* (J. F. Kennedy, Presidential inaugural address, 20 January 1961)

(5) *"One of the biggest responsibilities of the educated women today is how to synthesize what has been valuable and timeless in our ancient traditions with what is good and valuable in modern thought."* (Indira Gandhi, speech on "What Educated Women Can Do", 23 November 1974)

Note: Sentences (3) and (4) could each be split into two sentences and still retain parallel structure across sentences:

It is a far, far better thing that I do than I have ever done. It is a far, far better rest that I go to than I have ever known.

Ask not what your country can do for you. Ask what you can do for your country.

17.9 Summing up

Here are the main points of this chapter:

(1) Parallel structure is a strategy of writing that expresses similar ideas or elements in the same grammatical form (e.g., same word class, same type of phrase, same type of clause).

(2) Parallel structure makes your writing clear so that readers will find it easier to read and understand you.

(3) You should consider using parallel structure for a series or a set of related items. These items are the elements that should be expressed in the same grammatical form.

(4) The elements that are parallel can be single words, phrases, or clauses within a sentence or across sentences.

(5) Elements in a parallel structure can be linked by coordinating conjunctions (**and**, **but**, **or**, **yet**, etc.), correlative conjunctions (e.g., **both . . . and . . .**; **not only . . . but also . . .**; **either . . . or . . .**, etc.), or such words as **rather than**, **as opposed to**, and **more . . . than . . .**

(6) Pay special attention to long infinitive phrases.

(7) Note how some words, serving as parallel structure signals, introduce parallel elements. If the same signal word is used to introduce multiple elements, that word may need to be repeated.

(8) Elements appearing in a list (with elements in words, phrases, or even clauses) should be presented in parallel structure.

Exercises   Chapter 17

Exercise 17.1

Underline the elements in the following sentences that are parallel.

將下列每個句子中相互平行的元素劃上底線。

1. In the summer camp, children live together to learn how to care for and cooperate with one another.

2. Schooling offers development of the mind and of the body.

3. Success is not without fears and failure is not without hopes.

4. Mr. Wong has been teaching for many years, always disciplined but kind towards his students and serious but passionate in his work.

5. A church congregation consists of people who share a common religious faith and who develop a sense of identity in worship and prayer.

6. Service workers are worried that they were losing their jobs and that the government offered no assistance.

7. Hong Kong is known for its freedom of doing business, efficiency of financial institutions, and rule of law.

8. Any person intending to start a business is concerned with obtaining sufficient seed money, creating a need for the proposed business and finding a suitable location.

9. Competition is not just about winning but also about doing your best.

10. Children enjoy watching images on their smart phones rather than reading story books.

Exercise 17.2

Circle the letter representing the sentence that contains correctly set up parallel structure.

下面每組句子都有三個版本，只有一個含正確的平行結構。把代表正確句子的字母圈起來。

1. (a) A good manager must set goals, willing to hear criticism, and able in taking responsibility for decisions.

    (b) A good manager must set goals, willing to hear criticism, and able to take responsibility for decisions.

    (c) A good manager must be ready to set goals, willing to hear criticism, and able to take responsibility for decisions.

2. (a) Mommy will wash the vegetables, mince the pork, and steaming the fish.

    (b) Mommy will wash the vegetables, mince the pork, and steam the fish.

(c) Mommy will get the vegetables washed, mince the pork, and have the fish steamed.

3. (a) You can either choose soup or salad.

    (b) Either you can choose soup or salad.

    (c) You can choose either soup or salad.

4. (a) We not only visited Tokyo but also Osaka.

    (b) We visited not only Tokyo but also saw Osaka.

    (c) Not only did we visit Tokyo but we also saw Osaka.

5. (a) As Tony started university, his goals were to make new friends and to be well educated.

    (b) As Tony started university, his goals were making new friends and to be well educated.

    (c) As Tony started university, his goals were to make new friends and becoming well educated.

6. (a) We prepared a report in both Chinese and in English.

    (b) We prepared a report both in Chinese and in English.

    (c) We prepared a report both in Chinese and English.

7. (a) Our group consists of people who love travelling and taking pictures and who enjoy sampling exotic cuisines.

    (b) Our group consists of people who love to travel and taking pictures and who enjoy sampling exotic cuisines.

    (c) Our group consists of people who love travel and to take pictures and who enjoy to sample exotic cuisines.

8. (a) Choosing a topic and construct an outline are the first steps in the writing process.

    (b) To choose a topic and constructing an outline are the first steps in the writing process.

    (c) Choosing a topic and constructing an outline are the first steps in the writing process.

9. (a) We can vote for either candidate X or for candidate Y.

    (b) We can vote either for candidate X or candidate Y.

    (c) We can vote for either candidate X or candidate Y.

10. (a) Most people buy clothes for more of their style than how durable they are.

    (b) Most people buy clothes more for their style than for their durability.

    (c) Most people buy clothes more for style than they are durable.

Exercise 17.3

Revise the following sentences so that they contain elements parallel in structure. Rephrase (change wording) as necessary. There may be more than one solution.

改正下列病句，使句子含正確的平行結構。如有需要，措辭可作合適的改動。或有多種修改方法。

1. To get along with their teenage children, parents need to be patient, tactful, and to have tolerance.

    _____

2. The doctor warned her not to smoke, drink, or eating spicy foods.

    _____

3. Swimming in the pool and to ride a bicycle in the country park are his favourite pastimes.

    _____

4. In setting up our project team, we looked for members whose work was innovative, with diverse interests, and who had endless energy.

    _____

    _____

5. Optimism, sincerity, and being a good thinker are three important qualities of a successful sales representative.

    _____

    _____

6. Our dilemma is obvious: we must either reduce costs or we must diversify income sources.

    _____

7. It is not how you think but your action that counts.

    _____

8. Given adequate training, workers can acquire the skills and interest in a variety of jobs.

    _____

9. We watch movies not only to kill time but we can see the interplay between characters.

    _____

10. Before you write an essay or taking an examination, you need to organize your thoughts.

    _____

11.   We may realize the relativity of social reality and see that there is always a hidden side of society.

_____

12.   It is possible that most welfare recipients want to work rather than social welfare payments.

_____

Chapter 18	Strengthen Your Word Skills

What you will learn in this chapter

We have, in the previous chapters, examined a variety of specific skills of using English correctly and appropriately for writing good English. However, to be truly competent in writing, you need to also focus on words themselves.

How well do you know your English words? This question involves much more than just words' meanings. You will learn that good word skills include familiarity with word roots (such as prefixes and suffixes), word combinations, words in idiomatic phrases, synonyms and antonyms, compound words, and confusable words. Not an easy task!

我們在前面各章探討了許多正確恰當使用英語的具體技巧，能幫助我們寫出地道的英語。不過，要真正掌握寫作，還需在字詞方面多下功夫。

你對英語詞彙的認識有多深呢？這問題所包括的其實遠不止詞議。要真正認識英語的字詞，還要熟悉英語單詞的詞根〔包括前綴（prefixes）和後綴（suffixes）〕、詞的搭配、慣用短語中的用詞、同義詞與反義詞、複合詞和容易混淆的詞。所以，用詞要得心應手，實在不易。

18.1   **What are word skills?**

18.2   **Word roots: the foundation of word skills**

18.3   **Use a good dictionary.**

18.4   **Word class (part of speech)**

18.5   **Meanings**

18.6   **Spelling**

18.7   **Pronunciation**

18.8   **Collocations (common combinations with other words)**

18.9   **Idiomatic phrases**

18.10 **Words with similar and opposite meanings**

18.11 **Compound words**

18.12 **Confusable words**

18.13 **Summing up**

18.1 What are word skills?

Simply put, word skills constitute the ability to use words properly and effectively. These skills grow from familiarity with the following:

- Word class (part of speech)

- Meanings (a given word can have multiple meanings)

- Spelling (including spelling variation according to grammatical function)

- Pronunciation

- Common combinations with other words (collocations)

- Idiomatic phrases

- Words with similar (synonyms) and opposite (antonyms) meanings

- Compound words

- Confusable words

As will be shown later in this chapter, you can develop a wealth of knowledge of words in all these aspects if you have a regular habit of using a good dictionary.

18.2 Word roots: the foundation of word skills

Before surveying these aspects, let us first take a quick peep at "word roots". They are "fragments" (with Latin and Greek origins) from which words are made, including fragments that come at the beginning, called "prefixes", and those that come at the end, called "suffixes". If you know a fair number of them well, it helps to strengthen your knowledge of words and enhances your ability to recognize or guess the meaning of new words that you come across in reading. A good knowledge of word roots certainly is an advantage in boosting your word skills for writing good English.

To whet your appetite for the study of word roots, the following gives you only a listing of selected prefixes, suffixes, and other word roots. You are probably familiar with many of them; they are included here to give you a brief overview of their diversity. Each entry is accompanied by several example words to help you see and remember the meanings. You can try to add example words that you know of to reinforce your understanding.

18.2.1 Prefixes

Prefixes come at the beginning of a word to form a new word without any change to the spelling of the base word. Sometimes, a hyphen comes between the prefix and the base word (e.g., **pre-arranged**).

Prefix	Meaning	Examples
ab-	away from, not	*abnormal, abstract, absolve, abstain*
anti-	against	*anticlockwise, antibiotic, antisocial*
auto-	self	*autobiography, automatic, autonomous*
bi-	two, twice	*bicycle, bicentenary, bifocal, biweekly*
com-	together	*combine, commit, compare, compress*
de-	remove, undo	*decompose, deforest, defrost, dehydrate*
dis-	not	*disagree, dishonest, disrespect, distrust*
il-	not	*illegal, illegible, illiterate, illogical*
im-	not	*imbalance, immoral, impatient, impossible*
in-	not	*incomplete, incredible, indirect, inhuman*
inter-	between	*interface, intermission, international*
mini-	small	*miniature, minibar, minibus, minimum*
mis-	wrong, bad	*misfortune, misspell, mistake, misunderstand*
non-	not	*nonfiction, nonsense, nonstop, nonviolent*
pre-	before	*pre-arranged, predict, prepare, prevent*
pro-	for, forward	*proceed, pro-choice, proclaim, propel*
re-	again, back	*recurrent, repeat, report, return, revive*
tele-	from afar	*telecast, telephone, telescope, television*
trans-	across	*transform, transition, transmit, transport*
ultra-	extremely, beyond	*ultra-high, ultramodern, ultraviolet, ultrasound*
un-	not	*unclean, uncertain, unhappy, unsatisfied*

18.2.2 Suffixes

Suffixes can be added at the end of a word to form a new word, often changing the class of the word (e.g., from a verb or noun to an adjective). The spelling of the ending of the base word may change (e.g., **extend → extension**).

Suffix	Meaning	Examples
-able	able to	*enjoyable, memorable, portable, workable*
-ible	able to	*edible, permissible, possible, transmissible, visible*
-al	related to	*maternal, national, personal, regional, social*
-ance	state, quality, act	*attendance, dominance, performance, resistance*
-ence	state, quality, act	*competence, dependence, patience, residence*
-ary	related to	*documentary, elementary, preliminary, sanitary*
-ate	become, having the quality of	*affectionate, captivate, dehydrate, passionate*
-dom	state, quality	*boredom, freedom, kingdom, serfdom, wisdom*
-en	become, to make	*broaden, deepen, harden, loosen, strengthen*
-er	person who does a job	*baker, courier, lawyer, teacher, worker*
-er	more	*faster, harder, lower, nicer, prettier, tastier*
-ful	full of	*careful, cheerful, hopeful, powerful, restful*
-hood	state, quality	*childhood, likelihood, manhood, parenthood*

Suffix	Meaning	Examples
-ic	related to	basic, heroic, fantastic, organic, rhythmic
-ion, -tion	state, quality	action, completion, election, graduation, promotion
-ition	action, state	competition, opposition, position, repetition
-ish	fairly, related to	boyish, childish, foolish, selfish, yellowish
-ism	state, quality, action, belief, prejudice	absenteeism, escapism, impressionism, materialism ageism, collectivism, dogmatism, racism, sexism
-ity	state, quality	clarity, continuity, humility, nobility, reality
-ive	having the power of	active, expensive, compulsive, massive, productive
-ize	to make, to act	legalize, mobilize, popularize, realize, organize
-less	without	careless, endless, fearless, hopeless, speechless
-ly	in the manner of	erroneously, friendly, gently, motherly, personally, properly, readily, really, steadily, wickedly
-ment	state, quality, act	agreement, engagement, enjoyment, resentment
-ness	state, quality	dizziness, friendliness, goodness, happiness, softness
-ology, -logy	study of	archaeology, biology, psychology, physiology
-ship	state, quality	hardship, friendship, relationship, workmanship
-sion	state, action	conclusion, decision, extension, provision, revision
-some	having the quality of	awesome, burdensome, troublesome, worrisome
-y	having the quality of, full of	creamy, foggy, gloomy, grassy, hilly, icy, rocky, roomy, sandy, shady, steamy, tricky, watery

18.2.3 Other word roots

While prefixes and suffixes appear at the beginning and the end, respectively, of words, there are many other roots that can be present anywhere—front, middle, or end—in words. Familiarity with them, like familiarity with prefixes and suffixes, is helpful in understanding and remembering the meaning of many words. The following box contains just some such word roots.

Root	Meaning	Examples
aqua	water	aquarium, aquatic, aqueous
bio	life	biology, biography, biochemistry
cycl	circle	bicycle, cyclone, cyclical, recycle
graph	to write	graphic, paragraph, choreograph
hydr	water	hydrant, hydrogen, dehydrate
hyper	over, above	hyperactive, hypersensitive, hypertension
ident	same	identity, identical, identification
lingu	language	bilingual, linguistics, linguist
log	word, discourse	dialogue, eulogy, logic, monologue
memor	to remember	memory, memorandum, commemorate
min	less, little	diminish, minority, minimize
numer	number	enumerate, numerical, numerous
orn	to decorate	adornment, ornate, ornament

Root	Meaning	Examples
ped	foot	*pedal, pedestrian, impede*
phon	sound	*phonetics, phonograph, telephone*
qual	what kind	*quality, qualify, qualification*
rupt	to break	*abrupt, disrupt, interrupt, rupture*
san	healthy	*insane, sane, sanitary, sanatorium*
sci	to know	*conscious, conscience, science, omniscient*
sequ	to follow	*sequence, sequel, consequence*
tempor	time	*contemporary, temporary, temporal, tempo*

18.2.4 Why are word roots important?

When you read (books, magazines, newspapers), try to pay more attention to how some words begin and end, which will enable you to be more aware of prefixes and suffixes. Pick some words and see if you recognize any roots. Although the lists in 18.2.1 to 18.2.3 are not exhaustive, study them and use them as reference. Roots other than prefixes and suffixes may not be easy to identify.

Word roots are important for the following reasons:

(1)   **Word roots help you to understand and remember the meaning of a word**. For example, once you know and remember that **dis** means "not" or "negative" and **-ion** often signals the noun form of a word, you will find it easy to understand the meaning of the following words:

Word	Meaning
discolouration	colour becoming less attractive
disconnection	becoming not connected
disqualification	being stopped from doing something because of a certain inappropriate behaviour
disruption	a situation in which something cannot function normally
dissolution	the breaking up of a relationship or a system

Learning words this way makes the learning more interesting, which in turn strengthens your understanding and memory of words so learned.

(2)   **Word roots show patterns**. As you become more familiar with roots such as prefixes, you can recognize a certain pattern that will help you choose the appropriate prefix for a given word. Some examples follow:

Prefix	Meaning	Example words
mis- (often before verbs and nouns)	departure from accuracy or correctness	**miscalculate misconduct misinformation misrepresent**

Prefix	Meaning	Example words
dis- (often before verbs)	not doing something	**disagree** **discredit** **disengage** **dispossess**
un- (often before adjectives)	not	**unhappy** **uncommon** **unfavourable** **unscientific**

Complications exist, though. Thus, **non-, in-,** and **im-** (= not) are also quite commonly used before adjectives:

Prefix	Example words (all adjectives)
non-	**non-professional** **non-residential** **non-refundable** **non-specific**
in-	**inadequate** **incredible** **insane** **insensitive**
im-	**immobile** **imperfect** **impersonal** **impractical**

Further, an adjective may take two different prefixes to express somewhat different meanings. For instance, while **unscientific** means "not done in a scientific (careful, systematic) way", **non-scientific** means "not involving science". Similarly, **unprofessional** means not up to the standard in a particular profession whereas **non-professional** refers to "not holding any professional qualification" or "doing something not as a professional but only as an amateur".

(3) **Word roots help you to guess what a word means**. Of course, word roots are too numerous to remember correctly, but those that you know will help you to guess what an unfamiliar word means. This is especially so when you are already familiar with the basic meanings of certain prefixes and suffixes. You should keep in mind the meanings of the following groups of prefixes and suffixes:

Prefixes/suffixes	General meaning
de-, dis-, mis-, non-, un-	something negative, opposite, or removed
-ance, -dom, -ion, -ism, -ity, -ment, -ship	a condition or quality
-ate, -en, -ize, -sion	an action or process

Use your knowledge of these prefixes and suffixes as clues to guess what the following words probably mean. You should check your guess with your dictionary, though. If your guess is not correct, make sure you find out the correct meaning from the dictionary.

Word	Meaning
communicability	
depersonalize	
disintegration	
endurance	
insensitivity	
misalignment	
nonrefundability	
prefabrication	

18.2.5 Note the information on roots when you look up a dictionary.

If you use a good dictionary to look up a word, it may tell you the origin of the word by showing you the word's roots in Latin or Greek and what they mean.   Because the English language has various origins, word roots may vary in spelling. [Such variation may also depend on the word class (noun, verb, etc.) of the original root.]

Take the word **fabricate** for example. The *Concise Oxford English Dictionary* (12th edition, 2011) tells us it is from Latin *fabricat, fabricare*. It directs us to see the **fabric** entry, which tells us *fabric* is from French *fabrique* and from Latin *fabrica* meaning "something skillfully produced". So, **fabricate**, a verb, means (a) "invent in order to deceive" and (b) "construct or manufacture, especially from prepared components".

18.3   Use a good dictionary.

One main reason why many learners and users of English do not have a sufficiently strong vocabulary is that they do not make the effort to look up the meaning and related information of an unfamiliar word in a good dictionary. This is simply an essential task you cannot avoid if you wish to elevate your competence with words to a level at which you can write (and speak) with confidence.

You may already have an electronic dictionary in your mobile phone, which may or may not be detailed enough. Use it by all means, but you should also have a larger dictionary (hard copy) at home or your work place for more thorough checking and searching. It is an investment that is both instrumental and worthwhile.

Now we are ready to survey briefly the kinds of information you can get from a dictionary (mentioned earlier in 18.1):

- Word class (part of speech)

- Meaning

- Spelling (including spelling variation according to grammatical function)

- Pronunciation

- Common combinations with other words (collocations)

- Idiomatic phrases

- Words with similar and opposite meanings

- Compound words

- Confusable words

18.4 Word class (part of speech)

Note any suffix associated with the class (e.g., **-ment** and **-tion** for nouns; **-ive** for adjectives and nouns; **-ate** for verbs) of the word you are looking up. If the word is a verb, particularly an irregular verb, note how it inflects (= varies in form) according to time (e.g., **fly, flew, flown**).

A given word may function as one or more classes (e.g., **control** is noun and verb). When this is the case, you should examine how the word actually functions in these different roles by studying the example sentences in the dictionary.

Often, you will likely see other forms (different word classes) of the word as separate entries in the vicinity (e.g., **complete** and **completion**; **instant** and **instantaneous**). You should make an effort to read them also.

18.5 Meanings

A word may belong to more than one word class (e.g., noun and verb.) For a given class, the word may have multiple meanings, which are often classified into themes or contexts using appropriate short labels following different numbers. You can use these numbers and labels, when given, to guide you to the meaning you want.

Thus, for example, the meanings of **raise** may be given under such labels as *move higher* (**raise your hand**), *increase* (**raise public awareness**), *collect money* (**raise money for charity**), *mention a subject* (**raise the question of safety**), *cause* (**raise doubts and fears in people's minds**), *bringing up children* (**raising four children under harsh conditions**), *animals or plants* (**raised cattle and corn**), and *dead person* (**God raised Jesus from the dead**).

If you desire to know a word more thoroughly, you might as well read through all meaning groups or contexts. You will remember the various meanings if you study the example sentences given for each meaning group.

18.6 Spelling

Try to memorize the spelling of an unfamiliar word and pay attention to any doubling of certain letters.

Although English spelling does not always correspond with pronunciation, it is generally useful to memorize a word's spelling by the syllable (e.g., **environment** is spelled *en-vir-on-ment*, **consumer** is spelled *con-su-mer*, and **necessarily** is spelled *ne-ces-sar-ily*).

Take note of other words derived from a main word. The spelling changes according to their grammatical role. Thus, referring to the main word **necessary,** other words given in separate entries include **necessitate** as verb and **necessity** as noun.

Correct spelling is certainly one quality of good written English. To minimize misspellings, you must pay careful attention constantly to the spelling of words, especially those with double letters, multiple syllables, and silent letters. The following is only a short list of selected words that are commonly misspelled.

Some commonly misspelled words:

accommodation   alphabetical   approximately   boycott

claustrophobia   commitment   contemporary   definition

encyclopaedia   exaggerate   fluorescent   guarantee

immigrant   innovation   liaison   maintenance   miscellaneous

necessary   noticeable   possession   privilege   pronunciation

refrigerator   rhythm   rendezvous   symmetrical   schedule

twelfth   unanimous   vaccinate   vicious   Wednesday   yacht

18.7   Pronunciation

This is usually marked in IPA (International Phonetic Alphabet). If you do not know IPA, learn it to know how to pronounce words correctly with the right sounds and the proper stresses. Sometimes, a word may be pronounced in more than one way (e.g., **controversy, laboratory, medicine**), including possible differences between British and American English. In addition, the place of stress may be different for the noun form of a word and the verb form. Thus, **import** and **contract** as nouns have stress on the first syllable, whereas as verbs they have stress on the second syllable. If you do not know the difference, you are likely to make mistakes in speaking.

Although the main concern of this book is writing, some reminders about proper pronunciation are needed here because proper pronunciation calls for greater attention to the spelling of words and differentiation between words that may be confused (and confusing to listeners) if pronounced incorrectly. Let me mention just a few important points as follows:

(1) Distinguish between the long *ee/ea* sound and the short *i* sound.	long **ee/ea** sound: **beat, feel, heel, leave, seat, sheep** short **i** sound: **bit, fill, hill, live, sit, ship**

(2) Distinguish between the long *a* sound /eɪ/ as in *day* and the short *a* sound /æ/ as in *man*.	long **a** sound: **claim, main, plain, rain, sail, sale, game**
	     Some common errors: **sales** mispronounced as **sells**;
	     game (/geɪm/) mispronounced as "**gam**" (/gæm/);
	     claim (/kleɪm/) mispronounced as **clam** (/klæm/)
	
	 short **a** sound: **man, plan, ran, fan, sand, gamble**

(3) Distinguish between voiced (= vocal cords in vibration) *th* and unvoiced *th*.	voiced **th**: **this, these, that, those, then, they, though** (The initial voiced **th** must NOT be pronounced as a **d**.) unvoiced **th**: **thank, thick, thing, three, month, north**
(4) Distinguish between voiced *v/ ve* and unvoiced *f*.	voiced **v**: **believe, serve, starve, van, very, vine, over** unvoiced **f**: **belief, serf, staff, fan, ferry, fine, offer**
(5) Use the correct stress. (Note which syllable carries the stress.)	**purchase** (1st syllable) **mechanism** (1st syllable) **mandatory** (1st syllable) **Manchester** (1st syllable) **contribute** (2nd syllable) **Janet** (1st syllable) **controversy** (1st syllable; BrE also 2nd syllable) **record** (n, /'rekɔːd/1st syllable); **record** (v, /rɪ'kɔːd/ 2nd syllable) n = noun, v = verb Try saying this: The conversation will be recorded (/rɪ'kɔːdɪd/).
(6) Pay attention to words ending in *d, t, f, ce, se,* and *ve*. The ending may change when the class of the word changes. Get used to pronouncing them properly, otherwise you may misspell the word when you write it.	**complain** (v) → **complaint** (n) **constrain** (v) → **constraint** (n) **defend** (v) → **defence** (n) **expend** (v) → **expense** (n) **respond** (v) → **response** (n) **receive** (v) → **receipt** (n) **resident** (n, person) → **residence** (n, place) **repentant** (adj) → **repentance** (n) **fragrant** (adj) → **fragrance** (n) **worse** (adj, comparative) → **worst** (adj, superlative) **prove** (v) → **proof** (n) **half** (adj) → **halve** (v) adj= adjective

(7) Be sure to pronounce the *-ed* ending audibly in the past forms of verbs following a *d* or *t*. If you habitually ignore or miss this sound, your past tense verbs in your writing may miss the *-ed* ending too.	/dɪd/: **boarded, decided, extended, founded** (= established)
	     provided, intended, rounded, scolded, sounded, tended
	
	 /tɪd/: **credited, doubted, fainted, mounted, noted, pointed,**
	     rested, sighted, sorted, wanted

18.8 Collocations (common combinations with other words)

Words in English come together in a way that is natural to the native speaker of the language.

Collocations are simply the *natural and idiomatic combinations of words*. Thus, for example, we say

"**Did you have breakfast?**" and "**It's easy to make mistakes**", but not "**Did you eat breakfast?**" and not "**It's easy to have mistakes**". We generally say that **we make an effort** (not ~~pay an effort~~) **to do something** and we may want to conduct a **detailed** or **rigorous analysis** (but not ~~an intensive analysis~~ or ~~a deep analysis~~) of a problem.

Many expressions used in speech and writing are natural and idiomatic collocations, such as **bits and pieces, loud and clear, wear and tear, strike a balance**, **place an order, draw a conclusion**, **lay the groundwork**, **run the risk, set the pace**, **relieve pain**, and **gain trust**.

When you look up a word, your dictionary may give you some common collocations involving the word. Do pay attention to them and see how they are used in example sentences that the dictionary may also give you. Of course, there could be quite a variety of words that can combine idiomatically with a given word. The choice of which word to combine with often depends on the meaning intended. A different choice may well indicate a different shade of meaning (= slight or subtle difference in meaning). One advanced learner's dictionary, for example, offers quite a number of collocations under the headword **demand**. The following box shows just some of them (each with an example sentence not shown here):

Adjectives + **demand**

> *Huge demand*   *high/low demand*   *increasing/growing demand*   *falling demand*

Verbs + **demand**

> *Meet/satisfy demand*   *keep up with demand*   *cope with demand*   *boost/reduce demand*

Phrases

> *Be much in demand*   *supply exceeds demand*   *a lack of demand*   *a surge in demand*

Sometimes, you may be looking for a suitable adjective to go with a particular noun. Thus, for instance, **clear, thorough, full, complete, adequate,** and **correct** are some possible adjectives that can come before and modify the word **understanding**.

If you wish to describe the understanding of something as inclusive of all relevant details, you could consider **full** (implying richness), **adequate** (implying suitability for a particular purpose), **complete** (implying nothing missing), or **thorough** (implying sophistication). I have given, in the parentheses, only a rough interpretation of what these four adjectives might imply when used to describe **understanding.**

For a more careful evaluation of which adjective is closest to expressing what you mean, you should look up these words separately or, better still, consult a thesaurus, which is a dictionary of words with similar meanings. If you also consult a dictionary of collocations and look up the headword **understanding**, you will most likely see adjectives within different groups of meaning that you can choose to modify **understanding.**

Let us next look briefly at the choice of verbs with a generally similar meaning to combine with different nouns as subject. Take the idea of "happen" as an example. It is an intransitive verb (does not take an object). It shares the same general meaning with such verbs as **occur, exist, arise, emerge, result, take place,** and **take shape**. The choice of word or phrase depends, then, on what subject (noun) we are referring to. The following are some typical combinations:

Something **happens**:

> *A condition **exists**.*
>
> *A conflict **breaks out** or **erupts**.*
>
> *A consequence **results** from some action.*
>
> *A discussion **develops**.*
>
> *An event or process **happens** or **occurs**.*
>
> *An idea **emerges** or **evolves**.*
>
> *A meeting **takes place**.*
>
> *A pattern or trend **emerges**.*
>
> *A plan or programme **takes shape**.*
>
> *A problem **exists** or **arises**.*

Both a thesaurus and a dictionary of collocations can be particularly helpful when you are concerned about the question of word combinations. In general, you use a thesaurus to look for words with similar meanings (e.g., what words share similar meanings with **happen**?). You use a dictionary of collocations to look for words that can combine with a particular word such as **emerge** (e.g., **trend + emerge** as noun + verb; **emerge + gradually** as verb + adverb).

18.9 Idiomatic phrases

These are phrases formed from the base or key word. Their meanings are not always immediately clear from the phrase itself (e.g., **beat about the bush** under **beat**, **cross your fingers** under **cross**, **come to a head** under **head**, **make much of something** under **make**, and **pull out all the stops** under **pull**). Also reflecting idiomatic use are **phrasal verbs**, which are verbs consisting of two or three words (e.g., verb + preposition: **stand by, touch on, grow into**; verb + adverb: **get away, pay off, pull through**; verb + adverb + preposition: **put up with, cry out for, move out of**).

When you look up a verb, try to go beyond knowing its basic meaning to find out the ways in which this verb can link up with an adverb or a preposition or both to function as a phrasal verb with a different meaning. Here are just a few phrasal verbs to whet your appetite:

Phrasal Verb	Meaning
come down to something	may be stated in one main point
drop by or *swing by*	to pay a short, casual visit to somebody
fit in with something	coexist nicely with something
get something over with	to finish something unpleasant but necessary
go through something	to experience a process; to practise something for performance; to look at something in detail
go over something	to inspect or study something carefully
move ahead	to proceed, often after some delay
put somebody up	to have somebody stay at your home
put up with somebody	to tolerate somebody who is annoying
put something across	to explain something to somebody clearly
put something together	to produce something by collecting parts or ideas
run out of something	to use up all of something
shy away from something or *from doing something*	to avoid something or doing something because you are not confident

To use phrasal verbs correctly in writing is not easy. If you take the time to look up even seemingly simple words like **get, look, make, put, take**, and **turn**, you will find that they are associated with a great number of phrasal verbs, all with meanings you cannot easily tell from the component words themselves. You must first understand them well, which you can do by reading and studying the explanations and example sentences provided by your dictionary. Try to memorize them as units. If you get yourself a dictionary of phrasal verbs and use it to supplement a regular English dictionary, your groundwork in phrasal verbs will be firmer.

18.10   Words with similar and opposite meanings

To enhance your word skills, you need to be *both* familiar with *and* able to distinguish between words that have similar meanings. Such words are called "synonyms". Though similar in meaning, they often have different connotations beyond the basic meaning and are thus used somewhat, or perhaps quite, differently. Most advanced learner's dictionaries provide information on selected words that are synonyms of the one you are looking up, and give example sentences to illustrate their differences. In some such dictionaries, boxes marked "thesaurus" are provided for some headwords, making the learning of synonyms more convenient.

Try looking up an adjective, such as **enough**, and your dictionary may, in a thesaurus box or in a box giving advice on word choice, compare it with synonyms like **sufficient** and **adequate**. You will find that **enough** is what you usually say to mean "as much as you need", while **adequate** means "good enough (but could be better in quality) for a particular purpose". **Sufficient** means the same as **adequate** but may not have the "could be better" connotation. Both **adequate** and **sufficient** are more formal in tone than **enough**. Besides **adequate**, words such as **acceptable** and **satisfactory** have about the same meaning with the "could be better" connotation. Thus, when an employee's performance is evaluated as "adequate", it is not a particularly positive statement because it implies that the employee's performance is merely "satisfactory" and could have been better.

"Antonyms" are words that are opposite in meaning to a given word. Dictionaries tend to give more attention to synonyms than to antonyms, especially for commonly used adjectives that have multiple meanings. In such cases, opposites may be given for only some particular meanings. For example, **rich** means, among other things, "wealthy", "full of detail", "strong and attractive (in colour)", "luxuriant (vegetation)", "containing much cream (in food)", and "good for growing plants (soil)". You may see **poor** given as the opposite of "wealthy" and "good for growing plants (soil)" and **light** as the opposite of "containing much cream (in food)". That is, **poor** is not wealthy, **poor** soil is not good for growing plants, and **light** food is not creamy.

This of course is not the only way to learn antonyms. When you have in mind a specific meaning of a particular word A, you can select, from what you already know, a word B that you think may be the opposite word you want. Then check your dictionary whether that word (B) conveys the right opposite meaning for your purpose. Thus, taking **rich** again as example, you may think of **poor**, **deprived**, and **needy** as all conveying the opposite meaning of "wealthy". Check the meanings of these three words in your dictionary to see which one is the word you want. Your choice depends on your intended meaning or connotation, which is something more than just the basic meaning (**poor** = having little money; **deprived** = without enough things necessary for a comfortable life; **needy** = having very little money or food and thus in need of help)

You can always look up a thesaurus or dictionary of synonyms, which usually gives you more choices. Although it concentrates on synonyms, antonyms are also given where appropriate. If you need the opposite of **rich** in the sense of "strong and attractive in colour", try looking under **colourful** in a thesaurus and you may find **colourless** and **drab** as opposites. Use your dictionary to check these two words. If you want a word that has the sense of not only "not bright in colour" but also "dull or not cheerful", then **drab** is the word you want.

As you learn more about words, you will soon realize that some words have relatively direct opposites and others do not. Thus, there are straightforward pairs such as **good** and **bad**, **young** and **old**, **long** and **short**, **top** and **bottom**, **far** and **near**, **quick** and **slow**, **happy** and **sad**, **accept** and **reject**. Then there are a good number of words (including many nouns) that form opposites when attached to appropriate prefixes or suffixes, such as **agree** and **disagree**, **understand** and **misunderstand**, **pleasant** and **unpleasant**, **polite** and **impolite**, **eligible** and **ineligible**, **participation** and **non-participation**, **unity** and **disunity**, **truth** and **untruth**, **conformity** and **nonconformity**, **advantage** and **disadvantage**, **hopeful** and **hopeless**, **troublesome** and **trouble-free.** The list can go on; it shows how useful your knowledge of prefixes and suffixes can be in expanding your vocabulary.

However, you should be cautioned that many words can have opposites or near-opposites other than by attaching to some prefix. Take **pleasant** for example, you can use a thesaurus to search for synonyms of **unpleasant**. If it does not list **unpleasant** as a main entry, check its index where you are likely to find **unpleasant** mentioned under the entries **bad** and **mean**. By this search, you may find quite a few synonyms of **unpleasant**, such as **annoying**, **miserable**, **nasty**, **objectionable**, and **irritating**, each having some specific connotation underlying what makes a situation **unpleasant.**

Indeed, you often need to think carefully about specific meanings and connotations when looking for opposites of words. Sometimes, a near-opposite may have the right connotation for you. Think of words such as **kind**, **lively**, **graceful**, **impressive**, **strengthen**, **thorough**, **trusting**, and **meticulous**. Each of them can have more than one near-opposite with a certain contrasting meaning. Thus, while **unkind** and **kind** are treated as direct opposites, **inconsiderate** or **not generous** and **kind** are not exact but near-opposites. You may decide that **inconsiderate**, rather than **unkind**, has the connotation you want for a particular statement (e.g., **It was rather inconsiderate of him to keep us waiting for nearly half an hour**).

You will soon realize that your choice of opposites is helped greatly by your knowledge of synonyms simply because there can be many words with similar meanings all serving as possible opposites or near-opposites of a given word. So, to take one more example, if you know that **trusting** means "tending to believe that other people are sincere and honest", you will consider **doubtful, cynical,** or **sceptical** as possible opposites.

18.11   Compound words

Compound words result from the combination of two or more words (may or may not be hyphenated) to indicate the coexistence of two or more elements. With developments in technology and modern living, compound words increase rapidly. A compound word functions as a single entity. Compound words can be nouns, verbs, or adjectives. They are usually listed as separate headwords according to their alphabetical order alongside other word entries. Sometimes, though, they are listed under the entry of the main word of the compound word (e.g., **the man in the street** under **man**). Some idiomatic expressions, listed under a given word may also be used as compound adjectives after hyphens are added (e.g., **once and for all** and **once in a blue moon** under **once: We come here once in a blue moon → This is our once-in-a-blue-moon experience**). If any of the following example words are unfamiliar to you, please look them up in your dictionary:

Compound nouns	General remarks
autofocusing *air conditioning* *bookshop* *five-year-olds* *ice cream* *intensive care unit* (ICU) *job description* *passer-by* *self-awareness* *wishful thinking*	At least one word in a compound noun is usually a noun (or a verbal noun) (e.g., **passer** in **passer-by**, **focusing** in **autofocusing**). Some compound nouns are written as one word (e.g., **bookshop**), some as separate words (e.g., **ice cream***), others as hyphenated words (e.g., **self-awareness**) Compound nouns can be subject or object in a sentence: *Five-year-olds can be quite sociable.* *These clothes are fit for five-year-olds.*
	*Some compound nouns ordinarily written as separate words are hyphenated to become a compound adjective placed before a noun (e.g., **ice-cream soda**, **ice-cream parlour**, **air-conditioning technician**).

Compound Verbs	General remarks
cross-examine *double-check* *dry-clean* *force-feed* *mismanage* *misinterpret* *overexpose* *overreact* *self-destruct* *stir-fry*	Compound verbs are usually composed of two words, one of which—typically the second—is a verb. Be careful with the inflection of the verb according to number (singular or plural), time (present or past), and voice (active or passive). Examples: *We have **double-checked** all the statistics in the report.* *She **stir-fries** many dishes expertly.* *In France, geese are **force-fed** to grow heavier with bigger livers.*
Compound adjectives	**General remarks**
across-the-board *all-encompassing* *above-average* *better-known* *computer-literate* *happy-go-lucky* *home-made* *low-profile* *made-to-measure* *matter-of-fact* *mind-boggling* *non-profit-making* *once-in-a-lifetime* *real-time* *self-centred* *user-friendly* *whole-hearted*	A compound adjective is formed by two or more words. When used before a noun, compound adjectives are usually linked by one or more hyphens. When used after a noun, hyphens are often not used: *She obtained **above-average** results in most subjects.* *Her results in most subjects are **above average**.* Not all compound adjectives can be used after a noun (e.g., **real-time**) Note that compound adjectives are formed by different types of word combinations, including noun + adjective (e.g., **user-friendly**), noun + past participle (e.g., **home-made**), adjective + noun + **-ed** (e.g., **whole-hearted**), and noun + **-ing** verb form (e.g., **mind-boggling**). Some compound nouns can be used adjectivally (e.g., **low-profile behaviour**, **real-time occurrence**)

18.12   Confusable words

Words may be confusable because of similarity in spelling, pronunciation, or meaning. They may look alike (**through, thorough**), sound alike (**principal, principle**), or may be closely related (**replace, substitute**). A careless writer is likely to use the wrong word for what he or she means to say. I once saw in a bookshop a label at the top of some shelves holding things like files, envelopes, writing pens, and paper. The label was **stationary**. That, of course, should have been **stationery**.

What you can do is make a collection of confusable words and study them carefully with the help of your dictionary and its example sentences. You need to know their differences *precisely* so that you will learn to use them correctly. Some examples of easily confused words are:

affect vs. *effect*	*every day* vs. *everyday*
board vs. *broad*	*imply* vs. *infer*
clean vs. *cleanse*	*intense* vs. *intensive*
close vs. *closed*	*lose* vs. *loose*
contain vs. *constrain*	*moral* vs. *morale*
continual vs. *continuous*	*past* vs. *passed*

desert vs. *dessert*	*principal* vs. *principle*
dinner vs. *diner*	*replace* vs. *substitute*
discreet vs. *discrete*	*seat* vs. *sit*
doubtful vs. *dubious*	*stationary* vs. *stationery*
emerge vs. *evolve*	*thorough* vs. *through*
eminent vs. *imminent*	*wave* vs. *waive*

18.13 Summing up

Words are building blocks of sentences. There is inevitably a close connection between your use of words and the quality of your writing. Good word skills (note the plural) result from a multi-dimensional understanding of words. You need good word skills to write well.

The advantages of good word skills are as follows:

(1)   Understanding the grammatical function (as a noun, verb, adjective, etc.) of words increases your ability to use them in a grammatical sentence.

(2)   Knowing the various meanings and connotations of words with generally similar and opposite meanings helps you to choose the right word to say what you mean.

(3)   Familiarity with the common combinations of words and how some of these combinations are idiomatic phrases with specific meanings is an important asset of writers. It helps you write natural and expressive English.

(4)   The correct use of compound words that have entered the English language in large numbers is instrumental for effective communication in modern society.

(5)   The English language contains many words that may be easily confused because of similarity in spelling, pronunciation, or meaning. If you know these confusable words well, you are not likely to misuse them and mislead your readers.

Chapter 18

Exercise 18.1

The following are prefixes that appear commonly in many words. Write in the space the letter representing the correct meaning of each prefix. Consult a dictionary if you need help.

以下是一些較為常見的前綴。在空白處寫上代表每個前綴正確意思的字母序號。如有需要可以查閱字典。

	Prefix	Example words	Meaning		
1.	mis-	mistake, misspell	_____	a.	over, above
2.	dis-	disagree, dishonest	_____	b.	extremely, beyond
3.	re-	repeat, revive	_____	c.	together
4.	com-	combine, compare	_____	d.	inside
5.	de-	decompose, defrost	_____	e.	not doing something
6.	ab-	abnormal, abstain	_____	f.	water
7.	pro-	propose, pro-establishment	_____	g.	across
8.	hyper-	hyperactive, hypertension	_____	h.	not
9.	bio-	biodiversity, biography	_____	i.	undo, remove
10.	aqua-	aquarium, aqueous	_____	j.	away from, not
11.	mar-	marine, maritime	_____	k.	before
12.	inter-	interact, international	_____	m.	from afar
13.	ultra-	ultramodern, ultraviolet	_____	n.	sea
14.	fore-	forecast, foresee	_____	o.	against, opposite
15.	endo-	endocrine, endoscopy	_____	p.	again, back
16.	contra-	contradict, contraception	_____	q.	departure from accuracy/correctness
17.	trans-	translate, transport	_____	r.	forward, support for
18.	pre-	preheat, prepare	_____	s.	life
19.	tele-	telescope, televise	_____	t.	between
20.	im-	improper, impure	_____	u.	before

Exercise 18.2

The following are suffixes that appear commonly in many words. Write in the space the letter representing the correct meaning of each suffix. Some suffixes have the same meaning. Consult a dictionary if you need help.

以下是一些較為常見的後綴。在空白處寫上代表每個後綴正確意思的字母序號。有些後綴意思相同。如有需要可以查閱字典。

	Suffix	Example words	Meaning		
1.	-ible	possible, visible	_____	a.	person who does a job
2.	-ance	dominance, resistance	_____	b.	state, quality
3.	-ary	documentary, preliminary	_____	c.	related to
4.	-ate	dehydrate, passionate	_____	d.	to make, to act
5.	-en	deepen, loosen	_____	e.	in the manner of
6.	-er	baker, lawyer	_____	f.	study of
7.	-hood	childhood, likelihood	_____	g.	able to
8.	-ic	basic, organic	_____	h.	state, quality, action, belief
9.	-ish	foolish, reddish	_____	i.	having the power of
10.	-ism	escapism, racism	_____	j.	state, quality, act
11.	-ity	reality, humility	_____	k.	having the quality of
12.	-ive	active, productive	_____	m.	become, having the quality of
13.	-ize	legalize, mobilize	_____	n.	fairly, related to
14.	-logy	biology, geology	_____	o.	without
15.	-ship	hardship, workmanship	_____	p.	become, to make
16.	-some	awesome, troublesome	_____		
17.	-ence	dependence, patience	_____		
18.	-ment	agreement, enjoyment	_____		
19.	-ly	friendly, personally	_____		
20.	-less	hopeless, speechless	_____		

Exercise 18.3

In the parentheses write T if the statement is true and F if the statement is false.

假如你認為下面的陳述是正確，在括號裏寫 T，否則寫 F。

1.　(　　) Some word roots have very similar meanings.

2.　(　　) Suffixes can be added at the beginning of a word.

3.　(　　) The word **contemporary** contains both a prefix and a suffix.

4.　(　　) Word roots can come only in front or end positions.

5.　(　　) Knowledge of word roots can help you understand the meaning of a word.

6.　(　　) Word root patterns help you choose the appropriate prefix for a given word.

7.　(　　) A given word always functions as one word class only.

8.　(　　) Meanings of a word in a dictionary may be given under multiple themes or categories.

9.　(　　) The spelling of a word may change according to its grammatical role.

10.　(　　) Words may be confusable because of similarity in spelling.

11.　(　　) Collocations are the natural and idiomatic combinations of words.

12.　(　　) "**Did you eat lunch?**" contains a natural collocation.

13.　(　　) There is a common collocation involving the word **effort** in this sentence: "**We spent a great effort to complete the task**."

14.　(　　) Different shades of meaning may be indicated by a different choice of an adjective to combine with a given word.

15.　(　　) Because we can say that "**an event takes place**", we can also say that "**a problem takes place**".

16.　(　　) "**To go over something**" means to skip something.

17.　(　　) A thesaurus is a dictionary of synonyms.

18.　(　　) Compound words can be nouns, verbs, or adjectives.

19.　(　　) A compound adjective is formed by two or more words linked by hyphens, which must be kept whether the compound adjective is used before a noun or after it.

20.　(　　) The meaning of a phrasal verb is clearly shown by the words it contains.

Exercise 18.4

Each sentence in this exercise contains an idiomatic expression known as a phrasal verb. Choose one of the three given phrases to indicate the correct meaning of the phrasal verb <u>as it is used in the sentence</u>.

以下練習裏的每個句子都含一個稱為"短語動詞"(phrasal verb) 的慣用語。句子之下有三個短語，你認為哪一個表達了該短語動詞在該句內的意思？請作出選擇。

1. **go through something**   *Let's **go through the whole song** one more time, from the beginning of the strings' introduction.*

    a. to look at a document in detail

    b. to practise something for performance

    c. to use up a supply of something

2. **put something across**   *The pastor is very skilful at **putting his biblical interpretation across** to the congregation.*

    a. to explain ideas to an audience successfully

    b. to pass along an object to your friends

    c. to place something across the width of a table

3. **put up with something**   *She has to **put up with his crazy ideas** without any objection.*

    a. to support something with a frame

    b. to accept something unpleasant without complaint

    c. to raise something to a high level

4. **drop by**   *He just **dropped by** to see how we were doing.*

    a. to let something fall

    b. to put something down at a particular place

    c. to visit somebody without special pre-arrangement

5. **go for something**   *You have to be well prepared to **go for that job**.*

    a. to make some sacrifice

    b. to leave because of some reason

    c. to try to get or achieve something

6. **take up something**   *She **took up tai-chi practice** a few years ago.*

    a. to begin an activity as an interest

    b. to carry something

    c. to start a job

7. **take on something**   *Her singing of this song **took on a more emotional tone**.*

   a. to accept some work or responsibility

   b. to have a particular character or quality

   c. to become disturbed

8. **get away with doing something**   *How can you let him **get away with insulting you** like that?*

   a. to take something away from somewhere

   b. to manage to do something wrong without getting any bad consequences

   c. to steal something and take it away successfully

9. **get something over with**   *She wanted to **get the exam over with** as soon as possible.*

   a. to do something unpleasant just because it is necessary, but you want it to be finished

   b. to gain control of something

   c. to make something reach a particular condition

10. **look out for something**   ***Look out for** this award-winning film coming soon.*

   a. to look carefully trying to find something

   b. to try to avoid some mistake or accident

   c. to search for some object from among your things

Chapter 19   Use Punctuation Carefully to Enhance Your Writing

What you will learn in this chapter

Punctuation is to writing as voice and gestures are to speaking. You will learn the functions of various punctuation marks in English writing. Using punctuation properly is a valuable asset to writers of English who want their writing to be effective and clearly understood.

標點符號之於寫作猶如語調與姿勢之於說話。在這章裏，你會學習英語寫作中各種標點符號的用法。學會善用標點符號能讓你如獲至寶，你的寫作會因此流暢達意。

19.1   **Why do we need punctuation?**

19.2   **Full stop (.) (period in AmE)**

19.3   **Comma (,)**

19.4   **Semicolon (;)**

19.5   **Colon (:)**

19.6   **Question mark (?)**

19.7   **Exclamation mark (!)**

19.8   **Quotation marks (double: " "; single: ' ')**

19.9   **Parentheses ( ) (also known as round brackets)**

19.10   **Dash (--) (typed by two consecutive hyphens, with no space before and after it)**

19.11   **Apostrophe (')**

19.12   **Hyphen (-)**

19.13   **Ellipsis (. . .)**

19.14   **Summing up**

19.1 Why do we need punctuation?

When we speak, we indicate what we mean and how we feel with the help of our voice level, facial expression, gestures, and pauses. We pause shorter or longer at various moments to coordinate with our speech. In writing, we do not have these devices. We can only rely on punctuation marks to convey some of those feelings and to show where we are in a series of thoughts.

Unfortunately, many students and users of English have not learned to use punctuation marks properly in their writing. This may cause unclear or misleading statements. Readers may find it difficult to follow the writer's train of thought. So, I strongly advise that you go through this chapter slowly and carefully to recognize the correct ways of using punctuation to enhance the quality of your writing.

19.2 Full stop (.) (period in AmE*)

*AmE= American English; BrE= British English

19.2.1 Use a full stop at the end of a complete sentence or sentence fragment (sentence without a verb) that is not a question or an exclamation.

We went to the Peak yesterday.   Lots of people there.

19.2.2 Place a full stop and a space after initials in personal names. If all initials are used instead of the name, full stops may be omitted and the initials are not spaced.

S. C. Yao SCY

J. F. Kennedy JFK

19.2.3 Full stops may or may not be used with abbreviations.

(a) Full stops normally needed:

a.m. p.m.   i.e. (that is)   *e.g.* (for example)   *etc.*

A.D. B.C.

(b) Full stops may be omitted in common titles, academic degrees, and some country names:

Dr   Mr   Mrs   Ms

PhD BA   MPhil MBA

UK   USA PRC

(c) Acronyms formed from the first letters of the names of organizations and acronyms pronounced as a word do not require full stops after the letters:

HSBC (Hong Kong and Shanghai Banking Corporation)

IBM (International Business Machines)

BBC (British Broadcasting Corporation)

WHO (World Health Organization)

NATO (North Atlantic Treaty Organization)

ASEAN (Association of South East Asian Nations)

(d) Abbreviations consisting of the first part of a word should end with a full stop:

Monday → *Mon.   February* → *Feb.*

(e) Abbreviations beginning with the first letter of a word and ending with the word's last letter may end without a full stop:

manager → *mgr   important* → *impt*

19.2.4 A full stop is not added at the end of a sentence that ends with an abbreviation with a full stop that is the last character of the sentence.

He has travelled to many European countries, including France, Germany, Italy, Switzerland, etc.

but

He has travelled to many European countries (France, Germany, Italy, Switzerland, etc.).

19.3   Comma (,)

19.3.1 A comma is often used to separate main clauses joined by a coordinating conjunction such as *and, but, for, or, so, yet.* Place the comma before the coordinating conjunction.

*She had planned a number of social activities during the Chinese New Year period, **but** the coronavirus scare forced her to cancel them all.*

*The symphony ended with a quiet note, **and** there was soon thunderous applause from the audience.*

19.3.2 It is incorrect to use a comma to join two main clauses without a coordinating conjunction.

This error is known as a "comma splice". To correct it, you can (1) insert a suitable conjunction after the comma, (2) replace the comma with a semicolon, or (3) split the sentence into two.

(✗) ~~We like travelling very much, we take three or four trips a year.~~

(✓) *We like travelling very much, and we take three or four trips a year.*

(✓) *We like travelling very much; we take three or four trips a year.*

(✓) *We like travelling very much. We take three or four trips a year.*

19.3.3 When correlative conjunctions (such as *either . . . or . . .* , *neither . . . nor . . .* , and *not only . . . but also . . .*) join long main clauses, use a comma to separate them.

Either you buy just one box of milk at full price, or you can buy a pack of three boxes for the price of two.

Not only does she supervise her three boys' homework every day, but she also takes care of all household chores and prepares dinner for the family.

19.3.4 Do not use a comma to separate a subject from its verb:

(✗) ~~Those youngest in the gathering, will be taken care of first.~~

(✓) *Those youngest in the gathering will be taken care of first.*

19.3.5 Use a comma to set off introductory words, phrases, and clauses.

Thus, nations must do everything possible to protect Planet Earth.

In brief, children imitate adults' speech as an important way of language learning.

Since we still have a large amount of work remaining, we might as well call it a day now.

19.3.6 Use a pair of commas to set off a parenthetical element (a word or phrase that is not part of the main statement) or a transitional expression (e.g., *however, therefore, for example*).

Albert Einstein, world-famous physicist in the twentieth century, developed the theory of relativity.

"Schindler's List", as far as I am concerned, is the best film about the persecution of Jews by Nazi Germany during the Second World War.

It seems, however, that you have misunderstood me.

19.3.7 Use a pair of commas to set off a non-restrictive (non-defining) relative clause. (See also 12.5 in Chapter 12 and 13.1.1 in Chapter 13.)

The apples, which were a new shipment, sold very well. (The information in the *which* clause is only incidental to the main statement. The clause is non-restrictive, requiring two commas to set it off in mid-sentence.)

The apples that were a new shipment sold very well. (The information in the *that* clause is essential in specifying which apples are being referred to. The clause is restrictive, and so no commas to set it off.)

19.3.8 Use commas between items in a series.

Leisure can be seen as time, activity, and experience.

A set lunch consists of appetizer, main course, coffee or tea, and dessert.

The last comma comes before *and* in the last item. Called the "serial comma", it is commonly used in AmE but optional in BrE. In general, a serial comma helps to clarify individual items in a series, especially when some such items contain two elements always linked by **and** (for example, phrases such as **law and order, peace and quiet, research and development, bed and breakfast, bread and butter, trial and error**).

> *People here are particularly concerned about job opportunities, cost of living, and law and order.* (*Law and order* is the final item in the series.)

19.3.9 Use commas between adjectives coming before a noun.

> *He is a dynamic, outspoken person.*
>
> *It is a cold, damp, windy day.*

Do not use commas between adjectives if the last adjective is more closely related to the noun than the other(s).

> *a pretty young lady* (main term: **young lady**)
>
> *a fruity red wine* (main term: **red wine**)
>
> *a lovely old cottage* (main term: **old cottage**)

19.4 Semicolon (;)

19.4.1 Use a semicolon to join independent clauses (complete sentences) that are closely related.

(a)   The independent clauses may together represent an event:

> *The boat came rushing down a slide; all three of us screamed madly; everybody was soaked by the huge splash of water.*

(b)   The independent clauses may complement or parallel each other:

> *New York is a large metropolitan city with numerous skyscrapers; it is also a mecca for lovers of the performing arts.*
>
> *Food nourishes the body; books nourish the mind.*

(c)   The independent clauses may represent contrasting or incongruous ideas:

> *The steak dishes here are very good; the seafood dishes are disappointing.*
>
> *He once did poorly in science in school; now he is a professor of physics.*

(d)   The second independent clause is introduced by a conjunctive adverb (such as

consequently, for example, furthermore, hence, however, in addition, indeed,

moreover, nevertheless, therefore, and **thus**), which is customarily followed by a comma:

The job moulds the person; however, the person may also shape the job.

19.4.2 Use a semicolon as a stronger division in a sentence that already contains comma divisions.

He hurriedly left home, which was a short walk from the MTR station; but he suddenly realized he had forgotten to bring his mobile phone, and so had to return home to get it.

19.4.3 Use semicolons between items in a list when the items are long or contain commas.

We plan to invite the following guests: Mr Lee, chairman of our Board of Directors; Mr Wang, our main benefactor; and Mrs Johnson, who has always supported our overseas promotional work.

19.5   Colon (:)

19.5.1 Use a colon to introduce a series (list of items). Note that you must have an independent clause, not a phrase or sentence fragment, before the colon.

An essay usually contains the following: introduction, main body, and conclusion.

19.5.2 You can start with a series after which you can use a colon to introduce a summary statement.

Introduction, main body, and conclusion: all essays contain them.

Visiting museums, seeing scenic places, sampling local cuisines: these are the things that make a memorable vacation for me.

19.5.3 Use a colon to introduce speech or quoted material.

Martin Luther King once famously said: "I have a dream."

As the saying goes: "Rome was not built in one day."

19.5.4 You can use a colon to separate two independent clauses when there is a progression or development from the first clause to the second.

(a) From introduction to main point:

Cities are expanding: ease of transportation and mobility of people encourage the blurring of urban boundaries.

(b) From cause to effect:

The neglect of the study of Chinese history in schools is problematic: young people are growing up without a strong sense of national identity.

(c) From general statement to example:

Technology compresses time and space: what happens half a world away can be seen on television news "live" at the same time.

(d) From brief announcement or statement to explanation or elaboration:

His basic problem is this: he believes he is always right.

We came home late: we were totally exhausted after a day-long hike.

19.5.5 Use a colon to introduce descriptions.

The music was just like telling a story: peasants in the countryside were harvesting happily; a nearby stream was flowing gently with birds chirping; suddenly a storm came and the peasants ran for shelter; soon the storm subsided and everybody sang a joyful song.

19.5.6 Follow these conventions concerning capitalization after a colon.

(a) Always capitalize the first word of a subtitle after a colon.

(b) Do not capitalize the first word of a phrase after a colon.

(c) You may begin the first word of a clause with a capital letter or a lowercase (small) letter, but you need to be consistent.

19.6 Question mark (?)

19.6.1 Use the question mark at the end of a direct question. (Make sure you know the difference between a direct question and an indirect question.)

Would you like to have dessert? (Indirect question: *The waitress asked me whether I would like to have dessert.*)

"Do you think I am ready for the competition?" she asked her violin teacher.

19.6.2 The following use of the question mark is incorrect because it is not a direct question.

(✘) ~~We must ask somebody where is the high-speed train station?~~

Write it as an indirect question, like this:

(✓) *We must ask somebody where the high-speed train station is.*

To show a direct question, you can rephrase it as follows:

(✓) *We must ask somebody this question: Where is the high-speed train station?*

If you are writing a piece for your travel journal, you might say this:

We asked someone walking nearby, "Excuse me, where is the high-speed train station?"

19.6.3 Do not use a question mark for an indirect question in reported speech. An indirect question is a statement and therefore should be punctuated with a full stop.

The chairman asked if members had any questions about the minutes of the previous meeting.

19.6.4 Use the question mark in a pair of parentheses immediately after a word or phrase to show doubt or uncertainty about it. (Note that if this comes at the end of the sentence, a full stop must follow the parentheses.)

The current coronavirus pandemic may last for many more months (?).

The book of Romans in the Bible was written in about A.D. 60 (?) by the apostle Paul.

19.7   Exclamation mark (!)

19.7.1 Use the exclamation mark after a word, phrase, or sentence to express emphasis or any strong feeling (such as *joy, admiration, enthusiasm, warning, wonder*).

I'm so glad to see you!

Wow! Look at these flowers. Aren't they pretty! (Here, the exclamation mark replaces the normal question mark at the end of a question.)

Let me help you!

Take care and stay healthy!

What a super idea! Just wonderful!

19.7.2 Sometimes, you may use an exclamation mark in parentheses following a word or phrase in a sentence to draw more attention because you think it is amusing or ridiculous.

She said it was great fun walking in knee-deep snow (!) to return the library books.

He told his friend that eating fifty hot-dogs in fifteen minutes (!) at the competition was no big deal for him.

19.8   Quotation marks (double: " "; single: ' ')

19.8.1 Use quotation marks for direct speech and quotations. (AmE prefers double quotation marks; BrE prefers single quotation marks.)

My friend said, "Let's get together for lunch sometime soon."

"It is impossible to live without failing at something." (J. K. Rowling, commencement speech at Harvard University, June 5, 2008)

19.8.2 Use single quotation marks for a quotation within a quotation. (In BrE, it is double quotation marks inside and single quotation marks outside.)

"Then Jesus declared, 'I am the bread of life. He who comes to me will never go hungry, and he who believes in me will never be thirsty.'" (John 6:35)

19.8.3 Use quotation marks to enclose fragments, regardless of length, of quoted matter reproduced exactly as found in the original source.

At the early stage of the novel coronavirus epidemic, there were concerns that "limited human-to-human transmission" was possible.

19.8.4 Punctuation that divides a sentence in reported speech is placed inside the quotation marks.

"I'm going to get some fruit at the supermarket," she said, "and see if they have any fresh fish."

Note clearly that the comma after **supermarket** and the full stop at the end of the sentence are placed inside the quotation marks.

19.8.5 Use quotation marks to enclose words or phrases used in a special way.

Charles Cooley coined the term "looking glass self" to refer to the image of ourselves obtained from comments and evaluations of others.

The management "encouraged" employees to take short no-pay leaves to save operation cost.

19.8.6 Place the question mark inside the quotation marks when it is part of the quoted matter.

The chairman asked, "Do you realize the severity of the problem?"

19.8.7 Place the question mark outside the quotation marks when it is not part of the quoted matter.

What did the chairman mean when he said that "the problem was severe"?

19.8.8 Quotation marks are sometimes used to enclose words treated as words. (Boldface or italics can also be used for this purpose.)

Many students confuse "principle" with "principal".

19.8.9 If a quoted word or phrase comes at the end of a sentence, the ending full stop is placed before the closing quotation mark. (In BrE, the full stop comes after the closing quotation mark.)

See examples in 19.8.1, 19.8.2, 19.8.4, 19.8.8.

19.9 Parentheses ( ) (also known as round brackets)

19.9.1 Use a pair of parentheses to enclose explanations, additional information, or comment.

A set dinner usually consists of starters (appetizers), main course, and dessert.

We visited Harvard University (established in 1636) in Cambridge, Massachusetts.

Mr Chang is (as he always was) a dedicated teacher.

19.9.2 Use parentheses to enclose figures or letters when listing items.

This new vacuum cleaner is (a) powerful, (b) quiet, and (c) easy to use.

There are two reasons why we like cruises: (1) there are lots of things to do on the ship; (2) we do not have to pack our bags every night as we would in land tours.

19.9.3 Use parentheses to give citations of relevant academic studies.

Some scholars argued for studying leisure in the context of larger social structures (e.g., Heywood, 1988; Kelly, 1992; Stokowski, 1994).

19.9.4 Words enclosed by parentheses are sometimes treated as included within the sentence. If they come at the end of the sentence, place the full stop outside the closing parenthesis. If they come in mid-sentence, place a comma outside the closing parenthesis.

Interest in the performing arts varies directly with educational attainment (see Table 3).

These face masks have a very high level of bacterial and particle filtration (the kind that dentists use).

Other people may disagree with you (perhaps quite sharply), but you must stand firm if you are convinced that you are right.

19.9.5 If the enclosed words form a complete sentence, place the punctuation they end with inside the closing parenthesis.

Interest in the performing arts varies directly with educational attainment. (See Table 3.)

When Ashkenazi performed the piano concerto, he conducted the orchestra from the piano. (That is something pianists rarely do.)

19.10 Dash (--) (typed by two consecutive hyphens, with no space before and after it)

19.10.1 The dash is a mark of separation stronger than a comma. It is less formal and more relaxed than a colon. Both tend to draw attention to what you write after it. The dash is a better choice than the colon if what you mention

next contains an element of surprise. Type the dash with two consecutive hyphens, with no space before or after the mark.

19.10.2 Single dash. Use a single dash to introduce material that explains or elaborates what you say before it.

News as reported on television is not something that just happens—it is the result of what journalists and editors have agreed to put together so that there is a "story" to tell.

Whereas children assimilate technology rather easily as they grow up, adults must make a big effort to accommodate—a much more difficult learning process.

19.10.3 Use a single dash to introduce a phrase that summarizes what you say before it.

Friendly, approachable, humorous, and dynamic—all these are qualities of my business partner.

The digital transformation of society is producing a split between information haves and have-nots—a digital divide.

19.10.4 Use a single dash to introduce an afterthought which may become a point of emphasis.

Politics is part of the culture of organizations—schools are no exception.

She can memorize the long speech—and she will!

19.10.5 Two dashes. Use a pair of dashes to set off parenthetical material that is not part of the main statement. While you can also use a pair of commas to set off parenthetical material (see 19.3.6), the break produced by a pair of dashes is more distinct. That is, dashes are more emphatic than commas used this way.

Long hours of practice—no less than five or six hours a day—are common among professional pianists.

19.11   Apostrophe (')

19.11.1 Use the apostrophe (make sure it faces the correct way: ')

(a) to show the possessive of singular nouns not ending in **s**:

a day's work

the company's managing director

our city's population

(b) to show the possessive of singular names ending in **s**:

Dickens' novels (or *Dickens's novels*)

James' family   (or *James's family*)

Starbucks' coffee (or *Starbucks's coffee*)

(c) to show the possessive of plural nouns not ending in **s**:

children's books

women's shoes

men's washroom

people's opinions

(d) to show the possessive of plural nouns ending in **s**:

citizens' response

workers' union

the Chens' study (study by two or more authors of the same surname *Chen*)

19.11.2 To show joint possession held by two persons or parties (only the last person or party takes *'s* or just the apostrophe *'*)

Lee and Adams' book (The book is co-authored by Lee and Adams.)

The landlord and tenant's agreement (The agreement is jointly signed by the landlord and the tenant.)

19.11.3 To show joint possession held separately by two persons or parties

Cheng's and Wang's properties (Cheng's properties and Wang's properties)

Hans' and Lin's ideas (Hans' ideas and Lin's ideas)

19.11.4 You may use the apostrophe to express years in a particular decade or to form the plural of numbers and individual letters. Not using the apostrophe is becoming common (except for lower-case letters), but you have to be consistent.

the 1980's (or: *the 1980s*)

women in their 50's (or: *women in their 50s*)

Check all applicable items with X's. (or: . . . *with Xs*)

You should teach a child to cross all her t's and dot all her i's. (apostrophe preferred)

Here is a list of do's and don'ts.
(In *don'ts,* the apostrophe belongs to the contraction of *do not,* hence no need for another

apostrophe to indicate the plural. Just add **s** at the end.)

19.11.5 It is quite acceptable to omit the apostrophe for plural unpunctuated abbreviations using capital letters. If the abbreviation ends in lower-case letters, use the apostrophe before s to be clearer.

PhDs	*BAs*
MPhils (*MPhil's* would be clearer.)	*JPs*
MBAs	*CEOs*
UFOs (unidentified flying objects)	*TVs*

19.11.6 Use the apostrophe to indicate contractions.

aren't   (*are not*)

you're   (*you are*)

doesn't   (*does not*)

we'll   (*we will*)

they won't   (*they will not*)

there's   (*there is*)

it's   (*it is* or *it has*) (Note: *its* = of it. Using *it's* for this meaning is incorrect.)

can't   (*cannot*)

class of '15   (*class of 2015 or 1915 depending on the context*)

fish 'n' chips   (*fish and chips*) (Note the use of two apostrophes when *and* is shortened to *n*.)

19.11.7 Do not confuse contractions with possessive personal pronouns.

Contraction	Possessive pronoun
you're (*you are*)	*your*
they're (*they are*)	*their*
it's (*it is*)	*its* (belonging to *it*)
who's (*who is*)	*whose*

19.12 Hyphen (-)

Many compound words are written with hyphens. However, some compound words that used to be hyphenated may now be written as one word, such as **bookstore, facelift,** and **teabag.** The following are some main rules. When in doubt, consult a dictionary.

19.12.1 Compound adjectives formed with a noun and the present participle or the past participle of a verb. The combination of these two elements serves as a unit to modify the noun that follows. Compound adjectives so formed usually precede the noun they modify.

self-fulfilling prophecy

face-saving act

Hong Kong-based company

profit-oriented move

picture-framing shop

self-centred personality

mind-boggling problems

achievement-motivated frame of mind

19.12.2 Compound adjectives beginning with an adverb such as *better, half, hard, well, much, little, or best*. Do not hyphenate these compounds when they follow the noun they modify.

better-known artist	(*artist who is better known*)
half-cooked chicken	(*chicken that is half cooked*)
hard-earned reputation	(*reputation that is hard earned*)
well-trained specialists	(*specialists who are well trained*)
much-acclaimed film director	(*film director who is much acclaimed*)
little-understood idea	(*idea that is little understood*)
best-organized programme	(*programme that is best organized*)

However, compounds formed with **ill** tend to be hyphenated both before and after the noun it modifies:

ill-fated liner "Titanic"	(*The liner "Titanic" was ill-fated.*)
ill-conceived ideas	(*ideas that are ill-conceived*)

Compounds containing **least** and **most** are usually not hyphenated:

least affected countries	(*countries that are least affected*)
most respected statesmen	(*statesmen who are most respected*)

19.12.3 Do not use a hyphen in compound adjectives beginning with *very* or an adverb ending in *-ly*, followed by a present or past participle.

very complicated issue

rapidly changing society

deeply worrying situation

carefully considered action

thoroughly cleaned hands

jointly prepared proposal

widely read magazine

19.12.4 Hyphenate compound adjectives beginning with *all* both before and after a noun.

all-encompassing fog	(*fog that is all-encompassing*)
all-important decision	(*decision that is all-important*)
all-inclusive holiday package	(*holiday package that is all-inclusive*)
\all-powerful chairman	(*a chairman who is all-powerful*)
all-purpose tool	(*a tool that is all-purpose*)
all-round person	(*a person who is all-round*)

19.12.5 Compound adjectives made up of an adjective and a participle are usually hyphenated when used before a noun.

closed-ended question (Incorrect: ~~close-end~~ or ~~close-ended.~~)

hot-tempered people

half-hearted support

middle-aged woman

open-minded view

rapid-flowing river

wide-ranging variation

19.12.6 Compound adjectives made up of an adjective and a noun are usually hyphenated when used before a noun.

public-sector organizations

high-tech society

long-term benefits

mid-life crisis

middle-class neighbourhood

top-quality ham

19.12.7 Compound adjectives in which the first element is a cardinal or ordinal number and the second a noun are hyphenated before but not after a noun.

a six-day period	(*a period of six days*)
provides 24-hour service	(*provides service 24 hours a day*)
an 85-member orchestra	(*an orchestra of 85 members*)
a 120-page book	(*a book of 120 pages*)
a 12-year-old girl	(*a girl who is 12 years old,* or *a girl aged 12*)
a five-person team	(*a team of five persons*)
first-year effort	(*effort during the first year*)
twentieth-century history	(*history of the twentieth century*)
second-floor apartment	(*apartment on the second floor*)

Note: As in the first six examples above, the noun is always singular when it is hyphenated with a preceding cardinal number. So, for instance, it is incorrect to say **a five-hours period** or **this shop provides 24-hours service.** Say, instead, **a five-hour period** and **this shop provides 24-hour service.**

19.12.8 Compound adjectives consisting of two nouns, two verbs, or two adjectives representing two related or opposing elements are hyphenated and typically placed before a noun.

love-hate relationship

nature-nurture issue

soft-loud variation

win-win situation

zero-sum game

on-off switch

19.12.9   Compound adjectives formed by noun + adjective are hyphenated and usually placed before a noun.

carbohydrates-rich diet

computer-literate generation

duty-free shop

labour-intensive industries

user-friendly software

water-repellent coating

crystal-clear explanation

19.12.10   Compound adjectives consisting of three or more hyphenated elements, sometimes serving a temporary purpose, are placed before a noun.

15-to-19-year-old group

hard-to-please audience

matter-of-fact approach

once-in-a-lifetime experience

on-the-job training

question-and-answer period

take-it-or-leave-it attitude

work-hard-and-play-hard philosophy

19.12.11   Many compound words contain a preposition as prefix or as suffix. Some of these compounds are hyphenated while many are not. The following are some examples involving *in, out, over, up,* and *down*. The word class is indicated for each compound. Note that not all of them are adjectives; some are both adjective and adverb, others are verbs, nouns, or both.

Hyphenated	Not hyphenated
in	
in-group (n) *in-house* (adj, adv) *in-laws* (n) *break-in* (n) *walk-in* (adj)	*incoming* (adj) *indoor* (adj) *Badminton is an indoor game.* *indoors* (adv) *Badminton is played indoors.*

273

Hyphenated	Not hyphenated
out	
out-of-date (adj) *out-of-the-way* (adj) *out-of-doors* (adj)	*outdated* (adj) *outdoor* (adj) *outdoors* (adv, n) *out of doors* (adv) *outgoing* (adj) *breakout* (n) *dropout* (n) *drop out* (phrasal v) *takeout* (n) *take out* (phrasal v) *walkout* (n) *walk out* (phrasal v)
over	
over-the-counter (adj, = obtainable without doctor's prescription) *over-the-top* (adj, = too unreasonable) *over-optimistic* (adj) *carry-over* (n)	*over the counter* (adv) *overflow* (v, n) *overlap* (v, n) *overnight* (adj, adv) *overreact* (v) *changeover* (n) *change over* (phrasal v) *takeover* (n) *take over* (phrasal v) *turnover* (n) *turn over* (phrasal v)
up	
up-and-coming (adj, = likely to become successful) *up-to-date* (adj) *up-to-the-minute* (adj, = including all the latest; very modern) *build-up* (n) *grown-up* (adj) *hold-up* (n) *tie-up* (n) *warm-up* (n, adj)	*upbringing* (n) *upgrade* (v, n) *uphill* (adj, adv) *upstairs* (adv, adj, n) *update* (v, n) *backup* (n) *back up* (phrasal v) *breakup* (n) *break up* (phrasal v) *build up* (phrasal v) *grow up* (phrasal v) *hold up* (phrasal v) *setup* (n) *set up* (phrasal v) *tie up* (phrasal v) *warm up* (phrasal v)
down	
down-to-earth (adj) *put-down* (n, = remark that makes someone feel stupid) *run-down* (adj, = in a bad condition)	*downhill* (adv, adj) *downstream* (adv, adj) *downturn* (n) *rundown* (n, = a quick report)

Note a few important points about the compound words shown above:

(a)   When a compound word is hyphenated, it usually functions as a noun (e.g., **meeting *in-laws* during the Chinese New Year period**) or an adjective placed before a noun (e.g., ***over-the-counter* medicines**)

(b)   However, many compounds working as nouns (e.g., ***overflow* of water**), verbs (e.g., **a garden *overflows* with colour**), or adjectives (e.g., **the *outgoing* chairman**) are written as one word.

(c)   Many compounds have double roles (noun/verb; adjective/adverb).

(d)   Many one-word compounds used as nouns may become phrasal verbs when separated as two words. (e.g., **high *turnover* at a company**; ***Turn* this responsibility *over* to someone else**.) The phrasal verb use can have many different meanings in different contexts.

19.12.12 Use a hyphen for fractions and numbers from 21 to 99. Do not hyphenate numbers from 100 to larger ones (but retain hyphens for 21 to 99 within the larger number, such as 2,642 shown below).

one-third   one-half   three-quarters two-fifths   twenty-eight

ninety-nine   one hundred and fifty-two   two thousand six hundred and forty-two

19.12.13 Use a hyphen to indicate that two or more compounds have the same second element.

short- and long-term consequences

15- to 24-year-old age group (all in words: *fifteen- to twenty-four-year-old age group*)

ten- to fifteen-minute intervals

pre- and post-1997 social conditions

Note that, when referring to two compounds, as in the above four examples, there must be a space after the hyphen following the first element of the first compound.

The following is an example of three compounds with the same second element:

first-, second-, and third-quarter figures

19.12.14 Do not use a hyphen in familiar compound words consisting of two nouns.

bulk purchase	*life quality*
charity donation	*media event*
consumer market	*performance art*
customer relations	*table manners*
holiday sale	*quality control*
identity crisis	*travel insurance*
airport express	*fusion cuisine*
mail order	*family doctor*

lunch box   *country park*

package tour   *science fiction*

19.12.15 **In general, do not use a hyphen after prefixes. This applies to nouns, verbs, adjectives, and adverbs. However, use a hyphen when the prefix is followed by a capitalized word (e.g., *non-Chinese*) or a numeral (e.g., *post-1997*). If necessary, use the hyphen to improve readability or to clarify meaning. In some cases, either the unhyphenated or the hyphenated form is acceptable. But you must be consistent in using the chosen form.**

cooperate, coordinate   (also *co-operate, co-ordinate*)

coworker   but *co-author*

extraordinary   but *extra-curricular*

multifunctional   but *multi-disciplinary*

nonconformity   but *non-essential, non-Christian*

postwar   but *post-Cold War*

postindustrial   (also *post-industrial*)

                               but *post-colonial*

predominant   but *pre-eminent*

reproduce   but *re-enact, re-register, re-route*

*recreation** (= enjoyment)   but *re-creation** (= new creation)

semicircle   but *semi-skilled, semi-professional*

underdeveloped   but *under-served* (= not getting enough care)

*Note the difference in meaning.

19.12.16 **Hyphenate compounds that indicate relationships or positions.**

ex-chairman

ex-officio member

foster-family background

heir-to-be

mother-in-law

officer-in-charge

president-elect

vice-chancellor (also: *vice chancellor*)

would-be partner

19.13 Ellipsis (. . .)

Ellipsis, also called "ellipsis points", are three *spaced* dots used mainly to indicate (a) the omission of some part of an original text (= passage) when you quote from it, (b) a deliberately uncompleted sentence, and (c) pause or hesitation.

19.13.1   When quoting, you may use three spaced ellipsis dots to show that some part or parts of the original have been omitted. You do this because you believe this serves your purpose better (to be more to your point, for example). Consider the following statement from a reader's (Mr A) letter to the editor of a newspaper:

> *Most young people probably think of Peking opera as old-fashioned, but if they are given*
>
> *a taste of Peking opera, they will understand it better, their views may change and some*
>
> *of them may be interested to learn more and even to get involved.*

When someone quotes this statement, it could be shortened in various ways by omitting parts that are not essential for his or her purpose. The following are two possibilities:

Version 1
As Mr A says, "Most young people probably think of Peking opera as old-fashioned, but . . . their views may change and some of them may be interested to learn more and even to get involved."
Version 2
As Mr A says, "Most young people probably think of Peking opera as old-fashioned, but if they are given a taste of Peking opera, . . . some of them may be interested to learn more and even to get involved."
Note the inclusion of *but if they are given a taste of Peking opera* in Version 2 but omitted in Version 1.

Note that any punctuation mark present before an ellipsis, whether within or at the end of a sentence, should be kept in the quotation (such as the comma after **opera** in Version 2 above).

19.13.2 **The retention of a punctuation mark present before an omission following a sentence is also illustrated below. For this purpose, we will change slightly Mr A's statement in his letter to the editor.**

Mr A's statement slightly changed
Most young people probably think of Peking opera as old-fashioned. But their attitude can change. If they are given a taste of Peking opera, they will understand it better, and some of them may be interested to learn more and even to get involved.
A possible report containing selective omissions
As Mr A says, "Most young people probably think of Peking opera as old-fashioned. . . If they are given a taste of Peking opera, they will understand it better, and some of them may be interested to learn more. . ."
Note that the full stop following **old-fashioned** is retained, giving the omission the appearance of four points. Note also that since the last part of the statement **and even to get involved** is omitted, the end punctuation, a full stop, following the omission, is retained, again giving the omission the appearance of four points.

19.13.3 **Sometimes, you may use ellipsis points to show an intentionally unfinished sentence to mean that little more can be said or that something has been better left unsaid. The same can be done after completed sentences for the same purpose.**

Excessive mass market tourism can bring about increased crowding in public areas and additional road and public transport congestion. This is likely to arouse resentment, which will . . .

I don't think that is a very good option. . .

Note that in the second example above, the end-of-sentence full stop after **option** is retained, followed by the regular three-spaced-dot ellipsis, giving a total of four dots or points.

19.13.4 **You may use ellipsis points to show a hesitation or pause, even shaky or fragmented speech.**

"Oh my goodness! . . . I've made a terrible mistake!" cried my secretary.

Our waiter has never been so . . . well, so attentive and courteous.

"God! . . . What . . . what am I . . . what am I going to do? I . . . I . . . I can't . . . " sobbed Mrs Chen's daughter.

19.14 Summing up

Pay more attention than before to the proper use of punctuation. It is an important part of good writing. Used correctly, it can improve the quality of your writing by helping your readers to see and follow your ideas. They can even feel the emotions that you may have injected into your prose. Some punctuation marks may be more frequently used than others, but you should know them well enough so that you will have a wider choice of punctuation to suit your various purposes.

Here are some main points to bear in mind:

(1)   The punctuation marks that are most commonly used are the full stop, the semicolon, and the comma. The full stop ends a sentence; the semicolon joins clauses or sentences (as in this sentence you are reading); and the comma sets off various elements within a sentence.

(2)   Other punctuation marks are used for such purposes as elaborating a point, quoting, indicating possession, inserting remarks, and forming compound words.

(3)   Guard against overuse of the comma and its misuse of joining sentences. When you come to the completion of an idea, use a full stop. When you need to join two complete clauses, use a comma followed by a coordinating conjunction.

(4)   Study the rules and guidelines for each punctuation mark. Use good thinking and good sense to decide how to punctuate what you write.

Exercises Chapter 19

Exercise 19.1

Add commas, semicolons, apostrophes, and colons where appropriate. (But not all sentences here need them.)

在適當的位置加入逗號 (comma)、分號 (semicolon)、撇號 (apostrophe) 和冒號 (colon)。(但並非所有下面的句子都有這需要。)

1. The chief sources of air pollution in our city are cars factories and smoke from people who smoke.

2. Musicians are experimenting with new digital music audiences are not too receptive with such experiments.

3. Theres no point in living according to my friend if you dont slow down to enjoy life.

4. To me the most important things in life are as follows faith in God good health and harmonious relationships with family.

5. She takes physical exercise seriously she swims for an hour almost every day for example.

6. A business that wants to be successful must invest substantially in marketing and innovation.

7. Your general approach is a good one however I think there are some practical difficulties.

8. If you are in a hurry you can grab a hamburger at McDonalds.

9. Theyre thinking of joining a river cruise in Europe two years from now they are not going to Canada or the United States.

10. Take your time at the childrens books section which is on the third floor Ill wait for you in the Starbucks café on the ground floor.

11. The young lady who recently joined the company has two masters degrees.

12. Not enough Chinese history is taught in schools today young people are growing up without a clear sense of national identity.

Exercise 19.2

Use an apostrophe to indicate omissions in standard contractions.

用撇號表示標準縮略詞中省略的部分。

1. I am   →   _____

2. you are   →   _____

3. he is   →   _____

4. she is   →   _____

5.   we have   →   _____

6.   they had   →   _____

7.   they would   →   _____

8.   it cannot   →   _____

9.   it could not   →   _____

10.   we will   →   _____

11.   we will not   →   _____

12.   she does not   →   _____

Exercise 19.3

Rewrite the following phrases so that hyphens are used.

Example: *benefits in the long term* → *long-term benefits*

將以下的短語改寫為含連字號 (hyphens) 的短語。(見上面舉例)

1.   a store that opens 24 hours a day   →   _____

2.   a girl who is 11 years old   →   _____

3.   report covering the first year   →   _____

4.   achievements of the twenty-first century   →   _____

5.   my office on the third floor   →   _____

6.   a team of four persons   →   _____

7.   an orchestra of 88 musicians   →   _____

8.   a period of nine months   →   _____

9.   statistics that are up to date   →   _____

10.   a doctor who is well known   →   _____

11.   social conditions before and after 2020   →   _____

12.   (rewrite using all words) 142 pounds   →   _____

Exercise 19.4

Punctuate the following sentences. All are single sentences except #2, which contains two sentences. Punctuation marks needed include comma, colon, semicolon, apostrophe, quotation marks, dashes, question mark, and full stop.

在適當的位置加上合適的標點符號。除第二題含有兩句外,其他都是單句。所需的標點符號包括逗號 (comma)、冒號 (colon)、分號 (semicolon)、撇號 (apostrophe)、引號 (quotation marks)、破折號 (dashes)、問號 (question mark)、句號 (full stop)。

1. To write well we should recognize this basic requirement sentences must be grammatical and word combinations idiomatic

2. Good management copes with complexity it brings order and predictability to a situation in comparison good leadership learns to cope with change

3. Human agents reporters photographers editors and researchers all participate significantly in the construction of media practices

4. Many people confuse principal with principle

5. The fundamental sociological problem is not crime but the law not divorce but marriage not recreation but how leisure as idea and behaviour intertwines with social life

6. Television viewers in Hong Kong like those elsewhere are most interested in seeking entertainment

7. Do you think I am ready for the race he asked his coach

8. He is a sociable generous and outspoken person always ready to help someone in need

9. Freedom is valuable however it must not infringe on others rights

10. Your time should not be spent on trivial things instead more time should be spent on using your talent to serve others

Chapter 20   Know How to Write Reported Speech

What you will learn in this chapter

Reported (or indirect) speech is reporting what someone said in your own sentences. This is different from direct speech, which quotes the speaker's exact words as spoken, using quotation marks. In this chapter, you will learn the various changes necessary when you go from direct speech to reported speech. Two important structures are used: "reporting clauses" and "reported clauses". Writing in the form of reported speech, sometimes along with direct speech, is common in news reports and commentaries.

間接引語（reported speech）是以自己的話轉述別人說話的內容。這跟直接引語（direct speech）用引號轉述他人的原話不同。在本章裏，你會學習怎樣將直接引語改成間接引語，其中會用到兩個很重要的部分：轉述分句（reporting clauses）和被轉述從句（reported clauses）。間接引語有時會輔以直接引語，在媒體的新聞報導和評論中都很常見。

20.1 Recognizing direct speech and reported speech

Recognizing the differences between direct speech and reported (indirect) speech is a useful skill when you need to report someone's words, thoughts, and ideas in your own sentences. Sometimes, using the exact words in direct speech can be more effective when you want to highlight or emphasize some particular point. At other times, you need only give the meaning of what someone said. So, we will start with the basic picture followed by a closer look at the various changes necessary for turning direct words into part of your own sentences.

20.1.1 Comparing direct speech and reported speech

In direct speech, the speaker is mentioned first or at some natural breaks and the speaker's exact words, enclosed by quotation marks, are known as "quotes". The following examples show the speaker in front, middle, and end positions.

Direct speech
Mrs. Wong said, "I have forgotten to bring my mobile phone."
"These apples," said the salesgirl, "are on sale at half-price today."
"Where is the nearest MTR entrance?" asked the tourist.

In reported speech, a **reporting clause** containing the original speaker (**Mrs Wong said; the salesgirl said; the tourist asked**) opens the sentence, followed by a **reported clause** (often a subordinate clause introduced by **that** or a **wh-** word).

Reported speech (reported clause boldfaced)
Reporting clause + Reported clause:
*Mrs Wong said **that she had forgotten to bring her mobile phone**.*
*The salesgirl said **that the apples were on sale at half-price that day**.*
*The tourist asked **where the nearest MTR entrance was**.*

20.1.2 Two points to note

First, when the speaker in direct speech comes at positions other than the sentence beginning (that is, in mid-sentence or sentence-end), inversion (verb before subject) is possible. However, when the subject is a pronoun (e.g., **she, they**), inversion is not normally used and the subject comes before the verb. Thus, the first example sentence in 20.1.1 can be written as either (a) or (b), but not (c):

(a) *"I have forgotten to bring my mobile phone," said Mrs Wong.*

(b) *"I have forgotten to bring my mobile phone," she said.*

(c) (✗) *"I have forgotten to bring my mobile phone," said she.*

Second, when the reporting verb is in past tense, a change in tense is often required in reported speech. We shall have more to say on tense changes later.

20.2 Changing direct speech to reported speech

When we change direct speech to reported speech, we need to pay attention to the following:

- reporting verbs

- noun clauses

- the **to**-infinitive and the **-ing** gerund

- changes in person, place, time, and tense.

We can illustrate these with the following example sentences. Direct speech is marked (a), and reported speech is marked (b). The basic aspects are reviewed following the sentences.

Direct speech	Reported speech (**that** may be omitted)
1a. *Mr. Lee said, "I have brought my proposal."*	1b. *Mr. Lee said* (**that**) **he had brought his proposal**.
2a. *She asked me, "What do you think of the movie?"*	2b. *She asked me* **what I thought of the movie**.
3a. *My friend says, "I'm not happy with my present situation."*	3b. *My friend says* (**that**) **she is not happy with her present situation**.
4a. *The teacher asked the class, "Do you know what WHO stands for?"*	4b. *The teacher asked the class* **if/whether they knew what WHO stands for**.
5a. *Our fitness coach said, "Now I want you to do twenty sit-ups."*	5b. *Our fitness coach told us* **to do twenty sit- ups**.
6a. *The salesperson said, "We'll refund you for the damaged dress."*	6b. *The salesperson offered* (or *agreed*) **to refund the customer for the damaged dress**.

20.3 Reporting verbs

In reported speech, you use verbs to report what others (or sometimes you) said. The most common reporting verbs are **say** and **tell**. Other reporting verbs include **ask, reply, answer, explain, agree, offer, promise, suggest,** and **wonder**. The choice of the reporting verb depends on the context. Specifically, you need to know if the original speaker made a statement, asked a question, gave an instruction or advice, explained something, or made an offer, a promise, or a suggestion. Your reporting verb and the clause that follows should reflect this.

20.4 Noun clauses

The reported clause, often a noun clause (introduced by **that, if/whether, what, where, when, which, why,** or **how**), follows the reporting verb (see boldfaced part of sentences 1b, 2b, 3b, and 4b above) as its object. (Remember that a noun clause functions like a noun and thus can be subject or object in a sentence.) The reported clause indicates what is/was said or asked. The verb in the reported clause is referred to as the "reported verb".

In addition to **say** and **ask**, as illustrated in sentences 1b, 2b, 3b, and 4b, other reporting verbs such as **admit, advise, agree, remind,** and **suggest** can also be followed by a **that** noun clause:

Direct speech (only showing quotes; reporting clauses not shown)	**Reported speech** (**that** may be omitted)
7a. *"I did not take the medication as instructed."*	7b. *The patient admitted (**that**) **she did not take the medication as instructed**.*
8a. *"You ought to take plenty of rest."*	8b. *The doctor advised (**that**) **I take plenty of rest**.* (Reported verb **take** remains in present tense because statement is still valid.)
9a. *"We should postpone discussion on the funding issue."*	9b. *Members agreed (**that**) **they should postpone discussion on the funding issue**.*
10a. *"Don't forget we have a tough competition ahead."*	10b. *We reminded ourselves (**that**) **we had a tough competition ahead**.*
11a. *"Could we siblings get together once a month?"* Or *"Shall we siblings get together once a month?"*	11b. *She suggested (**that**) **she and her siblings could get together once a month**.* Or *She suggested **getting together with her siblings once a month**.*

20.5   The *to*-infinitive and the *-ing* gerund

When reporting orders, instructions, offers, agreements, and requests, you can use a **to-** infinitive. Some reporting verbs such as **admit, suggest, apologize for,** and **insist on** can be followed by an **-ing** gerund. In the following box, only the reported speech is shown. You can try to reconstruct the direct speech for each statement. Keep in mind differences in context and be aware of whether the reporter is the same person as the one in the original direct speech.

Note the use of a **to-**infinitive from sentence 12 to sentence 17:

12. *Our fitness coach told us **to do twenty sit-ups**.* (Order, sentence 5b above)

13. *His boss told him **not to say anything about it**.* (Order)

14. *There is a public announcement on television telling people **to wash hands in seven steps**.* (Instruction)

15. *Uncle John offered **to fix my computer the next day**.* (Offer)

16. *The salesperson offered (or agreed) **to refund the customer for the damaged dress**.* (Offer/ agreement, sentence 6b in 20.2 above)

17. *You asked the waitress **to change your drink from tea to iced coffee**.* (Request)

18. *The salesperson asked **to see my receipt**.* (Request)

Note the use of an **-ing** gerund in the next three sentences:

19. *I apologized for **arriving late**.* (Apology)

20. *It was raining hard, so my wife suggested **taking a taxi**.* (Suggestion)

21. *Most of us insisted on **keeping Vienna on the itinerary**.* (Insistence)

20.6   Changes in person, place, time, and tense

You normally need to make changes in reported speech. Such changes, which involve person, place, time, and tense, depend very much on the situation. You should bear in mind whether (a) you are reporting something another person has said or (b) you are referring to your own words or even thoughts. Sometimes, you may be reporting the ideas of a group of people including yourself. The box below illustrates these two kinds of situation.

(a) reporting something another person said	*The waiter said, "The chef's recommendation today is seafood risotto."* → *The waiter told us* **that the chef's recommendation that day was seafood risotto.** *She asked her brother, "What do you think of the movie?"* → *She asked her brother* **what he thought of the movie.**
(b) referring to your own words or words of your group	*I said, "I'm sorry for arriving late."* → *I apologized for* **arriving late**. *We said, "Don't forget: we have a tough competition ahead."* → *We reminded ourselves* **that we had a tough competition ahead**.

The following are some typical changes from direct speech to reported speech:

	If the speaker in direct speech said/ says this	**The reporter in reported speech changes it to**
Person	*I* *me* *my* *you* (referring to reporter) *you* (referring to another person)	*he, she* *him, her* *his, her* *I, me* Name of that person
Place	*here* *this place*	*there* *that place*
Time	*now* *today* *tomorrow* *yesterday* *this month/week* *last month/week* *an hour ago*	*then, at the time* *that day* *the next day, the following day* *the previous day, the day before* *that month/week* *the previous month/week* *the month/week before* *an hour earlier, an hour before*
Tense	*is/am/are* *have, has* *came* *was thinking, has been thinking*	*was/were* *had* *had come* *had been thinking*

All these changes are necessary because the reporting is usually done with *a changed viewpoint in a different place at a different time*. Although the changes listed above are typical, you still need to tailor them to the specific situation in question. For example, if the content of the direct speech is directed towards particular persons, the reported speech should reflect this fact.

Direct speech	Indirect speech
The doctor said to me, "Take plenty of rest." *The doctor said to my wife, "Take plenty of rest."*	*The doctor told me to **take plenty of rest**.* Or *The doctor advised **that I take plenty of rest**.* *The doctor told my wife to **take plenty of rest**.* Or *The doctor advised **that my wife take* plenty of rest**.* (This is a subjunctive use of a **that**-clause following verbs like **advise, decide, demand, propose,** and **suggest** to mean that the situation expressed in the **that**-clause should be realized. *The verb in the **that-** clause is the base form, without the **-s** ending for the third person singular.)

20.7   Choosing the right reporting verb

Some room exists for choosing the right reporting verb to represent the kind of statement being referred to. You have to decide whether it is, for instance, more an advice than an order, or more an offer than an agreement or a promise. Then choose your reporting verb accordingly (e.g., **advise, order, offer, agree, promise**). Of course, sometimes the same reporting verb, such as **tell,** may mean a bit of different things, including, for example, order, advice, and request.

20.8   Changes in tense: back-shifting

The basic direction of change is "back-shifting" or shifting back in time. Since the reporter's viewpoint is the present, the reporting verb in reporting a past event (someone said something) should be in the past simple tense (**said, told, advised, suggested**, etc.). Then, from the reporter's present viewpoint, anything expressed in the direct speech (the reported verb) must be cast in a past form that goes further back, as illustrated below:

Direct speech	Reported speech (changes in both reporting and reported verbs)
"I'm ready." (Present simple)	*He said he was ready.* (Past simple)
"We're preparing for the test." (Present progressive)	*They said they were preparing for the test.* (Past progressive)
"I have brought my proposal." (Present perfect)	*Mr. Lee said he had brought his proposal.* (Past perfect)
"I have been trying to call you." (Present perfect progressive)	*My friend said she had been trying to call me."* (Past perfect progressive)

20.9   Changes in tense: modal auxiliary verbs

Direct speech	Reported speech
can *"You can come anytime."*	***could*** *My neighbor said I could come anytime.*

Direct speech	Reported speech
may *"My wife and I may visit Iceland next year."*	*might* *Dave said he and his wife might visit Iceland the following year.*
must (= necessary to do something) *"Remember you must bring your passports."* *must* (= to conclude that something is true) *"I can't believe it. I must be dreaming!"*	*had to/must* *Our tour guide reminded us that we had to/must bring our passports.* *must* (not **had to** because of different meaning) *He said he couldn't believe it and thought he must be dreaming.*
shall *"I shall win if I practise enough."*	*should* *You said you should win if you practised enough.*
will *"The company will celebrate its 10th anniversary next month."*	*would* *The manager announced that the company would celebrate its 10th anniversary the following month.*

If **could, might, had to, should, would,** and **ought to** appear in direct speech, they stay unchanged in reported speech.

Direct speech	Reported speech
*"I hope I **could** help you."*	*He hoped he **could** help me.*
*"We **would** not discuss this issue any further."*	*They said they **would** not discuss that issue any further.*
*"I **might** change plans if it rains."*	*She said she **might** change plans if it rained.*

20.10 Optional tense changes

If the reported verb is in the past, you can either keep it the same or change it to the past perfect. If, however, the reported verb is past perfect, it stays the same.

Direct speech	Reported speech
*"We **visited** Disneyland many times."* (Past simple)	*They said they **visited** Disneyland many times.* (Past simple) Or *They said they **had visited** Disneyland many times.* (Past perfect)
*"We **had** never thought of coming here."* (Past perfect)	*They admitted that **they had never thought** of **coming** here.* (if the place is the same as the reporter's) (Past perfect) Or *They admitted that **they had never thought** of **going** there.* (if the place is different from the reporter's) (Past perfect)

If the statement is still valid at the time of reporting, or if the present tense reported verb has timeless meaning, you can leave the tense of the reported verb the same or change it.

Direct speech	Reported speech
"I like chocolate milkshake."	*You said you **like/liked** chocolate milkshake.*
"How much do you charge teaching a beginner?"	*She asked the piano teacher how much he **charges/charged** teaching a beginner.*
"Don't forget that the chairman can vote when there is a tie."	*He reminded us that the chairman **can/could** vote when there is/was a tie.*
"Woody Allen's pictures are not easy to understand."	*You told me that Woody Allen's pictures **are/were** not easy to understand.*

20.11 No tense changes

If the present tense reported verb in direct speech refers to something that is always true, you keep the present tense reported verb in reported speech:

Direct speech	Reported speech
*"People in the ancient world did not realize that the earth **is** round."*	*The teacher told the children that people in the ancient world did not realize that the earth **is** round.*
*"Young children **find** it hard to understand that two plus two **equals** four."*	*I told them that young children **find** it hard to understand that two plus two **equals** four.*
*"Remember, trains in Germany **are** always punctual."*	*My friend reminded me that trains in Germany **are** always punctual.*

When you use the present simple, future simple, and present perfect tense in your reporting verbs, you keep the tense of the reported verbs the same as in the original because there is probably little difference in time reference between you and the original speaker. You also use a present tense reporting verb to report something that is still true or relevant.

Direct speech	Reported speech (Note tense of reporting verb.)
"I'll wait till the end of the month to see how things are."	***He says** he will wait till the end of the month to see how things are.* (present simple)
"I'm doing fine in Boston."	***I'll tell** your parents you're doing fine in Boston.* (future simple)
"All schools will resume in early June."	***The government has announced** that all schools will resume in early June.* (present perfect)
"Alcoholic drinks are not sold to anyone under the age of 18."	***The law says** that alcoholic drinks are not sold to anyone under the age of 18.* (present simple)

However, if you are not sure whether what you are reporting is currently true, use a past tense for both the reporting verb and the reported verb.

Direct speech	Reported speech
"I have five domestic helpers."	*She told me that she **has** five domestic helpers.* (might mean this is currently true) *She told me that she **had** five domestic helpers.* (might mean this has never been true, or was once true but is no longer so)

20.12   Pay attention to pronouns.

The example sentences in the preceding section (20.11) should have shown you how pronouns are chosen in reported speech to indicate correctly the person(s) that the statement refers to. You need to understand the context that includes the change in viewpoint. Take, for example, the second box in 20.11. The first sentence there in reported speech reads **He says he will wait till the end of the month to see how things are.** This assumes the reporter is reporting to someone what a male person has said, hence ***he*** says ***he*** **will**. In the second sentence, however, the reporter is promising something to the original speaker. Thus, the appropriate wording is ***I'll*** **tell** ***your*** **parents** ***you're*** **doing fine in Boston.**

20.13   Reported questions (indirect questions)

20.13.1   Wh-questions

Wh-questions begin with words such as **when, what, where, which, why,** and **how**. In direct questions, the verb comes before the subject (this is called "inversion"). In reported (indirect) questions, the subject comes before the verb (as is usually true of statements) in the reported clause. In reported questions, common reporting verbs include **ask, wonder, want to know.**

Direct questions	Reported questions
"When will we next meet, Mr. Chairman?"	*She **asked** the chairman when they would next meet.*
"What day of the week is it?"	*The patient **asked** the nurse what day of the week it was.*
"Where would you like to eat?"	*I **asked** him where he would like to eat.*
"Which exit should we take?"	*They **wondered** which exit they should take.*
"Why is the weather so irregular?"	*We all **wanted to know** why the weather was so irregular.*
"How do you say good-bye in German?"	*I just **asked** my visitor from Munich how to say good-bye in German.*

20.13.2   Yes/no questions

These are questions the answers to which are either Yes or No, such as **Have you paid your income tax yet?** Use **if** or **whether**, which introduces a noun clause, in the reported question. You can understand the way the reported questions begin if you read the note in parentheses after each direct question.

Direct questions	Reported questions
"Has a vaccine for Covid-19 been produced yet?" (We all have this question in mind.)	*We are wondering **if/whether** a vaccine for Covid-19 has been produced yet.* (There is no change in time reference, thus entire statement is in present time.)
"Can you finish the job in a week?" (She asked me.)	*She asked **if/whether** I could finish the job in a week.*
"Do you have any old books to give away?" (I asked him.)	*I wanted to know **if/whether** he had any old books to give away.*
"Is it going to rain?" (I heard him asking.)	*He wondered **if/whether** it was going to rain.*

20.13.3 Asking for information

Sometimes, you can start with a phrase such as **Do you know, May I know,** or **Could you tell me,** followed by a reported question to ask politely for information. Note that now the question becomes direct speech:

*"**Do you know** if there's a bookstore in the mall?"*

*"**May I know** what time your restaurant closes on weekends?"*

*"**Could you tell me** how much a taxi ride to the airport would cost?"*

To strengthen your familiarity with reported speech, you can turn them into reported questions, adding possible questioners and objects of the questions, as follows:

I asked the receptionist at the information counter if there was a bookstore in the mall.

My friend asked the restaurant manager what time they close on weekends. (The statement is still up to date, thus the verb tense in the reported clause remains the same.)

My travel companion asked the hotel's concierge how much a taxi ride to the airport would cost.

20.14   Using a *to*-infinitive or a *that*-clause

As indicated earlier, a **that**-clause (noun clause, see 20.4) or a **to**-infinitive (see 20.5) can follow a reporting verb in reported speech, as is often the case in requests and orders. To illustrate this further, study the next set of sentences to see how you can change from one to the other after some reporting verbs, including those for requests and orders (such as **ask, request, tell**). You should remember that your choice of the reporting verb should reflect the nature of the situation in which the original speaker spoke.

Direct speech	Reported speech using a *to*-infinitive	Reported speech using a *that*-clause
"Can I see your receipt, please?"	**ask** *The salesperson asked **to see** my receipt.* Or *The salesperson asked me **to show** her my receipt.*	**ask** *The salesperson asked **that I show her my receipt**.*
"Leave your shoes outside."	**request** *We were requested **to leave** our shoes outside. (Passive construction common)*	**request** *The attendant requested **that we leave our shoes outside**.*
"Wash your hands."	**remind** *His mother reminded him **to wash** his hands.*	**remind** *His mother reminded him **that he should wash his hands**.*
"No photos allowed!"	**tell** *The guard told us not **to take** photos.*	**tell** *The guard told us **that no photos were allowed**.*
"We need to find a common purpose."	**agree** *We agreed **to find** a common purpose.*	**agree** *We agreed **that we needed to find a common purpose**.*
"I had no prior knowledge of the problem."	**claim** *He claimed **to have** had no prior knowledge of the problem.*	**claim** *He claimed **that he had had no prior knowledge of the problem**.*
"We better leave earlier."	**decide** *They decided **to leave** earlier,*	**decide** *They decided **that they should leave earlier**.*
"I'll see you back soon."	**expect** *I expected **to see** him back soon.*	**expect** *I expected **that I would see him back soon**.*
"I hope to see you at Christmas."	**hope** *She hoped **to see** me at Christmas.*	**hope** *She hoped **that she would see me at Christmas**.*
"I would rather stand."	**prefer** *He preferred **to stand**.*	**prefer** *He preferred **that he stand**.*
"I'll complete the task on time."	**promise** *You promised **to complete** the task on time.*	**promise** *You promised **that you would complete the task on time**.*
"Let's celebrate Father's Day differently this year."	**propose** *Their brother proposed **to celebrate** Father's Day differently this year. (**that year** if not the current year at reporting time)*	**propose** *Their brother proposed **that they celebrate Father's Day differently this year**. (**that year** if not the current year at reporting time)*

However, please note that this dual change is not always possible. Some reporting verbs, such as those in the following box, may take a **that**-clause but not a **to**-infinitive clause.

Direct speech	Reported speech using a *that*-clause but not a *to*-infinitive
"I've completely forgotten about my appointment."	**admit** *You admitted **that you had completely forgotten about your appointment**.*
"I was very upset and didn't want to see anyone."	**explain** *She explained **that she was very upset and didn't want to see anyone**.*
"We cannot give up!"	**insist** *I insisted **that we could not give up**.*
"You have all ignored one important fact."	**mention** *The chairman mentioned **that they had all ignored one important fact**.*
"The epidemic may not be fully controlled for perhaps a year."	**predict** *The infectious disease expert predicted **that the epidemic might not be fully controlled for perhaps another year**.*
"The government can try relaxing social distancing restrictions gradually."	**suggest** *The doctor suggested **that the government could try relaxing social distancing restrictions gradually**.*

20.15 Conditional sentences

Recall, from Chapter 16, that there are three basic types of conditional sentences. In reported speech, they are treated as follows:

Direct speech	Reported speech
Type 1 (probable events)	(Change in tense)
"If the meeting finishes early I'll come home for dinner."	*He told his wife that if the meeting finished early he would go home for dinner.*
"If you are planning to eat out on Mother's Day, you had better make a reservation soon."	*My friend reminded me to make a reservation soon if I was planning to eat out on Mother's Day.*
Type 2 (content of the **if**-clause is unreal)	(No change in tense)
"If I had a million dollars I would give half of it to charity."	*She said if she had a million dollars she would give half of it to charity.*
"If I were you I would move somewhere else."	*I told him that if I were him I would move somewhere else.*
Type 3 (situation in the **if**-clause did not happen)	(No change in tense)
"If we had visited Japan in early March, we would have seen cherry blossoms."	*My neighbours said that they would have seen cherry blossoms in Japan if they had gone there in early March.*
"If I hadn't overslept and missed the interview, I might have got the job."	*John told me that if he hadn't overslept and missed the interview, he might have got the job.*

20.16   Using reported speech along with direct speech

If you observe carefully, you will note that reported speech is often used along with direct speech in various kinds of text, such as journalistic reports and essays, minutes of meetings, novels, and biographies. In general, reported speech gives summaries of events while direct speech gives the reader a chance to see the exact words used by someone about a particular point. Through the combined use of both forms of speech, the reader is likely to gain a clearer and more vivid picture of a story or some happening. Read the following example:

Most committee members expressed concern at yesterday's meeting that something constructive must be done following the recent wave of complaints from the club's members about facilities at the clubhouse. Acting quickly, they said, was crucial to safeguarding the club's reputation. Sharing their sentiment, the chairman declared, "We run the risk of losing the trust and support of our members if no positive action is taken soon."
Note: The first two sentences are in reported speech.

20.17   Summing up

Reported speech is used to show other people's, and our own, words and thoughts. The following are some important points about the writing of reported speech:

(1)   Be clear about who the original speaker is and who is reporting. Often, you may be reporting what someone said. Sometimes the two may be the same person (when you are reporting your own words). Any pronouns and specified persons in the reported speech should reflect the context correctly.

(2)   Choose your reporting verb(s) according to the nature of the words used or thoughts expressed (such as statement, question, order, request, advice, offer, suggestion, admission, complaint, reminder, apology, and promise).

(3)   When there is a significant difference in time reference (or viewpoint) between the speaker and the reporter, you need to back-shift the tense of the verb(s) in the reported clause. Thus, a current event described by a present tense verb in the speaker's direct speech is treated as a past event when reported.

(4)   Sometimes you can keep the past tense verb or the present tense verb unchanged in the reported clause.

(5)   Many reporting verbs take a **that**-clause after them; some can, alternatively, take a **to**-infinitive clause. However, some reporting verbs can only be followed by a **that**-clause.

(6)   For conditional sentences in reported speech, tense change applies to only Type 1 conditionals but not Type 2 and Type 3 conditionals.

Exercises	**Chapter 20**

Exercise 20.1 Changes in reported speech (person, time, place)
間接引語中的變動（人稱、時間、地點）

Read what the following persons say and then fill in the blanks to complete the meaning. You may need to add words to clarify the context.

Example: Mr. Lee: My boss gave me a difficult task last week. → Mr. Lee's boss had given him a difficult task *the previous week*.

先把下面每個人物所說的話讀一遍，然後按照原話意思將空白處補充完整，以構成一句間接引語。你或需額外加詞來表述清楚相關情境。參看上面的例子。

1. Shirley: I tried to see my doctor, but he was fully booked this month. → Shirley's doctor was fully booked _____ .

2. Hoi-Man: My teacher tells me I have been chosen to join the school's swimming team. → _____ has been chosen to join the school's swimming team.

3. Joan said to me: I will meet you at the General Post Office this afternoon at two. → Joan would meet _____ at the General Post Office _____ .

4. Peter (to you on the phone): I'll see you at Starbucks this Saturday morning. → You (at Starbucks on Saturday): Peter said he would see me _____ .

5. Siu-ling (several days ago): I'm visiting my aunt tomorrow. → You (today): When I saw Siu-ling, she told me she _____ .

6. Cary to Amy (on Monday): I am sorry that I did not return your call yesterday. → Amy (on Tuesday): Cary apologized to me _____ .

Exercise 20.2 Using indirect questions in reported speech
間接引語中用的間接問句

Use a noun clause based on the given direct question to complete the sentence in reported speech. The reporting clause is given for each sentence.

把下面的直接問句改為名詞從句 (noun clause)，並填在空白處，使之與前面的轉述分句 (reporting clause) 共同構成間接引語。

1. "What is the problem?"

   She asked me _____ .

2. "Why haven't you finished the report?"

   I didn't know why he _____ .

3. "Where will the meeting be held?"

   He asked the chairman _____.

4. "Do you have a record of the transaction?"

   She asked her husband whether _____.

5. "Shall I ever see my friends again?"

   He wondered _____.

6. "What is she doing?"

   Her mother wants to know _____.

7. "Can I post some letters here?"

   Tom asked at the front desk _____.

8. "How long does the concert last?"

   I have no idea _____.

Exercise 20.3   Using a *to*-infinitive or a gerund in reported speech
間接引語中的帶 **to** 不定式 (**to-infinitive**) 或動名詞 (**gerund**)

Based on each given statement in direct speech, complete the sentence with the given reporting clause using a *to*-infinitive or a gerund (an **ing-**form) as appropriate.

試把下面每句直接引語用帶 to 不定式或動名詞作改寫，放在已有的轉述分句後構為間接引語。

1. "Please stay for a few more days."

   I persuaded my friend _____.

2. "You must explain the plan once again."

   We urged our team leader _____.

3. "I really must leave early tonight."

   She insisted on _____.

4. "Please come again!"

   The manager invited us _____.

5. "Shall we go to the beach today?"

   Their two children suggested _____.

6. "I'm sorry that I forgot to bring my assignment."

The student Janet apologized for _____.

7. "Don't touch the switch when your hand is wet!"

    His mother warned him _____.

8. "I'll surely prepare well for the tutorial discussion next week."

    You promised _____.

Exercise 20.4　Modal verbs and conditional sentences in reported speech
間接引語中的情態動詞（**modal verbs**）和條件句（**conditional sentences**）

Change the direct speech in each of the following sentences to reported speech.

把下面每句直接引語改寫為間接引語。

1. Tai-Ming said to me, "You should have called me earlier."

    _____

2. Jenny told her cousin, "I could bring some chicken curry to the pot luck dinner."

    _____

3. The technician said, "The problem cannot be fixed."

    _____

4. Unable to find her credit card, she said, "I must have left it in the supermarket."

    _____

5. Tony said to his father, "I'll be home by 10 p.m."

    _____

6. Mother said, "If the whole family is going to eat out, we'll need to book a large table."

    _____

7. Her coach said, "If she tries harder she might win the competition."

    _____

8. "Had I known that the sale was on, I would have gone to look for bargains," said my aunt.

    _____

Exercise 20.5

Change the direct speech in each sentence to reported speech. Bear in mind the following: (1) whether the statement is still valid (up to date), (2) whether a present tense reported verb refers to an eternal truth,

(3) whether the reporting verb and the reported verb are both in the past (then you may choose back-shifting or no back-shifting), and (4) whether there is little or no change in time reference between the original speaker and the reporter. Also, pay attention to the use of appropriate pronouns to reflect all persons referred to properly.

將下列每個句子由直接引語改寫為間接引語。你應當考慮以下各點：

(1) 所陳述的情景是否仍然存在，(2) 如果被轉述從句裏的動詞 (reported verb) 是現在時態，所涉及的是否為恆常真實的事，(3) 轉述動詞 (reporting verb) 與被轉述動詞是否都屬過去時態 [如是，你可以選擇用或不用往後轉移 (back-shifting)]，(4) 原陳述者與轉述者的表達是否無大時差。此外，注意所用的代詞在指涉方面是否恰當。

1.　　"The position makes the person," he always said.

　　　_____

2.　　"You must study hard for the examination," the professor reminded us.

　　　_____

3.　　Our friend told us, "It would be helpful when you travel in Japan if you understand Japanese."

　　　_____

4.　　"I saw Ricky at the IFC Mall the other day," Mandy said to Angela.

　　　_____

5.　　"I think Albert Einstein is the most important scientist of the 20th century," his sister said.

　　　_____

6.　　My student who works with the orchestra said, "I hope you'll enjoy the concert."

　　　_____

7.　　"It has not been possible to solve the problem so far," the chairperson repeated.

　　　_____

8.　　"That wasn't our idea of a relaxing holiday, I must say," my neighbour said.

　　　_____

9.　　"If you feel sick," his mother said, "you had better go to bed."

　　　_____

10.　　"I've been wondering," said John, "whether our daughter might postpone her wedding plans under the present pandemic situation."

　　　_____

　　　_____

Chapter 21 — Write Clearly and Effectively I

What you will learn in this chapter

You will learn seven important strategies that help you to write clearly and effectively. The first four of them are covered in this chapter, and the remaining three will be taken up in the next chapter: (1) eliminate unnecessary words; (2) prefer plain words and choose words carefully; (3) let your characters stand out as subjects of actions, and use verbs for actions; (4) use the active or passive voice judiciously; (5) vary the length and structure of your sentences; (6) emphasize your ideas at suitable places; and (7) establish cohesion and coherence when writing paragraphs.

你會學習七項重要的策略，有助於你的英文寫作清晰而達意。本章將介紹前四項。餘下的三項，接著在下章討論。這七項策略分別是：（1）消除冗詞；（2）用詞要簡明，選詞要謹慎；（3）介入行動的人物要明顯，講述行動最好用動詞；（4）使用主動或被動語態應當審慎；（5）句子長短和造句方式要隨情況而有所變化；（6）根據需要而強調所述內容；（7）句子構成段落時，要留意它們之間的銜接（cohesion）和整體的條理（coherence）。

21.1 Aim to write clearly and effectively.

21.2 Eliminate unnecessary words.

21.3 Prefer plain words and choose words carefully.

21.4 Let your characters stand out as subjects of action and use verbs for actions.

21.5 Use active or passive sentences judiciously.

21.6 Summing up

21.1   Aim to write clearly and effectively.

You have in this book learned a large variety of skills in the correct use of English. When you use these skills to write, of course you expect to be able to write better. But it may not be easy all at once. Some additional skills are needed to make that happen steadily in due course.

Many books have been written on writing well because it is undeniably an important subject. In these two final chapters, I like to share with you several fundamental principles of how to write clearly and effectively.

Focus, for a moment, on the words "clearly" and "effectively". They are at the core of what is meant by "better writing". Writing is not just writing individual sentences but sentences that together form passages or paragraphs. So, writing that is clear means not only sentences that are grammatically and idiomatically correct, straightforward, not confusing, but also sentences in groups logically related so that ideas "flow" smoothly, just as you can think clearly, to be all about a certain theme. If you can achieve this goal, you are writing effectively as well as clearly.

Let us now begin to consider seven strategies that together can help you to write clearly and effectively. They are not difficult to understand, and you should try to keep them in mind when you write. This chapter covers the first four; the next chapter will describe the remaining three.

(1)   Eliminate unnecessary words.

(2)   Prefer plain words and choose words carefully.

(3)   Let your characters stand out as subjects of actions and use verbs for actions.

(4)   Use active or passive sentences judiciously.

(5)   Emphasize your ideas at suitable places.

(6)   Vary the length and structure of your sentences.

(7)   Establish cohesion and coherence when writing paragraphs.

21.2   Eliminate unnecessary words.

Bear in mind that, whatever you write, try to use no more words than necessary to convey what you have to say. That is, your writing should be concise. You may not see it all at once, yet you will need to be both careful and patient in cutting out words from your draft without losing any intended meaning. If you find yourself writing sentences like **This three-year project, which is going to be very complex in nature, will . . . ,** read it again with a little thinking and you are then likely to change your sentence to **This complex three-year project will . . .** It is now about half the length, without losing any meaning.

Let us see three main situations where unnecessary words may be eliminated: (1) saying something twice (tautology); (2) roundabout expressions (circumlocution); and (3) long-winded phrases.

21.2.1 Saying something twice (tautology)

Occasional use of tautology is acceptable, but you should remove its excessive use.

Avoid	Prefer
glanced through the report briefly	glanced through the report
repeat this exercise again soon	repeat this exercise soon
their consensus of opinion	their consensus
the reason for the delay is because	the reason for the delay is that
absolutely essential preparation	essential preparation
at a later date	later
disappear from sight	disappear
visitors are fewer in number	visitors are fewer
responsible for forward planning	responsible for planning
in actual fact	in fact
two bodies in mutual cooperation	two bodies in cooperation
the new beginning	the beginning

21.2.2 Roundabout expressions (circumlocution)

Roundabout expressions always result in wordiness. Try to express an idea directly.

Avoid	Prefer
a greater length of time	longer
we are of the same opinion	we agree
at a later date	later
at an early date	soon
bright red in colour	bright red
despite the fact that	although
due to the fact that, for the reason that	because
during the month of August	in August
in connection with	about, concerning
in excess of	more than
in the foreseeable future	soon
in the vicinity of	near
spell out in detail	explain
that being the case	if so
there is no doubt that	undoubtedly

21.2.3 Long-winded phrases

Many long-winded phrases are clichés, which are *overused* and tend to become weak or even almost meaningless. Although politicians and various public speakers may still use them, you should avoid them in your writing.

Avoid	Prefer
it all comes down to this	*in summary*
as a matter of fact (or: *the fact of the matter is*)	*the truth is*
at the end of the day (or: *when all is said and done*)	*finally*
at this point in time	*now*
at your earliest convenience	*as soon as possible*
by and large	*generally*
face the music	*face it, confront it*
in the final analysis	*finally, to sum up*
in this day and age	*today, presently*
matter of life and death	*quite serious*
the name of the game	*the true purpose, the heart of the matter*
with regard to, with reference to	*about*

21.3   Prefer plain words and choose words carefully.

Prefer plain words and choose words that mean what you want to say. Plain words, as opposed to more abstract ones, are commonly used and more likely to be recognized and understood. While the more abstract words often appear in legal and other formal documents to sound more impersonal and authoritative, you can train yourself to write better by using plain words competently.

Instead of	Try
aggregates	*groups*
amend*	*change*
approximately*	*roughly, about*
assistance*	*help*
commence*	*begin*
comprehend	*understand, grasp, see*
demonstrate	*show, prove*
detrimental	*harmful, damaging*
diminish	*reduce*
disseminate	*spread*
encounter	*meet*
endeavour*	*try*
facilitate*	*help*
identical	*same*
institute (verb)	*begin, start*
magnitude	*size*
per annum	*a year*
terminate*	*end, stop*
thereafter	*then, afterwards*
utilize*	*use*
*Pay particular attention when you find yourself using these words.	

303

When there are several plain words corresponding to the same basic idea, you will need to choose carefully. Take the word **understand** for example. Other plain words with a similar meaning include **see, follow,** and **grasp**. The following phrases illustrate the uses of these words, together with the use of the more abstract word **comprehend**.

Understand: to **understand** the meaning of a word, what someone says.

See (especially spoken): to **see** what someone means, what something looks like.

Follow: to **follow** an explanation or argument, a story's plot.

Grasp: to **grasp** (= understand) an idea or concept, how something works.

Comprehend (often in negative statements): to **comprehend** something that is complicated or difficult (e.g., *The vastness of the universe is almost impossible for us to* **comprehend.**); to **comprehend** a theory or a totally outrageous idea.

You can see that they are not completely the same in meaning but have somewhat different shades or references. Thus, you need to choose one to reflect the shade or reference you have in mind.

Study the sentences of the following passage containing all these five words.

We **saw** *that the topic of the lecture, "Protection against Viral Infection", was a timely one. The speaker, an experienced physician, seemed to have a good* **grasp** *of why a viral epidemic is so hard to control. However, we did not fully* **understand** *all that he said and found some of the processes of infection he described not easy to* **follow***. This came as no surprise, because the intricate mechanisms of viral infection are indeed too complicated for ordinary people like us to* **comprehend***.*

21.4 Let your characters stand out as subjects of actions and use verbs for actions.

This is a basic principle of clear writing. Make your characters as subjects of actions and use verbs, rather than nouns or nouns made from verbs, for actions. Read the four sentences in the left part of the box. Compare them with their revised versions in the right. You should find the revised versions shorter, clearer, more direct, and hence more readable, because now you see clearly the characters as subjects of actions and actions in verbs (boldfaced).

Less clear	Clearer
1a. *Our carelessness is a cause of our mistakes.*	1b. *We **make** mistakes if we **are** careless.*
2a. *Japan was the destination of our flight.*	2b. *We **flew** to Japan.*
3a. *There is disagreement among us about the modification of our marketing tactics.*	3b. *We **disagreed** about how to **modify** our marketing tactics.*
4a. *Children's reading ability tends to decrease with their increased television watching time.*	4b. *Children who **watch** a lot of television tend to **become** less able readers.*

21.4.1 Be familiar with nominalizations and think clearly.

You will notice that all the less clear sentences contain abstract nouns, especially those formed from verbs and adjectives. The nouns so formed are called "nominalizations" (**nom** = name). A few other commonly appearing nominalizations are also included in the following box.

Nouns (including gerunds) derived from verbs	Nouns derived from adjectives
fly (past tense: *flew*) → *flight*	*able* → *ability*
disagree → *disagreement*	*careless* → *carelessness*
modify → *modification*	*destined* → *destination*
watch → *watching*	*patient* → *patience*
play → *playing*	*accurate* → *accuracy*
appear → *appearance*	*attentive* → *attentiveness*
discover → *discovery*	*reliant* → *reliance*

Of course, some nominalizations have the same form as the verb, such as **answer, change, hope, increase, process, reply**, and **shape**. The point is, however, if you use nominalizations to express an idea, your sentences will most likely be longer and not easy to read. If you are familiar with the nominalized forms and the verbs or adjectives from which they are derived, try using these verbs or adjectives instead. Your sentences will then be more concise and direct. Study the following sentences using **increase, process**, and **reply** first as nominalizations and then as verbs.

Less concise and less direct	More concise and direct
5a. *There will be an **increase** of 1 per cent in the management fees.*	5b. *Management fees will **increase** by 1 per cent.*
6a. *All admission applications will be handled by the school in a **process** taking a few weeks.*	6b. *The school will take a few weeks to **process** all admission applications.*
7a. *We would like to receive your **reply** at your earliest convenience.*	7b. *Please **reply** as soon as possible.*

Examine, once again, sentence (1a) in 21.4. **Our carelessness is a cause of our mistakes. Our carelessness** is a subject, but that is not a character doing something. Use **we** as the subject in **We make mistakes**, you at once bring the character into the picture as subject of **make mistakes**. Now, a wordy sentence can always be reworded to become clearer.   Thus, you can reword the first part of the original sentence to **if we are careless** (using **we** a second time as a character and replacing the nominalization

carelessness by the adjective **careless**). You can put this clause in the second part of the sentence as a reason why **we make mistakes.** Thus, the revised sentence (1b) is **We make mistakes if we are careless.** Alternatively, you can also say **If we are careless, we make mistakes.**

21.4.2 Times when nominalizations can be useful

While avoiding nominalizations is in general desirable to keep your sentences concise and clear, there are occasions when nominalizations can be useful. For instance, a nominalization can help you to refer to a preceding sentence in a way that establishes cohesion (= flow, dependence) between the two sentences. Take as an example sentence (3b) in 21.4: **We disagreed about how to modify our marketing tactics.** A sentence that follows might be: ***This disagreement* led to a delay in the promotion of several new products.** By repeating the idea mentioned in the preceding sentence, the nominalization **disagreement** establishes cohesion to help the reader pick up a new element (promotion delay).

Remember we said in 21.4 that characters should stand out as subjects in sentences. This is even more important than having verbs describe actions. Sometimes, a nominalization refers to an idea or concept that is familiar to readers because it is very much a part of life in modern society. Such nominalizations, despite being abstract nouns, may stay in your sentences. The following are some examples.

> ***Protection of privacy*** *is nowadays an important concern.*
>
> *Many restaurants have innovatively designed **fusion cuisines**.*
>
> *Under the influence of the Covid-19 pandemic, people are generally practising **social distancing**.*
>
> *Hardly is any issue as controversial as **racial discrimination**.*

21.5   Use active or passive sentences judiciously.

As you probably already know, a sentence written in the active voice shows the "doer" (or "agent") as the subject of an action. If the verb of the action is transitive, an object follows. For example:

Our team leader wrote the proposal. (Focus: **wrote the proposal**)

This is an active sentence, using an active voice verb. If we change **the proposal** to be the subject, it is not a doer and the verb must be changed from active **wrote** to passive **was written**. The original subject **our team leader** is moved to the end, where it is introduced by the preposition **by**. The sentence then becomes a passive sentence because it uses a passive voice verb:

The proposal was written by our team leader. (Focus: **our team leader**)

21.5.1 Write in the active as far as possible.

This is generally good advice because "who does what" is clear in an active sentence. Verbs, probably the most important class of words in writing, usually are more effective in active sentences. They are more effective in that they enable us to see an activity more easily. Read the following passage in which you find only active sentences using active verbs (boldfaced).

> *There is no doubt children **are** capable of learning a great deal from reading. Reading **exposes** them to descriptive language involving people and the things they **do**. When such language **tells** an adventure story, children **learn** a variety of behaviour that **shows** such values as bravery, honesty, decisiveness, and cooperation. They **pick up** new words, **identify** with the story's characters, and **develop** their imagination.*

However, there are exceptions to this advice.

21.5.2 When do you write in the passive?

(1)   We do not know the doer, or it is difficult to say, or it is not important.

> *Kiwi fruit **is imported** from New Zealand.*
>
> *Movable type printing **was** first **used** in China.*
>
> *Cars illegally **parked** here will be ticketed.*
>
> *The film "Dunkirk" **was screened** in Hong Kong two years ago.*
>
> *She **was** completely **carried away** working on her computer.*
>
> *This problem will have to **be dealt with** right away.*
>
> *We **are reminded** when using our mobile phone that time is **compressed** and distances are **removed**.*
>
> *Over a million citizens **have been tested** for Covid-19 in the universal community testing programme.*

(2)   We use the passive (sometimes it may be the active) if it helps moving smoothly from one sentence to the next.

> Note that in passage (1), the second sentence begins with new information seemingly unrelated to the first sentence. The flow is not smooth.
>
> (1) *We had planned a dinner gathering for about twenty friends, but decided to postpone it. Careful consideration of health risks under the recent alarming surge in local coronavirus cases brought about this decision.*
>
> In passage (2), the second sentence opens with **the decision**, which is familiar information as it is already mentioned in the first sentence. The second sentence is passive, using **was based on**, but makes a smoother flow from the first sentence.
>
> (2) *We had planned a dinner gathering for about twenty friends, but decided to postpone it. The decision **was made** after careful consideration of health risks under the recent alarming surge in local coronavirus cases.*

21.5.3 Choose the active or the passive judiciously (= carefully and sensibly).

Simply put, both the active and the passive have their merits. Active sentences are more direct while passive sentences are more indirect. Not all active sentences can be converted to the passive (e.g., **She got up** early; **The two groups** *will cooperate* to launch the new service), and some sentences are usually written in the passive (e.g., **Dinner** *is served*; **Many goods** *are made* in China or some southeast Asian country).

Sometimes, a long clause as subject makes the active sentence awkward. Changing it to the passive would sound more natural and would be easier to understand with the proper "end-focus" as a point of emphasis. See, for example, how the second sentence (passive) is better than the first (active) in the following:

Awkward	More natural
(1) *The rich sounds of the strings, the great variety of emotions expressed, and the close rapport between conductor and musicians deeply **impressed** us.*	(2) *We **were** deeply **impressed by** the rich sounds of the strings, the great variety of emotions expressed, and the close rapport between conductor and musicians.*

At times, you may want to focus attention on one perspective rather than another. One perspective is conveyed better by the active and another by the passive. In the following, the first passage focuses on the teacher while the second focuses on the pupil.

The teacher	The pupil
(1) *What happens in the classroom? The teacher **tells** her pupils many things. She **asks** them questions to see whether she has explained things clearly. She also **gives** them homework, which she **demands** to be returned at the next class.*	(2) *What happens in the classroom? The pupils **are told** many things by their teacher. They **are asked** questions to see whether they understand what she has explained. They **are** also **given** homework, which they are to return at the next class.*

Therefore, when it comes to using the active or the passive in your writing, try reading them yourself a few times and listen to how they sound. Are they clear? Do they sound natural? Do they present the proper focus or convey the right perspective? You need to be careful and sensible so that you produce sentences that are natural and right for your intended focus. In other words, do it *judiciously*.

21.6 Summing up

To write clearly means that your sentences should be not only grammatically free of errors but also straightforward and unambiguous as a result of how you use words to express ideas. To write effectively goes further. Do your sentences say what you want them to say? Do they produce an effect (e.g., agreeing with you about something) on your readers just the way you intended?

You may want to describe, explain, persuade, encourage, criticize, excite, support, praise, suggest, or whatever that is your purpose. Your concern should be: *Do my sentences succeed in doing that?*

You have learned the following four important strategies to write both clearly and effectively (three more strategies will be discussed in Chapter 22):

(1)   **Eliminate unnecessary words**. Watch out for unnecessary words. You should not develop the habit of saying the same thing twice when one word is sufficient. Neither should you include in your writing roundabout expressions or overused clichés that are both wordy and empty in meaning. Avoid wordiness and keep your writing concise.

(2)   **Prefer plain words**. Plain words are more recognizable and easier to understand. When you can think of more than one word to express the same idea, choose carefully the one that better fits your

purpose. Consult a good dictionary if necessary.

(3)   **Let characters be subjects and use verbs for actions**. Try to have characters (people) as subjects of actions and use verbs, rather than nouns or nouns made from verbs, for actions. Avoid nominalizations (nouns formed from verbs and adjectives) if possible. Follow this principle and you will more likely write convincing and readable sentences.

(4)   **Use active or passive voice sensibly**. While you should in general write in the active voice, this is not always feasible or advisable. Be careful and sensible so that you produce sentences that are natural and right for your intended focus or perspective. In other words, you need to be judicious (= careful and sensible) in choosing the active or the passive in writing.

| Exercises | **Chapter 21** |

Exercise 21.1

Rewrite each sentence so that unnecessary words are cut out, roundabout expressions are simplified, and cliché-like phrases are replaced by plain words.

改寫下列句子，剔除贅餘的詞，簡化迂迴不明的詞，並以淺易的詞代替陳腔濫調。

1.　He has chosen the field of business administration as his major subject in university.

　　_____

2.　We should study the figures given in Table 1.

　　_____

3.　Writing the report will take a greater length of time than originally estimated.

　　_____

4.　Her bag is completely filled with grocery.

　　_____

5.　We have plans to open a branch in the foreseeable future.

　　_____

6.　There is no doubt that prevention is better than cure.

　　_____

7.　We encountered many problems in the course of the last two years.

　　_____

8.　I am of the opinion that she has made impressive progress.

　　_____

9.　It all comes down to this: no one is sure about the effectiveness of the new vaccine.

　　_____

10.　In this day and age, we cannot function well without our mobile phone.

　　_____

11.　As a matter of fact, none of us understands what he was saying.

　　_____

12. Considering the present difficult situation, the government's subsidy to small businesses is by and large much needed.

Exercise 21.2

Equate each word in column A with a plain word or phrase in column B.

將 B 列中較簡易的詞或短詞與 A 列中的詞相對應。

	Column A		Column B
1.	advantageous	_____	a. cut
2.	commence	_____	b. try
3.	detrimental	_____	c. make easier
4.	diminish	_____	d. best
5.	eliminate	_____	e. main
6.	encounter	_____	f. go ahead
7.	endeavour	_____	g. place
8.	expedite	_____	h. reduce
9.	facilitate	_____	i. useful
10.	implement	_____	j. meet
11.	locality	_____	k. harmful
12.	optimum	_____	m. end
13.	predominant	_____	n. begin
14.	proceed	_____	o. carry out
15.	terminate	_____	p. speed up

Exercise 21.3

In Part A, turn verbs and adjectives into nominalizations. In Part B, turn nominalizations into verbs and adjectives. Note that some verbs and nominalizations are the same words.

在 A 部分中，把動詞和形容詞改為名詞（名詞化）。在 B 部分中，把名詞轉為動詞和形容詞。須注意：有些詞既是動詞也是名詞。

Part A

Verb	Nominalization	Adjective	Nominalization
1. appear		13. accurate	
2. argue		14. careless	
3. arrange		15. close	
4. decrease		16. comprehensive	
5. define		17. conservative	
6. discover		18. different	
7. discuss		19. efficient	
8. examine		20. fragile	
9. explain		21. fruitful	
10. fail		22. magnificent	
11. fulfil		23. same	
12. gain		24. similar	

Part B

Nominalization	Verb	Adjective (can be more than one)
1. ability		
2. accommodation		
3. articulation		
4. brightness		
5. clarity		
6. completion		
7. depression		
8. deprivation		
9. embarrassment		
10. evaluation		
11. generation		
12. hardness		
13. improvement		
14. initiation		
15. knowledge		
16. limitation		
17. modernization		
18. preparation		

Nominalization	Verb	Adjective (can be more than one)
19. realization		
20. reinforcement		
21. rejection		
22. satisfaction		
23. sensitivity		
24. transformation		

Exercise 21.4

Rewrite the following sentences so that the subjects are no longer descriptions expressed in abstract nouns but characters whose actions are expressed in verbs.

試把下面句子重寫，使主語不是以抽象名詞構成的陳述，而是用動詞來表達行動的人物。

1.   Expectation now exists among Hong Kong people that social distancing restrictions under Covid-19 will be a new normalcy of life.

     _____

     _____

2.   There is a belief among many customers that their shopping in supermarkets could be more efficient if there were installations of touch screens to indicate location of items.

     _____

     _____

3.   Children's music appreciation ability will increase with greater exposure to music.

     _____

     _____

4.   There has been rapid growth in the market for sport equipment because of the common desire among young people for outdoor activities.

     _____

     _____

5.   Because her preparation for the singing contest was thorough, none of the other competitors was a threat to her.

     _____

     _____

Exercise 21.5

Part A Change the following sentences into the passive. (Note: agents of actions are not always mentioned in the passive.)

試把以下的句子改寫成被動語態。（注意：在被動語態中，行為的施動者不一定出現。）

1. My friend explained the situation to me.

   _____

2. All committee members elected him chairman.

   _____

3. The principal is going to explain the changes in extra-curricular activities to the students.

   _____

4. They saw the car knocking over a pedestrian.

   _____

5. Our project leader hopes to include Tony in his team.

   _____

6. People use the pedestrian escalators all the time.

   _____

Part B Change the following sentences into the active.

試把以下句子改寫成主動語態。

1. Their home was broken into when they were on holiday.

   _____

2. It was believed that the project would not finish on time.

   _____

3. Consideration will be given to the new recruitment procedure at the next meeting.

   _____

4. The data in the report should be checked carefully.

   _____

5. Everyone in the audience was amused by the subtle humour of the speaker.

   _____

6. That elderly man should have been offered some help when he fell.

   _____

Chapter 22   Write Clearly and Effectively II

What you will learn in this chapter

Following the preceding chapter, you will learn in this chapter three more strategies that help you to write clearly and effectively: (1) emphasize your ideas at suitable places; (2) vary the length and structure of your sentences; and (3) establish cohesion and coherence when writing paragraphs. While the four strategies in Chapter 21 focus more on words, the three in this chapter are largely concerned with sentences and how they can work together in a paragraph.

本章內容接續前章，你將繼續學習另外三項重要的策略，幫助你書寫清晰而達意的英語：（1）按需要在適當之處表示強調；（2）句子長短和造句方式隨情況而有變化；（3）句子構成段落時，要留意它們之間的銜接（cohesion）和整體的條理（coherence）。上一章所介紹的四項策略，重點在於字詞的使用；這一章所講的三項策略，主要討論句子的處理和句子怎樣在段落裏產生效用。

22.1 Beyond words

22.2 Emphasize your ideas at suitable places.

22.3 Vary the length and structure of your sentences.

22.4 Establish cohesion and coherence when writing paragraphs.

22.5 Summing up

22.1 Beyond words

In Chapter 21, you have seen how to write clearly and effectively through four basic strategies: removing unnecessary words, using plain and appropriate words, preferring verbs for actions rather than using nominalizations, and using active and passive voice judiciously. In various ways, the main focus of these strategies is words. In this chapter, while words are still important for expressing ideas, we will be more concerned with sentences and how they can work together in a paragraph. Specifically, you will learn three more strategies:

(1)   Emphasize your ideas at suitable places.

(2)   Vary the length and structure of your sentences.

(3)   Establish cohesion and coherence when writing paragraphs.

22.2 Emphasize your ideas at suitable places.

Unlike a speaker who can emphasize his or her points by such means as voice level, speed, facial expressions, and gestures, the writer can emphasize ideas only by choosing words and using them in particular ways. To write clearly and effectively, you need to know the tools available for putting emphasis in your sentences.

Emphasis is attention or importance given to an element or idea. Reasons for this include: you may feel strongly about something, you may want to show a contrast with something, or you may say that something unexpected actually happened. The following are the main ways of showing emphasis:

* Use particular words.

* Use rhetorical questions.

* Place the more important idea at end of sentence.

* Use inversion.

* Use fronting.

* Use cleft sentences.

22.2.1 Use particular words.

(1) Repeat a word or restate the same idea with a strong tone.
*It's **clear** to me. Crystal **clear**.*
*They know **everything** about our plans. **Everything!***
*Listen carefully, because this is **very**, **very** important.*
***I cannot** do this. **Not me**.*
*The sight of the mountains **takes your breath away**! It's **out of this world**!*

(2) Stress an auxiliary verb. (Use boldface or capitals in writing; say the word with stress in speech)

I AM telling you the truth!

DO read this agreement carefully.

He DOES have a sense of guilt in this matter.

They SHOULD NOT treat us like this.

(3) In *negative* statements, add **at all** after the negative word or later in the sentence, use **whatever** after a negative noun phrase, or use **not a** or **never** at the beginning of the sentence.

*We know nothing about it—nothing **at all**.*

*I cannot find any fault **at all** with her performance.*

*They did not care about customers' complaints **at all**.*

*There is no reason **whatever** for rejecting this proposal.*

*It was a bad failure and we have no excuse **whatever**.*

***Not a sound** was heard in the hall before the violinist started playing.*

***Never** have I seen such a lofty mountain.*

(4) Use *forceful* verbs (or verbs in strong expressions) to say something specific about an action.

*I **relish** the opportunity to take a river cruise in Europe next year.*

*It's our time to **shine**. (= to show our achievement/glory)*

*With her excellent persuasion skills, she can surely **hammer out** a good deal. (= to decide on a plan or reach an agreement after much discussion)*

*With rising Covid-19 cases, restaurants got severely **clobbered** (= hit very hard) as the government had to ban evening dining in eateries.*

*She **scrutinized** (= examined very carefully) the document before signing.*

*We **bent over backwards** (= tried very hard to help) to overcome the project's difficulties.*

*You need to **think** at least **five steps ahead**.*

*He **knows** the tourism industry **from A to Z**.*

(5) Use intensifying adjectives and adverbs. (Note: Some modifiers such as **great, terrific, tremendous,** and **fantastic** are commonly used as emphatic ways of saying **good** or **nice**: **We had a great time**. When overused, however, they tend to lose their emphatic meaning. Note also that **awfully** and **terribly** can be used in both a positive and a negative sense.)

*That he could finish the marathon was a **complete** surprise to us.*

*When the examinations were over, she had an **overwhelming** sense of relief.*

*It was just **sheer** luck that he was unhurt in the traffic accident.*

*The publicity campaign was a **total** failure.*

*I have **absolute** confidence in you.*

> *He said it was his best achievement in his **entire** life.*
>
> *This is **definitely** one of the best Italian restaurants in town.*
>
> *We had a **truly** relaxing time in the Blue Lagoon of Iceland.*
>
> *The weather was **terrific**, and we met some **awfully** nice people in the village.* (*awfully* used in a positive sense)
>
> *I felt **awfully** embarrassed when I forgot a line in my speech.* (*awfully* used in a negative sense)
>
> *It's **terribly** important for children to enjoy learning.* (*terribly* used in a positive sense)
>
> *The plan went **terribly** wrong.* (*terribly* used in a negative sense)

22.2.2 Use rhetorical questions.

A rhetorical (= using speech or writing in a special way to persuade or influence) question is asked not to solicit an answer but to make an *emphatic statement*. If the rhetorical question takes a positive form, it is equivalent to making a strong negative statement. If the rhetorical question is negative, it is actually making a strong positive statement.

> Positive form
>
> *Is this a reason for rejecting his idea?* (= Of course it is NOT.)
> <u>Negative statement</u>
>
> Negative form
>
> *Didn't we warn you of possible criticisms from our readers?*
> (= Surely, you must remember we warned you of possible criticisms from our readers.)
> <u>Positive statement</u>

You can have rhetorical **wh-**questions. The following are examples using **what, why, when,** and **who**.

> Positive form
>
> *What use will it have?* (= It will have NO use.)
> <u>Negative statement</u>
>
> *Why should we pretend that the problem does not exist?*
> (= We should NOT pretend that the problem does not exist.)
> <u>Negative statement</u>
>
> Negative form
>
> *Aren't we going to stop polluting the air?* (= We must stop polluting the air.)
> <u>Positive statement</u>
>
> *Who doesn't know that prevention is better than cure?*
> (= Certainly, everybody knows that prevention is better than cure.)
> <u>Positive statement</u>

22.2.3 Place the most important idea at the end of sentence.

In general, save the most important idea for the end of your sentence. That is usually where you leave a stronger impression on your reader. Compare the following two sentences:

> *She plays the piano beautifully, and she also plays guitar and the flute.*
>
> *She plays guitar and the flute,* ***but she plays the piano beautifully***.

Although both sentences are grammatical and can communicate, the second sounds more natural because it obviously brings out the main point announced at the end of the sentence.

In the next pair of sentences, the first is written using coordination (two equally important ideas linked by a coordinating conjunction, see Chapter 15). Two ideas are linked by **but**. The second is written using subordination, in which you see a subordinate adverbial clause introduced by a subordinating conjunction **although**. The main clause, carrying the main idea (never having been to Hokkaido), comes at the end. To place emphasis on this idea, the second sentence is a better choice. Since the main clause normally contains the main idea, such emphasis is now combined with the emphasis appearing at the end of the sentence. Choosing the second sentence enables you to achieve double emphasis.

> *We have visited Japan many times before,* ***but*** *have never been to Hokkaido.*
>
> ***Although*** *we have visited Japan many times before, we have never been to Hokkaido.*

Now read the following short passage I have written on climate change. If you read it carefully, you can see at the end of each sentence the emphasis of a point expressed by a word or phrase.

> *We have come to **a critical point**. Climate change is such an important issue that no country can afford to **ignore it any longer**. Global warming is not fiction but **a scientific fact**. To safeguard the welfare of future generations, governments must **cooperate and take firm action**. Opportunity to minimize grave consequences is still **possible**. As individuals, we must take brave steps to change our lifestyle **before it is too late**.*

22.2.4 Use inversion.

The subject of a sentence normally comes before the verb. *Inversion occurs when the verb comes before the subject.* When you do so, you reorder the information in the sentence so that an element appears later in the sentence where it receives attention. For example:

A large statue *stands in the middle of the square.* → *In the middle of the square stands* ***a large statue***.

The following are some main situations where you can use inversion:

> A. Main verb before the subject
>
> > *Up **goes** the hot-air balloon.*
> >
> > *On that wall **hangs** a large painting of flowers.*
> >
> > *Here **are** the books you wanted.*
> >
> > *Into the pool **dived** two playful teenage boys.*
> >
> > *The opening movement was slow and subdued. Then **came** the contrast of the second movement's lively and brilliant dance tempo.*

B. Short answers beginning with **so, neither, nor,** followed by auxiliary verb + subject

*"We enjoy visiting museums." "**So do I.**"*

*"She cannot speak French." "**Neither/Nor can we.**"*

*"We do not eat raw fish." "**Neither/Nor do I.**"*

*"He has decided to study medicine, and **so have his best friends.**"*

C. After **as, than,** and **so**

*She was very happy with her achievement, **as were her parents**.* (She was just as happy with her achievement as her parents were.)

*Women in general have a longer life expectancy **than do men**.*

***So** well **did the orchestra play** that the audience applauded thunderously.*

D. After adverbs with negative or restrictive meanings, use auxiliary verb (**do, have, can,** etc.) + subject.

***At no time did he** notice he was waiting for his friend at the wrong place.*

***Hardly ever does he** pay attention to details.*

***Little did I** realize how dangerous escalators can be.*

***Only later did she** manage to correct her mistake.* (Note: To use inversion of subject and auxiliary after **only, only** must be followed immediately by some time expression, e.g., **only when the meeting began, only after a long while, only on weekends.**)

***No sooner had we** sat down than waiters brought us water and the menu.*

***Not only does he** love steaks, **he also** craves for desserts.*

***Never have I** seen such a chaotic sight.*

***Under no circumstances can purchased underwear** be exchanged.*

E. After expressions of place and direction

***Behind the counter were** two courteous and smiling receptionists.*

***On the podium stood** a smartly dressed young conductor.*

***Down these stairs is** the department selling household items.*

***About two kilometres to the east** lies a small village by the side of a stream.*

F. Conditional sentences

***Had you tried** harder, you would have done better.*

***Had we found** this shorter route earlier, we might have saved a lot of time.*

***Were I** the manager, I would do things differently.*

22.2.5 Use fronting.

Fronting is moving a part of the sentence to the front position to give it some prominence. This can be a word, phrase, or clause. Fronting often comes with inversion (see D, E, F in box of 22.2.4), especially when the fronted words have negative meaning (e.g., **hardly, little, rarely**). In effect, then, fronting catches attention immediately at the start of a sentence while also putting emphasis on what comes later in the sentence.

If some already-known information is placed at the beginning of a sentence, it relates more noticeably to something mentioned in the preceding sentence, thus helping the flow of thought. This occurs, for instance, when you want to show some detail or make an attention-catching comparison with a point already mentioned. (See B in the box below.)

A. Adverbials of place and time

   ***In Canada** houses have kitchens larger than those in Hong Kong.*

   ***On Sunday** we will go to church.*

   ***Last Christmas** our classmates had a wonderful reunion.*

   ***In the middle of the square** is a large fountain.*

B. Adverbials connecting with earlier information and adverbials that show writer's comments

   *The final episode of the exploration series just finished. **Next is** the evening news.*

   *There has been a serious surge in local infection cases. **Consequently**, the government announced some more stringent measures of social distancing.*

   *Her suggestion was not bad. **However**, not everybody agreed.*

   *To reduce cost, we employed fewer staff in the last quarter. **As you might expect**, this affected our service really hard.*

C. Fronting with **so** with inversion to say that something is *also true* of someone

   *"They have prepared well."   "**So** have we."*

   *"She enjoyed the play." "**So** did you."*

   *"We will do our best to increase our market share." "**So** will our competitor."*

D. Fronting with **so** without inversion to *affirm* that something is true.

   *"You have forgotten to bring your phone." "**So** I have!"*

   *"Robots will soon be working in restaurants." "**So** they will be!"*

   *"The Covid-19 pandemic is changing the way we live." "**So** it is."*

E. Fronting with **as** or **though** after an adjective or adverb to express an *emphatic contrast*

   ***Strange as it may seem**, I never learned swimming until I was 45.*

   ***Tough as the job was**, we got it done.*

   ***Much as I like Chinese calligraphy**, I do not really have the time to practise it.*

   ***Hard though she tried**, she did not win in the singing contest.*

F. Fronting the object to become the topic, making it more important

We have thoroughly discussed this problem. → **This problem** *we have thoroughly discussed.*

It is certainly a good choice. → **A good choice** *it certainly is.*

I never understand how a poem can be written on a rice grain. → **How a poem can be written on a rice grain** *I never understand.*

22.2.6 Use cleft sentences.

A cleft (= divided) sentence divides a sentence into two parts, each with its own verb and one part is given greater emphasis. One type of cleft sentence begins with **it is/was.**

Normal sentence pattern (single clause, one verb): **My daughter gave me a shirt for Father's Day**.

Cleft sentence (two clauses, two verbs):

It is *my daughter*	**who gave me a shirt for Father's Day.**

In this form, the cleft sentence gives emphasis to part of the sentence (here: **my daughter**). It can be reworded to give emphasis to other parts of the same sentence:

---

*It was **a shirt** that my daughter gave me for Father's Day.*

*It was **for Father's Day** that my daughter gave me a shirt.*

More examples of **it**-type cleft sentences compared with the normal pattern:

Normal pattern	**It-type cleft sentences**
1. *Sovereignty over Hong Kong was returned to China in July 1997.*	*It was **in July 1997** that (or when) sovereignty over Hong Kong was returned to China.*
2. *We can get excellent vegetables in the market on Cage Street.*	*It is **in the market on Cage Street** where we can get excellent vegetables.*
3. *Human error, not bad weather, usually causes traffic accidents.*	*It is **usually human error**, not bad weather, that causes traffic accidents.*
4. *She discovered she had forgotten her passport when she was on her way to the airport.*	*It was **only when she was on her way to the airport** that she discovered she had forgotten her passport.*

Note: You cannot use an **it**-clause to emphasize the verb associated with the action. Instead, you must use a **wh**-type cleft sentence. Read on to see how this is done.

Another type of cleft sentence begins with a clause introduced by a **wh**-word (often **what**, but also **when, where,** and **why**) to highlight an action. Again, the cleft sentence contains two clauses, each with its own verb. Take, for example, **She took her son to the museum**. The **wh**-clause is followed by a suitable form of **be**.

What she did was *(to) take her son to the museum*. (emphasized part in italics)

As you can see, **wh**-type cleft sentences are suitable for emphasizing actions. For example, sentence 3 in the preceding box can be rewritten as follows to emphasize "causes traffic accidents": **What usually causes traffic accidents is human error, not bad weather.**

More examples of **wh**-type cleft sentences compared with the normal pattern:

Normal pattern	Wh-type cleft sentences
1. We need a holiday after all the hard work.	**What** we need after all the hard work is a holiday.
2. He has wasted too much time.	**What** he has done is waste too much time.
3. We gave them some ideas for improvement.	**What** we gave them was some ideas for improvement.
4. She spent last Sunday in Stanley.	The place **where** she spent last Sunday was Stanley. (to emphasize the place) Or in an informal style: Stanley was **where** she spent last Sunday. The day **when** she went to Stanley was last Sunday. (to emphasize the day)
5. Wagner's operas are rarely performed because they are too long.	The reason (**why**) Wagner's operas are rarely performed is they are too long.
6. Prof. D. C. Lau translated The Analects of Confucius to English.	**What** Prof. D. C. Lau **did** was (to) translate The Analects of Confucius to English.
7. You must never give up trying.	**What matters is** you must never give up trying. (to emphasize the whole sentence)
8. His application was not accepted.	**What happened was** (that) his application was not accepted. (to emphasize the whole sentence)

Other cleft sentences emphasizing time and place:

Normal pattern	Cleft sentences
9. Polio was almost eliminated with the introduction of effective vaccines in the 1960s.	**It was not until** the 1960s when effective vaccines were introduced that polio was almost eliminated.
10. I realized that the concert was cancelled when I read the email from the organizer.	**It was only when** I read the email from the organizer that I realized (that) the concert was cancelled.
11. You can get a quick haircut here.	**This is where** you can get a quick haircut. (Or: **Here is where** you can get a quick haircut.)
12. My school was there in the 1950s.	**That is where** my school was in the 1950s.

22.3   Vary the length and structure of your sentences.

To write well, you have to put all the English skills you have learned to work for you in such a way that you convey your ideas clearly and effectively to your readers. Your sentences must be carefully constructed to be clear, lively, and easily understood. To do so, observe the following three principles that help you build more variety in your sentences:

(1) **Your sentences have different lengths**. Some sentences are short; some are long. Some simple sentences can be long (e.g., **More than four months later, she received a reply from only one of the many international companies on her application list.**) while some complex sentences can be very short (e.g., **She listens when the pastor speaks.**)

There is no clear-cut quantitative definition of "short" and "long". Indeed, sentence length depends on the writer's purpose. If you are writing a project progress report for busy executives, you may use concise, succinct sentences to be clear and readable. On the other hand, if you are writing a speech for a fundraising meeting, you may use longer sentences to appeal to donors' generosity but one or two forceful short sentences occasionally and at the end to stress an important point. Sentence length does depend on what you want to say and how you want to shape your ideas.

(2) **Include different sentence types**. What you write may contain simple sentences (a single independent clause, but can contain a few or many modifying elements), compound sentences (two or more independent or coordinated clauses), complex sentences (main clause + one or more subordinate clauses), and, where appropriate, compound-complex sentences. Of course, you do not have to have all these types in a particular document that you write. The point is: *try to have some variety. It makes your writing more interesting.*

(3) **Begin your sentences in different ways to avoid repetitious sentence structure**. Beginning a sentence in different ways often means adopting different sentence structures to achieve different objectives even though you may be toying with the same idea. Try different sentence constructions to express roughly the same idea and choose one that suits your purpose and also adds variety to the sentences that make up the paragraph or passage you are writing.

Let us now go over a few tips for achieving sentence variety.

22.3.1 Avoid a series of short, simple sentences because they sound choppy.

If you write many short sentences in a row, they tend to sound choppy (= disjointed or not well connected). Readers may easily lose interest. You can rewrite a group of short sentences by using coordination or subordination to show how the ideas are related.

Choppy:	Remarks:
Hong Kong and Shenzhen are neighbouring cities. The Shenzhen River is a boundary between them. They are different in many ways.	Sentences feel (or sound) choppy if they seem to be unrelated and contain many different topics. Simple sentences surely have their uses, including serving as brief statements of fact or important points. However, do not overuse them. Sometimes, you can combine them (or the ideas they contain) to form a more focused statement.
Improved:	
Separated by the Shenzhen River, Hong Kong and Shenzhen are neighbouring cities that, however, differ in many ways.	The three simple sentences on the left are combined to begin with a participial phrase, followed by a main clause (**Hong Kong and Shenzhen are . . .**) with another subordinate clause (**that, however, differ in many ways.**)

22.3.2 Use compound and complex sentences suitably.

Sometimes a **compound sentence** (two or more independent clauses joined by conjunctions) is clear and sensible enough, requiring little or no change.

*The company will no longer support this project, **and** there is little we can do.*

*The demand is decreasing, **but**, strangely enough, the price has not come down.*

There are times when a compound sentence should be rewritten as a **complex sentence** (one main clause with one or more subordinate clauses) with probably better effect. An idea may stand out more noticeably in a main clause.

Original: *Hong Kong is now part of China, and its legal system remains as autonomous as before.*

Revised: <u>**Hong Kong**, (which is) now part of China,</u> <u>**keeps its legal system as autonomous as before.**</u>
                (dependent clause)   (main clause)

Or: *Now part of China, Hong Kong keeps its legal system as autonomous as before.*

Original: *The task of cleaning the data was laborious, and we had no idea how long it would take.*

Revised: <u>When we took up the laborious task of cleaning the data,</u> <u>**we had no idea how long it would take.**</u>
                  (dependent clause)   (main clause)

Original: *The golf club is near Dongguan, and it attracts many visitors from Hong Kong.*

Revised: <u>Located near Dongguan,</u> <u>**the golf club attracts many visitors from Hong Kong.**</u>
       (dependent clause)   (main clause)

Sometimes you may consider writing a **compound-complex sentence**. Each of the following two sentences contains two independent/main clauses and one dependent/subordinate clause.

<u>*Given that there are many similar products in the market,*</u> <u>***a new product must be advertisded***</u>
               (dependent clause)   (main clause 1)

or <u>**the public will never ask for it**</u>.
      (main clause 2)

<u>**He finished his exam paper early**</u>, *and* <u>**he kept checking it**</u> <u>*until the time was up.*</u>
     (main clause 1)   (main clause 2)   (dependent clause)

In the following sentence, there are two independent clauses and two dependent clauses:

<u>*Although it was hot,*</u> <u>**I walked the whole way**</u>, *and so* <u>**I was soaked with sweat**</u> <u>*when I got home.*</u>
(dependent clause 1)   (main clause 1)   (main clause 2)   (dependent clause 2)

22.3.3 Guard against elements of unequal rank, excessive use of *and*, and vague linkage.

Do not use conjunctions to link phrases or clauses of unequal rank.

Not: ~~I went to the cinemas area, **and** a family of four appeared and talked loudly.~~

But this: *I went to the cinemas area **where** a family of four appeared and talked loudly.*

Or this: *I went to the cinemas area. A family of four appeared and talked loudly.*

Not: ~~Our company employs over 2,000 people and was founded in 1965.~~

The following two rearrangements have different meanings/emphases:

But this: **Our company**, *which employs over 2,000 people*, **was founded in 1965**. (main clause: *Our company was founded in 1965.*)

Or this: **Our company**, *founded in 1965*, **employs over 2,000 people**. (main clause: *Our company employs over 2,000 people.*)

Excessive or loose use of *and* leads to lengthy sentence and weakens flow of thought.

Not: ~~She was home by herself and there were few things she could do, and she felt quite unhappy.~~

But this: *Home by herself with few things to do,* **she felt quite unhappy**. (ideas linked more tightly)

Not: ~~The participants listened to a talk, and then they practised role play, and then they evaluated each other's performance.~~

But this: *The participants listened to a talk, practised role play, and then evaluated each other's performance.*

Use a more specific conjunction to link clauses to express their relationship.

Not: ~~People avoid going out in the epidemic~~ **and** ~~shop owners are losing a lot of business.~~

But this: *Shop owners are losing a lot of business* **because** *people avoid going out in the epidemic.*

Or this: *People avoid going out in the epidemic,* **so** *shop owners are losing a lot of business.*

Or this: *The epidemic has cost shop owners a lot of business* **since** *people avoid going out.*

22.3.4 Always look for opportunities of expressing ideas in parallel forms.

Parallel forms (see Chapter 17) help to clarify the relationship between ideas or between parts of a single idea, thus making your sentences more readable. Parallel forms also enable you to write coherent paragraphs, a point we will come to in 22.4. Do you notice the parallel elements in the preceding two sentences (both within a sentence and across sentences)?

Parallel forms or structures can consist of nouns, verbs, adjectives, adverbs, and various phrases and clauses:

Single words

> The children **ate**, **sang**, and **played**. (past tense verbs)

> His acting was **convincing**, **natural**, and **brilliant**. (adjectives)

> At home I have books on **history**, **art**, **music**, and **languages**. (nouns)

> The bomb disposal expert worked very **slowly** and **carefully** to disable the explosive device. (adverbs)

Phrases

> Last year we travelled to Iceland **by air**, **by sea**, and **by land**. (prepositional phrases)

> Her hobbies include **painting** and **playing the piano**. (gerund phrases)

> He spends his time **reading magazines** and **listening to old songs**. (participial phrases)

> Fortunately, he has a high-salary job **to support his family** and **to pay for his home's mortgage**. (infinitive phrases)

> *She was excited to hear that she was **accepted by the university, awarded a scholarship**, and **offered a hostel room**.* (finite verb phrases)

Clauses

> *An executive **who focuses on opportunities** and **who takes responsibility for decisions** will be respected by his or her colleagues.* (adjective clauses)
>
> *I remembered **that my two library books were due last Friday** and **that I had a reserved book to pick up on the same day**.* (noun clauses)

Sometimes you need to have **parallel subjects** at the beginning of clauses:

Faulty: *We are glad that you are interested in our school, **and** please call us if you need further information.*

Revised: ***We are glad that** you are interested in our school, and **we hope that** you will call us if you need further information.*

22.3.5 Begin your sentences in different ways.

Do not habitually begin your sentences with an ordinary subject (such as a person or thing). That would be monotonous to read. Try to achieve a more varied and interesting style by putting different words, phrases, or even clauses before the subject of a sentence. The following are some of the many possibilities.

A. Begin with an adverb (that modifies the whole sentence)
***Occasionally**, doing something different is desirable.*
***Finally**, the soloist walked to the front of the stage.*
B. Begin with an adverbial clause (subordinating to a main clause)
***Although the work is exhausting**, you are learning many new things.*
***If I practise persistently**, I will soon be able to play this difficult song.*
C. Begin with a prepositional phrase
***In spite of its shortcomings**, the study is still a respectable pioneering work.*
***Given its innovativeness**, the pyramidal glass entrance to the Louvre is a great landmark.*
D. Begin with an infinitive
***To succeed**, you must adopt a sound strategy.*
***To pay**, just scan this QR code with your mobile phone.*
E. Begin with an infinitive phrase
***To tell the truth**, this is a very serious problem.*
***To serve you** is our pleasure.*
F. Begin with a participle
***Smiling**, she came to the podium to give a speech.*
***Frustrated**, he left without saying a word.*

G. Begin with a participial phrase (as modifier of subject in the main clause)
Not discouraged by failure, *they kept on trying with better ideas.*
Studying people's behaviour, *Confucius learned a great deal about human nature.*

H. Begin with a gerund phrase (as subject)
Seeing him so thin and pale *shocked her.*
Repairing the vacuum cleaner *will be expensive.*

I. Begin with a noun clause (as subject)
That life may exist on other planets *is seriously considered by many scientists.*
What you are doing now *may have unintended consequences.*

J. Begin with a transitional word or phrase (when the context justifies it)
However, *not everybody agrees.*
At the same time, *we need to consider possible alternatives.*

K. Begin with an appositive (An appositive, usually a noun phrase, serves to identify, explain, expand, or supplement the meaning of other nouns or noun phrases. Commas are used to set off an appositive.)
A cosmopolitan commercial city, *Hong Kong is easily accessible from other places.* (The appositive can also come after the subject: *Hong Kong,* ***a cosmopolitan commercial city***, *is easily accessible from other places.*)
An expert in immunology, *Dr. K. gave an informative talk on how health food can help prevent many illnesses.*

L. Begin with an "absolute phrase." (An absolute phrase contains a noun phrase modified by a participle, an adjective or adjective phrase or a prepositional phrase with adjectival function). It modifies the sentence as a whole. It has its own subject and is grammatically independent of the sentence it modifies.) In the following sentences, the underlined part is an absolute phrase.
(Present participle) *Dinner* ***being*** *ready, she asked her guests to be seated.*
The epidemic ***spreading*** *alarmingly, more stringent isolation measures were imposed.*
(Past participle) *The project once* ***completed***, *he will feel immensely relieved.*
(Adjective phrase) *His lips* ***trembling with stage fright***, *he soon started to cry.*
(Prepositional phrase with adjectival function) *His baton* ***in his hand***, *the conductor walked cheerfully to the front of the orchestra.*

22.4 Establish cohesion and coherence when writing paragraphs.

22.4.1 Cohesion

Cohesion refers to the flow of ideas from one sentence to the next. If there is connection between ideas from one sentence to the next, you can feel the "flow", meaning that the sentences are cohesive. Sentences that are cohesive help the reader to follow you in the intended direction.

Notice that the three sentences in the preceding paragraph are actually written to illustrate that ideas can flow more easily if you observe one requirement: Pay some attention to how each sentence ends and the next begins.

Cohesion refers to the flow of ideas from one sentence to the next. If there is connection between ideas from one sentence to the next, you can feel the "flow", meaning that the sentences are cohesive. Sentences that are cohesive help the reader to follow you in the intended direction.	Note that the beginning of the second sentence says "If there is connection between ideas from one sentence to the next", which is announced towards the end of the first sentence. The second sentence ends with " . . . the sentences are cohesive". Then, that idea is repeated in the first words of the next sentence. In general, cohesion occurs when the information given at the end of one sentence appears at the beginning of the next.

To drive home the principle that beginning a sentence with something just mentioned in a preceding sentence is useful for achieving smoother flow of thought, let us see another example. This is a longer passage from a hypothetical essay about friendship and loneliness. Read it carefully and you will see how the principle works.

① *Friendships are changeable.* ② *We choose to be socially closer to some friends and more distant from others.* ③ *We see some often and others rarely.* ④ *In any case, friends become our social support that makes life more interesting.* ⑤ *Nevertheless, we are not in full control over how we choose and relate to people whom we broadly call "friends".* ⑥ *Our involvement in work and the stress it brings us can affect the way we choose and keep friendships.* ⑦ *Modern life may leave us little room for friendships, which then begin to fade.* ⑧ *That is when loneliness grows.* ⑨ *Little do we realize that loneliness can become a health problem because it weakens our safety net of social support.*	The sentences on the left demonstrate cohesion as follows: • Sentence ① announces the theme. • Sentence ② picks up and expands the idea introduced in sentence ① to specify how friendships are changeable. • Sentence ③ expands this point even more. • Sentence ④ states that while friendships are changeable, they form our "social support". • Sentence ⑤ brings out a new idea of "we are not in full control" of choosing and relating to friends. • Sentence ⑥ picks up this idea and attributes it to work and stress. • Sentence ⑦ goes further to say that friendships "begin to fade" when there is "little room for friendships." • Sentence ⑧ tells us clearly that this is also "when loneliness grows". • Tightly connected to this announcement of "loneliness", sentence ⑨ warns that loneliness can become a "health problem" because "it weakens our safety net of social support".

22.4.2 Coherence

Coherence refers to how well or how strongly your sentences in a paragraph "hang together." They hang together well if they clearly are related in a way that they speak about the same theme. In other words, your sentences have a recognizable common focus.

Cohesion, which shows the connection from one sentence to the next, is an important part of what makes your writing coherent. But there are other elements that help to bring about coherence as an attribute of the entire paragraph. They include the presence of a topic sentence and use of suitable pronouns, and transitional words and expressions as "sign posts" to guide your reader along the way (to see how ideas in the paragraph are related and elaborated or explained).

Six elements will help you write a coherent paragraph:

(1) Start with a topic sentence
Each paragraph ought to be concerned with one main idea, which is announced by a "topic sentence" placed at or near the beginning of the paragraph. The topic sentence guides you in writing the rest of the paragraph to develop that main idea.
(2) Use appropriate pronouns
As words standing for or referring to nouns, pronouns serve as cues that help your readers to follow characters (actors), actions, and other objects of attention. Thus, you should keep the references of your pronouns consistent and clear. Check to make sure. (e.g., What does this **it** in your text refer to?)
(3) Use proper verb tenses
Do not make tense errors or shift from one tense to another without any reason. Otherwise, you will weaken the relationship among the elements making up your sentences.
(4) Repeat important words and phrases
Restate important points by repeating certain words and phrases. You may use synonyms or other phrases with similar meanings to help your readers see your points of emphasis.
(5) Use parallel structures
Remember that parallel structures or constructions are grammatically the same for expressing similar or related ideas. This can be quite effective to strengthen the connection of ideas within and between sentences.
(6) Use transitional markers or expressions (See more in 22.4.3.)
These expressions (e.g., **but, moreover, however, in other words**) usually come at the beginning, sometimes in the middle, of a sentence to show how it relates to what is said in a preceding or even earlier sentence. They serve as "sign posts" to guide your readers to follow your train of thought. Nevertheless (this is a transitional marker), do not overuse them or they are likely to weaken the intended effect.

Let us read two example passages to see how some of the above techniques are used. The first passage comes from my own valedictory speech as a representative of the graduating class delivered at the graduation ceremony of Chung Chi College of The Chinese University of Hong Kong in July 1966. The second is from a speech given by former US president Ronald Reagan in West Berlin in June 1987 before the reunification of Germany in 1989.

Passage 1*	Remarks
① *I believe that higher education aims at promoting freedom of thought, discussion, and critique.* ② *Looking back on the education we have received here, we need to remind ourselves that education is life itself.* ③ *Life on our campus has been full of opportunities for thinking, discussing, and critiquing.* ④ ***Truly***, *we need to be aware that, in more ways than one, we have been trained through all these opportunities to be our own critics, our own masters, and our own executives.* * From the author's valedictory speech at Chung Chi College, The Chinese University of Hong Kong, July 3, 1966.	• Sentence ① is a topic sentence announcing the main idea about the purpose of higher education. • Except for the opening word (**I**), the first-person plural pronoun (**we, our**) is used in every sentence. • The present verb tense is used throughout to indicate what is said is still valid. • The three elements mentioned in sentence ① —thought, discussion, critique—are central in this paragraph. • Sentence ② coheres with the first sentence by mentioning "the education we have received here" and focusing on the idea of "education is life." • Sentence ③ puts the three elements (thought, discussion, critique) in the context of campus life. Note that the word **life**, appearing at the end of sentence ① , begins sentence ③ , thus establishing cohesion between these two sentences. • The "opportunities," mentioned in sentence ③ , have enabled students, sentence ④ continues to say, to become "our own critics, our own masters, and our own executives." • Note the use of parallel construction in sentences ① , ③ and ④ . This parallelism adds emphasis.

Passage 2*	Remarks
① *There is one sign the Soviets can make that would be unmistakable, that would advance dramatically the cause of freedom and peace.* ② *General Secretary Gorbachev, if you seek peace, if you seek prosperity for the Soviet Union and Eastern Europe, if you seek liberalization: come here to this gate!* ③ *Mr. Gorbachev, open this gate!* ④ *Mr. Gorbachev, tear down this wall!* ** * From a speech delivered by former US President Ronald Reagan before the Brandenburg Gate in West Berlin, June 12, 1987. **Wall refers to the wall separating West Berlin and East Berlin.	• Sentence ① announces the topic, "*one sign the Soviets can make.*" • Sentence ② picks up the two important ideas at the end of the preceding sentence—*freedom* and *peace*. Thus, there is cohesion between the first two sentences. • The phrase "*if you seek . . .*" is repeated three times in a parallel construction in sentence ② . • "*Gate*" is the last word of sentence ② . It is mentioned in sentence ③ . • Note the two emphatic phrases "*open this gate!*" and "*tear down this wall!*" are in parallel form. • The name *Gorbachev* is mentioned three times. President Reagan obviously wanted Mr. Gorbachev's attention. • The present verb tense is used throughout.

22.4.3 Use suitable transitional markers to connect ideas.

As pointed out earlier (in first box of 22.4.2), transitional markers serve as "sign posts" to guide your readers to follow your train of thought. Your readers can follow you to see how ideas are connected.

Transitional markers may appear as sparsely or as frequently as needed. You saw the presence of one such marker (**truly**) in Passage 1 of 22.4.2. Let us see another passage in which several transitional markers appear to connect ideas. Can you identify them?

We arrived in Copenhagen in the afternoon, fully one day before our cruise to Norway and Iceland was to set sail. First, we checked into our pre-booked hotel where we rested briefly. Then, we collected some information about how to spend the rest of the day in town. Although we were complete strangers, the hotel staff were admirably helpful to advise us where to go and how to get there. As it turned out, we had a pleasant walk along the waterfront near the hotel and enjoyed a lovely dinner in a cosy restaurant.

The following are some commonly used transitional markers:

Transitional markers (some are phrases) usually appear at the beginning of sentences, sometimes in mid-sentence (normally following the subject), or even at sentence-end:

He was blind from birth. **Nevertheless,** *he became a successful pianist.*

With full support from his mother, he, **nevertheless,** *became a successful pianist.*

With full support from his mother, he became a successful pianist **nevertheless.**

a. **To reinforce or add ideas**

> *again   in addition   also   indeed   certainly   undoubtedly*
> *moreover   furthermore   surely   besides   clearly   more importantly*
> *equally important   as a rule   in fact   the fact is   truly   the truth is*

b. **To repeat**

> *as has been said   in other words   in short   that is   to put it differently*
> *in simpler terms   in brief*

c. **To show cause and effect**

> *as a result   as a result of   because   because of   since   therefore*
> *consequently   hence   thus   then   if ... then   subsequently*

d. **To show concession or contrast**

> *although   but   despite   in spite of   even if   given   given that*
> *even though   however   nevertheless   in contrast   instead   still*
> *on the contrary   on the other hand   by comparison   whereas*

e. **To give examples**

> *for example   for instance   to illustrate   in particular*

f. **To show sequence**

> *first   second   third   next   then   finally*

---

g. **To show similarity**

    in the same way   likewise   similarly   just as   also

h. **To show time**

    after   afterwards   as soon as   at last   before   during   earlier   later
    now   immediately   meanwhile   in the meantime   recently   shortly   soon
    then   until   when   since   since then   soon after that

i. **To show place**

    here   there   everywhere   elsewhere   beyond   opposite to
    above   next to   near   below

j. **To conclude or summarize**

    in conclusion   to conclude   in a nutshell   in short   therefore   thus
    to sum up   finally

22.5   Summing up

In this chapter, you have learned the following three important strategies (following four described in Chapter 21) to write both clearly and effectively:

(1) **Emphasis**. When you feel that an idea is important enough to draw more attention, choose a way to give that idea suitable emphasis. Your tools to do so include particular words, rhetorical questions, end focus, inversion, fronting, and cleft sentences.

(2) **Sentence length and structure**. To produce clear and effective sentences, you should pay more attention to their length and structure. Your writing should contain both shorter and longer sentences as the context requires. You should also try to have variety in sentence types and patterns. No less important, try to adopt different ways of starting your sentences to add richness and originality to what you write.

(3) **Cohesion and coherence**. Do not confuse these two words although they look and sound alike. Cohesion focuses on the connection between one sentence and another, which gives flow to ideas. Coherence is about the coming together of all sentences in the paragraph to speak about the same theme. Learning to write well involves not only writing well-constructed individual sentences but also producing paragraphs or passages that are both cohesive and coherent.

Exercises   Chapter 22

Exercise 22.1

Each of the following sentences uses a method to express emphasis. Identify what method is used (refer to the given list) and write the appropriate letter in the parentheses.

下面每句都含對內容的強調。辨認所用的強調方法（參看下表），把適當的字母序號寫在括號裏。

a. stress an auxiliary verb
b. use a forceful verb
c. use an intensifying adjective or adverb
d. repeating a word and adding **at all**
e. use a rhetorical question to make a positive statement
f. use a rhetorical question to make a negative statement
g. use end focus
h. use inversion
i. use fronting
j. use a cleft sentence

1. (   )   Although I have lived in Hong Kong for more than thirty years, I have never been to Tai O of Lantau Island.

2. (   )   We have nothing to do now—nothing at all.

3. (   )   What she told me was how she managed to overcome all difficulties.

4. (   )   There goes our train; we must take the next one.

5. (   )   We were simply *overwhelmed* by the sight of the Grand Canyon.

6. (   )   She *does* know how to solve the Rubik's Cube.

7. (   )   It may take years before the coronavirus can be effectively controlled, but you never know.

8. (   )   Weren't we warned of another wave of outbreak of the disease?

9. (   )   On the waterfront near the Star Ferry pier is the former Kowloon-Canton Railway clock tower.

10. (   )   Difficult as the puzzle was, she got it solved.

11. (   )   Little did he expect that he would win the first prize.

12. (   )   It was in July 1998 that Hong Kong's Chek Lap Kok International Airport was opened.

13. (   )   I was absolutely certain that I had already submitted my application.

14. (   )   He has already decided to cancel all travel plans this year, and so have we.

15. (   )   An excellent candidate for the job she definitely is.

16. (   )   What help will it give the disabled?

17. (   )   If effective means of controlling road use were not introduced, our city's traffic problems would soon become unmanageable.

18. (   )   Ocean Park was where the children went on Chinese New Year day.

19. (   )   It was the happiest moment in her entire life, she said.

20. (   )   Hardly had the meeting started when the air conditioning broke down.

Exercise 22.2

Decide whether each of the following statements is true (T) or false (F). Write T or F in the parentheses.

判斷下面的陳述是否屬真？如果屬真，在括號裏寫 T，否則的話，寫 F。

1.   (   )   A simple sentence must not be more than 12 words long.

2.   (   )   Shorter sentences are always better than long sentences.

3.   (   )   **He watches television when he comes home** is a simple sentence.

4.   (   )   This is a simple sentence: **About a year ago, she started to think about changing jobs from a local law firm to an international one.**

5.   (   )   Sentences sound choppy if they contain many different subjects from one sentence to another.

6.   (   )   A coordinating conjunction (e.g., **and, but, so**) joins two independent clauses to form a compound sentence.

7.   (   )   A compound sentence cannot be rewritten as a complex sentence.

8.   (   )   There is only one subordinate (dependent) clause in a complex sentence.

9.   (   )   Parallel forms may be applied to single words only.

10. (   )   The subordinate clause may appear at the beginning of a complex sentence.

11. (   )   You cannot begin a sentence with an infinitive phrase.

12. (   )   The opening noun phrase in **A cosmopolitan city, Hong Kong has more than seven million inhabitants** is called an "appositive".

13. (   )   You can use a participle or a participial phrase to begin a sentence.

14. (   )   A transitional marker at the beginning of a sentence may be repositioned at the end.

15. (   )   **Given that** can be used to begin a main clause.

Exercise 22.3

Read the given passage (illustrating sentence cohesion) and answer the questions that follow:

閱讀以下這段展示句子銜接的文字，然後回答問題。

Forest fires in Australia and California have caused considerable losses of life and property, and have brought environmental and ecological damages to vast regions. The major cause of these losses and damages points to human actions that have led to climate change. Humanity's stupendous consumption of fossil fuels and worsening conditions of air pollution from car exhausts, factories, and cigarette smoke have given us a hotter world with drier forests. Global temperatures will keep rising and drought conditions intensifying, so that the threat of large-scale forest fires will loom even larger in the years to come.

1.   What "losses" and "damages" are referred to?

      Losses:_____

      Damages: _____

2.   What "human actions" have led to climate change?

      _____

      _____

3.   How is climate change described briefly?

      _____

4.   How is this brief description repeated with somewhat more detail?

      _____

5.   Which two words capture the overall theme of this passage?

      _____

Exercise 22.4

Listed in the box below are some of the purposes of using transitional markers in writing paragraphs, but not all of them apply to the passage below. Identify the transitional markers contained in the passage and indicate the purpose of each. Use the table following the passage for your answers.

下面方框內列出了文章段落裏會出現的 "轉變標誌" (transitional markers) 的作用，但它們並不全都適用於以下這段文字。試找出該段文字裏的轉變標誌，並指出每個標誌的作用。把答案寫在該段文字後的表裏。

a. to reinforce or add ideas

b. to give a reason or show cause and effect

c. to repeat a point

d. to show concession

e. to show time

f. to conclude

Summary writing may seem simple. Because it is about others' ideas rather than your own, summary writing seems peripheral to the main task of writing. As a result, students may not pay as much attention to summary writing as they should. The truth is, writing a summary is not as simple as it appears since it depends so much on identifying the most important information contained in the original work. Given that learning depends on grasping the essential information of something, summary writing is intricately connected with the activity of learning.

When you write a summary in your own words, you need to examine the text's meaning carefully before you can find suitable words to express the gist of that meaning. Consequently, you are more likely to remember what you have read. Moreover, your summary should express the author's point of view even if your view is different. A good summary is, as a rule, both clear and accurate. Indeed, the ability to write clear and accurate summaries is one of the most important skills you need to do well academically.

Use this table for your answers:

Transitional marker	Purpose (Write the letter representing the purpose listed above or the words in full)

PART 3   Guide to Using Words Properly
(Alphabetically arranged)

English words are not easy to understand and master well. Most learners face difficulties of word use, as a word may or may not change spelling according to different grammatical functions, may look confusingly similar to some other words, and may have particular idiomatic meanings in specific phrases or expressions. Unless you make a sustained effort to both widen and deepen your knowledge of words, you may make mistakes in using them.

This section of the book aims to raise learners' awareness of the intricacies involved in using words correctly in sentences and appropriately to express their intended meanings. Of course, the words making up this section are selective, but they are among words frequently used in many fields and should be seen as within the basic vocabulary of educated people. While this section serves as a convenient guide to using certain words, it does not replace your dictionary. If you have an advanced learner's dictionary, consult it if you have doubts about a word or if you want to look for further details.

A good writer is always a careful writer who pays close attention to the use of words. Read the explanatory notes (in numbered paragraphs) and study the example sentences to make sure that you understand well the word in question. You should note the indicated class(es) of each word because it is important that you know how to use a word according to its grammatical function in a sentence.

Abbreviations used			Symbols used		
n	=	noun	(✗)	=	Incorrect or not proper
v	=	verb			
adj	=	adjective	(✓)	=	Correct or proper
adv	=	adverb			
conj	=	conjunction			
prep	=	preposition			
n phr	=	noun phrase			
n plural	=	plural form of a noun			
adv phr	=	adverbial phrase			
prep phr	=	prepositional phrase			
pron	=	pronoun			
AmE	=	American English			
BrE	=	British English			

able (adj), capable (adj)

1.   **be able to do something** (= to have the skill or opportunity to do something)

*If we have sufficient funds, we will **be able to** start a small business.*

*Not knowledgeable about art, we **are** not **able to** fully appreciate the objects on display in the*

Art Museum.

2.   **capable** (= skilled or competent)

    *A **capable** teacher is always aware of the learning difficulties of her pupils.*

3.   **be/become capable of (doing) something** (= having the ability or qualities needed for doing something) (Note: **capable of** must be followed by a noun phrase or an **-ing** gerund phrase.)

    *With commitment and discipline, some seemingly ordinary people **are capable of** great achievements.*

    *If children are spoiled they may become not **capable of** taking care of themselves.*

aboard (adv, prep), abroad (adv)

1.   Some writers carelessly use one of these two words when they mean the other:

    (✗) ~~I plan to study **aboard** after finishing university.~~

Of course, what the writer of the above sentence means to say is:

    *I plan to study **abroad** after finishing university.*

2.   Both words are adverbs, but **aboard** is also a preposition.

    Aboard as an adverb:

    *Large cruise ships take hours to load all passengers **aboard**.*

    *When you join an organization, you are likely to be greeted "Welcome **aboard**".*

    Aboard as a preposition:

    *Her flight will depart in a few minutes; she should be **aboard** the plane now.*

achieve (v), accomplish (v), attain (v)

1.   You **achieve** something (e.g., success, victory, honour) through your effort, especially when you have exerted such effort for a fairly long time.

    *Piccaso **achieved** considerable fame and success as an artist.*

    *For a woman with Asian background to become the manager of a professional American baseball team is no small **achievement**.*

2.   Both **achieve** and **attain** can mean successfully reaching a goal or objective. Both words, especially **achieve**, can involve effort or merit, but **attain** is open to other factors, such as good connections, leading to the success.

    *Every year, a handful of students **attain** top grades in five or more subjects in the school leaving public exams.*

3.   If you have **accomplished** something, you have done what you have aimed to do: you have completed a designated task that requires certain special qualities or technical skills.

>   *Neil Armstrong, along with two other astronauts, **accomplished** the moon landing mission in 1969 and became the first man to set foot on the moon.*

accurate (adj), precise (adj)

1.   **Accurate** implies fact or truth; **precise** emphasizes exactness of detail.

2.   If your watch is ten minutes slow, the time it shows is not **accurate**. On the other hand, if you know your watch is no more than one minute slow, you can claim that the time it shows is quite **accurate**. If you use it to tell the time as, let's say, 7:13 a.m., your report is both **precise** and **accurate**.

3.   The noun form of **accurate** is **accuracy**; the noun form of **precise** is **precision**.

>   *I trust the **accuracy** of my watch.*

>   *The GPS system helps us to locate a place with great **precision**.*

adapt (v), adopt (v), adjust (v)

1.   Both **adapt** (**adaptation**, n) and **adjust** (**adjustment**, n) mean changing or modifying something to make it suitable in a different environment or for a different purpose.

>   *My granddaughter will have to **adapt** to a new school in September.*

>   *A good speaker **adjusts** his or her language to the age of the audience.*

2.   **Adapt** can also be used when something is modified for presentation in a different way. **Adjust** is not used for this meaning.

>   (✓) *The story of Exodus in the Bible has been **adapted** for film more than once.*

>   (✗) ~~*The story of Exodus in the Bible has been **adjusted** for film more than once.*~~

3.   When you **adopt** (**adoption**, n) something, you take it up.

>   *The government **adopted** the new rule of no dine-in in eateries for only two days.*

advice (n), advise (v)

1.   **Advice** is an uncountable noun. Like other uncountable nouns, it is never preceded by the indefinite article (**a/an**) and does not have a plural form ending in **s**.

>   (✗) ~~*I gave him many advices.*~~

>   (✓) *I gave him a lot of advice.*

2.   You can, however, use a countable noun such as **piece** or **word** to say **a piece of advice** or **a word of advice**. People may **take** or **follow** a piece of advice, or act in some way **on someone's advice**.

*Let me give you **a piece of advice**.*

*She joined the study group **on her teacher's advice**.*

3.   The verb **advise** can be used in many ways: You may **advise** someone to do something or **advise** someone against doing something. An expert may **advise that** something needs to be done. You may ask a lawyer to **advise** you **on** legal matters. In formal use, an organization may **advise** its members **of** certain developments.

*Doctors **advise** us to be always vigilant during this epidemic.*

*Scientists **advise** strongly that we must make great changes in our lifestyle to avoid the ill effects of global warming.*

*The school will **advise** students' parents **of** changes in examination arrangements.*

affect (v), effect (n)

1.   **Affect** is a verb meaning "to influence".

*How does the coronavirus epidemic **affect** our daily life?*

2.   **Effect** is a noun (with both countable and uncountable uses).

*The visual **effect** of impressionistic paintings is quite noticeable.* (uncountable use)

*We should be aware of the harmful **effects** of plastic bags on the environment.* (countable use)

3.   **Effects** (plural noun, used in formal documents) (= personal possessions)

*This travel insurance policy covers all personal **effects** used during the trip.*

4.   Some common phrases containing the word **effect**:

*The insurance policy will **take effect** from July 1ˢᵗ to July 15ˢᵗ.*

*Interest rates will be cut **with effect from** next Monday.*

*The lawyer's letter says something **to the effect that** the lease is still valid.*

***With immediate effect**, Mr Wong is the new chairman of the board.*

*The doctor has warned me about the **harmful long-term effects** of the drug.*

5.   **Effect** can be used as a verb, meaning "to bring about".

*We need charismatic leaders to **effect** change in a large company.*

agree (v), agreeable (adj)

1.   **agree with**

You **agree with** something or **agree with** someone **about** something:

*We can **agree about** the general direction of the proposal but not about every detail.*

*The management and the workers' union **agreed on** a new benefits package.*

The sentence can also be written as, using **be agreed on**:

*The management and the workers' union **were agreed on** a new benefits package.*

3. **agree + that-**clause

    The **that-**clause describes the object of agreement.

    *Not all doctors **agree that** antibiotics should be prescribed for influenza.*

4. **agree to**

    You can **agree to** someone's request or some plan:

    *She performed so well that her boss **agreed to** her request for a pay rise.*

    You can **agree to do something:**

    *She **agreed to** return to Hong Kong after completing her exchange programme in Canada.*

5. **agreeable** (= pleasant, acceptable)

    *We spent a most **agreeable** afternoon together chatting about almost anything.*

    *The art of negotiation requires that any compromise must be **agreeable** to both sides.*

all ready (ready here is adj), already (adv)

1. **all ready** means "completely ready".

    *Our bags are packed; we are **all ready** to start our journey.*

2. **already** (one word) means "before a particular time". Note that it can come before a main verb (*completed*) or after the auxiliary (*have*) leading a verb phrase. It can also come at the end of the sentence.

    *We **already** completed the job.*

    *We completed the job **already.***

    *I have **already** done my part.*

    *I have done my part **already.***

all right (adj, adv)

1. Note the standard spelling of **all right** as two words. **Alright**, though common in informal usage, is incorrect in standard formal English.

2. Used as an adjective (only after noun):

342

*The food of that restaurant is **all right**.* (= satisfactory, but not too good)

*Your answers to the questions are **all right**.* (= all correct)

3.   Used as an adverb to mean "no problems":

    *Their son is getting on **all right** at school.*

    *Don't worry. She seems to be doing **all right**.*

all-round (adj), all round (adv)

1.   An **all-round** person is someone who is able to do many different things or who has many different skills. In AmE, **all-around** has the same meaning. Do not, however, write **all-rounded**, which is not standard, but **well-rounded** is an accepted equivalent of **all-round.** Note that as a compound adjective, **all-round** (with the hyphen) is used before a noun.

    *A good **all-round** education consists of learning both intellectual and social skills.*

    *Liberal arts colleges in the States try to offer a **well-rounded** educattion to students.*

2.   An **all-round** person can be described as an **all-rounder.**

    *Given adequate training, some people can become **all-rounders** in sports.*

3.   When used without the hyphen, **all round** is an adverb meaning in all respects:

    *This is a well-written speech **all round.***

all together (pronoun + adv), altogether (adv)

1.   **All together** means "everyone together" or "everything in one place".

    *On Chinese New Year's eve, the whole family would have dinner **all together**.*

    *I just put the gifts I bought **all together** in one bag.*

2.   **Altogether** means "in total" or "entirely".

    *There are **altogether** 16 decks on this cruise ship.*

    *They were not **altogether** convinced that their ship was about to face a severe storm.*

ambiguous (adj), ambivalent (adj)

1.   **Ambiguous** means "unclear" or "can be understood in more than one way". The word can refer to people, things, ideas, words, or situations. The noun form is **ambiguity.**

    *So far, he has been **ambiguous** about whether he wants a different job.*

    *This tenancy agreement is **ambiguous** on when the tenancy may be terminated.*

2.   **Ambivalent** means "having both positive and negative feelings about something". The word can only be used to refer to people because only people have feelings. The noun form is **ambivalence.**

343

*Many young couples are **ambivalent** about having children.*

*Some older people have an **ambivalent** attitude towards the mobile phone.*

apply (v)

1. Pay attention to the use of prepositions following **apply** to convey different meanings.

2. **Apply to** a place, organization, or person **for** something

   *Many foreign students **apply to** well-known universities **for** admission.*

   *Competition is tough when thousands of graduates **apply to** the top banks **for a** handful of management trainee positions.*

3. **Apply** something **to** something

   *Many restaurants have **applied** new technology **to** ordering food from their menus.*

   *We can **apply** the concept of achievement motivation **to** our understanding of human behaviour.*

4. **Apply to** something (= to have an effect or be relevant) (not used in the progresive/continuous tenses)

   *Special discounts on public transport fares **apply** only **to** senior citizens.*

   *Social distancing in seating arrangement **applies to** all restaurants.*

as (prep, conj, adv)

1. As a preposition (placed before a noun) :

   *She works in a restaurant **as** a waitress.*

   *You can use this glass bottle **as** a vase.*

2. As a conjunction (placed before a clause):

   *Communication becomes so much easier **as** mobile phones are so common.*

   ***As** time passed, his work performance seemed to get better.*

   *She enjoys classical music, **as** I do.* (In informal style, some people would say ~~She enjoys classical music like I do~~. This is not correct in formal standard English.)

   *Migrants starting new life in another country face many problems of adjustment, **as** they are unfamiliar with the country's language and culture.* (See more at **because, as** and **since**)

3. **the same . . . as . . .** (In this construction, **as** functions again as a conjunction.)

   *I went to **the same** school **as** you did.*

   *We consult **the same** family doctor **as** our neighbours do.*

4.   **as . . . as . . .** (adv) (= to the same extent)

> *Ethan is now **as** tall **as** his mother.*

> *The problem is not **as** difficult **as** I thought.*

> *Please reply **as** soon **as** possible.*

as if (conj), as though (conj)

1.   These two phrases describe what we think a situation is like.

> *He looked **as if/though** he had not slept for days.*

> (✗) *He looked **like** he had not slept for days.* (Although such use of **like** is common in informal speech, avoid it in writing. **Like** cannot be followed by a verb.)

2.   Using **as if** or **as though** with an "unreal" past tense verb in a sentence with present time meaning:

> *Alex is acting **as if/though** he was the boss.* (The use of the past tense *was* here has a present time meaning that Alex is not the boss but acts that way.)

as well (adv phr), also (adv), too (adv)

Note the position of these words in clauses. *Also* usually comes before the verb, while *as well* and *too* come at the end of a clause.

> *He not only speaks English; he **also** speaks French and Italian.*

> *He not only speaks English; he speaks French and Italian **as well**.*

> *He does not just speak English; he speaks French and Italian **too**.*

as well as (prep phr)

1.   **as well as** is not equivalent to **and**.

The clause introduced by **as well as** represents less important information or something already known.

> *I like some dessert **as well as** coffee.* (I will have coffee, but I like some dessert too. Wanting dessert is being emphasized.)

> *I like some dessert **and** coffee.* (I will have both dessert and coffee. The implied emphasis on dessert is not present here.)

2.   Note that, in the following sentence, the verb **has signed** agrees with the singular subject **Emily**. The phrase introduced by **as well as** is treated as additional information rather than as a part of the subject. Do not, therefore, use **have signed.**

> (✓) *Emily, **as well as** two of her best friends, **has** signed the petition.*

> (✗) *Emily, **as well as** two of her best friends, have signed the petition.*

3. Note the difference in subject-verb agreement between the following two sentences:

    *Dessert **and** coffee **make** a meal complete.* (**Dessert and coffee** is a compound or plural subject.)

    *Dessert, **as well as** coffee, **makes** a meal complete.* (**Dessert** is a singular subject.)

4. If a verb is present in the phrase introduced by **as well as**, it is often in **-ing** form:

    *Smoking is hazardous to health **as well as** polluting the air.* (Do not say: ~~Smoking is hazardous to health as well as it pollutes the air.~~)

5. Note that the phrase introduced by **as well as** can be placed in initial or final position in the sentence. Thus, the preceding sentence can be reworded as:

    ***As well as** polluting the air, smoking is hazardous to health.*

at last (adv phr), lastly (adv), last but not least (adv phr)

1. **At last** (= eventually) always refers to time. It implies you have been waiting or working for something a long time.

    ***At last** we reached our destination, Big Wave Bay, after hiking for over two hours.*

2. You can use **at long last** to stress that there has been a long wait or delay before you get to your goal:

    ***At long last,** our application for opening a group bank account was approved.*

3. **Lastly** (= finally). You use **lastly**, not **at last**, when you come to the last item in a list.

    ***Lastly**, we will consider ways of improving our memory.*

4. **Last but not least** is used to say that the last item or point in a list is just as important as the ones already mentioned or discussed.

    ***Last but not least**, let us thank all our support staff for their work in this project.*

    Note that this adverbial phrase is **last but not least**, and NOT ~~lastly but not least~~ or ~~last but not the least~~. (Do not use **the** before **least**.)

attitude (n), opinion (n)

1. An attitude is a disposition in some general direction; an opinion is a specific view or position regarding an issue.

    *They are studying the **attitude** of Hong Kong people **towards** organ donation.*

    *It is important that the mass media help to shape public **opinion** on social issues.*

2. We speak of an **attitude to/towards** someone or something. The attitude can be positive, supportive, sympathetic, or, on the contrary, negative, non-supportive, and unsympathetic.

3.   We describe an **opinion about**, **of**, or **on** a person, an object, an idea, or a problem.

aware (adj)

1.   **Aware** is not a verb and must not be used as such. The following constructions, all using **aware** as a verb, are incorrect:

> (✗) ~~I **aware** that parking is a big problem in the city.~~
>
> (✗) ~~Do you **aware** the difference between "leisure" and "recreation"?~~
>
> (✗) ~~No one **awared** that a few pages were missing from the report.~~

The above three sentences should be revised as follows:

> I am **aware** that parking is a big problem in the city.
>
> Are you **aware of** the difference between "leisure" and "recreation"?
>
> No one was **aware** that a few pages were missing from the report.

2.   **aware of**   Typical construction is **be** + **aware** + **of** + **noun phrase**.

> Organizations need to be **aware of** the value of investing more in people.
>
> We are well **aware of** the problem facing us.

3.   **aware that** (**that** introduces a noun clause)

> They are not **aware that** time is running out and something must be done.

4.   **aware what/why/when/how** (these words also introduce a noun clause)

> People born after the 1980s are not **aware what** Hong Kong was like in the 1950s.
>
> They were painfully **aware why** they lost the competition.
>
> He does not seem to be **aware when** his rental lease will end.
>
> We need to be **aware how** damaging rumour is to social stability.

5.   You can begin a sentence with a phrase starting with **aware of**:

> **Aware of** the need of homeless people, the government will adopt suitable measures to help them.

6.   **awareness** (n.) (can be followed by a **that** noun clause)

> Scientists have been very vocal to raise people's **awareness that** global warming will bring worrying consequences to everybody.

because, as, since (all subordinating conj), therefore (conjunctive adv)

1.   **Because, as,** and **since** all introduce a reason clause as a subordinate clause (that is why they are called subordinating conjunctions). The main clause so linked is given greater emphasis.

2.   **As** and **since** (more formal than **as**) are more often used at the beginning of a sentence:

   Since she has a lot of homework to do during Christmas break, her parents are planning only a short weekend trip for the family.

   As electronic resources are easily accessible, the learning of almost any subject is more efficient and interesting.

3.   Be careful with **as**: it can mean both "because" and "while". The meaning of **as** is ambiguous in the following sentence. To remove the ambiguity, you can use **since** or **while,** depending on what you mean to say.

   As the economy continued to deteriorate, the government devised a set of actions to increase employment opportunities.

4.   **Because** can also be used to introduce a reason clause at the beginning of a sentence, but it comes more often after the main clause:

   Small businesses find it difficult to operate in the central city because the rents are just too high.

5.   **Therefore** introduces a result of something just mentioned as a reason. This can be done in different ways as shown below. The first example sentence is set up as a typical compound sentence using coordination. Note the use of a semicolon after the first clause and a comma after **therefore.** The second example uses **and** to link the two parts without commas and without repeating the subject **he.** The third example splits the statement into two sentences: the first states the reason and the second states the result. In the second sentence, a different subject **we** is used and **therefore** is set off by commas.

   *He knows Japan very well; **therefore**, he can serve as our guide there.*

   *He knows Japan very well and **therefore** can serve as our guide there.*

   *He knows Japan very well. We can, **therefore**, ask him to be our guide there.*

6.   You must not use **because**, **as**, or **since** in the same sentence in which **therefore** introduces the result. Conversely, if you use **because**, **as**, or **since**, you must not use **therefore**.

   (✗) *Because rents are rising rapidly, therefore some kind of control is needed.*

   (✓) *Rents are rising rapidly; **therefore**, some kind of control is needed.*

   (✓) *Because rents are rising rapidly, some kind of control is needed.*

because of (prep), **because** (subordinating conj)

1.   Both **because of** and **because** are used in subordination.

2.   As a preposition, **because of** takes a noun or a noun phrase as its object:

   Because of the typhoon, our meeting has been cancelled.

Because of rising labour cost, manufacturers have to relocate their factories to places where there is cheaper labour. (**rising labour cost** is a noun phrase)

3.   **Because** must be followed by a clause with its own subject and verb:

Because we have plenty of time, we need not rush through our lunch. (**We have plenty of time** is a clause with **we** as subject and **have** as verb.)

below (prep, adv)

1.   The following is a frequently occurring error:

(✖) *Please see the **below** notes for reference.*

Placed before **notes, below** seems to be an adjective modifying **notes**. However, **below** is not an adjective. The sentence can be corrected to read:

*Please see the notes **below** for reference.*

In this corrected sentence, **below** is an adverb. It tells us where you can see the notes (at the bottom of the page). (Remember: An adverb modifies a verb, an adjective, or another adverb. In the sentence here, **below** says something about how an action (seeing the notes) is performed, thus functioning as an adverb.)

2.   As an adverb

*My friend lives two floors **below**.*

*Children aged six and **below** are not admitted to most serious music concerts.*

3.   As a preposition

*On a very cold day the temperature can fall **below** freezing.*

*His academic performance was somewhat **below** average in his class.*

beside (prep), besides (prep, adv), moreover (adv)

1.   **Beside** means "next to".

*Their children's school is right **beside** a large public park.*

2.   **Besides** as a preposition means "in addition to". Use it before a noun or noun phrase:

Besides a story book, I bought a junior dictionary for my granddaughter's birthday.

*Television programmes can cultivate tastes **besides** providing entertainment.*

3.   **Besides** as an adverb means "in addition". Use it before a clause or a new sentence to give *another reason for something*, or to make an extra comment, with emphasis, on what you have already said:

*This restaurant's food is not expensive. **Besides**, their dishes are all well prepared.*

*He is an expert in his field; **besides**, he has an excellent reputation among his peers.*

349

4.   In the preceding sentence, **besides** links the two clauses, both of which are treated as equally important.   It is thus called a conjunctive adverb. Note the use of a semicolon at the end of the first clause and a comma after **besides.**

5.   Like **besides**, **moreover** is a conjunctive adverb to coordinate two equally important ideas. It introduces additional information that may support what you have already said. If placed at the beginning of a sentence, **moreover** serves as a sentence adverb.

> *Living here near the park is desirable because the air is better. **Moreover**, the view is unbeatable.*

The two sentences can be joined as follows (note the punctuation):

> *Living here near the park is desirable because the air is better; **moreover**, the view is unbeatable.*

6.   Do not use **besides** to refer to something that is not really an extra comment or reason, such as the following:

> (✗) *This restaurant's food is not expensive. Besides, I go there quite often.*

Better say this:

> *This restaurant's food is not expensive. So, I go there quite often.*

beware (v)

1.   You use **beware of** to warn someone to be careful because something is a threat or danger.

> *Open the door gently: **beware of** hitting someone behind the door.*

> ***Beware of** wet and slippery floor.*

2.   The following is an incorrect use of **beware of:**

> ~~*Beware of your belongings.*~~ (This sign is often seen in public toilets in Hong Kong. People's belongings cannot be a threat to their owners, so it does not make any sense to tell people to beware of their belongings. The sign is supposed to remind people to be careful with their belongings and not to forget taking their belongings with them when they leave. Thus, the reminder should be simply this: ***Take care of** your belongings.*)

3.   You can use **beware** without the preposition **of** in the following ways:

> *Heavy rain warning was announced this morning. People going outdoors were cautioned to **beware**.*

> ***Beware**, buying overseas properties involves many problems.*

bought (v), brought (v)

1.   Pay attention to the difference in spelling and pronunciation of these two words. Do not ignore the **r** sound in **brought.**

2. **Bought** is the past tense and past participle of **buy** (v). **Brought** is the past tense and past participle of **bring** (v).

    *She **bought** (not **~~brought~~**) her jacket in the Christmas sales.*

    *We **brought** (not **~~bought~~**) our friend to church last Sunday.*

classic (adj, n), classical (adj)

1. If a literary work or artistic creation is considered the best of its kind, is typical, and has lasting quality, it is described as **classic.**

    *"The Dream of the Red Chamber" is a famous **classic** Chinese novel.*

    *Abraham Lincoln's "Gettysburg Address" is a **classic** example of a short but powerful speech.*

    Classic is an adjective in the above two sentences. It can also be used as a noun:

    *"A Tale of Two Cities" is Charles Dickens' **classic.***

2. **Classical** (adj) refers to the quality of being traditional in style and well established enough to have a lasting value as in classical music.

    *Mozart and Beethoven were important **classical** composers.*

3. **Classical** also means having to do with the history and culture of ancient Greece and Rome.

    A "classical scholar" is a specialist in Greek and Latin.

close (adj, adv, v, n), closed (adj)

1. The core meaning of **close** (adj) is "near". You can **be close to** some place by coming near it. When you are close to success, you are almost there.

    *China and the United States are **close** to reaching an agreement in their trade talks.*

2. **Close** also means "careful" and "friendly" or "intimate". You pay **close attention** to something important, such as how to stay **close to** your family.

    *Talking to a **close** friend helps when you are in trouble.*

    *If we take a **closer** look at the situation, we can see it is not as simple as it seems.*

3. **Close** is also an adverb, as in the following sentences:

    *Our daughter lives **close by.***

    *Runner No. 7 is now in first position, with No. 3 following **close** behind.*

4. **Close** can be used as a verb:

    *They have **closed** the shop for renovation.*

    *The bank **closes** early on Saturdays.*

5. In formal English, **close** (n) refers to the end of an activity or a period of time:

    *The meeting has come to a **close** after three hours' deliberation.*

    *Near the **close** of the 20ᵗʰ century, people worried about whether computers could distinguish between the year 1900 and the year 2000.*

6. **Closed** (adj) means "not open". A **closed society** isolates itself from outside influences. A person not willing to consider different ways of doing things or new ideas has a **closed mind.** In surveys, a question with preset response categories is a **closed-ended** question as opposed to an open-ended question, which asks for a freely written response.

    *One cannot approach this sensitive issue with a **closed** mind.*

    *This village used to be **closed to** outsiders.* (Outsiders were not allowed to visit.)

    A shop that is not open for business may put a sign at its door that says "***closed***". Shop owners must be careful not to write "***close***", which is incorrect for this purpose. The shop may have another sign on weekends that reads "***We close at 8 p.m. today***". (**Close** here is a verb.)

    *They will discuss the matter in a **closed-door** meeting.*

    *The public library is **closed** on Wednesday mornings.* (Or: *The public library **closes** on Wednesday mornings.*)

common sense (n phr), common-sense (compound adj, note the use of hyphen)

1. Always write **common sense** as two words when you use it as a noun.

    *It is only **common sense** that you should avoid risky actions.*

2. When hyphenated, **common-sense** is a compound adjective placed before a noun.

    *Most people adopt a **common-sense** view of what happens to them.*

compare (v) with, compare to

1. When you **compare** A **with** B, you want to consider their similarities and differences.

    ***Compared with** gardens in Western countries, Japanese gardens contain philosophical ideas in their design.*

2. When you **compare** A **to** B, they are being likened to each other. (A is like B.)

    *We can **compare** buildings and shops in the older central city area of Macao **to** those of Hong Kong in the 1950s and 1960s.*

complain (v), complaint (n)

1. Note that the noun **complaint** ends with a **t**, which should be audible when spoken.

2. **complain about**

*We often **complain about** the high cost of living.*

3.   **complain to someone about something**

*Some customers at the restaurant **complained to** the manager **about** the poor service.*

4.   **have a/no complaint about something**

*Shoppers have no **complaint about** the new self-service check-out machine.*

5.   **make a complaint to someone against something**

*Many residents of our building want to **make a complaint to** the management office **against** the latest increase in management fees.*

complement (v, n), compliment (v, n)

1.   These two words, pronounced the same way, are almost the same in spelling—except for one letter—but are completely different in meaning. Be careful.

2.   To **complement** (v) something is to add to it or to make it better or more attractive. The same idea applies to people. (The following sentences can be rewritten using the adjective form **complementary**.)

*Red wine **complements** steaks very well. (Red wine and steaks are **complementary**.)*

*They are all different characters but can **complement** each other in a team.*

*(They are all different characters but can be **complementary to** each other in a team.)*

3.   When A is a **complement** (n) **to** B, A's presence improves the quality of B.

*Fine wines are nice **complements to** Chinese dishes.*
*(Fine wines and Chinese dishes are **complementary**.)*

4.   **Complement** (n) also means, in grammar, a word or phrase following a verb to say something about the subject of the verb. In **She is happy** and **He became a famous pianist**, **happy** and **famous pianist** are complements.

5.   When you **compliment** (v) someone **on** something, you say something nice to praise them for what they have done.

*Her violin teacher **complimented** her on her outstanding performance in the competition.*

6.   You praise someone when you give him or her a **compliment** (n). The plural **compliments** is often used when you want to praise a person or when you send someone a formal gift.

*I will take your remark as a **compliment**.*

*The food is delicious. Please give the chef our **compliments**.*

7.   When you have praises to say about someone's work you are **complimentary** (adj) **about** it. **Complimentary** also means "given free of charge". Some restaurants may offer a **complimentary**

dessert when you order a set dinner.

complex (adj), complicated (adj)

1. Both **complex** and **complicated** share the common meaning of "involving many details and not easy to understand".

2. **Complex** can be used to describe organizations, procedures, and behaviour in a neutral way, referring essentially to their containing many parts or details without any negative connotations.

    *Large companies are usually quite **complex** in their structure and ways of doing things.*

3. **Complicated** is not entirely interchangeable with **complex**. Besides their common meaning of "involving many details and not easy to understand", **complicated** has elements of "irregular, tricky, even mysterious". Something described as "complicated" is seen as having considerations beyond logical analysis and thus particularly difficult to deal with or understand.

    *She has been in and out of jobs and leading a very **complicated** life.*

4. From the above, you can see **complex** is more formal and stresses its technical meaning (elaborate in structure). **Complicated** is more informal, with emphasis on "difficult to understand". The following two sentences illustrate these two words in use.

    *Setting up a will can be a **complex** matter because many legal details must be looked into.*

    *In a large family involving several generations and different kinds of assets, personal expectations and feelings may come into the picture and make the matter of setting up a will much more **complicated**.*

5. The verb **complicate** can be used to refer to the act of making something complicated.

    *Such factors **complicate** the matter of setting up a will.*

    *He was hurt in a car accident in his trip to Canada. Then his passport was missing, which really **complicated** things for him.*

comprise (v), compose (v), consist (v), constitute (v)

1. These four words are often confused and used incorrectly.

2. If we start with a whole, W, and refer to the parts, A, B, and C that make up W, we say that W **comprises** A, B, and C. Note that **comprise of** and **is comprised of** are always incorrect. Although some dictionaries accept **be comprised of** (as used by some people), it should be avoided by careful writers.

    (✓) *Hong Kong **comprises** eighteen districts.*

    (✗) *Hong Kong **comprises of** eighteen districts.*

    (✗) *Hong Kong **is comprised of** eighteen districts.*

3. Three other ways of saying the same thing:

*Hong Kong **is composed of** eighteen districts.*

*Hong Kong **consists of** eighteen districts.* (Never say ~~**is consisted of.**~~)

*Hong Kong **is made up** of eighteen districts.*

4.   If we start with the parts A, B, and C that make up W, we can have the following:

*Teaching departments, research units, an administrative structure, and students **compose** a university.*

*Eighteen districts **make up** Hong Kong.*

*Eighteen districts **constitute** Hong Kong.*

Although **Eighteen districts *compose* Hong Kong** is not wrong, it sounds not as natural as the sentences using ***make up*** and ***constitute***.

concern (n, v), concerned (adj), concerning (prep)

General comments:

These are among the most frequently misused words. Learn them and distinguish carefully how they are used in good correct English. First, bear in mind their functions as different word classes. **Concern** is both a noun and a verb. **Concerned** is an adjective. **Concerning** is a preposition.

Many learners tend to use **concern about** too freely but improperly. The following three sentences illustrate the incorrect use of **concern about**. Note carefully how they can be corrected:

1. (✗) ~~*Many people just **concern about** their own interest and ignore others.*~~

   (✓) *Many people **are** just **concerned with** their own interest and ignore that of others.*

   (✓) *Many people just **concern themselves with** their own interest and ignore that of others.*

2. (✗) ~~*Both parents and teachers are greatly **concern about** children's learning problems.*~~

   (✓) *Both parents and teachers **are** greatly **concerned about** children's learning problems.*

   (✓) *Children's learning problems are **a matter of great concern to** both parents and teachers.*

3. (✗) ~~*The workers **concern about** their employers will not renew their contracts.*~~

   (✓) *The workers **are concerned that** their employers will not renew their contracts.*

   (✓) *The workers **are concerned about** their employers' not renewing their contracts.*

concern (n)

1.   A **concern** is something that is important enough to be considered seriously or worried about. Use **concern** or **concerns** depending on the sense intended.

*We all have **concerns** as consumers.*

*Wages are the main **concern** of many workers.*

*Air pollution is a matter of serious public **concern**.*

2. **a cause** (n) **for concern**

   *Safety of children at school is **a cause for** their parents' **concern**.*

3. **be of concern to someone**

   *How customers feel about service can **be of great concern to** restaurant owners.*

4. **concern with something** (= attention given to something)

   *Doctors have great **concern with** treating their patients appropriately.*

5. **not someone's concern** or **none of someone's concern**

   *Some people think that what happens in far-away places is **not their concern**.*

   *It's naive to assume that the consequences of global warming are **none of our concern**.*

6. **concern about/for/over someone or something** (all involving some worry)

   *There is growing **concern about** air pollution in the city.*

   *When you show **concern for** some people, you worry about their well-being.*

   *The report expressed **serious concern over** rapidly rising property prices.*

7. You can use a **that-**clause to spell out the nature or content of a concern.

   *Our **concern that** Hong Kong's competitiveness is declining is not unfounded.*

concern (v)

1. **Y concerns something (** = Y is about something)

   *This movie **concerns** racial discrimination.*

2. **Y concerns someone** (=Y affects someone or makes someone worried)

   *New regulations governing income tax **concern** all tax payers.*

3. **concern oneself with**

   *Students are increasingly **concerning themselves with** getting good grades.* (Here, **concerning** is the progressive tense of the verb **concern** and not the preposition **concerning**.)

concerned (adj)

1. **concerned** (= affected by or involved in something) (placed after noun)

   *The management is trying to reach an agreement with all employees **concerned**.*

2.   **concerned** (= worried or troubled) (placed before noun)

*The patient looked at her doctor with a **concerned** expression.*

***Concerned** parents hope to hold a meeting with their children's teachers.*

3.   **be concerned with**

(a) be involved with or in

*Parents **are concerned with** caring for and protecting their young children.*

(b) have interest in

*Scientists **are** often **concerned with** the practical implications of their research.*

(c) be about

*Religious faith **is concerned with** spiritual growth.*

4.   **be concerned about/for** (= be worried about)

*Mrs Wong **is concerned about** her daughter's not having a healthy diet.*

*Parents **are** usually **concerned for** the welfare of their children studying overseas.*

5.   **be concerned that** (introducing a noun clause)

*Many people **are concerned that** quality of life in this city is deteriorating.*

6.   **be concerned to do something** (= to think that it is important to do something)

*Many of our church members **are concerned to** donate to support the church's programmes.*

7.   **as far as** (or **where**) **something/somebody is concerned** (can be placed at beginning or end of sentence)

***As far as** education background **is concerned,** these applicants are fine candidates for the job.*

*Hong Kong is a very liveable city, **where** public transport **is concerned.***

***As far as I am concerned,** the government is not doing a good enough job to support the development of the arts.*

concerning (prep) (= about, involving)

1.   **be + concerning** is always wrong. Instead, say either (a) **It/this is a matter concerning + noun phrase**, or (b) **It/this** (or **this matter**) **concerns + noun phrase.**

(✗) ~~This question is concerning the preservation of clean air.~~

(✓) *This is a question **concerning** the preservation of clean air.*

2.   You can rewrite this sentence in any of the following ways without changing its meaning:

*This question **concerns** the preservation of clean air.* (**concern** as v)

*The **concern** of this question is the preservation of clean air.* (**concern** as n)

*This question **is concerned with** the preservation of clean air.* (**concerned** as adj)

3. Remember this pattern: noun/noun phrase + **concerning** + noun/noun phrase

*We have read several <u>books</u> **concerning** <u>the early history of Hong Kong</u>.*
      (noun)   (noun phrase)

*The customer asked the manager <u>questions</u> **concerning** <u>the shop's policy governing return of</u>*
                    (noun)   (noun phrase)
<u>unsatisfactory goods</u>.

consider (v)

1. **consider as** (= think of someone or something as)

   *We **consider** Hong Kong **as** our home.*

   *Haydn is **considered as** father of the symphony.*

2. **consider to be** (= have a particular opinion of something or somebody) The words **to be** may be omitted.

   *Many **consider** Churchill **(to be)** the most charismatic statesman in the 20ᵗʰ century.*

   *Cantonese people generally **consider** steaming **(to be)** the best way to cook fresh fish.*

3. **consider doing something** (= think seriously about doing something)

   *I'm **considering** taking up Chinese calligraphy.*

constrain (v), restrain (v)

1. Both **constrain** and **restrain** contain the idea of preventing some behaviour from happening. We can feel **constrained** or **restrained** by some force so that we cannot do a particular thing. However, we use **constrain** when the restricting force comes from within ourselves, such as a character trait or certain moral principles. We use **restrain** when the limiting force comes from some external condition.

2. Given the difference pointed out above, the following two sentences illustrate a more careful use of **constrain** and **restrain**. Note the two different prepositions (**constrain against**, **restrain from**).

   *A sense of intellectual inadequacy **constrained** me **against** joining the discussion.*

   *That I attended the meeting as merely an observer **restrained** me **from** joining the discussion.*

content (adj, v), contented (adj)

1. **Content** (adj, accent on second syllable) (= happy and satisfied) (not before noun)

*It was a tough competition; she was **content** to have obtained a merit award.*

2.   **Content** (v, accent on second syllable) (= to make someone feel satisfied)

*Today, I **contented myself with** a simple sandwich for lunch.*

3.   **Contented** (adj, accent on second syllable, and **-ted** must be voiced) (can come before noun)

*With two substantial pensions, the Wongs are living a **contented** life.*

content (n), contents (n)

1.   **Content** (n, singular, uncountable, accent on first syllable)

*I cannot recall the **content** of his speech.*

*This brand of luncheon meat claims to have a low salt **content**.*

2.   **Contents** (n plural)

Sense (a): the objects in a container

*The **contents** of the safe deposit include several antique watches and some jewellery.*

Sense (b): the things written in a document or book

*The book's table of **contents** at the beginning shows the chapters making up the book.*

continual (adj), continuous (adj)

1.   **Continual** means "repeating frequently" or "recurring".

*As customer service manager, he handles **continual** complaints from customers.*

*Travel guidebooks to popular destinations are **continually** (adv) updated.*

2.   **Continuous** means "happening without interruption".

*He was in **continuous** employment at the same company until his retirement.*

*In preparation for her upcoming piano examination, she practises **continuously** (adv) for five hours each day.*

correct (adj), right (adj)

1.   These two words are sometimes used interchangeably, as when we refer to a **correct answer** or a **right answer**. However, **correct** stresses freedom from error, or accuracy; **right** stresses being in full accordance with fact, truth, or a standard.

2.   **Correct** (= proper, accurate) is used in sentences such as the following:

*Children start learning **correct** manners at an early age.*

*Her spelling of "accommodate" is **correct** with two c's and two m's.*

3. **Right** (= appropriate, suitable, desirable)**,** rather than **correct**, is used in the following:

   *Making the **right** decision at the **right** time is not easy.*

   *Your new job has great potential; you have taken a step in the **right** direction.*

cure (v), heal (v)

1. **Cure** is a transitive verb. That is, it takes an object. Medicine can **cure** a person **of** a disease or illness. (Note that **of** is needed in such a construction.)

   *Doctors may prescribe an antibiotic to **cure** an infection.*

   *Many infected with Covid-19 have been **cured**.*

2. **Heal** is often used as an intransitive verb (taking no object) although it can also be used transitively.

   *For older people, broken bones take longer to **heal**.* (intransitive use)

   *The two brothers found it very difficult to **heal** the misunderstanding between them.* (transitive use)

   *We pray that God will **heal** her through doctors and their care.* (transitive use)

definite (adj), definitive (adj)

1. The stress is on the first syllable in **definite**, but on the second syllable in **definitive**. In **definite**, **de** is pronounced /de/ (the e as in **ten**); in **definitive**, **de** is pronounced /dI/ (the I sound as in **sit**).

2. Something that is definite is "clear, firm, not likely to change".

   *In the tenancy lease, there is a **definite** statement about the tenant's responsibilities.*

3. Something that is definitive is "best, complete, final, authoritative".

   *My friend told me she has found a **definitive** biography of Beethoven.*

delay (v, n), postpone (v)

1. Many things can **delay** (v) an event, but it is specifically a person's action that **postpones** something.

   *The arrival of many flights will be **delayed** because of bad weather.*

   *Drivers usually face long **delays** (n) in cross-harbour traffic on weekends.*

   *The opening of the new music season has been **postponed** from September to October.*

   *Given the present coronavirus situation, we have **postponed** our travel plans until at least two years from now.*

2. We can speak of **delaying** an action.

*The chairman **delayed** his decision on whether to call a special meeting on the matter.*

3.   We use the term **delaying tactics** to refer to doing something deliberately to delay a decision or process.

   *Committee members may make long speeches as **delaying tactics** to avoid a vote.*

dependant (n), dependent (adj, also n in AmE)

1.   In BrE, **dependant** (n) is a person who depends on someone to live. In AmE, the word with the same meaning is **dependent.**

2.   In BrE, **dependent** is always an adjective.

   *She is a single mother with two **dependent** children. She has two **dependants**.*

3.   Something or someone is **dependent on** (or **upon**) someone or something **for** something.

   *His elderly parents are **dependent on** him **for** food and shelter.*

   *The orchestra is **dependent on** Government subsidy and public donations **for** its smooth operation.*

despite (prep), in spite of (prep phr)

1.   **Despite** means that something is true even though something else might have affected it. It means the same as **in spite of**.

2.   **Despite** is not followed by a preposition. (DO NOT write ~~despite of~~.) Both **despite** and **in spite of** are followed by a noun, noun phrase, or noun clause. You can use **despite** to start a sentence or in mid-sentence.

   ***Despite** the hot weather, they went hiking yesterday. (Or: They went hiking yesterday **despite** the hot weather.)*

   *Her paintings are quite intricate and beautiful **in spite of** the fact that she has never taken any painting lessons.*

detail (n), detailed (adj)

1.   **Detail** is used as a countable noun in the following two sentences:

   *This is one **detail** that I missed.*

   *I will tell her **details** of the story later.*

2.   **in (great/full) detail** (used as an uncountable noun)

   (✓) *She told me her success story **in detail**.*

   (✗) ~~*She told me her success story **in details**.*~~

   (✓) *The issue will be discussed **in great detail**.*

(**✗**) ~~The issue will be discussed **in great details**.~~

3. **detailed** (adj)

    *He is reading a **detailed** study of the second World War.*

    *Having lived in Shanghai for over ten years, she has a **detailed** knowledge of the city.*

difficult, easy, possible, impossible (all adj)

1. Chinese learners of English may use **difficult** incorrectly in such a sentence as **I am difficult to remember people's names.** This is likely the result of a literal translation from the Chinese 我是很難記得人名的 , which is acceptable in Chinese.

2. Never say **I am difficult to . . . ,** but say **I find it difficult to . . .** or **It is difficult for me to . . . .** Thus, the incorrect sentence mentioned in 1. can be corrected as:

    *I **find it difficult** to remember people's names.*

    *It is **difficult for me** to remember people's names.*

    Or you can use a gerund phrase as the subject of the sentence:

    *Remembering people's names **is difficult for me**.*

2. Similarly, note the three ways of expressing the same meaning:

    (**✗**) ~~She **is difficult** to get to work on time.~~

    (**✓**) *She finds it **difficult** to get to work on time.*

    Or: *It is **difficult** for her to get to work on time.*

    Or: *Getting to work on time is **difficult** for her.*

3. Sometimes, we use **difficult** and **easy** to describe something without referring to people:

    *Finding a place to eat is **easy** in this part of town.*

    *It is **difficult** to see how peace can be achieved in the Middle East.*

    *Contemporary music is **difficult** to understand.*

4. The construction of the preceding sentence (**Contemporary music is *difficult* to understand**) is possible only if the verb is transitive (= takes an object).

    *This story book is **easy** to read for young children.* (**Read** is transitive. Its object is **book** in this sentence.)

    (**✗**) ~~Conflict becomes **easy** to happen.~~ (Incorrect, because **happen** is intransitive.)

    We can say "understand some kind of music" or "read a book", but we cannot say "happen a conflict". A conflict simply **happens** (intransitive verb, requiring no object to complete its meaning). Thus, the sentence needs to be rewritten as follows:

*It is/becomes **easy** for conflict to happen.*

5.   When **difficult** is used to describe a person, it means the person is hard to please or hard to work with:

*His boss is a **difficult** manager, always stubborn and often unpredictable.*

6.   The words **possible** and **impossible** are used in a similar way. They usually refer to things or actions.

(✘) ~~*We are possible that we cannot come.*~~

(✔) *It is possible that we cannot come.*

*You bought this dress a month ago. It is **impossible** for you to return it for exchange or refund.*

7.   You can use **impossible** to describe someone whose behaviour is unreasonable and even annoying:

*Some people habitually jump the queue at service points and will argue with you if you ask them not to do so. They are just **impossible**!*

difficulty (n)

1.   As a noun, **difficulty** can be countable or uncountable. In the countable sense, the plural **difficulties** refers to things, situations, or problems that cause trouble:

*Soon after moving into the new flat, he ran into **difficulties with** the plumbing.*

*Mentally disabled children have learning **difficulties**.*

2.   Used as an uncountable noun, **difficulty** may refer to a general difficult situation.

*Their research project soon ran into **difficulty**.*

3.   In its uncountable sense, **difficulty** can be followed by **in, of**, or **with**, but with somewhat different connotations.

*The students have **difficulty in** translation from English to Chinese.* (The emphasis is on what students experience in the process of translation.)

Using **difficulty** in this sense, you can supply an **-ing gerund** to follow **difficulty** without the preposition **in**:

*The students have **difficulty** translating from English to Chinese.*

To stress the <u>quality of being difficult</u> found in the task of translation, you can say:

*It is not easy to understand the **difficulty of** translation.*

When you are faced with something unpleasant or when you have a tough task, you can use **difficulty with** although you may omit **with**:

*We all have **difficulty** (**with**) coming to terms with the loss of a loved one.*

*She has **difficulty** (**with**) solving the problem.*

dilemma (n), problem (n)

1. Do not use **dilemma** as a fancy word for "problem" or "difficult decision" unless the decision involves two uneasy choices.

2. You would **be in a dilemma** or **face a dilemma** when you have two equally unattractive choices.

   *His work hours are irregular, making it difficult to spend time with his wife and children. He is really facing the **dilemma** of choosing between work and family commitments.*

discuss (v), discussion (n), mention (v, n)

1. Do not make the common error of using the preposition **about** after **discuss** and **mention.** We **discuss** something, or we **mention** something. It is always wrong to say ~~we discuss about something~~ or ~~we mention about something~~.

2. To **discuss** something is to examine it in some detail, whereas to **mention** something is to say something about it without giving many details. The following sentence illustrates the difference:

   *The group **discussed** the benefits of urban development to the economy but only **mentioned** briefly the effects of urban development on the environment.*

3. While it is incorrect to say ~~discuss about something~~, it is correct to say **to have a discussion about something.**

   (✗) *~~The TV programme discusses about the effects of diet on health~~.*

   (✓) *The TV programme **discusses** the effects of diet on health.*

   (✓) *We had a useful **discussion about** the meaning of a healthy diet.*

4. Do not use a **that**-clause immediately after **discuss.** Use such words as **the idea**, **the proposal**, or **the suggestion** before the **that**-clause. You can also use words like **how, what, when, where,** and **why** to refer to objects that are discussed.

   (✗) *~~We will discuss that a little knowledge is a dangerous thing~~.*

   (✓) *We will **discuss the idea** that a little knowledge is a dangerous thing.*

   (✓) *Let us **discuss how** the dispute may be settled and **when** an agreement can be signed by the two parties involved.*

5. **Don't mention it.** This is a polite answer when someone thanks you for something.

   "Thanks so much for all your help."

   "Don't mention it!" (You can also say *"You are welcome"* or *"No problem"*.)

6. **Mention** is also a noun, as in the following two examples:

   *In the discussion, there is no **mention of** what "public opinion" really means.*

*Unfortunately, the report **makes no mention of** why the response rate was so low.*

disregard (v), ignore (v)

1.　Both **disregard** and **ignore** suggest total inattention to something.

2.　**Disregard** implies inattention after conscious consideration.

*Please **disregard** this notice if you have already paid.*

*The judge reminded the jurors to **disregard** statements not based on evidence.*

3.　**Ignore** suggests rejecting something without any conscious consideration.

*When you are walking on a busy street, you are likely to **ignore** the noise around you.*

*It is really dangerous for some people to **ignore** typhoon warnings and venture to the waterfront in the middle of strong winds.*

distinct (adj), distinctive (adj), distinguished (adj)

1.　**Distinct** means "clearly different".

Young people today hold values distinct from those of young people a few generations ago.

You can say that something is **distinct** if it is clearly seen, heard, or felt.

*Her gymnastic performance showed **distinct** improvement after two months' training.*

2.　**Distinctive** means "having a special and easily recognized quality".

*Pavarotti, the famous Italian tenor, sang with a very **distinctive** voice.*

3.　**Distinguished** means "successful, respected, and famous".

*Stephen Hawking was probably the most **distinguished** scientist since Albert Einstein.*

doubtful (adj), dubious (adj)

1.　Some people believe these two adjectives may be used interchangeably.

*I am **doubtful** about the claim that Vitamin C can cure colds.*

*I am **dubious** about the claim that Vitamin C can cure colds.*

2.　Careful writers reserve **dubious** for meaning "suspect" (adj, accent on first syllable) or "untrustworthy". A claim, a thing, or an arrangement can be described as **dubious,** e.g., **a dubious lab report**, if you cannot trust it. Only persons are capable of doubting, and so **doubtful** is used to refer to someone who is sceptical or suspicious.

*Many people are **doubtful** whether the new coronavirus vaccines will be safe.*

due (adj) to, owing to (prep)

1. **Due** is an adjective and should be used to modify a noun. Careful writers should write like the following:

    *The cancellation of the meeting **is due to** bad weather.* (**Due** modifies the head word, **cancellation**, of the noun phrase.)

    *Her career success **was due largely to** her innovativeness.*

2. The following constructions using **due to** are always incorrect in standard English, although they are commonly adopted in the media and in various official documents:

    (✗) ~~The meeting is cancelled **due to** bad weather.~~

    (✗) ~~**Due to** popular demand, there will be three additional performances.~~

3. **Owing to** is used prepositionally, meaning "because of".

    *The meeting is cancelled **owing to** bad weather.* (Or: ***Owing to** bad weather, the meeting is cancelled.*)

    ***Owing to** popular demand, there will be three additional performances.*

effective (adj), efficient (adj)

1. **Effective** is working in the intended way or producing the desired result. **Efficient** is working well through sensible use of resources such as time and money. We usually speak of a plan or an action as being **effective,** but people or a system as being **efficient.**

    *We wonder if the government's plans to create artificial islands to deal with the housing problem will be **effective.***

    *Airlines now offer **efficient** on-line check-in for passengers.*

2. The noun of **effective** is **effectiveness;** that of **efficient** is **efficiency.**

    *Pharmacologists often test the **effectiveness** of new drugs before they can be used.*

    *Writers using the computer in their work can achieve unparalleled **efficiency.***

effort (n), effortless (adj)

1. Do not say **~~pay an effort~~** or **~~spend much effort~~**. This is always incorrect. Instead, use the correct idiomatic collocation **make an effort.** In this construction, **effort** is treated as a countable noun, meaning an attempt to do something involving hard work and determination:

    *I am prepared to **make a great effort** (or **make every effort**) to do well in my job.*

    *This programme is made possible through the **efforts** of many people.*

2. You may use **effort** as an uncountable noun (without **-s** ending) when you think of it as physical or mental energy. Thus, you can say that you have **put much effort into** a project or running a new

business. For emphasis, you can even say you will **redouble** or **step up** your effort.

*Learning a foreign language takes much **effort**.*

*I have put a lot of **effort** into the writing of this book.*

3. Adjectives that modify **effort** include **considerable, constant, determined, great, enormous,** and **sustained.**

*To be fluent in a language requires **sustained effort**.*

*The authorities exerted an **enormous effort** to rebuild the town after the earthquake.*

4. Work done by a skilled craftsman or artist may seem **effortless.** It looks easy although it is the result of hard work, discipline, and much practice.

*Mr. Perlman's playing of this very difficult violin piece looked so **effortless** for him.*

either (determiner, pron, adv)

1. **Either** as a determiner can be placed before a noun or noun phrase to show which one you are referring to. It means one or the other of two things.

*You can park on **either** side of the street here.*

2. **Either** is also a pronoun when used as follows:

*We have orange juice or plain tea—you can have **either**.*

*Could **either** of you go to the restaurant to secure a table first?*

3. As an adverb, **either** is used following a negative phrase to say that it is also true of you or another person or thing:

*My wife doesn't like durians, and I don't **either**.*

Note that many students make the mistake of using *too*. You must not say:

(✘) ~~My wife doesn't like durians, and I don't *too*.~~

Alternatively, you can use *neither* to express the same meaning:

*My wife doesn't like durians, and **neither** do I.*

4. **Either . . . or . . .** are a pair of correlative conjunctions to refer to two equally important things. Note the positioning of these two words. Errors occur usually with **either**.

(✘) ~~John is not here yet. He is *either* delayed by traffic *or* something is keeping him at home.~~ (The elements after **either** and **or** are <u>not</u> parallel.)

(✓) *John is not here yet. **Either** he is delayed by traffic **or** something is keeping him at home.* (The elements after **either** and **or** are parallel.)

That is, observe parallel construction when you use **either . . . or . . .** , as in both of the following sentences. What comes after **either** and **or** must be grammatically the same:

*We can vote **either** for candidate A **or** for candidate B.*

*We can vote for **either** candidate A **or** candidate B.*

emigrate (v), immigrate (v), migrate (v)

1. People **emigrate from** a country or a territory to another. They are, in this view, **emigrants.** The movement is **emigration.**

    *In the 1980s, many Hong Kong people **emigrated** to Canada, the United States, and Australia.*

    *Large numbers of people **emigrated from** various European countries to the United States in the early decades of the 20th century.*

2. People **immigrate to** a country or territory from another. They are **immigrants.** Such movement is **immigration.**

    *When Donald Trump was president of the United States, his administration implemented policies to restrict **immigrants from** Mexico.*

    *Many people **immigrated to** Hong Kong from mainland China in the 1950s.*

3. When people move from one part of a country or territory to another (such as from rural areas to urban areas within the same country), they **migrate.** They are called **migrants.** Birds also **migrate** from colder to warmer places before winter arrives.

    *Rural-urban **migration** can cause problems of underemployment and overcrowding in the cities.*

eminent (adj), imminent (adj)

1. **Eminent** means famous, important, and respected.

    *Akira Kurosawa was an **eminent** film director whose career spanned over 50 years.*

2. An **imminent** event is one, usually unpleasant, that is likely to happen soon.

    *Many coastal cities are facing the **imminent threat** of flooding if global warming continues.*

emphasize (v), emphasis (n)

1. These two words are different in pronunciation. **Emphasize** (also spelled **emphasise**) is verb and rhymes with *size*; **emphasis** is noun and rhymes with *crisis*.

2. **Emphasize** never takes a preposition. ~~**Emphasize on something**~~ is always incorrect.

    (✗) *~~The restaurant's operation **emphasizes on** courteous customer service.~~*

    (✓) *The restaurant's operation **emphasizes** courteous customer service.*

    emphasize that   The preceding sentence can be rewritten as follows:

    *The restaurant's management **emphasizes that** they always give customers courteous service.*

3. **Emphasis** (n.) This is the singular form when **emphasis** is used as an uncountable noun. Note the use of a preposition after or before **emphasis.** You can **put** or **place** or **lay emphasis on** something. You can also say something **with emphasis.**

    *General education **places much emphasis on** the use of critical thinking.*

    *The committee chairman said **with emphasis** that, after so much discussion, the proposed action would be put to a vote.*

4. **Emphasis** can be used as a countable noun, sometimes requiring its plural form **emphases** (the last syllable is pronounced /-si:z/ to rhyme with *seize*):

    *Three **emphases** are evident in the education this primary school provides: politeness, team spirit, and obedience.*

especially (adv), specially (adv)

1. **Especially** means "notably", "even more so".

    *This restaurant serves exquisite desserts, **especially** tiramisu and mango pudding.*

2. **Specially** means "for a particular purpose".

    *I bought this brooch **specially** for my wife's birthday.*

even if, even though (both subordinating conj)

1. Both **even if** and **even though** introduce a subordinate clause containing an idea that is less important than that contained in the main clause of a sentence.

2. **Even if** introduces something that may happen:

    ***Even if** the United States and China can come to some agreement to end their trade war, the United States will continue to feel threatened by the ascendance of China..*

3. **Even though** introduces something that happens or has happened:

    ***Even though** many people say that critical thinking is important, most of them do not know exactly what critical thinking is.*

every day (two words, adv phr), everyday (one word, adj)

1. **Everyday** is one word when used as an adjective before a noun.

    *The Internet and mobile phone have become part of our **everyday** life.*

2. If you use it to modify an action, it must be written as two words and placed after the action it modifies. In this role, **every day** is an adverbial phrase.

    *Read something **every day** to keep well informed.* (Do not hyphenate **well informed** because the phrase is used adverbially. But do hyphenate it when you use it as an adjective before a noun, as in **a well-informed person.**)

everyone (indefinite pron), **every one** (**every** as adj modifying **one**)

1. Like **everybody**, **everyone** is written as one word. Use a singular verb after **everyone.**

    *Nearly **everyone** is not happy with the steep rise in property prices.*

2. When you use **every one**, make sure its reference is clear.

    *There are three main reasons for the new arrangement, but you can find something wrong in **every one** of them.*

except (conj, prep), **except for** (prep)

1. **Except** as a preposition is used between two nouns. **For** following **except** may be omitted after such words as **all, any, every, anybody, nobody, nowhere** and **nothing.**

    *The clinic is open every day **except** (**for**) Sundays.*

    *He has been to all Asian countries **except** (**for**) North Korea.*

    *She has seen nobody in the past month **except** (**for**) her aunt.*

2. If **except** is used at the beginning of a sentence, you should use the phrase **except for.**

    ***Except for** Sundays, the clinic is open every day.*

    ***Except for** North Korea, he has been to all Asian countries.*

    ***Except for** modern abstract art, I like most Western paintings.*

3. You can use **except for** to modify a whole statement. This means the purpose is not to single out any item or items for exclusion but to express some qualification to the statement. In the following sentence, some qualification is made to the whole statement *The concert hall was totally silent.*

    *The concert hall was totally silent **except for** the occasional coughs of a few individuals.*

    The sentence can be recast to begin with **except for:**

    ***Except for** the occasional coughs of a few individuals, the concert hall was totally silent.*

4. Use object form pronouns after **except** (**for**).

    *We all like cruising **except** (**for**) her.* (Not . . . ~~except she.~~)

    *Everybody has seen the announcement **except** (**for**) me.* (Not . . . ~~except I.~~)

5. Use **except**, not **except for**, before prepositions and **that.**

    *Their dog never barks at home **except when** they have visitors.*

    *This old dictionary, a prize I got in secondary school, is of little use now **except as** a sentimental souvenir.*

    *Restaurants normally add a service charge to bills **except in** tea cafes.*

*This trip to South America sounds attractive **except that** it is too expensive.* (Here, **that** is a conjunction , which must be followed by a clause.)

6.   Do not confuse **except (for)** with **besides. Except (for)** excludes something; **besides** includes something.

*I like all seafood dishes **except** raw fish.* (= I like all seafood dishes but not raw fish.)

*I like all seafood dishes **besides** raw fish.* (= I like all seafood dishes including raw fish.)

excited (adj), exciting (adj), excite (v), excitement (n)

1.   Like **interested** and **interesting** (also **surprised** and **surprising** among many others), **excited** and **exciting** are a pair of adjectives (one using the **-ed** past participle and the other using the **-ing** present participle) that have to do with our emotional response to some event or experience.

2.   Distinguish between (a) our response (**interested, surprised, excited**), using the past participle, and (b) the nature of some thing, event or experience (**interesting, surprising, exciting**), using the present participle, that causes our response. Thus, something can be **exciting** to us, and we become **excited** or feel **excited** as a result.

*Young people are easily **excited** (not ~~exciting~~) by the presence of popular idols.*

*They find popular music quite **exciting** (not ~~excited~~).*

3.   Note the use of the verb **excite** and the noun **excitement** as follows:

*Nothing **excites** him more than the sight of beautiful flowers.*

*Our grandchildren were filled with **excitement** when they arrived at Disneyland.*

4.   Here is a list of some commonly used adjective pairs to describe things/experiences and people's feelings in response to them. Be careful to use them correctly.

Things or experiences *Something is . . .*	People's responses *You are/feel . . .*
amazing	*amazed*
amusing	*amused*
annoying	*annoyed*
comforting	*comforted*
confusing	*confused*
depressing	*depressed*
disappointing	*disappointed*
discouraging	*discouraged*
disturbing	*disturbed*
encouraging	*encouraged*
entertaining	*entertained*
exciting	**excited**

Things or experiences *Something is . . .*	**People's responses** *You are/feel . . .*
exhausting	exhausted
fascinating	fascinated
frightening	frightened
heartening	heartened
horrifying	horrified
inspiring	inspired
insulting	insulted
interesting	interested
motivating	motivated
moving	moved
overwhelming	overwhelmed
puzzling	puzzled
relaxing	relaxed
satisfying	satisfied
shocking	shocked
soothing	soothed
stimulating	stimulated
surprising	surprised
terrifying	terrified
threatening	threatened
thrilling	thrilled
tiring	tired
troubling	troubled
worrying	worried

extent (n), **extend** (v), **extension** (n), **extensive** (adj)

1. Do NOT confuse **extend** (v) with **extent** (n). **Extend,** a verb, means to continue or to make longer; **extent,** a noun, means degree. When you speak, the appropriate ending **-d** or **-t** sound should be clear. The word is **extent,** not **extend,** in these phrases: **to a certain extent, to some extent, to a large extent,** and **to the extent that.**

    To a large extent, the progress a student can make in language learning depends on how much attention he or she pays to grammar and usage.

2. **To the extent that** (= as far as, so far as)

    To the extent that the cruise terminal may be used by thousands of passengers embarking and disembarking several times a week, the authorities need to have an effective design for transportation between the terminal and other parts of the city.

3. **Extend** (v), **extension** (n)

    Our study of racial minorities in Hong Kong extended over almost three years.

    Because she expects to be away from Hong Kong for several weeks, she is asking the Inland Revenue Department to extend the deadline of tax return by one month.

    She is asking the Inland Revenue Department to grant her a one-month extension of the deadline of tax return.

4.   **Extensive** (adj)

Extensive means large in size or covering a large area or amount:

*The vacation resort they visited in Indonesia has **extensive** grounds.*

Extensive also means including or dealing with a lot of information:

*There is **extensive** research on the connection between colon cancer and diet.*

facility (n), facilitate (v)

1.   **Facility** is usually used in the plural form, **facilities**, to mean rooms, buildings, equipment, or services provided for a particular purpose. Schools and universities have educational and training facilities such as playground, athletic field, library, laboratories, lockers, and gyms. Hotels have facilities for leisure, conference, storage, banquets, and laundry services.

2.   **Facility**, in the singular form, refers to a natural ability to do something well.

*This teenage girl has an amazing **facility** for mathematics.*

3.   **Facilitate** (v) means to make a process or activity possible or easier. You can make something more likely to happen when you **facilitate** it. Remember that you must use this word for processes or activities, not people.

(✘) ~~His experience in the hospitality industry **facilitated** us in the planning of the new hotel.~~

(✓) *His experience in the hospitality industry **facilitated** the planning of our new hotel.*

(✓) *His experience in the hospitality industry **helped** us in the planning of our new hotel.*

familiar (adj), familiarity (n), familiarize (v)

1.   You cannot use **do** or **does** before **familiar** (adj). Use the verb **be** instead: **be + familiar with +** noun/noun phrase.

(✘) ~~We **do not familiar** with this part of Hong Kong.~~

(✓) *We **are not familiar with** this part of Hong Kong.*

(✓) *If you **are familiar with** the MTR system, then you can go anywhere in Hong Kong.*

2.   Note the different use of **familiar to** vs. **familiar with**. While person A is **familiar with** an object or someone, an object or someone is (or looks) **familiar to** person A. An idea may sound **familiar to** person A. He/she may be **familiar with** that idea.

*This place **looks familiar to me**: I may have been here before.*

*The idea of pot-luck **sounds familiar** (to us): different families bring different dishes.*

3.   **Familiarity** (n) **with**

*We had a wonderful trip in Japan largely because our guide has intimate **familiarity with***

Japanese society and culture.

4. **Familiarize** (v) **oneself with**

*If you intend to study in France, you must first **familiarize yourself with** the French language.*

fewer (adj), less (determiner)

1. As a rule, use **fewer** for countable nouns and **less** for uncountable nouns.

    *Water is precious: use **less** of it.*

    *There were **fewer** than twenty people in the cinema.*

    (✗) *Protect the environment: use **less** plastic bags.*

    (✓) *Protect the environment: use fewer plastic bags.*

2. If you refer not to individual objects but to a single period, a distance, or a sum of money, use **less** rather than **fewer:**

    *The contractors promised to complete the renovation job in **less than** three months.*

    *The nearest mass transit station is only **less than** two street blocks away.*

    *Tickets for the charity concert sold so well that **no less than** two million dollars were raised. No **fewer** than 1,000 tickets were sold.*

the following (adj, n), as follows (as in place of a subject)

1. **The following** may be used as an adjective pre-modifying a noun.

    *We shall do it in **the following** way.*

    *The unemployment rate in 1999 was 5 per cent. In **the following** year, it started to rise.*

2. **The following** may be used as a noun, used with a singular verb (for one person or thing) or a plural verb (for multiple people or things). Note that you must not add an **-s** ending to the word **following** even when it is used with a plural reference.

    ***The following** is the story of his business success.*

    ***The following** (not **followings**) guests are invited to the grduation ceremony.*

3. **As follows**   **As** takes the place of a subject in this phrase. Used to introduce a list, it always keeps the **-s** ending regardless of whether it comes after a singular or plural noun.

    *The agreement after a long discussion is **as follows**.*

    *Their terms of employment are **as follows**.*

for example (**example** is n) (= **for instance**)

1. The word **example** (n) in this phrase is always singular, no matter how many examples follow this phrase. The same applies to **for instance**. Never write ~~for examples~~ or ~~for instances.~~

    (✗) ~~Many icons exist in popular culture, for examples, Bruce Lee, Michael Jackson, and Tom Cruise.~~

    (✓) *Many icons exist in popular culture,* **for example***, Bruce Lee, Michael Jackson, and Tom Cruise.*

2. The plural **examples** can be used if you rewrite the sentence as follows:

    Many icons exist in popular culture. **Examples** *include Bruce Lee, Michael Jackson, and Tom Cruise.*

    Bruce Lee, Michael Jackson, and Tom Cruise are **examples** *of icons in popular culture.*

3. The following are different ways of using **for example** in sentences:

    (a) *Many countries levy a sales tax on goods and services****; for example,*** *Canada, the USA, and Britain.*

    (b) *Many countries levy a sales tax on goods and services—****for example,*** *Canada, the USA, and Britain.*

    (c) *Many countries****, for example*** *Canada, the USA, and Britain, levy a sales tax on goods and services.*

    (Here, **for example** introduces items that together form a phrase set off from the main clause **Many countries levy a sales tax on goods and services.** In this sentence pattern, do not use comma after **for example**.)

    (d) *Many countries levy a sales tax on goods and services. They include****, for example,*** *Canada, the USA, and Britain.*

    (e) *Many countries levy a sales tax on goods and services.* **For example,** *they include Canada, the USA, and Britain.*

    (f) *A sales tax is levied on goods and services in other countries****,*** *Canada and Britain* ***for example.*** (No comma before **for example**)

    (g) *A sales tax is levied on goods and services in other countries****, for example*** *Canada and Britain.* (No comma after **for example**)

fourth (adj), **forth** (adv), **forthcoming** (adj)

1. There is a **u** in **fourth** if you mean "4 th".

    This is her **fourth** *attempt to win the competition.*

2. The word **forth** is used in some common phrases:

back and forth (going in one direction and then in the opposite direction)

*Pacing **back and forth** in the hallway, he was thinking about the problem.*

put forth (put forward an idea)

*Many different suggestions were **put forth** in the meeting.*

and so forth (and so on)

*She bought lots of fruit at the supermarket, including apples, pears, strawberries, **and so forth.***

3.   As an adjective, **forthcoming** is used before a noun when it means "going to happen":

*They are already preparing for their **forthcoming** tour to Japan in November.*

Forthcoming is used after a noun when it means available or given when needed:

*As development director, she is confident that financial support for the planned gala event will be **forthcoming**.*

historic (adj), historical (adj)

1.   **Historic** means "important in history". A historic event has some special significance in history and is therefore likely to be remembered for a long time. We also speak of historic buildings and monuments for their noteworthiness in history.

*Omaha Beach at Normandy, France is an area of great **historic** importance associated with the Second World War over 70 years ago.*

2.   **Historical** means "connected with the past or with the study of history".

*The Opium War is at the core of the **historical** background of Hong Kong.*

horizon (n), horizons (n plural)

1.   **The horizon** is the line where the land or sea seems to touch the sky far away.

*When evening approahes, the sun sinks gradually below the **horizon**.*

2.   **On the horizon** is an idiomatic expression to mean that something is likely to happen.

*The company is doing well now, but there are problems **on the horizon**.*

3.   **Broaden/widen/expand one's horizons** is another idiomatic expression meaning increasing a person's range of knowledge or experience. Note that you must use the plural **horizons** in this phrase.

*Travelling or studying abroad will surely **broaden your horizons**.*

While **broaden/widen/expand** is a verb in the above construction, you can use the gerund form to make the expression a gerund phrase to become the subject of a sentence or the object of a preposition such as **to**.

Expanding our horizons *is an important part of life.*

Travelling or studying abroad will surely contribute to ***broadening your horizons.***

imply (v), infer (v)

1. To imply is to suggest an idea without saying it directly.

   If you say that a certain movie is "all right", you may be ***implying*** *that it is mediocre.*

2. To infer is to guess that something may be true according to the information you have. If an author implies something in what he or she writes, the reader tries to infer what it is. Thus, **imply** and **infer** are used from two different points of view: a speaker or writer ***implies***, while a listener or reader ***infers***.

   We can ***infer from*** *what he said about the movie that it was rather boring.* (Note the use of the preposition **from** after **infer.**)

3. The noun of **imply** is **implication;** the noun of **infer** is **inference.**

   She praised the chairman and, by ***implication,*** *the whole committee.*

   I don't know what ***inference*** *we can draw from the research data.*

in addition to (prep phr)

In addition to means the same as **as well as** and is used similarly. It is followed by a noun, noun phrase, or gerund phrase.

She directed the play ***in addition to*** *being its author.*

In addition to *confidence in what we hope for, faith is assurance of what we do not see.*

indoor (adj), indoors (adv)

1. **Indoor** is an adjective. An indoor activity takes place inside a building.

   Like volleyball, badminton is usually an ***indoor*** *game.*

2. **Indoors** is an adverb. Activities such as meetings and concerts take place indoors.

   Tennis can be played ***indoors*** *if there is a large enough hall.*

intense (adj), intensive (adj), extensive (adj)

1. **Intense** = very strong or great. People may work under **intense pressure**. Deserts are places with **intense heat** under the sun. You may want to spend much time on something because you have an **intense interest** in it.

   When thousands of applicants are trying to be considered for just one position, the competition is extremely ***intense.***

2. **Intensive** = involving a lot of attention and effort. A training course may require **intensive work**.

If you study something **intensively**, you want to go into many details carefully.

*Patients suffering from burns need **intensive** care in a hospital.*

3.   Do not confuse **intensive** with **extensive** (= involving a large area, size, or amount). See also **extensive** in the entry on **extent, extend, extension, extensive.**

*The explosion due to gas leak caused **extensive** damage to the apartment.*

interest (n, v)

1.   **Interest** (n). You may develop an **interest in** (not **on**) something from some special experience. You may watch something **with interest** because it is new or curious to you. When you have (an) **interest** in something, you want to know more about it.   Of course, it is also possible that you may **lose interest in** something if something else draws your attention away from it.

2.   **In the public interest** = necessary for the good of the people

*It is **in the public interest** that the details of the accident are made known.*

3.   **In the interest of safety/justice =** in order to be safe/just

*Car passengers should wear seat belts **in the interest of safety**.*

In the interest of justice, the accused is entitled to a fair trial.*

4.   **Interest** (v). When something **interests** you, it draws your attention.

*It may **interest** you to know that you can now take a high speed train from Hong Kong to Beijing.*

*Greasy food does not **interest** me.*

*She has always **interested herself in** volunteer work.*

interested (adj), interesting (adj)

1.   It is important to distinguish between these two adjectives. An object of interest can be said to be **interesting to** a person; a person is **interested in** an object. In other words, use **interesting** to describe a thing or an experience; use **interested** to describe the person who sees the thing or responds to the experience. Simply put, an **interesting** experience makes you **interested.**

*Many visitors find Ocean Park an **interesting** place to visit.*

*Not too many people are **interested in** serious films.*

2.   A person can also be said to be **interested** to do something.

*Our neighbour's daughter has long been **interested to study** nutrition.*

3.   People who are affected by a particular situation or who may expect to gain from it are called an **interested party** or **interested group.**

*The project director will discuss this proposal with all **interested parties.***

its (determiner), **it's** (= it is/has)

1.   Do not think that an apostrophe always accompanies possessives. Many (too many) people make the error of writing **it's** for the possessive form of **it**, which is **its**. **Its** is a determiner (to show which thing we are talking about).

   *China is an expansive country. **Its** capital is Beijing.*

2.   Remember this: **it's** = **it is** or **it has**, depending on the context.

   ***It's** raining hard now* = *It is raining hard now.*

   ***It's** been a long time since I last saw you* = *It has been a long time since I last saw you.*

joyful (adj), joyous (adj), happy (adj)

1.   Both **joyful** and **joyous** imply a sense of pleasure and excitement more intense than **happy**.

   Happy is commonly used in social exchanges, such as **We are happy** (or **glad**) **to see you**.

2.   **Joyous** suggests the potential of high spirits arising from the nature of the occasion, such as a wedding, a reunion of school alumni, or a New Year celebration. These are **joyous** occasions. When people attend such occasions, they are likely to feel and express joy: they are **joyful**. However, this is a distinction not always observed, with **joyous** used as a synonym for **joyful**.

   *The New Year concert was attended by a **joyous** audience.*

   Better write: *The New Year concert was attended by a **joyful** audience.*

   *New year is always a **joyous** time.*

3.   As far as possible, try to follow this guideline: **Joyous** is best used for events or occasions, while **joyful** should be used for people.

   *Beethoven's Pastoral Symphony contains a section about peasants' **joyous** celebration of harvest.*

   *She received the good news of her success with a **joyful** heart.*

lack (n, v), lacking (adj)

1.   Distinguish between **lack** as a verb and **lack** as a noun. The verb **lack** needs no preposition; the noun **lack** needs the preposition **of**.

   (✓) *Many people **lack** patience.* (Here, **lack** is verb.)

   (✗) *Many people are lack of patience.*

   (✓) *People's **lack** of patience can be seen in whether they obey the lights when crossing the road.* (Here, **lack** is noun.)

*(✓) Your health may suffer if you **lack** exercise.*

*(✓) **Lack of** exercise may affect your health.*

2. You can say that something happened **through lack of** or **for lack of** something, as in:

    *The project could not be completed **through lack of** funds.*

3. **Lacking** is an adjective used after, but never before, the noun it modifies. You can say that something is **lacking** (=absent or not present) or that somebody is **lacking** in certain aspects.

    *Given the fast pace of life in our metropolis, courtesy is often sadly **lacking**.* (Here, **lacking** modifies **courtesy**.)

    *When you attend a job interview, never give the impression that you are **lacking** in confidence.* (Here, **lacking** modifies **you**.)

last (adj), latest (adj), lastly (adv), at last (adv phr)

1. **Last** and **latest** can both mean "most recent" but not always. In the second of the following two sentences, **latest** is not appropriate.

    *The famous violinist Itzhak Perlman's **last** (or **latest**) visit to Hong Kong was more than five years ago.*

    *"Harry Potter and the Deathly Hallows" is the **last** novel of the Harry Potter series.*

2. Because **last** may mean "latest" (most recent) or "final", you must be careful to avoid ambiguity. If, for instance, you refer to the most recent episode of a television series, say **the latest episode** instead of **the last episode** unless the context makes it clear that you mean the most recent one.

3. **Lastly** is used when you refer to the final point in a list. Do not say **at last**, which introduces somehting that happens in the end.

    ***Lastly**, I want to thank you all for your support.*

    ***Last but not least**, I want to thank you all for your support.* (To stress that the final point is still important.)

    ***At last**, after several hours' happy reunion, it was time to leave.*

    At long last may be used to emphasize the effort spent:

    ***At long last**, though totally exhausted, we reached the summit.*

lie (v), lay (v)

1. **Lie** is always intransitive (taking no object):

    *It feels good to **lie** on the grass.*

    *We know that statistics can **lie**, depending on how figures are presented.* (Here **lie** = to say something that is not true.)

2.   **Lay** is always transitive (taking an object):

> *Before dinner, we need to **lay** place mats on the dining table.*

> *Traditional Chinese culture **lays** great emphasis on filial piety.*

3.   Study the principal forms of **lie** and **lay** (**lie** has two sets of verb forms depending on its meaning).

	Base form	-ing participle	Past form	Past participle
lie (= to say something that is not true)	lie	lying	lied	lied
lie (= to be on a surface; to be in a particular place; to consist of or to exist)	lie	lying	lay	lain
lay (= to put down; to plan and prepare)	lay	laying	laid	laid

4.   Study the following sentences to understand the various meanings of **lie** and **lay.**

lie (= to say something that is not true)

> *Respondents in a survey can **lie** about personal information such as age and income.*

lie (= to be on a surface)

> *Joe never bothers to tidy up his room, with clothes **lying** about on the floor.*

lie (= to be in a particular place)

> *Macau **lies** about 50 miles to the west of Hong Kong.*

lie (= to consist of or to exist): **lie in**

> *The difficulty of measuring "happiness" **lies in** finding suitable indicators.*

lay (= to put down)

> *She **laid** piles of books on her desk and selected some to give away to libraries.*

lay (= to plan and prepare)

> *Learning English early **lays** the groundwork for good mastery of the language.*

like (prep), as (conj)

1.   These two words have functions other than those specified here (**like** as a preposition; **as** as a conjunction). But it is in these functions that they are commonly confused when used to refer to similarity:

> (✓) *You should operate the printer **as** the manual tells you.*

> (✗) ~~*You should operate the printer **like** the manual tells you.*~~

2.   Remember this guideline: **Like** as a preposition is used before a noun, pronoun, or noun phrase; **as** as a conjunction is used before a clause or a prepositional phrase:

*He runs **like** the wind.*

***Like** me, you are entitled to the $2 privileged fare on public transport.*

***Like** her mother, she can play the violin.*

*He won the 100-metre race, just **as** I said he would.* (**as** followed by a clause)

*She plays the violin, **as** do many of her classmates.* (**as** followed by a clause)

*In Hong Kong, **as in Japan**, people eat a lot of fish.* (**in Japan** is a prepositiona phrase)

3. Although many people, including some English native speakers, use **like** as a conjunction when it should be a preposition, it is non-standard (as in the first two sentences below). Use **as**, **as if**, or **as though** instead (as in the last two sentences below).

   (✗) *It looks **like** it is going to rain.*

   (✗) *Nobody knows my friend **like** I do.*

   (✓) *It looks **as if** it is going to rain.* (You could also say: *It looks **like** another rainy day.*)

   (✓) *Nobody knows my friend **as** I do.*

look forward to something (phrasal v)

1. A sentence like the following one, using a **to**-infinitive after **look forward**, is always wrong:

   (✗) *I look forward to hear from you.*

2. In the phrase **look forward to**, **to** is a preposition, not a part of the infinitive form of a verb. The preposition takes an object, usually in the form of an **-ing** gerund or verbal noun. Thus, the sentence in 1. should be corrected to:

   *I **look forward to hearing** from you.*

   Other similar constructions:

   *I am **looking forward to seeing** you soon.*

   *We **look forward to having** a great time with you.*

lose (v), loss (n), loose (adj)

1. **loss** is noun and **lose** (pronounced /luːz/) is verb. The past tense of **lose** is **lost** (also past participle), which ends with a **-t** sound. Do not confuse **loss** with **lost**. In the following, **lose** and **lost** are used as verbs:

   (✗) *We may **loss** much in any investment.*

   (✓) *We may **lose** much in any investment.*

   (✓) *We have **lost** much in our recent investment.*

2. The following sentences use **loss** correctly as a noun. In the first sentence, it is a countable noun; in the second, it is uncountable.

    *When the economy is not going well, there will be many job **losses.***

    *Terrorist attacks often cause senseless **loss** of life.*

3. Do not confuse **loose** (adj) and **lose** (v). **Lose** is pronounced /lu:z/, ending in a voiced **z** sound; **loose** is pronounced /lu:s/, ending in a soft unvoiced **s** sound. Their meanings are totally different. While **lose** means to no longer have something because it has been stolen or destroyed, **loose** means not tight, not packed together, or not tied to something.

    *I feel quite comfortable wearing a **loose** shirt.*

    *Oranges in supermarkets are sometimes sold **loose** and sometimes in bags.*

lots of, a lot of (both determiner)

1. These expressions, while common in spoken English, should be avoided in formal writing.

2. For countable nouns, use **many** or **a large number of**; for uncountable nouns, use **much** or **a great deal of**. For example:

    lots of/a lot of participants → **a large number of** participants

    lots of/a lot of different explanations → **many** different explanations

    lots of/a lot of discussion → **a great deal of** discussion

    lots of/a lot of interest → **much** interest

maybe (adv), may be (may as a modal auxiliary verb)

1. **Maybe** (one word) is an adverb to mean you are not certain or to make a suggestion.

    *We can finish the work in ten, **maybe** fifteen days.*

    ***Maybe** we can discuss this issue at the next meeting.*

    In both of the above two sentences, **maybe** can be replaced by **perhaps**, with the same meaning. **Maybe,** more informal than **perhaps**, is used more in AmE than in BrE.

2. **May be** must be two words when you use **may** as a modal auxiliary verb.

    *What he said **may** or **may not be** true.*

    *This issue **may be** taken up for discussion at the next meeting.*

much (adj), many (adj)

1. Do not use **many** when you should use **much** and vice versa. The general guideline is that **many** is used for countable nouns and **much** for uncountable nouns.

2. Some examples of correct and incorrect uses of **many** and **much**: (Note that some nouns are countable in some contexts but uncountable in others.)

CORRECT	INCORRECT
many questions	much questions
many ideas	much ideas
many people	much people
many times (here **time** means occasion)	
much time (here **time** refers to a quantity of time)	many time
much labour	many labour
much energy	many energy
much effort	many effort
much argument (as an activity)	many argument

but:

many arguments (here "argument" refers to a statement offered as evidence)

one of

Take note of three patterns of sentence construction involving the phrase **one of** and requiring a singular or plural verb.

1. **Y is one of** the (multitude of items) + **that/who** + plural verb

    *"Democracy" is one of those concepts that **require** careful definition.*

2. **One of** the (multitude of items) + singular verb

    *One of the best known scientists **is** Stephen Hawking.*

3. **Y is the only one of** the (multitude of items) **that/who** + singular verb

    ***She is the only one of** over 100 applicants who **speaks** Putonghua, English, and Japanese.*

other (adj, pron), other than (prep), others (pron)

1. **Other** is used as an adjective or a pronoun.

    As an adjective:

    *The meeting was longer than scheduled, so we had no time to discuss **other** questions.*

    *Teaching meets her aspiration; there is no **other** job she would rather do.*

    As a pronoun:

    *I have tried all but one of the set lunch main courses; I will try **the other** next time.*

2. **Other than** (= except) is a two-word preposition, used usually after a negative.

    *We were so tired after walking for two hours that we could think of nothing **other than** finding some place to sit down.*

3.   **Others** is used only as a pronoun. It is the plural of **another.**

   *I've read some of the articles in the current issue of TIME; I won't have time to read **the others.***

outdoor (adj), outdoors (adv)

1.   **Outdoor** is an adjective used only before a noun. An outdoor activity takes place outside a building.

   *Our granddaughter likes **outdoor** activities such as hiking, running, and swimming.*

2.   **Outdoors** is an adverb. Games involving a lot of running are more suitably played outdoors.

   *Most children enjoy playing **outdoors** running around chasing each other.*

3.   The expression ***the outdoors*** is a noun. Despite its **-s** ending, it is singular in meaning.

   *Canada is great for living if you have a love of **the outdoors**.*

partly (adv), partially (adv)

1.   Both **partly** and **partially** mean "not completely". They are sometimes interchangeable but they have slightly different meanings.

2.   **Partly** is used usually in two situations. First, when you refer to physical things and emphasize the part(s) in contrast to the whole.

   *A piece of music can be **partly** slow and **partly** fast.*

   *His new book is only **partly** finished.*

   *The fabric of this dress is **partly** cotton and **partly** polyester.*

   Second, when your sense is "to some extent".

   *The change in plan is **partly** due to time restriction.*

   *Schools are **partly** responsible for the moral development of children.*

3.   **Partially** applies best to a condition or state in the sense of "to a certain degree" or "not fully". Interestingly, it emphasizes the whole rather than the part.

   *The fish is only **partially** cooked.*

   *She has become **partially** deaf.*

past (prep, adv, adj, n), passed (v, past tense of pass)

1.   Take care when you use the word **past** because it belongs to four word classes: preposition, adverb, adjective, and noun.

2.   **Past** as preposition:

   *The Star Ferry is only a short walk **past** the Cultural Centre.*

3. **Past** as adverb:

    *Several months went **past** but we still had not been able to sell our property.*

4. **Past** as adjective:

    *I have been extremely busy over the **past** three months.*

5. **Past** as noun:

    *In the **past**, before the appearance of the mobile phone, people used phones in shops or coin-operated roadside public phones.*

6. **Passed**, pronounced just like **past**, is the past tense form of the verb **pass:**

    *She **passed** the examination with flying colours.* (= with great success)

    *You **passed** me at the mall entrance without noticing me !*

person (n), people (n)

1. **Person** refers to an individual.

    *She is a nice **person**.*

    *The charge for tea at this restaurant is twenty dolloars per **person**.*

2. When you have a few individuals, you can use the plural **persons** or **people. Persons** for this use is more common in AmE.

    *May I have a table for two **persons/people** please?*

    *A taxi can seat four, sometimes five, **persons/people.***

3. **People** (a collective noun) is used to refer to human beings in general.

    *There are nearly eight million **people** in Hong Kong.*

    *In a famous short speech during the American civil war in 1863, Abraham Lincoln, then president, said that they would strive so that "government of the **people**, by the **people**, for the **people** shall not perish from the earth".*

4. **People** always takes a plural verb when referring to human beings generally.

    ***People are** having a difficult time because of the pandemic.*

    *Not many **people know** that there was no wireless television in Hong Kong before 1967.*

5. **People** is also a singular noun (plural **peoples**) meaning "nation", "race", or "tribe".

    *The **peoples** of South-east Asia have different languages and cultures.*

phenomenon (n singular), phenomena (n plural), phenomenal (adj)

1. Notice the difference in spelling and pronunciation between **phenomenon** and **phenomena**.

    The ubiquity (= presence everywhere) *of the mobile phone is a modern **phonomenon**.*

    *Instantaneous telecommunication, cashless consumption, high-speed trains: these are some of the major **phenomena** of the twenty-first century.*

2. Because **phenomena** is plural, you cannot say **this phenomena**. Say **this phenomenon** and **these phenomena**.

3. The adjective **phenomenal** means "very great or impressive". We speak of **phenomenal success**, **phenomenal growth/expansion**, **phenomenal increase**, and **phenomenal rise**.

    *Hong Kong experienced a **phenomenal** growth in population after 1949.*

    *The McDonald's restaurant chain has been a **phenomenal** success globally.*

possible (adj), impossible (adj)

See **difficult, easy.**

possible (adj), probable (adj)

1. Something is **probable** when it is likely to happen or to be true, but is **possible** if you are not sure.

    *Given her hard work, success is **probable**.*

    *As the saying goes, anything is **possible** under the sun.*

2. The adverbs are **possibly** and **probably**.

    *He is **possibly** the best magician in the world.*

    *As you **probably know**, we are planning for a family trip this summer.*

practical (adj), practicable (adj)

1. When we say that something (e.g., a tool) is **practical**, it is useful. A **practical** person is sensible and down-to-earth.

    *My friend always adopts a **practical** approach to handling problems.*

2. **Practicable** means feasible (can be done) or possible.

    *She finally found a **practicable** method of resolving the rivalry between her two sons.*

3. Note that **practical** can be applied to a person or a thing, but **practicable** cannot be applied to a person.

preceding (adj), previous (adj)

1. **Preceding** means "immediately before".

*I have described various ways to write clearly in the **preceding** two chapters.*

2. **Previous** means "existing before" without necessarily specifying the immediate connection to the time mentioned.

    *At the job interview he was asked whether he had any **previous** relevant experience.*

3. Both **preceding** and **previous** can only come before the noun they modify.

principal (n, adj), principle (n), in principle (adv phr)

1. As a noun, **principal** is the amount of money you borrow or invest. A **principal** is also the head of a school, the main person in a business, the most important performer in a play or ballet, or the leader of an orchestra section.

2. As an adjective, **principal** means "most important" or "main".

    *Selling vegetables in the market is her **principal** source of income.*

    *What are the **principal** characteristics of Christianity?*

3. **Principle** is always a noun, meaning a basic belief or standard about what is right and wrong. It may be used in the singular if you refer to one clearly identifiable belief or standard:

    *Protection of the environment is a guiding **principle** of responsible living.*

    If you refer to a number of basic beliefs and assumptions, such as those of fairness and equality, use the plural **principles.**

    *Schools should teach children the **principles** of good behaviour.*

4. **In principle** (always singular) (= in general or in theory)

    ***In principle** a mellow sound in choral singing is possible if singers follow the conductor closely, but in practice this is not easy.*

prohibit (v), inhibit (v)

1. **Prohibit,** usually used in the passive form, means that something is not allowed by law or by certain rules:

    *Smoking is **prohibited** in all public places.*

    *Airplane passengers are **prohibited from** having sharp objects in their carry-on baggage.*

2. To **inhibit** is to discourage or prevent someone from doing something. The inhibition can be due to embarrassment, lack of confidence, stress, or fear.

    *Recording an interview may **inhibit** the respondent from expressing his or her true opinions.*

    *Inexperience in facing an audience **inhibits** a young person from performing on stage.*

3. A process can also be **inhibited** from continuing or developing normally:

*The lack of confidence in the viability of investment can **inhibit** economic growth.*

*Chinese students are **inhibited from** studying in the West by discrimination against minorities there.*

provide (v), provided that (conj)

1. Be careful with the use or non-use of prepositions when you use **provide.** You don't use any preposition following **provide** in a sentence such as this one:

    *They will **provide** light refreshments and drinks at the reception.*

2. **provide** somebody **with** something

    *This new hospital **provides** patients **with** the best medical and health services.*

3. **provide** something **for** somebody

    *This new hospital **provides** the best medical and health services **for** patients.*

    *The school **provides** an opportunity **for** students to develop intellectual and social skills.*

4. When you **provide for** some people, you give them the things like food and money they need to live.

    *He works hard to **provide for** his family.*

    *He works hard to ensure that his children **are** well **provided for**.*

5. **Provide that** is used formally for rules or laws.

    *The law **provides that** a person must have lived in Hong Kong contiuously for seven years to become a permanent resident.*

6. **Provided that** (or **providing that**) sets a condition for something to happen. The word **that** may be omitted.

    *A person becomes a permanent resident of Hong Kong **provided that** he or she has lived there continuously for seven years.*

    *Customers will return to eat at a restaurant **provided** they find good value for their money.*

rather (adv)

1. **Rather** means "fairly" or "to some degree".

    *My boss is **rather** happy with my team's performance.*

    *She is **rather** a patient and methodical worker.*
    (Or: *She is a **rather** patient and methodical worker.*)

2. When **rather** is used with a verb, it softens the tone of the statement.

    *I **rather** hope that he would do as he promised.*

3. **Would rather, would rather . . . than** (both used for showing preference)

The restaurant is close by. **Would** *you take a bus or* **rather** *walk?*

Their coffee is good, but I **would rather** *have tea today.*

He would **rather** *be called "chicken"* **than** *take the bungee jump from the bridge.*

rather than (conj, prep)

1. **Rather than** can function as a conjunction (the more common use) and as a preposition.

   When used as a conjunction, there must be parallel elements on each side of it.

   She gets her grocery from wet markets **rather than** *supermarkets.*

   We should discuss this matter rationally **rather than** *emotionally.*

   This television series is about Einstein as a person **rather than** *as a scientist.*

   His speech caused young people to think and ask questions **rather than** *just sit and listen.*

2. When **rather than** comes between two verbs, the verbs are often used in the gerund form.

   I have always liked reading **rather than** *watching movies.*

   But the above sentence can be reworded with a bare infinitive (without **to**) following **rather than**:

   I have always liked to read **rather than** *watch movies.*

3. As a preposition, **rather than** usually begins a sentence to introduce a subordinate clause, and can connect nonparallel elements.

   Rather than *risking getting infected, we are staying home most of the time.*

   Rather than *hanging around aimlessly, it is better for students to do something interesting or useful during the long summer vacation.*

   You can reword the sentence to begin with the main clause, putting **rather than** in mid- sentence:

   It is better for students to do something interesting or useful during the long summer vacation **rather than** *hanging around aimlessly.*

recent (adj), recently (adv)

1. **Recent** and **recently** mean "not long ago", which could cover a period up to the present.

   Two verb tenses are commonly used with these two words: simple past and present perfect.

   We received an email from him **recently**. (Simple past)

   In **recent** *years, the proportion of Hong Kong's population aged 60 and above has increased.* (Present perfect)

2. The simple past or past progressive may be used with the phrase **until recently**:

    *We did not know about these new requirements **until recently**.* (Simple past)

    ***Until recently** their son was living in Sidney.* (Past progressive)

regard (v, n)

1. Two common uses of **regard** as verb (= to think of someone or something in a particular way) are illustrated in the following sentences:

    *His artistic designs are highly **regarded**.*

    *The dog is **regarded as** man's best friend.* (Note the use of the preposition **as**.)

2. Use **as regards something** (prep phr) when you want to write about a particular thing.

    ***As regards** the treatment of cancer, many advances have been made in the past decade.*
    (Note the use of present perfect **have been made** to cover a period up to now.)

3. **Regard** as noun means thought, attention, or respect. When we have much respect for someone, we hold that person ***in high regard.***

    *People sometimes act without **giving proper regard to** the needs of others.*

    *Physicians are generally held **in high regard**.*

    *City planning should **demonstrate proper regard for** environmental issues.*

4. **Regard** as noun appears in two prepositional phrases often used in business correspondence and certain formal documents: **with regard to**, **in regard to**. They are used in the same way as **with reference to**, **with respect to**, **in reference to**, and **in respect of**. They all mean "regarding", or "concerning". Avoid using these phrases because they are wordy and cause the writing to sound impersonal. Instead, try using other words such as **about**, **for**, **of**, **on**, **concerning**, or **regarding**.

    (✗) ~~*With regard to your recent enquiry, our customer relationship manager will be in contact with you soon.*~~

    (✓) ***Concerning** your recent enquiry, our customer relationship manager will contact you soon.*
    Or: *Our customer relationship manager will soon contact you **about** your recent enquiry.*

    (✗) ~~*The company's position **in regard to** maternity leave is stated clearly in the terms of service.*~~

    (✓) *The company's position **on** maternity leave is stated clearly in the terms of service.*

regarding (prep) (= concerning)

*Let me know if you have any questions **regarding** your assignment.*

regardless (adv), regardless of (two-word prep)

1. When you keep on doing something **regardless** (adv), you do it without being influenced by a bad situation.

*They all said it was an impossible task, but he carried on **regardless**.*

2.   As a preposition, **regardless of** must be followed by a noun, noun phrase, or noun clause.

*The meeting will take place, **regardless of** weather.* (**regardless of** + noun)

***Regardless of his inexperience**, he gave a respectable performance.* (**regardless of** + noun phrase)

*The orchestra is prepared to play at its best, **regardless of** what the music critics might say afterwards.* (**regardless of** + noun clause)

related (adj) to, relating to (two-word prep)

1.   When two things are related, they are connected in some way.

*Mental health is **related to** stress at work.*

This sentence can be reworded without using **to:**

*Mental health and stress at work are **related**.*

2.   When two persons are related, they are connected by kinship (family relationship).

*Joan is **related to** Mandy.*

*They have the same last name and are **related**.*

3.   **Related to** also means "belonging to the same group".

*English and German are **related to** the same branch of the Indo-European language family.*

4.   **Relating to** is a preposition meaning "about" or "concerning". A noun or noun phrase is used both before and after **relating to.**

*Many scientists are studying problems **relating to** climatic change.*

relation (n), relationship (n)

1.   The basic meaning of **relation** is "connection" between people or things. Thus, we speak of fishermen's relation to the sea or the relation between tourism and the economy.

2.   We use the plural form **relations** to refer to the way two groups, organizations, or countries act towards each other. Thus, we speak of business relations, public relations, and international relations.

*China wants to maintain good **relations** with many Western countries.*

3.   **In relation to** (three-word prep) (= compared with; concerning)

*Women's social status **in relation to** men's has changed greatly in the last few decades.*

*The Chief Executive just made some important announcements **in relation to** the coronavirus situation.*

4.   While people may be connected in a relation, they need time to accumulate common experience and develop mutual acceptance. The result is a **relationship**.

> *A good manager is interested in developing a good working **relationship** with his or her co-workers.*

relatively (adv)

1.   Always use a non-comparative adjective after **relatively.**

> (✘) ~~Macau is a relatively smaller city.~~

> (✓) *Macau is a relatively small city.*

2.   **Relatively** (= fairly, rather) implies some standard of comparison. The question is: compared with what? If the standard of comparison is explicitly stated or at least implicitly understood, the use of **relatively** is unproblematic. Otherwise, the use of **relatively** is loose.

> *Compared with Hong Kong, Macau is a relatively small city.*

To be safe, use some other word instead, such as **fairly** or **moderately.**

> *Macau is a **fairly** small city.*

> *This is a **moderately** expensive restaurant.*

relax (v), relaxed (adj), relaxing (adj)

1.   As a verb, **relax** can be intransitive (taking no object) or transitive (taking an object).

> *I felt so tired that I just wanted to lie in my sofa and **relax**.* (intransitive use of **relax**)

> *Do you think the Government might **relax** the qualifying requirements for foreign-trained doctors?* (transitive use of **relax**, with **qualifying requirements** as object)

2.   The present participle **relaxing** and the past participle **relaxed** can be used as adjectives. Be careful that **relaxing** refers to some thing or experience while **relaxed** refers to how a person feels as a result of the experience.

> (✘) ~~The restaurant has a relaxed atmosphere and I felt quite relaxing dining there.~~

> (✓) *The restaurant has a **relaxing** atmosphere and I felt quite **relaxed** dining tthere.*

replace (v), substitute (v, n)

1.   In standard English, you **replace** something old **with** something new. Or, you **substitute** something new **for** something old. Do NOT say you **substitute** the old **with** the new.

2.   **A replaces B (B is the original one)**

> *This is the revised proposal that **replaces** the original one.*

3.   **replace B with A**

*Let us **replace** the original proposal **with** the revised one.*

*Our piano is more than thirty years old. We are thinking of **replacing** it **with** a new one.*

4. **B is replaced by A**

    *Our 30-year-old Yamaha piano is **replaced by** a new Petrof piano.*

5. **substitute A for B** (= put **A** in the place of **B**) **Substitute** (v) is always used with the preposition **for,** not **with** or **by.**

    (✓) *Let us **substitute** the revised proposal **for** the original one.*

    (✗) ~~*Let us **substitute** the original proposal **with** (or **by**) the revised one.*~~

6. **A is substituted for B** (= **A** is put in the place of **B**)

    (✓) *The revised proposal is **substituted for** the original one.*

    (✗) ~~*The original proposal is **substituted by** (or **with**) the revised one.*~~

7. Thus, when eating out, if you order pork chop that is normally served with potatoes but you want rice instead of potatoes, you can give either of the following two instructions:

    *I would like to **replace** potatoes **with** rice, please.*

    *I would like to **substitute** rice **for** potatoes, please.*

8. **Substitute** is also a noun. In the restaurant situation above, you can say this if you are happy with pork chop served with rice:

    *Rice is a good **substitute for** potatoes.*

respond (v), response (n)

1. Many people confuse these two words. The verb ends in **-d**; the noun ends in **-se**. The confusion lives on with many failing to pronounce these endings properly when uttering a sentence.

2. In the following sentences, the verb form is used:

    *I don't know how to **respond** to her letter.*

    *"I'm not sure," he **responded**.* (Be sure to pronounce the **-ded** ending.)

    *His skin problem did not **respond** to the cream he used.*

3. In the following sentences, the noun form is used:

    *I phoned several times, but there was no **response**.*

    ***In response to** our recent tax inquiry, the Inland Revenue Department gave us some helpful answers.*

rise (v, n), **raise** (v, n)

1. As verbs, **rise** is intransitive (not taking an object), but **raise** is transitive (taking an object):

    *The sun **rises** in the east.*

    *You have to **raise** your voice, or no one can hear you.*

2. **Raise** is a regular verb (past tense: **raised**; perfect tense: **have/has/had raised**). **Rise** is an irregular verb (past tense: **rose;** perfect tense: **have/has/had risen**).

    *She **raised** many questions during the meeting.*

    *The nice weather has certainly **raised** our spirits.*

    *Through hard work, he **rose** to become general manager.*

    *Food prices have **risen** sharply over the last few months.*

3. **Rise** is used as a noun in the following sentences:

    *There has been a **rise** in the life expectancy of the population of Hong Kong.*

    *Knowledge of global warming has given great support to the **rise** of environmentalism.*

4. **Rise** as a noun is commonly used in these phrases: **give rise to** (*The controversial bill **gave rise to** unfounded fears*); **rise to power/fame** (*His **rise to power** in the company is dramatic.*)

5. In AmE, **raise** can be used as a noun to mean an increase in pay or salary. The corresponding word in BrE is **rise** (n).

    *In a weakened economy, people generally do not expect to have a pay **raise** (**rise**) of more than two per cent.*

safe (adj), **save** (v)

1. Do not confuse these two words. The adjective **safe** and the verb **save** are not pronounced the same. The **f** sound in **safe** is voiceless; the **v** sound in **save** is voiced.

2. The two words are related in meaning as shown in the following sentences:

    *The life guard **saved** the boy from drowning. The boy is now resting at a **safe** place.*

3. **Safe** occurs in some idiomatic phrases, such as **on the safe side** and **play safe:**

    *It may rain today; I'd better bring my umbrella just to be **on the safe side.***

    *I have stored the data in three separate files: it's always better to **play safe**.*

4. You can **save** money in the bank in a **savings account;** you can also **save** some time by working faster or **save** some of your energy by taking longer rests.

satisfy (v), **satisfied** (adj), **satisfactory** (adj), **satisfying** (adj), **satisfaction** (n)

1. The base word, **satisfy**, is verb

    Taikooshing, as a residential complex, has a variety of shops and facilities that can satisfy residents' daily needs.

    She has satisfied the basic requirements for entry to local universities.

2. **Satisfied**, the past form of **satisfy**, is also adjective, which is often followed by **with.**

    The workers were satisfied with the pay rise that the management promised.

    Sometimes, **with** may be omitted, especially when **satisfied** describes a feeling:

    After much negotiation, the workers felt satisfied.

    Customers not satisfied can ask for a refund.

    Satisfied can pre-modify a noun:

    That little boy showed a satisfied smile after hearing that his parents would take him to Disneyland.

3. **Satisfactory** and **satisfying** are both adjectives. If something seems good to you, but not wonderful or outstanding, you can describe it as **satisfactory.** If something makes you feel pleased and happy, it is **satisfying** to you. It could be you have done something you enjoy, or it could be a meal that is quite filling.

    His exam results are just satisfactory.

    They all enjoyed a satisfying dinner at their favourite restaurant.

4. **Satisfaction** is noun, referring to the result of being satisfied.

    I get great satisfaction from helping my students to learn.

    Parents cherish the satisfaction and joy of seeing their children graduate from university.

seat (n, v), **sit** (v)

1. A **seat** (n) is where you sit, such as in a hall, a theatre, or a bus.

    This bus has 45 seats.

    When you ask someone to sit down, you say: *Please take a seat.*

2. **Sit** (v) is often used with prepositions to show different meanings. You **sit down in/on** a chair. When you study or read, you may **sit at** a desk.

    You may **sit on** some task committee as a member. Leaders of political parties may **sit** as members in the Legislative Council. When you **sit in for** someone, you are performing that person's duties while he/she is away.

If you **sit in** a course at university, you are not taking it for credit but only listening to its lectures. In BrE, to **sit (for)** an examination means to take an examination. This is rather formal use of **sit**. In Hong Kong, students who have completed secondary school **sit** the DSE (Diploma of Secondary Education) Examination.

3. A few more idiomatic phrases using **sit**: **sit still** (without moving), **sit back** (in a comfortable or relaxed position), **sit up straight** (with a straight back), **sit around** (doing nothing particularly useful)

    *Young children rarely **sit still** for even a few minutes.*

    *Now you can **sit back** and relax with the Blockbuster movie coming up .*

    ***Sit up straight!** A good posture will keep you healthy.*

    *We are **sitting around** all night with nothing special to do.*

4. **Sit** is an irregular verb: **sit** (present), **sat** (past), **sat** (past participle)

    *We have **sat** here for a long and leisurely lunch.*

5. **Seat** can be used as a verb:

    *This bus can **seat** 45 passengers.*

    *Please wait to be **seated**.* (in a retaurant)

6. **Seated** is also used as an adjective. When you ask people politely to sit down, you would say, *"Please be **seated**"*. When you travel by plane, you will hear this instruction when the plane is landing:

    *Please remain **seated** until the aircraft has come to a complete stop.*

seem (v) (not used in progressive tenses)

1. **Seem** is a linking verb (see 6.15 of Chapter 6) that joins an adjective or a noun phrase to a subject.

    *He seems **smart**.* (adjective)

    *This seems **an impossible job**.* (noun phrase)

2. **Seem to be** (when referring to objective facts)

    *This restaurant **seems to be** full.*

    *You don't **seem to be** ready yet; you need more practice.*

    *There **seems to be** some mistake in this matter.*

3. **Seem (to be)** (dropping **to be** when referring to subjective feelings)

    *She **seemed** unhappy after reading the letter.*

    *You **seem** very puzzled about the rearrangement.*

*It may **seem** a small thing, but it is actually quite important.*

4. **Seem** + **to**-infinitives of other verbs

    *This shopping mall **seems to need** some renovation.*

    *You **seem to have misunderstood** me.*

    *She **doesn't seem to remember** what happened.*

    (More formally) *She **seems not to remember** what happened.*

5. **Seem like** (followed by a noun or noun phrase). See also **like** (prep), **as** (conj).

    *We waited at the station for what **seemed like** hours.*

    *Cruising the Mediterranean **seems like** a wonderful holiday idea.*

    *It **seems like** you have caught a cold.* (informal speech)

    This use of **seem like**, followed by a clause, is acceptable only in informal speech. More properly, use **seem as if** when you have a clause following:

    *It **seems as if** you have caught a cold.*

    *It **seems as if** the rain will never stop.*

    *He felt devastated by the failure. To him, it **seemed as if** it was the end of the world.*

6. **It seems that** or **it seems likely that**

    *It **seems to me that** we have got lost.*

    *It **seems that** we have solved the problem.*

    (Polite, or not too sure) *It **would seem that** we have solved the problem.*

similar (adj), like (prep)

1. Two things are **similar.** One of them **is similar to** the other. (X is similar to Y.) Or you can say that one of them is just **like** the other.

2. The use of **similar** in the following sentence is not correct:

    (✗) ~~*Similar to Hong Kong, Macau is a special administrative region of China*~~. To use **similar to Hong Kong** in a sentence, you must place before it a noun phrase followed by **be** (X is similar to Y), as in this sentence:

    *Macau's status as a special administrative region of China **is similar to** Hong Kong.*

    *Renoir's painting style **was similar to** that of many other impressionist painters.*

3. If you have a clause X (now X is **Macau is a special administrative region of China**) with its own subject and verb, the element Y with which it is compared will be introduced by **like**:

Like Hong Kong, Macau is a special administrative region of China.

Similarly, if, like somebody, you have some specific interest, your sentence would be:

Like my cousin, I am greatly interested in collecting stamps of Hong Kong during the colonial period.

some (determiner) (= a word that begins a noun phrase to indicate which one or how many/much)

1. When **some** is used with an uncountable noun, it takes a singular verb:

    Some of the failure of his business is a result of mismanagement..

    Some of her work has nothing to do with her training.

    Some hardship comes with this particular position.

2. When **some** is used with a plural countable noun, it takes a plural verb:

    Some of the items in the special exhibit are on loan from the Louvre in Paris.

    Some of the company's problems have been around a long time.

    Some participants in our reunion have come from the United States and Canada.

someday (adv), some day (n phr)

1. **Someday** (adv) (= at a certain time in the future, but without specifying precisely when)

    This word is used much like **sometime**.

    We will come back someday.

    Let's try to plan a reunion someday/sometime next February.

2. **Some day** (n phr, in which **some** is a determiner modifying **day**)

    Let us pick some day (not **someday**) *next February to have our reunion.* (Can you sense the difference in meaning compared with the preceding sentence?)

sometimes (adv), sometime (adj, adv), some time (n phr)

1. Be careful with the difference in meaning and use between **sometimes** (with **-s** ending) and **sometime** (no **-s** ending). **Sometimes** (= occasionally, not often) is an adverb. **Sometime** is an adverb when it means at a time (either in the future or in the past) that you are not sure of, but an adjective when it refers to what someone used to be.

2. **Sometimes** (adv)

    She sometimes goes to swim with her sister.

    Sometimes the weather can be quite unpredictable.

3. **Sometime** (adv) (= at some point in the future or in the past)

*Let us get together **sometime** this summer.*

*I remember he came from Canada to visit us **sometime** last year.*

4. **Sometime** (adj) (= former) (only used before noun)

    *Mr. Wong, the **sometime** principal of our school, was present at the school's 50ᵗʰ anniversary celebrations.*

5. **Some time** (n phr) (= a period of time, usually implying that the period is not a short one)

    *They have been studying the problem for **some time** now.*

speak (v), talk (v)

1. **Speak** is generally a bit more formal than **talk.**

    *I should **speak to** my lawyer about this matter.*

    *In a lunch gathering with my former classmates, we **talked about** our good old days for more than three hours.*

2. **Speak**, not **talk**, is used in sentences like the following:

    (On the telephone) *May I **speak to** Mr. Ma please?*

    *The **speaker** is **speaking** so softly that I just cannot hear him.*

    *Her boss **speaks highly of** her.*

    *He is only twelve years old, but he **speaks** five languages, including Putonghua Chinese.*

3. **Talk** is used in these sentences:

    *I haven't **talked with** Katie in years.*

    *They can **talk business** all day.*

    *These medical experts will **talk about** the side effects of taking the new Covid vaccines.*

    *He has lived in Japan all his life, so **he knows what he is talking about**.*

staff (n, v)

1. **Staff** is a collective noun referring to the people who work in a particular organization or some part of it. It is plural in meaning and has no singular form. Individuals can be referred to as **members of staff** or **staff members**.

2. In BrE **staff** can be used with both singular and plural verbs.

    *The staff **has/have** done its/their best to improve the operation of the office.*

    AmE prefers the use of singular verbs.

*The staff **is** doing its best.*

3.   People sometimes use numbers before **staff** to mean the number of members of staff. This use is acceptable but be careful not to add **-s** to **staff.**

*We have five **staff** working on the project.*

However, using **staffs** for such meaning is incorrect.

(✗) *We have five **staffs** working on the project.*

4.   Since **staff** is a collective noun, **staffs** can only be used to mean different groups of employees. Thus, when staff members from two different units or departments come together for a meeting, you can say that the two **staffs** have discussed something and exchanged views on some idea.

5.   The word **staff** appears in many collocations (compound nouns) such as **staff association, staff meeting, staff development, staff room, staff canteen** and **staff benefits**. If you work for a company, you are **on the staff of the company**. (BrE) You are a **member of staff** of the company. (AmE) You are a **staff member** of the company.

6.   **Staff** can also be a verb meaning to provide workers for an organization. Thus, a welfare service programme may be **staffed** by volunteers.

stationary (adj), stationery (n)

1.   Be careful not to confuse these two words. **Stationary**, an adjective, means "not moving".

*The taxi collided with a **stationary** bus.*

2.   **Stationery**, a noun, refers to the materials for writing and things like files, clips, erasers, glue, staplers and so on. **Stationery** is an uncountable noun, but you can refer to different items of stationery. It is convenient to remember the **e** in this word if you remember that stationery includes envelopes.

*There is a **stationery** section in this bookshop.*

3.   The person in charge of a stationery shop is called a **stationer**. Such a shop is known as a **stationer's**.

*I'm looking for a **stationer's**. Is there one nearby?*

succeed (v), success (n)

1.   Do not confuse these two words. One is a verb, the other a noun. Note the spelling of each.

(✗) *I can **success** if I work hard.*

(✓) *I can **succeed** if I work hard.*

(✓) *To **succeed**, I must work hard.*

(✓) *I had little **success** because I didn't work hard enough.*

2. One can **succeed in** something (such as business, science, politics, and music)

    *One needs to be both innovative and aggressive to **succeed in** business.*

3. One can also **succeed in** doing something or **succeed as** somebody.

    *She **succeeded in** gaining admission to the university's law school.*

    *He is more likely to **succeed in** capturing his listeners' attention if he uses actual stories to explain things simply.*

    *To **succeed as** a concert pianist, you need not only talent but also a great deal of disciplined practice.*

4. **Succeed** also means to be the next one to take up somebody's position.

    *Do you remember who **succeeded** Jiang Zemin as China's president?*

5. **Successful** is an adjective. One can be **successful in** something or doing something.

    *She was **successful in** gaining admission to a medical school.*

    *To be a **sucessful** business person, you need to be innovative and alert to market conditions.*

suppose (v), supposed (adj), supposedly (adv), supposing (conj)

1. **Suppose** (v) (= to believe or to think in some way, implying some uncertainty)

    *I **suppose** (that) the food in this old restaurant is as good as ever.*

    *Do you **suppose** (that) the Covid-19 pandemic will end soon?*

2. **Supposed** (adj) (= "expected" in the phrase **be supposed to**)

    *We **are supposed to** meet our friends at the lobby of the City Hall.*

    *She was **supposed** to return to Hong Kong after completing her studies in the States.*

3. **Supposed** (adj) (only before noun to show that you think a claim is probably not true)

    *I'm not sure about the **supposed** health benefits of these mixed tea-fruit drinks.*

4. **Supposedly** (adv) (= according to what many people believe or what ought to be true)

    *Why are some **supposedly** well-educated people so prejudiced?* (**supposedly** modifying the adjective **well-educated**)

    ***Supposedly**, his daughter is coming from Australia to visit him this summer.*
    (Here **supposedly** is a sentence adverb modifying the entire sentence.)

    (Many Hong Kong people, when mixing Cantonese and English in speaking, use **suppose** rather than **supposedly** to modify a statement: 佢地 **suppose** 係唔會遲到。（他們 **suppose** 是不會遲到的。）(*They won't be late, **supposedly**.*) This is probably because of lack of knowledge of the difference between the two words and a general inability to pronounce clearly the ending of

supposedly (last two syllables /zɪdlɪ/).

5.   **Supposing** (conj) You can use **supposing (that)** to talk about a possible situation and imagine what may result. As a conjunction, **supposing** links the situation and the result.

   Supposing (that) *the government decided to levy goods and services tax, how would the people of Hong Kong react?* (The past tense **decided** is not a real past tense but shows something is merely hypothetical.)

   The present tense can be used in the **supposing** clause if you refer to what may happen:

   Supposing (that) *you fail the test, what will you do then?*

surprise (n, v), surprised (adj), surprising (adj)

1.   Many students have difficulty with these words. Note that they have to do with our emotional response to an event. There are three elements involved: (a) the person, (b) the event, and (c) the emotional experience. (See similar consideration at the entries **excited**, **interested**, and **satisfied**.)

2.   Using this framework, study the following statements. Note in particular the difference in use between **surprising** and **surprised:**

   The event **surprises** (v) the person.

   The event gives the person a **surprise** (n). (the emotional experience)

   The event is **surprising** (adj) to the person.

   The person is **surprised** (adj) **by** the event. (He does not at all expect it.)

3.   The following sentences are all about the same idea, but are worded somewhat differently:

   *It does not **surprise** (v) us that some cancer patients can recover completely.*

   *That some cancer patients can recover completely comes to us as no **surprise** (n).*
   (Note that the **that**-clause is a singular subject, which takes a singular verb, **comes**.)

   *We are not **surprised** (adj) that some cancer patients can recover completely.*

   *That some cancer patients can recover completely is not **surprising** (adj) at all to us.*

   *It is not **surprising** (adj) that some cancer patients can recover completely.*

   The last sentence can be recast by using the adverb **surprisingly** to modify the entire clause:

   *Not **surprisingly** (adv), some cancer patients can recover completely.*

4.   Study these other ways of using **surprised (**adj):

   *We were happily **surprised** to learn that they finally succeeded.*

   *We would not be **surprised** if this child prodigy will become a world class cellist.*

   *We were greatly **surprised at** the news.*

Surprised by the poor sales of the new product, the marketing people had to rethink their promotion strategy.

5. Learn these two idiomatic expressions: **take somebody by surprise, much to somebody's surprise.** In both expressions, **surprise** is noun.

    *The rapid rebuilding of the city after the earthquake **took us by surprise.***

    ***Much to everyone's surprise**, she went on to become a successful hotelier.*

take something/somebody for granted

1. When you **take something/somebody for granted**, you assume or expect that something or somebody is always there without really appreciating how important or valuable they are.

    *Children tend to **take their parents for granted**.*

    *We **take many things for granted**: running water, electricity, mobile phones, and even breathable air.*

2. **Take something /it for granted** also means to believe that something is or will be true or will happen without making sure.

    *Do not **take it for granted** that the pandemic will disappear anytime soon.*

    *We **took freshness of produce in this market for granted**, only to discover that some of the apples we bought were rotten inside.*

time (n), times (n)

1. As an uncountable noun, **time** is always used in the singular:

    *Given the right conditions, it does not take too much **time** for a stranger to become a good friend.*

    ***Time** is often a critical factor in crisis management.*

    *We were **just in time** for the movie when we got to the theatre.*

2. **Time** can be a countable noun to mean "occasion". When you refer to "occasions", you can say **times**.

    *The company is handling the problem more cautiously this **time.***

    *There are **times** when parents learn much from their children.*

    *At **times** (= sometimes), the pressure to conform to peers is strong, especially in a closely knit group.*

3. In the following sentences, **time** is also a countable noun meaning "period" (as in a person's life or in the history of a society):

    *She described her secondary school years as the happiest **time** of her life.*

*Hong Kong had gone through many difficult **times** in the 1950s and the 1960s before the economy improved significantly in the 1970s.*

Other phrases using **time** in this sense include **wonderful time, good times, hard times**, and **challenging times**.

4.   Some common phrases using **time: ahead of time, kill time** (= make time pass by doing something**), over time** (= as time passes**), keep up/move with the times**

*Our plane arrived almost half an hour **ahead of time.***

*It was raining heavily the whole morning, so we stayed in the hotel and watched televsion to **kill time.***

*A language changes **over time** because of changes in technology, ideas, and lifestyle.*

*We may love to preserve good old traditions, but we also must **keep up with the times.***

too (adv), either (adv)

1.   Placed before adjectives and adverbs, **too** means "more than is good, acceptable, ordinary, possible and so on".

*The classroom is **too** small to accommodate 50 students.*

*He got news that he was accepted by Harvard University with a full fellowship. It seemed **too** good to be true!*

*Some careless mistakes in using English happen **all too often.*** (= much too often)

2.   When speaking positively, **too** means "also". **Too** usually comes at the end of a clause.

*They have been to Japan many times. I have been **too.***

*When she has finished reviewing this lesson, she is going to read the next lesson **too**.*

3.   In formaal writing, **too** can be placed after the subject or after a prepositional phrase at the beginning of a clause.

*We **too** must do our best to stay healthy.*

*In this case, **too**, gathering evidence will take a long time.*

4.   When responding to a negative statement to say that it is also true about another person or thing, you cannot use **too**. You must use **either**.

Person A: I don't drink coffee.

*Person B: I don't drink coffee either. OR I don't **either.** (NOT ~~I don't drink too.~~)*

She: My dish isn't tasty at all.

*You: Mine isn't **either.***

405

5.   You can use **either** to add another negative statement about someone or something.

*Joe is not a very good manager, and he is not friendly **either**.*

*This vacuum cleaner is not easy to operate, and it is not cheap **either**.*

uninterested (adj), disinterested (adj)

1.   If you are **uninterested** in something, you have no interest in it.

*He has always been **uninterested** in politics.*

2.   You can be a **disinterested** (impartial) onlooker when two parties are having an argument if you are not affected by any personal benefit that might come from the situation.

*We expect a lawyer, as a **disinterested** party, to give us objective legal advice.*

3.   Do not use **disinterested** when you mean **uninterested.**

unique (adj)

1.   **Unique** means "the only one of its kind". Hence, if something is unique, it cannot be compared with anything else. You must not say that it is "very unique", "most unique", or "really unique". It is just "unique". If something is not quite unique, you can say it is **almost** or **nearly** unique.

2.   Some people, including advertisers, may say "very unique" or "most unique" to mean "very special". If something is very special, say so or use such adjectives as **unusual** or **rare**. Both "most unusual" and "very rare" are legitimate phrases.

3.   Because the initial sound of **unique** is a consonant sound (u = /ju/), you say something is "a unique" not "an unique" object.

update (v, n), up-to-date (adj)

1.   **Update** is both verb and noun (see below). Many people in Hong Kong erroneously use **update** as an adjective when speaking in Cantonese interspersed with English words. For example:

呢個 software 唔夠 update。（這個 software 不夠 update。）(✗) ~~This software is not update enough.~~

The sentence should be: (✓) *This software is not sufficiently **up to date**.*

If you have to use a sentence using both Cantonese and English, it would be:

呢個 software 唔夠 up to date。（這個 software 不夠 up to date。）

If you must use the word **update**, use it as a verb, even when you mix Cantonese Chinese

and English (not recommended practice) in the same sentence:

呢個 software 三年都冇 update 過。（這個 software 三年都沒有 update 過。）
(See 4 below for the English sentence.)

2.   The phrase **up to date** is not hyphenated if used after the noun (or pronoun) it modifies. When the phrase comes before the noun it modifies, you must insert hyphens to have **up-to-date** as a compound adjective.

> *We can keep **ourselves up to date** with the latest developments in any field by consulting various electronic data sources.*

> *There are many magazines about **up-to-date fashion**.*

3.   The opposite of **up to date** is **out of date.** Observe the same rule of using or not using hyphenation. Alternatively, you can use **outdated** both before and after the word it modifies.

> *The **figures** you quote in your paper are **out of date/outdated**.*

> *You should not use **out-of-date/outdated figures** in your paper.*

4.   To **update** (v) something is to make it more modern or **up to date** by adding something new or changing it to meet new requirements.

> *This software has not been **updated** for nearly three years.* (Be sure to pronounce the third syllable /tɪd/ of **updated**.)

> *The observatory **updates** its weather report several times each day.*

5.   **Update** is also a noun, as in this sentence:

> *The late news on television gives us an **update** on the day's events.*

use (n, v), usage (n)

1.   **Use** is both a noun and a verb.

> *The **use** (n) of digital payment is becoming popular.* (Note that **use** takes a singular verb.)

> *Both managerial skills and professional expertise are **used** (v) in large organizations.*

2.   Some common phrases: **make use of**, **have no use for**, **put something to good use**

> *She is **making the best use of** her contacts in the UK to get settled there.*

> *We **have no use for** the table and chairs because they won't fit in our small new home.*

> *He has just got a job where he can **put his computer skills to good use.***

3.   **Usage** refers to (a) the action of using something, or (b) how much something is used.

> *Land **usage** (sense a) is an important matter to the government.*

> *Electricity **usage** (sense b) usually rises sharply in the summer months.*

4.   In language, **usage** is how words and phrases are used. **Usage** has a general sense while **use** has a specific sense. We speak of **proper** or **improper** usage generally, but the **proper** or **improper use** of a particular word or phrase.

*The learning of English grammar and **usage** is instrumental for writing well.*

*The **use** of an adjective before the word "unique" is not recommended.*

used to do something, be used to (doing) something, get used to (doing) something

1. **Used to** is a modal auxiliary verb that exists only in the simple past tense. You say **used to** to refer to a condition that no longer exists. What follows is usually an infinitive (base verb form).

    *Before the first cross-harbour tunnel was built, cars **used to** cross the harbour on the vehicular ferry between Jordan Road in Kowloon and Central on Hong Kong Island.*

    *I **used to live** in the New Territories.*

    *Did Hong Kong people in the 1960s **use to** like Mandarin popular songs?* (The past tense is indicated by **did,** so you must write **use to** instead of **used to** in this question form.)

2. **Be used to (doing) something**. In this phrase, **used** is an adjective that modifies the subject placed before it. **To** is a preposition (unlike **to** as an infinitive marker in **used to do something),** which is followed by an object (a noun phrase or an **–ing** gerund phrase). You use the phrase **be used to doing something** the same way you use the phrase **be accustomed to doing something.**

    *Westerners **are used to** having red or white wine with their meals.*

    *Many Hong Kong people **are not used to** watching an English-speaking film without Chinese subtitles.*

3. **Be used to** can be part of a noun clause (introduced by **what**) that comes at the end of a sentence:

    *Life in a foreign country can be completely different from **what we are used to.***

4. **Get used to (doing) something**. After **get used to** you must use a noun phrase or a gerund (**–ing** form).

    *Filipino domestic helpers in Hong Kong need to **get used to speaking some Cantonese** with their employers.*

    *Living in a foreign country for the first time, you have to **get used to** customs that may seem strange to you.*

valuable (adj), invaluable (adj)

1. Do not confuse these two words although both words have **value** as their common meaning. A **valuable** thing is worth much money or is important or useful. An **invaluable** thing is extremely important or useful, so much so that you cannot place any quantitative value on it. It is priceless.

    *Basic research is **valuable** to the advancement of science.*

    *An effective coronavirus vaccine will be **invaluable** to controlling the pandemic.*

2. The opposite of **valuable** is **valueless** or **worthless**, and not **invaluable**.

vocabulary (n)

1. **Vocabulary** means all the words that you know. Since there are words that you may know but rarely use, the vocabulary that you normally use may be smaller. This smaller vocabulary is your *active vocabulary.* In any case, the word **vocabulary** always refers to the whole collection of words rather than individual words that you know or use. Some students make the mistake of using the plural form **vocabularies** to mean "words".

    > (✗) *I have learned many vocabularies this summer.*

    > (✓) *I have learned many words this summer to expand my **vocabulary**.*

    > (✓) *You can enrich your **vocabulary** through reading and listening.*

2. People in different kinds of work are likely to be in contact with different kinds of words. There are thus **vocabularies** corresponding to different specializations in science and technology, medicine, law, art, music, religion, business and commerce, logistics and so on. Naturally, each field has its collection of special terms not normally used in other fields.

3. As a result of the preceding point, people would use words taken from or relevant to some special field when they talk about a particular subject, such as health, entertainment, or politics. If they do this often, these words become part of their *active vocabulary.*

4. Adjectives used to qualify **vocabulary** include **large**, **extensive**, **rich**, **limited**, **restricted**, **shared**, **scientific**, and **formal**. You can take actions (such as reading, watching English dialogue movies and television documentaries, and talking to English speakers) to **broaden**, **widen, enlarge**, **expand**, **enrich**, or **strengthen** your vocabulary.

worth (n, adj), worthless (adj), worthy (adj), worthwhile (adj)

1. **Worth** (n) (= value)

    *Museums have items of great **worth** in their exhibits.*

    *Contestants have put in three months' **worth** of training.*

    *Some cruise itineraries are so well planned that passengers joining them can **get their money's worth.***

2. **Worth** (adj) (= having a certain value) Used after **be**: **be** + **worth** + gerund or noun phrase.

    *This book **is** really **worth** reading.*

    *Any method that can increase sales **is** well **worth** a try.*

3. **For what/whatever it is worth.**   Use this phrase to show that you are willing to share an idea with others although it may not be very useful.

    *Here is my suggestion **for whatever it is worth**.*

4. **Worthless** (adj) (= having no value)

*In the years (1930s) of the Great Depression, stocks became **worthless** overnight.*

5.   **Worthy** (adj) Used before a noun to mean "deserving respect or admiration".

*Yundi Li was a **worthy** winner of the first prize in the International Chopin Piano Competition in 2000.*

*Donating money to charity is a **worthy** thing.*

6.   **Be worthy of something, -worthy** (e.g., **praiseworthy, noteworthy, trustworthy**)

*His leadership in reviving his failing business **is worthy of** praise.*

*His leadership in reviving his failing business **is praiseworthy**.*

*It is **noteworthy** (= deserving attention) that many professional cooks are men.*

*Our friends are fortunate to have hired a very **trustworthy** helper.*

7.   **Be worthy of somebody** (= to be as good as what a particular person might do)

*The cellist gave a performance that **was worthy of** Yo Yo Ma.*

8.   **Worthwhile** (adj), **worth somebody's while** (if it is important enough for the person)

*Considering the health implications involved, all the effort made in cancer research has been **worthwhile**.*

*Singing in the choir is a **worthwhile** service helping the congregation to praise God.*

*It is **worthwhile** to make customers happy if this means better sustained business.*

*It is **worth your while** to do volunteer work if that gives you satisfaction.*

Appendix (Irregular verbs)

BrE = British English   AmE = American English

Base form (bare infinitive)	Past form	Past participle
arise	arose	arisen
awake	awoke	awoken
be	was, were	been
bear	bore	borne
beat	beat	beat
become	became	become
begin	began	begun
bend	bent	bent
bet	bet	bet
bite	bit	bitten
bleed	bled	bled
blow	blew	blown
break	broke	broken
bring	brought	brought
broadcast	broadcast	broadcast
bring	brought	brought
build	built	built
burn	burnt (or: burned)	burnt (or: burned)
burst	burst	burst
buy	bought	bought
cast	cast	cast
catch	caught	caught
choose	chose	chosen
come	came	come
cost	cost	cost
creep	crept	crept
cut	cut	cut
deal	dealt	dealt
dig	dug	dug
do	did	done

Base form (bare infinitive)	Past form	Past participle
draw	drew	drawn
dream	dreamt (or: dreamed)	dreamt (or: dreamed)
drink	drank	drunk
drive	drove	driven
eat	ate	eaten
fall	fell	fallen
feed	fed	fed
feel	felt	felt
fight	fought	fought
find	found	found
fly	flew	flown
forbid	forbade	forbidden
forget	forgot	forgotten
forgive	forgave	forgivern
foretell	foretold	foretold
freeze	froze	frozen
get	got	got (AmE also: gotten)
give	gave	given
go	went	gone
grind	ground	ground
grow	grew	grown
hang	hung hanged (= executed)	hung hanged (= executed)
have	had	had
hear	heard	heard
hide	hid	hidden
hit	hit	hit
hold	held	held
hurt	hurt	hurt
keep	kept	kept
kneel	knelt	knelt
knit*	knit	knit
know	knew	known

*When *knit* means "to join closely together", it is an irregular verb, as shown in the table; but when it means "to make clothing out of cotton or wool", it is a regular verb *(knit/knitted/knitted)*.

Base form (bare infinitive)	Past form	Past participle
lay	laid	laid
lead	led	led
lean	leaned (BrE also: leant)	leaned (BrE also: leant)
leap	leapt (or: leaped)	leapt (or: leaped)
learn	learned (BrE also: learnt)	learned (BrE also: learnt)
leave	left	left
lend	lent	lent
let	let	let
lie**	lay	lain
light	lit (or: lighted)	lit (or: lighted)
lose	lost	lost
make	made	made
mean	meant	meant
meet	met	met
mistake	mistook	mistaken
misunderstand	misunderstood	misunderstood
overcome	overcame	overcome
overtake	overtook	overtaken
pay	paid	paid
prove	proved	proven
put	put	put
quit	quit (or: quitted)	quit (or: quitted)
read	read#	read#
ride	rode	ridden
ring	rang	rung
rise	rose	risen
run	ran	run
say	said	said
see	saw	seen
seek	sought	sought
sell	sold	sold
send	sent	sent

**When *lie* means "to say something that is not true", it is a regular verb (lie/lied/lied).
Pronounced /red/.

Base form (bare infinitive)	Past form	Past participle
set	set	set
sew	sewed	sewn (or: sewed)
shake	shook	shaken
shine	shone	shone
shoot	shot	shot
show	showed	shown
shrink	shrank (or: shrunk)	shrunk
shut	shut	shut
sing	sang	sung
sink	sank	sunk
sit	sat	sat
sleep	slept	slept
slide	slid	slid
smell	smelled (BrE also: smelt)	smelled (BrE also: smelt)
sow	sowed	sown (or: sowed)
speak	spoke	spoken
speed	sped (or: speeded)	sped (or: speeded)
spell	spelt (AmE also: spelled)	spelt (AmE also: spelled)
spend	spent	spent
spill	spilled (BrE also: spilt)	spilled (BrE also: spilt)
spin	spun	spun
split	split	split
spoil	spoiled (BrE also: spoilt)	spoiled (BrE also: spoilt)
spread	spread	spread
spring	sprang	sprung
stand	stood	stood
steal	stole	stolen
stick	stuck	stuck
sting	stung	stung
stink	stank (or: stunk)	stunk
strew	strewed	strewed (or: strewn)
strike	struck	struck
strive	strove	striven
swear	swore	sworn

Base form (bare infinitive)	Past form	Past participle
sweep	swept	swept
swell	swelled	swollen (or: swelled)
swim	swam	swum
swing	swung	swung
take	took	taken
teach	taught	taught
tear	tore	torn
tell	told	told
think	thought	thought
throw	threw	thrown
tread	trod	trodden
undergo	underwent	undergone
understand	understood	understood
undertake	undertook	undertaken
uphold	upheld	upheld
upset	upset	upset
wake	woke	woken
wear	wore	worn
weave	wove	woven
weep	wept	wept
wet	wet (or: wetted)	wet (or: wetted)
win	won	won
wind	wound	wound
withdraw	withdrew	withdrawn
withhold	withheld	withheld
withstand	withstood	withstood
wring	wrung	wrung
write	wrote	written

Answers to Exercises (Chapters 4 - 22)

Chapter 4

Exercise 4.1

Noun	Verb	Adjective	Adverb
paintings	is	typical	particularly
space	adds	Chinese	even
meaning	seems	empty	seemingly
quality	gazing	certain	together
hermit	come	philosophical	poetically
pavilion	tell	aesthetic	
stream		distant	
trees			
hills			
story			

Exercise 4.2

1. verb	2. noun	3. noun	4. verb	5. verb	6. adjective
7. verb	8. adjective	9. noun	10. verb	11. verb	12. adjective
13. noun	14. verb	15. adjective	16. verb	17. noun	18. verb

Exercise 4.3

1. bad, badly
2. different, recently
3. anxious, nervously
4. beautifully, beautiful
5. hard, well
6. completely, inexpensive
7. readily, ready
8. various, satisfactorily
9. uneasy, difficult
10. tired, fast, mad
11. carefully, incorrect
12. usually, fair

Chapter 5

Exercise 5.1

1. bought	2. reviewed	3. won	4. began	5. forgot	6. taught
7. waited	8. spread	9. left	10. hid	11. caught	12. cost

Exercise 5.2

1. heard   2. rains   3. discovered, was   4. has

5. was working   6. has been received   7. boils, reaches   8. flew

9. had lived, returned   10. have been trying   11. believe, improve   12. has been learning

13. have visited   14. were   15. had done   16. are planning, or plan

17. will be, or are   18. is going to   19. have finished   20. had given, felt

Exercise 5.3

1. are, AV   2. has been, AV   3. is, MV   4. does not, AV

5. have, MV   6. has, AV   7. had, AV   8. do, MV

9. do, AV   10. do, MV   11. had, MV   12. were, MV

Exercise 5.4

1. i   2. c   3. f   4. g   5. j   6. d

7. b   8. e   9. h   10. g   11. a   12. i

13. e   14. b   15. a   16. f   17. j   18. h and f

Chapter 6

Exercise 6.1

1. reasons   2. They   3. you   4. pressures   5. Not stopping for a red traffic light

6. mother   7. Swimming and ice-skating   8. Tai Chi   9. clock tower   10. time

Exercise 6.2

1. is   2. do   3. are   4. works   5. have   6. has   7. hopes, is

8. was   9. are   10. thinks, are

Exercise 6.3

1. remain   2. has   3. gave   4. has, paid   5. is   6. get   7. worries

8. is   9. is   10. is   11. are   12. are

Exercise 6.4

1. have   2. makes   3. was   4. CORRECT   5. has   6. has, is   7. live

8. CORRECT   9. CORRECT   10. is   11. requires   12. have, does   13. are

14. are   15. CORRECT

Chapter 7

Exercise 7.1

1. Every	2. much	3. more	4. fewer
5. much	6. some	7. less	8. Few
9. Many	10. several	11. fewer	12. little

Exercise 7.2

1. groceries	2. contact	3. demand	4. strength
5. hours	6. reservations	7. weight	8. essentials
9. power	10. emphasis		

Exercise 7.3

1. f	2. m	3. b, c	4. f, i	5. b, c	6. a, f
7. f, h	8. j	9. d	10. e, f	11. f, k	12. g

Exercise 7.4

1. savings account	2. desserts	3. watches	4. taxi stand
5. CORRECT	6. eyeglasses need	7. women's department	8. McDonald's
9. five-day vacation	10. CORRECT	11. by hand	12. twelve-year-old

Chapter 8

Exercise 8.1

1. have, their	2. he, keeps	3. its	4. his or her	5. are, our
6. its	7. their	8. their	9. their, minds	10. its (**their** also acceptable)

Exercise 8.2

1. it	2. its	3. CORRECT	4. their	5. which
6. his/her	7. themselves	8. CORRECT	9. them	10. his or her

Chapter 9

Exercise 9.1

1. T	2. F	3. T	4. T	5. F	6. F
7. T	8. T	9. F	10. T	11. T	12. T

Exercise 9.2 (Ø = no article is needed)

1. the	2. the, the	3. Ø, Ø, Ø	4. A, a, Ø
5. a, the, an	6. The, Ø, a, a	7. The, Ø, Ø	8. a, Ø, Ø
9. The, the, the	10. the, the	11. the, a, the, the	12. the, Ø, the

Exercise 9.3

1. an	2. Ø	3. a	4. a	5. the	6. Ø
7. the	8. the	9. a	10. The	11. an	12. Ø
13. Ø	14. Ø	15. Ø	16. the	17. a	18. Ø
19. a	20. the	21. the	22. a	23. the	24. an
25. a	26. the	27. Ø			

Chapter 10

Exercise 10.1

T = true   F = false

1. F	2. F	3. T	4. T	5. T
6. F	7. T	8. F	9. T	10. T

Exercise 10.2

1. ADV	2. ADJ	3. ADV	4. ADV	5. ADJ
6. ADV	7. ADV	8. ADJ	9. ADJ	10. ADV
11. ADJ	12. ADJ			

Exercise 10.3

1. warmer	2. more carefully, honestly	3. demanding	4. closest
5. more efficiently	6. worst	7. more frequently	8. harder
9. faster, faster	10. less interesting	11. more pleasant, less chilly	12. well

Exercise 10.4

1. OK	2. OK	3. OK	4. P	5. OK	6. OK
7. P	8. OK	9. P	10. OK	11. OK	12. P

Chapter 11

Exercise 11.1

1. for	2. on	3. at	4. under	5. over
6. in	7. out of	8. through	9. across	10. Owing to
11. as well as	12. in, at	13. to	14. at, on	15. from

Exercise 11.2

1. on	2. in	3. NP	4. for	5. to, at	6. to, with
7. in	8. for	9. NP	10. at	11. to	12. on

Exercise 11.3

1. Because of	2. along with	3. prior to	4. away from	5. next to
6. in spite of	7. For all	8. in front of	9. except for	10. in relation to
11. by means of	12. in contrast to			

Exercise 11.4

1. She said she has come up with an idea to share with us.

2. My granddaughter recently took up the recorder.

3. He is doing all he can to get at the truth of the matter.

4. Harmony between two conflicting parties can come about if both sides agree to compromise.

5. I don't know how you could put up with the noise from the renovation work next door.

6. He was lucky to come through the dangerous operation.

7. She takes after her father in the pursuit of excellence.

8. Mango ice cream is a great dessert, but it does not agree with me.

9. Don't ever think you can get away with cheating in your tax return.

10. Politicians need to be good at putting their ideas across to the public.

Chapter 12

Exercise 12.1

1. T	2. F	3. T	4. T	5. F	6. F
7. T	8. F	9. T	10. T	11. F	12. F
13. T	14. T	15. F			

Exercise 12.2

1. f, 1	2. c, 6	3. d, 1	4. f, 1	5. e, 1	6. a, 7	7. d, 1
8. c, 1	9. f, 3	10. a, 6	11. e, 2	12. c, 7	13. d, 2	14. e, 3
15. f, 5	16. b, 6	17. b, 7	18. f, 4	19. a, 6	20. e, 1	

Chapter 13

Exercise 13.1

1. c	2. e	3. c	4. c	5. d	6. d
7. b	8. a	9. b	10. c		

Exercise 13.2

1. (NR) The ability to write well, <u>which is not commonly found among learners of English</u>, can be consciously cultivated.

2. (R) We can all learn from the mistakes <u>that we have made</u>.

3. (R) She carelessly left in the taxi the gift <u>that she had just bought</u>.

4. (NR) Symptoms of Covid-19, <u>which can take a long time to emerge</u>, are not the same for all the infected.

5. (NR) Hong Kong, <u>which began as a small fishing village</u>, has developed into a large cosmopolitan city.

6. (NR) I'll see you at the City Hall, <u>where we met last time</u>.

7. (NR) The Grand Canyon, <u>which is over 300 kilometres long</u>, has to be seen to be believed.

8. (R) The concert <u>that we are all looking forward to</u> is next Sunday.

9. (R) According to an article <u>that appeared in National Geographic</u> scientists are studying the possibility of travel to Mars.

10. (R) This is the house <u>where we lived while we were in Cambridge in 1977</u>.

11. (R) He does not like to drive at times <u>when the roads are dark</u>.

12. (NR) Albert, <u>whom you met yesterday</u>, works in an international company.

Exercise 13.3

1. Formal: Finding affordable housing is a problem **about which** many young people are concerned.

    Informal: Finding affordable housing is a problem **that** many young people are concerned **about.**

2. Formal: We have a new task **on which** we will need to spend a great deal of time.

Informal: We have a new task **that** we will need to spend a great deal of time **on.**

3. Formal: This is an attractive position **for which** everybody wants to apply.

    Informal: This is an attractive position **that** everybody wants to apply **for.**

4. Formal: This is the medical research **to which** he referred.

    Informal: This is the medical research **that** he referred **to.**

5. Formal: Here are the buildings **of which** you have heard so much.

    Informal: Here are the buildings **that** you have heard so much **of.**

6. Formal: They are the main supplier **from which** many wine sellers get their wines.

    Informal: They are the main supplier **that** many wine sellers get their wines **from.**

Chapter 14

Exercise 14.1

1. wearing a green jacket
2. Generally speaking
3. NIL
4. Opened since 2018
5. Always trying to do well
6. playing with their phones
7. NIL
8. crowded with people
9. looking for a place to park
10. Calling his opponent a liar

Exercise 14.2

1. **Having completed the project,** John took a vacation.

2. **Arriving at the party,** they found that everyone was singing.

3. **Not knowing where the Museum of History was,** she asked for directions at the Tourist Information Office.

4. **Widely known as an influential physicist,** Einstein has given us the idea of relativity.

5. **Having been invited to give a speech at the meeting,** I better get prepared.

6. **While crossing the road,** an old lady was hit by a car.

7. **Applauding excitedly when the concert ended,** the audience would not leave.

8. **Having read the book many times,** she can tell you the whole story.

9. **Not knowing anyone in her department,** the new employee feels quite disoriented at times.

10. **Surrounded by reporters,** the company chairman made an important announcement.

Exercise 14.3

1. CORRECT

2. <u>Having failed numerous times</u>, success was finally hers.

    Revised: **Having failed numerous times, she finally succeeded.**

3. CORRECT

4. <u>Passing by the village</u>, some rice fields were visible.

    Revised: **Passing by the village, we saw some rice fields.**

5. <u>Looking out of the window</u>, a fantastic view of the harbour was before our eyes.

    Revised: **Looking out of the window, we saw a fantastic view of the harbour before us.**

6. CORRECT

7. <u>Completely absorbed in watching her drama videos</u>, hours went by without notice.

    Revised: **Completely absorbed in watching her drama videos, she was not aware that hours went by.**

8. <u>Never having learned to swim properly</u>, swimming in the deep pool was too scary.

    Revised: **Never having learned to swim properly, he was too scared to swim in the deep pool.**

9. <u>Comparing television and news magazines</u>, each type of medium has its strengths and limitations.

    Revised: **Comparing television and news magazines, we can see that each type of medium has its strengths and limitations.**

10. <u>Hoping to sustain the economy</u>, large sums of employment subsidy are being given to both big and small companies.

    Revised: **Hoping to sustain the economy, the government is giving large sums of employment subsidy to both big and small companies.**

Chapter 15

Exercise 15.1

1. coordinating conjunctions: c) **but**   f) **or**   j) **and**

2. conjunctive adverbs: a) **however**   b) **indeed**   k) **in fact**   n) **therefore**

3. correlative conjunctions: d) **if . . . then . . .**   h) **both . . . and . . .**

4. subordinating conjunctions: e) **although**   i) **while**   m) **given that**

5. relative pronouns: g) **who**   o) **that**

Exercise 15.2

1. Swimming allows movement of the whole body, **and** it is enjoyable and relaxing.

2. The project is highly challenging, **but** we managed to complete it in time.

3. This is our rough plan; **however,** it will be modified and improved.

4. Writing well is not easy; **indeed,** you need to have good language skills and well-organized ideas.

5. **If** we learn to recognize errors, **then** we are more likely to avoid those errors when we write.

6. We cannot work effectively without a good plan, **nor** can a good plan succeed without a good leader.

7. **Just as** television serves as our window to the world, **so** the smart phone acts as our connector with people.

8. She put in many hours of practice every day; **consequently,** she won first prize in the public speaking contest.

9. **Both** writing grammatical sentences **and** using words properly are important for writing well.

10. Credit cards make consumption easy, **so** consumers are lured into debt.

Exercise 15.3

1. **Although** you may not succeed right away, you should keep on trying.

2. **Impressed** by the young lady's qualifications, they offered her the position.

3. **Because** (or **Since**) tourists are unfamiliar with places here, they often need to ask locals for directions.

4. **In spite of** (or **Despite**) the task's difficulty, we did it successfully.

5. The new hospital, **which** is located at a quiet setting, has over 500 beds.

   Or: The new hospital, **which** has over 500 beds, is located at a quiet setting.

6. He will consider setting up a shop there **provided that** the site is easily accessible.

7. **Because of** (or **As a result of**) poor planning, the project operated at a great loss.

8. The new teacher, **eloquent and friendly**, soon gained the trust and respect of her students.

9. **While** (or **Although**, **Even though**) we have seen sunrise on the peak many times, we still enjoy the view these days.

10. The news **that** the daily number of locally infected Covid-19 cases remains at low single digits is comforting.

Chapter 16

Exercise 16.1

1. Type 1   2. Type 3   3. Type 2   4. Type 2   5. Type 1

6. Type 2   7. Type 3   8. Type 3   9. Type 2   10. Type 3

Exercise 16.2

1. (c)   2. (c)   3. (b)   4. (a)   5. (b)

6. (c)   7. (c)   8. (a)   9. (c)   10. (b)

Exercise 16.3

1.   If I had known what to do, I would have done it.

2.   It would have cost the company too much money if it had agreed to the compensation package.

3.   Our project would fall behind schedule if it were not for her help.

4.   Had it not been for the sudden bad weather, our cruise ship would have berthed at the last port of call.

5.   If you should run into Ben (but not likely), give him my regards.

6.   I would think about it again if I were in your position.

7.   If you would wait here, I'll see if the manager is free.

8.   If you liked to go to that concert, you could have asked me.

9.   She probably would have studied if she had known that there was a test yesterday.

10. I am not a good cook, but if I were I would not have to eat out so often.

Chapter 17

Exercise 17.1

1.   In the summer camp, children live together to learn how to **care for** and **cooperate with** one another.

2.   Schooling offers development **of the mind** and **of the body**.

3.   Success is **not without fears** and failure is **not without hopes**.

4.   Mr. Wong has been teaching for many years, always **disciplined but kind towards his students** and **serious but passionate in his work**.

5.   A church congregation consists of people **who share a common religious faith** and **who develop a sense of identity in worship and prayer**.

6. Service workers are worried **that they were losing their jobs** and **that the government offered no assistance**.

7. Hong Kong is known for its **freedom of doing business**, **efficiency of financial institutions**, and **rule of law**.

8. Any person intending to start a business is concerned with **obtaining sufficient seed money**, **creating a need for the proposed business** and **finding a suitable location**.

9. Competition is not just about **winning** but also about **doing your best**.

10. Children enjoy **watching images on their smart phones** rather than **reading story books.**

Exercise 17.2

1. (c)   2. (b)   3. (c)   4. (c)   5. (a)   6. (b)

7. (a)   8. (c)   9. (c)   10. (b)

Exercise 17.3

1. To get along with their teenage children, parents need to be patient, tactful, and tolerant.

   Or: To get along with their teenage children, parents need to have patience, tact, and tolerance.

2. The doctor warned her not to smoke, drink, or eat spicy foods.

3. Swimming in the pool and riding a bicycle in the country park are his favourite pastimes.

4. In setting up our project team, we looked for members whose work was innovative, whose interests were diverse, and whose energy was endless.

   Or: In setting up our project team, we looked for members with innovative work, diverse interests, and endless energy.

5. Optimism, sincerity, and good thinking are three important qualities of a successful sales representative.

6. Our dilemma is obvious: we must either reduce costs or diversify income sources.

   Or: Our dilemma is obvious: either we must reduce costs or we must diversify income sources.

7. It is not how you think but how you act that counts.

   Or: It is not your thinking but your action that counts.

8. Given adequate training, workers can acquire the skills for and interest in a variety of jobs.

9. We watch movies not only to kill time but (also) to see the interplay between characters.

10. Before you write an essay or take an examination, you need to organize your thoughts.

    Or: Before writing an essay or taking an examination, you need to organize your thoughts.

11.   We may realize the relativity of social reality and see a hidden side of society.

Or: We may realize that social reality is relative and that there is always a hidden side of society.

12.   It is possible that most welfare recipients want work rather than social welfare payments.

Or: It is possible that most welfare recipients want to work rather than accept social welfare payments.

Chapter 18

Exercise 18.1

	Prefix		Meaning
1.	*mis-*	q.	departure from accuracy/correctness
2.	*dis-*	e.	not doing something
3.	*re-*	p.	again, back
4.	*com-*	c.	together
5.	*de-*	i.	undo, remove
6.	*ab-*	j.	away from, not
7.	*pro-*	r.	forward, support for
8.	*hyper-*	a.	over, above
9.	*bio-*	s.	life
10.	*aqua-*	f.	water
11.	*mar-*	n.	sea
12.	*inter-*	t.	between
13.	*ultra-*	b.	beyond, extremely
14.	*fore-*	k.	before
15.	*endo-*	d.	inside
16.	*contra-*	o.	against, opposite
17.	*trans-*	g.	across
18.	*pre-*	u.	before
19.	*tele-*	m.	from afar
20.	*im-*	h.	not

Exercise 18.2

	Suffix		Meaning
1.	*-ible*	g.	able to
2.	*-ance*	j.	state, quality, act
3.	*-ary*	c.	related to
4.	*-ate*	m.	become, having the quality of
5.	*-en*	p.	become, to make
6.	*-er*	a.	person who does a job
7.	*-hood*	b.	state, quality
8.	*-ic*	c.	related to
9.	*-ish*	n.	fairly, related to
10.	*-ism*	h.	state, quality, action, belief
11.	*-ity*	b.	state, quality
12.	*-ive*	i.	having the power of
13.	*-ize*	d.	to make, to act
14.	*-logy*	f.	study of
15.	*-ship*	b.	state, quality
16.	*-some*	k.	having the quality of
17.	*-ence*	j.	state, quality, act
18.	*-ment*	j.	state, quality, act
19.	*-ly*	e.	in the manner of
20.	*-less*	o.	without

Exercise 18.3

1. T   2. F   3. T   4. F   5. T   6. T   7. F   8. T   9. T   10. T

11. T   12. F   13. F   14. T   15. F   16. F   17. T   18. T   19. F   20. F

Exercise 18.4

1. b   2. a   3. b   4. c   5. c   6. a   7. b   8. b   9. a   10. a

Chapter 19

Exercise 19.1

1. The chief sources of air pollution in our city are: cars, factories, and smoke from people who smoke.

2. Musicians are experimenting with new digital music; audiences are not too receptive with such experiments.

3. There's no point in living, according to my friend, if you don't slow down to enjoy life.

4. To me, the most important things in life are as follows: faith in God, good health, and harmonious relationships with family.

5. She takes physical exercise seriously: she swims for an hour almost every day, for example.

6. (No additional punctuation marks needed.) A business that wants to be successful must invest substantially in marketing and innovation.

7. Your general approach is a good one; however, I think there are some practical difficulties.

8. If you are in a hurry, you can grab a hamburger at McDonald's.

9. They're thinking of joining a river cruise in Europe two years from now; they are not going to Canada or the United States.

10. Take your time at the children's books section, which is on the third floor; I'll wait for you in the Starbuck's café on the ground floor.

11. The young lady who recently joined the company has two master's degrees.

12. Not enough Chinese history is taught in schools today: young people are growing up without a clear sense of national identity.

Exercise 19.2

1. I'm	2. you're	3. he's	4. she's	5. we've	6. they'd
7. they'd	8. it can't	9. it couldn't	10. we'll	11. we won't	12. she doesn't

Exercise 19.3

1. a 24-hour store	2. an 11-year-old girl	3. the first-year report
4. twenty-first-century achievements	5. my third-floor office	6. a four-person team
7. an 88-musician orchestra	8. a nine-month period	9. up-to-date statistics
10. a well-known doctor	11. pre- and post-2020 social conditions	
12. one hundred and forty-two pounds		

Exercise 19.4

1. To write well, we should recognize this basic requirement: sentences must be grammatical and word combinations idiomatic.

2. Good management copes with complexity; it brings order and predictability to a situation. In comparison, good leadership learns to cope with change.

3. Human agents—reporters, photographers, editors, and researchers—all participate significantly in the construction of media practices.

4. Many people confuse "principal" with "principle".

5. The fundamental sociological problem is not crime but the law, not divorce but marriage, not recreation but how leisure as idea and behaviour intertwines with social life.

6. Television viewers in Hong Kong, like those elsewhere, are most interested in seeking entertainment.

7. "Do you think I am ready for the race?" he asked his coach.

8. He is a sociable, generous, and outspoken person, always ready to help someone in need.

9. Freedom is valuable; however, it must not infringe on others' rights.

10. Your time should not be spent on trivial things; instead, more time should be spent on using your talent to serve others.

Chapter 20

Exercise 20.1

1. Shirley's doctor was fully booked that month.

2. Hoi-Man has been chosen to join the school's swimming team.

3. Joan would meet me at the General Post Office that afternoon at two.

4. Peter said he would see me here this morning.

5. When I saw Siu-ling, she told me she was visiting her aunt the next day.

6. Cary apologized to me yesterday for not returning my call the day before.

Exercise 20.2

1. She asked me what the problem was .

2. I didn't know why he hadn't finished the report.

3. He asked the chairman where the meeting would be held.

4. She asked her husband whether he had a record of the transaction.

5.　He wondered <u>if/whether he would ever see his friends again</u>.

6.　Her mother wants to know <u>what she is doing</u>.

7.　Tom asked at the front desk <u>whether/if he could post some letters there</u>.

8.　I have no idea <u>how long the concert lasts</u>.

Exercise 20.3

1.　I persuaded my friend <u>to stay for a few more days</u>.

2.　We urged our team leader <u>to explain the plan once again</u>.

3.　She insisted on <u>leaving early that night</u>.

4.　The manager invited us <u>to come again</u>.

5.　Their two children suggested <u>going to the beach that day</u>.

6.　The student Janet apologized for <u>forgetting to bring her assignment</u>.

7.　His mother warned him <u>not to touch the switch when his hand was wet</u>.

8.　You promised <u>to prepare well for the tutorial discussion the following week</u>.

Exercise 20.4

1.　Tai-Ming said I should have called him earlier.

2.　Jenny told her cousin that she could bring some chicken curry to the pot luck dinner. Or (better): Jenny offered to bring some chicken curry to her cousin's pot luck dinner.

3.　The technician said that the problem could not be fixed.

4.　Unable to find her credit card, she said she must have left it in the supermarket.

5.　Tony promised his father that he would be home by 10 p.m.

6.　Mother said that if the whole family was going to eat out, we would need to book a large table.

7.　Her coach remarked that if she tried harder, she might win the competition.

　　Or:　Her coach reminded her that she might win the competition if she tried harder.

8.　My aunt said that if she had known that the sale was on, she would have gone to look for bargains.

Exercise 20.5

1.　He always said (that) the position makes the person.

2.　The professor reminded us (that) we must study hard for the examination.

　　Or:　The professor reminded us to study hard for the examination.

3.   Our friend told us (that) it would be helpful when we travel in Japan if we understand Japanese.

Or: Our friend told us (that) if we understand Japanese, it would be helpful when we travel in Japan.

Or: Our friend told us (that) some knowledge of Japanese would be helpful when we travel in Japan.

4.   Mandy told Angela (that) she saw/had seen Ricky at the IFC Mall the other day.

5.   His sister thought (that) Albert Einstein is the most important scientist of the 20th century.

6.   My student who works with the orchestra hopes (that) I'll enjoy the concert.

7.   The chairperson repeated that it had not been possible to solve the problem so far.

8.   My neighbour admitted (that) it wasn't their idea of a relaxing holiday.

9.   His mother advised him to go to bed if he felt sick.

Or: His mother said (that) if he felt sick, he had better go to bed.

10.   John said (that) he had been wondering whether their daughter might postpone her wedding plans under the present pandemic situation.

Chapter 21

Exercise 21.1

1.   He has chosen ~~the field of~~ business administration as his major ~~subject~~ in university.

    →He has chosen business administration as his major in university.

2.   We should study the figures ~~given~~ in Table 1.

    →We should study the figures in Table 1.

3.   Writing the report will take ~~a greater length of time~~ than originally estimated.

    →Writing the report will take longer than originally estimated.

4.   Her bag is ~~completely~~ filled with grocery.

    →Her bag is filled with grocery.

5.   We ~~have~~ plans to open a branch ~~in the foreseeable future~~.

    →We plan to open a branch soon.

6.   ~~There is no doubt that~~ prevention is better than cure.

    →Undoubtedly, prevention is better than cure.

7.   We encountered many problems ~~in the course of~~ the last two years.

→We encountered many problems over (or *in*) the last two years.

8. I am of the opinion that she has made impressive progress.

    →I believe she has made impressive progress.

9. It all comes down to this: no one is sure about the effectiveness of the new vaccine.

    →Most importantly (or **in the end/simply put**), no one is sure about the effectiveness of the new vaccine.

10. In this day and age, we cannot function well without our mobile phone.

    →Today (or **nowadays/now**), we cannot function well without our mobile phone.

11. As a matter of fact, none of us understands what he was saying.

    →Actually (or **indeed/in fact**), none of us understands what he was saying.

12. Considering the present difficult situation, the government's subsidy to small businesses is by and large much needed.

    →Considering the present difficult situation, the government's subsidy to small businesses is much needed.

Exercise 21.2

1. i (useful)   2. n (begin)   3. k (harmful)   4. h (reduce)   5. a (cut)   6. j (meet)

7. b (try)   8. p (speed up) 9. c (make easier)   10. o (carry out)   11. g (place)   12. d (best)

13. e (main)   14. f (go ahead) 15. m (end)

Exercise 21.3

Part A

Verb	Nominalization	Adjective	Nominalization
1. appear	*appearance*	13. accurate	*accuracy*
2. argue	*argument*	14. careless	*carelessness*
3. arrange	*arrangement*	15. close	*closeness*
4. decrease	*decrease*	16. comprehensive	*comprehensiveness*
5. define	*definition*	17. conservative	*conservatism*
6. discover	*discovery*	18. different	*difference*
7. discuss	*discussion*	19. efficient	*efficiency*
8. examine	*examination*	20. fragile	*fragility*
9. explain	*explanation*	21. fruitful	*fruitfulness*
10. fail	*failure*	22. magnificent	*magnificence*
11. fulfil	*fulfilment*	23. same	*sameness*
12. gain	*gain*	24. similar	*similarity*

Part B

Nominalization	Verb	Adjective (can be more than one)
1. ability	enable	able
2. accommodation	accommodate	accommodating
3. articulation	articulate	articulate
4. brightness	brighten	bright
5. clarity	clarify/clear	clear
6. completion	complete	complete/completed
7. depression	depress	depressed/depressing
8. deprivation	deprive	deprived
9. embarrassment	embarrass	embarrassed/embarrassing
10. evaluation	evaluate	evaluative
11. generation	generate	generational/generative/generated
12. hardness	harden	hard
13. improvement	improve	improved
14. initiation	initiate	initial
15. knowledge	know	knowledgeable
16. limitation	limit	limited/limiting
17. modernization	modernize	modernized/modern
18. preparation	prepare	prepared/preparatory
19. realization	realize	realized
20. reinforcement	reinforce	reinforced
21. rejection	reject	rejected
22. satisfaction	satisfy	satisfactory/satisfying/satisfied
23. sensitivity	sensitize	sensitive
24. transformation	transform	transformed

Exercise 21.4 (suggested rewrites)

1. Hong Kong people now expect that social distancing restrictions under Covid-19 will be a new normalcy of life.

2. Many customers believe that they could shop more efficiently in supermarkets if touch screens were installed to indicate location of items.

3. Children who are more exposed to music will be more able to appreciate what they hear.

4. The market for sport equipment has grown rapidly because young people generally like outdoor activities.

5. Because she prepared thoroughly for the singing contest, she felt no threat from any of the other competitors.

Exercise 21.5

Part A.

1. The situation was explained to me by my friend.

2. He was elected chairman by all committee members.

3. The changes in extra-curricular activities are going to be explained by the principal to the students.

4. The car was seen knocking over a pedestrian.

5. Tony hopes to be included by the project leader in his team.

6. The pedestrian escalators are used all the time.

Part B.

1. Someone broke into their home when they were on holiday.

2. Everybody believed that the project would not finish on time.

3. They will consider the new recruitment procedure at the next meeting.

4. They (or some appropriate person) should check the data in the report carefully.

5. The subtle humour of the speaker amused everyone in the audience.

6. Somebody should have offered that elderly man some help when he fell.

Chapter 22

Exercise 22.1

1. g   2. d   3. j   4. h   5. b   6. a   7. g   8. e   9. i   10. i

11. h   12. j   13. c   14. h   15. i   16. f   17. g   18. j   19. c   20. h

Exercise 22.2

1. F   2. F   3. F   4. T   5. T   6. T   7. F   8. F   9. F   10. T

11. F   12. T   13. T   14. T   15. F

Exercise 22.3

1. Losses: losses of life and property. Damages: environmental and ecological damages.

2. "stupendous consumption of fossil fuels and deteriorating conditions of air pollution from car exhausts, factories, and cigarette smoke"

3. "a hotter world with drier forests"

4. "Global temperatures will keep rising and drought conditions intensifying"

5. Forest fires

Exercise 22.4

Transitional marker	Purpose
because	b. to give a reason or show cause and effect
as a result	b. to give a reason or show cause and effect
the truth is	a. to reinforce or add ideas
since	b. to give a reason or show cause and effect
given that	d. to show concession
when	e. to show time
before	e. to show time
consequently	b. to give a reason or show cause and effect
moreover	a. to reinforce or add ideas
even if	d. to show concession
as a rule	a. to reinforce or add ideas
indeed	a. to reinforce or add ideas

Suggested References (with annotations)

There is so much to know about the use of English that you need to cultivate the habit of using various references as tools to enrich your knowledge of the language. There are times when you may be curious about a certain aspect of grammar (e.g., using the present tense to talk about the future) or when you have specific questions about idiomatic expressions (e.g., What is the difference between "put you up" and "put up with you"?). This book may or may not have the answers to all your questions, thus you are encouraged to read more and look further to enhance your English skills.

For the benefit of readers, the following list of suggested references, mostly with annotations, includes regular and special dictionaries and books on English grammar and usage. Some of them, marked with an asterisk (*), are relatively concise and are suitable for quick reference.

A. Regular dictionaries

Dictionaries are instrumental for enriching word skills (as explained in Chapter 18). Excellent English dictionaries for advanced learners are available from such reputable publishers as Oxford, Cambridge, Collins Cobuild, Longman, and Macmillan. I strongly recommend that you have at least one for your use. It is an investment that you will never regret.

Some of these publishers have also produced English-Chinese editions. These and their English editions all provide useful example sentences for different meaning categories and for such matters as word use, synonyms, collocations, and idiomatic expressions. Never underestimate how much you can learn from these sentences!

B. Special dictionaries and guides

(1) Synonyms

*Crozier, J., Gilmour, L., & Robertson, A. (Eds.). (2006). *Collins thesaurus A-Z* (Compact Edition). Glasgow: HarperCollins.

This is a volume convenient for quickly checking synonyms of a given word. As in many thesauruses, it lists synonyms according to different senses of the word. Each sense category starts with a key synonym to guide the user. Where appropriate, opposites and related words are also given.

Oxford University Press (China) (2012). *Oxford learner's thesaurus: A dictionary of synonyms* (English-Chinese Edition).《牛津英語同義詞學習詞典》英漢雙解版 . Hong Kong: Author.

This thesaurus, designed for learners interested in gaining a fuller knowledge of the meaning and use of words, contains a wealth of information about not just synonyms but also useful patterns and collocations. Attention is given to contexts (e.g., formal vs. informal, written vs. spoken) and differences between pairs of synonyms (e.g., **strange** or **unfamiliar**? **plain** or **simple**?).

(2) Collocations

McCarthy, M., & O'Dell, F. (2005). *English collocations in use.* Cambridge, England: Cambridge University Press.

This guide on collocations covers the grammatical aspects of collocations and a wide variety of topics (such as "travel and the environment" and "leisure and lifestyle") with practice exercises for each topic.

Oxford University Press (China) (2006). *Oxford collocations dictionary* (English-Chinese Edition).《牛津英語搭配詞典》英漢雙解版. Hong Kong: Author.

This reference helps you to treat the idiomatic or natural combination of words seriously. Collocations are presented according to meaning category, clearly showing the grammatical structure. For example, one meaning category of **effort** is "attempt to do something". Collocations are given as adjective + **effort** (e.g., **special effort**), verb +**effort** (e.g., **renew effort**) and shown in example sentences. Both this dictionary and *Oxford learner's thesaurus* contain useful study pages with practice exercises.

(3) Idioms and phrasal verbs

Oxford, Longman, Cambridge, and HarperCollins all have published dictionaries of idioms and phrasal verbs for English learners. The English-Chinese editions from Oxford are particularly user-friendly for Chinese-speaking readers.

McCarthy, M., & O'Dell, F. (2002). *English idioms in use.* Cambridge, England: Cambridge University Press.

McCarthy, M., & O'Dell, F. (2004). *English phrasal verbs in use.* Cambridge, England: Cambridge University Press.

These two guidebooks by McCarthy and O'Dell are just as helpful as their similar work on collocations. The meanings and use of idioms and phrasal verbs are clearly explained in their typical contexts and accompanied by helpful practice exercises.

*Oxford University Press (China) (2005). *Oxford idioms dictionary* (English-Chinese Edition).《牛津英語習語詞典》英漢雙解版. Hong Kong: Author.

With a rich coverage of English idiomatic expressions, clear example sentences, and references to other idioms at different key words, this dictionary is compact enough for easy use but detailed enough for deepening learners' understanding of idioms.

*Oxford University Press (China) (2005). *Oxford phrasal verbs dictionary* (English-Chinese Edition).《牛津短語動詞詞典》英漢雙解版. Hong Kong: Author.

Like *Oxford idioms dictionary*, this dictionary of phrasal verbs is clear and has many useful details. In addition to meanings and illustrative sentences, you can see (a) the grammar patterns of phrasal verbs, (b) information on commonly used subjects and objects of many of the verbs, and (c) where applicable, useful notes on grammar or usage.

(4) Verbs and Prepositions (These areas are particularly troublesome for learners of English.)

Leech, G. N. (2004). *Meaning and the English verb* (3rd ed.). London: Longman.

> The proper use of verbs to convey different meanings involving time and context is a particularly weak spot of learners whose first language is not English. This very practical reference, suitable for teachers and advanced students, deals with such trouble points as tense, progressive (continuous) and perfect aspects, mood, and the modal auxiliaries.

*Sinclair, J. (Ed. in chief). (1991). *Collins Cobuild English guides 1: Prepositions.* London:

HarperCollins.

Sinclair's work is also available in a Chinese bilingual edition:

* 任紹曾（主編）(2004)。《Cobuild 英語語法系列：介詞》。香港：商務印書館。

> This useful reference contains two parts: (1) explanations of over 100 alphabetically listed prepositions, and (2) an extensive list of words (nouns, verbs, adjectives) commonly used with prepositions. Example sentences are given in both parts. The book is suitable for anyone wishing to gain a clearer understanding of the use of prepositions.

C. Grammar

(selected for their practical use and broad coverage of topics explained clearly)

Biber, D., Susan, C., & Leech, G. (2002). *Longman student grammar of spoken and written English.* Harlow, England: Pearson Education.

> An excellent reference for teachers and advanced students (university), this grammar examines patterns of the use of English in real contexts based on a corpus or a large, systematic collection of texts. Special topics include "word order choices" and "the grammar of conversation".

*Gucker, P. (1966). *Essential English grammar.* New York: Dover.

> This grammar, suitable for both teachers and students for quick reference, is wonderfully concise yet covers all the main points of grammar, with each topic taking only a few pages and accompanied by one or more practice exercises (with answers).

*HarperCollins (2009). *Collins grammar & punctuation.* Glasgow: Author.

> This brief overview of grammar, suitable for anyone who wants to improve his or her English, includes phrases, clauses, determiners, and punctuation, with a clear and accessible format.

*Jackson, H. (2005). *Good grammar for students.* London: Sage.

> This grammar is suitable for students and others who need to write good quality papers or reports with accuracy. There are useful tips on pitfalls to avoid and helpful information on spelling and punctuation.

Leech. G., & Svartvik, J. (2003). *A communicative grammar of English* (3rd ed.). Harlow, England: Longman.

For decades, this has been a book helpful to advanced learners, undergraduates, and teachers of English. It adopts an approach that emphasizes the uses of grammar rather than grammatical structure. It also contains an alphabetically arranged guide to grammar topics.

*Pearson Education Asia (1999). *Longman dictionary of grammar and usage* (2nd ed.). Singapore: Author.

The contents are arranged in such a way that you can use the book as a dictionary to answer questions about grammar and usage. A detailed alphabetical list of topics is provided at the front of the book to help the reader find what he or she wants.

Thomson, A. J., & Martinet, A. V. (1986). *A practical English grammar* (4th ed.). Oxford, England: Oxford University Press.

This classic work has been widely used for decades as a textbook or reference for intermediate and post-intermediate students. More advanced students and teachers of English will also find this book useful as it explains grammar topics clearly through numerous examples.

任紹曾（主譯）(2014)。《Collins Cobuild 英語語法大全》（全新版）。香港：商務印書館。

This is the Chinese bilingual edition of HarperCollins (2011). *Collins Cobuild English grammar* (3rd ed.). Comprehensive and authoritative, it is suitable for those who want a deeper understanding of grammar. Tables of words with common characteristics in usage, an extensive English-Chinese Glossary of grammatical terms, and a detailed index are special features.

D. Usage and words

While some of the books in the preceding category also deal with matters of usage, the references in the present category focus on words and their use.

(1) Word roots

Glazier, T. F., Knight, L. D., & Friend, C. E. (2005). *The least you should know about vocabulary building: Word roots* (5th ed.). Boston: Thomson Wadsworth.

Learning word roots is a quick and effective way to expand your vocabulary. Word roots are arranged alphabetically, clearly explained and demonstrated in many examples. Each root or set of roots is given a set of exercises for practice.

(2) Use of words

*Alexander, L. G. (1994). *Right word wrong word: Words and structures confused and misused by learners of English.* Harlow, England: Longman.

As indicated by its title, this reference shows both correct and incorrect ways of using words through numerous example sentences. Entries include words close or related in meaning. The book provides many test exercises for intermediate and advanced learners.

Cutts, M. (2013). *Oxford guide to plain English* (4th ed.). Oxford: Oxford University Press.

This is one of the best references for writing in good, clear, and plain English. There is much to learn beyond good grammar, as can be seen from the chapter headings such as "Writing tight", "Using vertical lists", and "Using reader-centred structure".

*Karjalainen, J. (2012). *The joy of English.* Oxford: How To Books.

A concise and easy-to-read reference, Karjalainen explains each of 100 topics or language items directly and interestingly in only two to three pages. The book is as useful to students as it is to writers, teachers, and other users of English.

*Manser, M. H. (Ed.). (2011). *Good word guide* (7th ed.). London: Bloomsbury.

This is a comprehensive but compact reference giving clear and authoritative guidance on how to write and questions concerning grammar, spelling, punctuation, and confusable words. It is well laid out and easy to use.

Swan, M. (2016). *Practical English usage* (4th ed.). Oxford: Oxford University Press.

No doubt a most helpful reference for teachers of English and advanced learners, Swan's work examines a wide range of problems about grammar and structures used with particular words. The explanations, examples of correct usage and of typical errors are concise and clear. The index is sufficiently detailed to guide the reader to locate the grammar point or specific word in question (e.g., **can** or **could**? **may** or **might**? **altogether** or **all together?**).

(3) Common errors and confusable words

*Bunton, D. (2010). *Common English errors in Hong Kong* (New ed.). Hong Kong: Pearson Education Asia.

*Bunton, D. (2011). *More common English errors in Hong Kong.* Hong Kong: Pearson Education Asia. ("For senior secondary or university students and young adults.")

These two volumes by Bunton, in an easy-to-read format, present common errors in a number of groups of different aspects of English. Each group (chapter) gives a brief overview of the problems involved. Each entry in every chapter shows an incorrect sentence and its corrected version, followed by short explanations of the error and, if appropriate, some related constructions.

Carey, S., Lee, K. S., & Hue Ng, M. L. (2011). *Common English mistakes of Hong Kong students* (New HKDSE & IELTS Edition). Hong Kong: Northumbria Educational Press.

This reference deals with over 180 points of grammar and usage classified into 29 units. These points, most troublesome for students, are explained concisely to show correct usage in sentences. There are plenty of practice exercises (with answers) for all these troublesome points.

*Carpenter, E. (1991). *Collins Cobuild English guides 4: Confusable words.* London: HarperCollins.

Containing nearly 400 entries, covering over 900 items, this handy book gives clear explanation of differences in meaning and use. The many example sentences, drawn from real sources, show how the words in question are typically used in modern English.

*Heaton, J. B., & Turton, N. D. (1994). *Longman English-Chinese dictionary of common errors.*《朗文常用英語正誤詞典》Hong Kong: Longman Asia.

Looking up errors is quick and easy with this dictionary that lists each incorrect sentence against its corrected version followed by a brief explanation of the problem underlying the error. Many errors commonly made by Chinese learners of English are included.

*Leetch, P. (2007). *The 1... 2... 3... book of common errors.* Hong Kong: SCMP Book Publishing.

This book is based on real samples of English written by Chinese learners in Hong Kong. Students, secondary and tertiary, and other adult users of English will find it helpful.

Index

The numbers refer to sections.